#9 BLOOD SIEGE

WARBOTS

G. HARRY STINE

I0627746

IMHOLT
PRESS

Imholt Press

Originally published by Pinnacle Books

Copyright © 1990 by G. Harry Stine

Currently Published by Imholt Press, LLC

ISBN: **978-1-951810-02-3**

For more information contact **tim@timothyimholt.com**

SIERRA CHARLIE TAKEDOWN!

"Stop right there, Carson!" the mere, General Steve Calder, yelled at the warbot commander, aiming his 9-millimeter directly at his chest.

Carson didn't miss a step. "Calder, give it up. I've got the whole damned Seventeenth Iron Fist Division all over you."

"All I see is one lousy company. I've got reinforcements on the way," he said, jerking his head to indicate a bevy of troop trucks coming up the broad avenue.

Hawk Wizard Seven, take out the four trucks enroute to Grey Head, Carson tacommed on his NE link to the Sierra Charlie Harpy driver hovering up-sun to the west.

Roger that, Grey Head, the man replied, and a split second later, the explosions of M300A 25-millimeter cannon shells tore the air as they destroyed the approaching convoy.

"No!" Calder screamed, whirled and brought his Mendoza SMC to bear.

In impulse response, Curt activated his laser-directed Novia and pulled off a single 7.62-millimeter round. Calder's head exploded in crimson mist; then his body jerked in spasms from the impact of dozens of Novia rounds at close range. What crumpled to the ground was only the ragged, bullet-torn remains of what had been a miserable excuse for a soldier.

TO:

Gary C. Rosenfield,
former airman,
United States Air Force

"In view of the complexity of...warfare, the control of a nation's armed forces has passed beyond the capacity of any individual commander. This means that the field commander needs to operate as a part of a team of planners, working to individual strengths and pooling ideas to produce a cogent strategy. This has not lessened the task of the commander. On the contrary, he must now be able to receive, process, and transmit information with machinelike efficiency, even though he is not a machine and is prone to breakdown as the demands exceed his capacity to meet them. Thus, the...commander faces pressures of a psychological kind which are far removed from those of his warrior-commander predecessors."

- Geoffrey Regan, from "Great Military Disasters, A History of Incompetence on the Battlefield," 1987.

Forward

In this ninth installment of Warbots, G. Harry Stine takes us further into the world of robotic warfare that G. Harry saw as the future, we see it as the present. The technology we use for this task improves every day. G. Harry reminds us that no good weapon or tactic development program goes unnoticed.

The satellite systems zooming around over our heads seem to get better all the time. What happens when the Russians see a private group secretly building large missiles and want those missiles destroyed?

Will the United States allow the foreign nation to deal with our internal problem, or will we use our military on our own soil, against our own citizens?

This is a topic we struggle with today. Can the United States deal with a world where we may have to use our military to gain control over what is going on inside our own borders?

Is that something we should do? What if those citizens are holding other US citizens hostages and the police aren't equipped well enough to solve the problem?

It is a challenging question to answer.

I hope you enjoy this installment into Warbots, I give you Warbots Book 9: Blood Siege.

Timothy Imholt PhD

Chapter One

Twenty-four M60A Mary Ann warbots suddenly emerged out of an arroyo six hundred yards across the grassy pampa.

Cougar Leader, this is Puma Leader! I have targets! came the cool report from Lieutenant Lew Pagan on the voiceless tactical command channel as the skin electrodes in his battle helmet picked up his neural impulses and transmitted them as voice analogues to his company commander.

Hold your fire! was the quick but terse command from Captain Kitsy Clinton. She knew that tactical doctrine required the warbots to precede their human counterparts in a skirmish line. Clinton's Cougars had a good defensive-offensive position, and she intended to let the enemy expend warbots and soldiers assaulting her company's position. Then she'd launch a counterattack. She thought her platoon leaders understood this plan since it was part and parcel of standard operating procedure. *Wait for their Sierra Charlies so you have warm bodies to shoot at. Let them close the range.*

Whites of their video sensors and all that? Roger! However, Lew Pagan didn't intend to hunker down in the scrub oak and take incoming without returning it.

Scorpion Leader, can you turn their flank? Neuroelectronic tacomm was not only silent because it picked up and transmitted thought waves, but it was also very fast. The Special Combat or Sierra Charlie troops of the 3rd Robot Infantry Regiment, (Special Combat), familiarly known as the Washington Greys or The Third Herd, not only "talked" to one another on the battlefield through this high-tech system hut also commanded their war robots with it. Until the fire fight started, a twenty-first century battlefield was strangely silent. Unlike soldiers of other nations who sang or yelled or followed pipers going into battle, Americans moved silently, something they had learned centuries ago from the Amerindians. This behavior scared the hell out of the more vocal troops of Africa and Asia against whom the American Sierra Charlies had fought in years past.

Negatory, Kitsy. But when they start leap-frogging, I think I can take them from their left quarter, was the immediate voiceless reply from Captain Adonica Sweet.

This isn't Stand-up in the Club! Follow tacomm protocol! This was Captain Kitsy Clinton's first company command. And her first field operation since being discharged from Walter Reed Army Hospital. She was rusty on tactical procedures and still a tyro when it came to leadership.

Her two platoon leaders, Captain Adonica Sweet and Lieutenant Lewis Pagan, didn't reply. They were giving her some slack. Besides, the enemy warbots were closing the range, and this was no time for idle chatter. The hunkered forms of the enemy troops were now visible, advancing in a skirmish line behind the warbots, taking advantage of the cover provided by their Mary Anns and providing smaller targets than the larger warbots.

Okay, I have a laser-designated range, Lew Pagan reported. *Four-five-three meters to the lead Wolfhound warbot.*

Dammit, Pagan, you know better than to break stealth! Kitsy reprimanded him.

It was a single pulse laser bounce. They shouldn't detect it-

Pagan's reply was interrupted by an enemy Mary Ann firing its 25-millimeter autocannon. Warbots didn't miss. The jelly round splattered crimson dye over his M33A2 General Purpose Warbot or Jeep, whose laser ranger he'd used.

They detected it, Kitsy pointed out. *Puma Leader, form the fire base. Scorpion Leader, go to maneuver mode and-*

But at that instant, the "mad minute" began. The first part of any combat engagement quickly became a maelstrom of firing and activity as both sides sought to exploit surprise and discover the opponent's weakness. And Captain Kitsy Clinton immediately lost control of the fight.

That was new to her. As a platoon commander, she'd always had close communications and even visual contact with her sergeants during most of the fight. Leading a combat company was a slightly different matter. She had to depend more on communications and the tactical display projected on her helmet visor by the helmet's nanoelectronics. It was confusing at first and even more intense because she'd been away from the Washington Greys for almost two years.

Pagan knew his job, and so did his platoon sergeant, Betty Jo Trumble. Both of them had been in every fracas of the Washington Greys since the regiment had converted from a pure warbot unit and pioneered the new Sierra Charlie doctrine. Making the transition from running remotely controlled neuroelectronic warbots while located safely in a rear area warbot control van to the far more lethal environment of actual personal combat was a change most warbot brainies could handle, especially if they were as aggressive as Lew Pagan. But in the situation, Pagan had been designated by his company commander as the company's fire base. It was up to him to keep the enemy pinned down while the other platoon leader, Captain Adonica Sweet, moved to seek their flank.

"Hold 'em by the nose with fire and kick 'em in the ass with maneuver!" That was classical Patton tactical doctrine. The Washington Greys had resurrected and perfected it as the basic Sierra Charlie doctrine where soldiers and their warbots operated together on the battlefield, each taking advantage of the strong points of the other to cover their own weak points.

Even with Mod 7/11 artificial intelligence circuitry, a warbot was the equivalent of a stupid grunt infantry soldier with an IQ of about seventy. On the other hand, a warbot rarely missed when it shot. And it was more heavily armored. A warbot was like an intelligent light tank. At least this was true of the M60 Mobile Assault warbots, the Mary Anns. (See Appendix IV.)

No robot had yet been built that was as intelligent, resourceful, mobile, compact, small, adaptable, and unpredictable as a human being. Warfare was a human activity. Machines didn't fight one another. Machines didn't care whether they won or lost. No amount of tinkering and experimenting by the robotic experts had ever been able to make a robot give a damn. Robots had always been tools for humans to use, not competition or even a substitute for a human being. At one time, the United States Army had thought so...until the Washington Greys had come up against tactical situations that remotely controlled neuroelectronic warbots couldn't handle.

And, as the Washington Greys maintained, human beings could be readily produced by relatively unskilled labor...and it was a lot more fun that way.

Lew Pagan and his Pumas used their Mary Anns as heavy fire against the enemy Mary Anns while he and his three sergeants concentrated on the eight human targets out there. *Company strength assault,* he reported to Kitsy. *We can hold 'em if we go to stealth mode. Which we've just done. And we're going for the warbot eyes.* He knew that the 25-millimeter M300 automatics on his Mary Anns wouldn't breach the armor of the opponent's Mary Anns, even if this hadn't been a war game with the 27th R.I. Regiment, the Wolfhounds. So, he'd instructed them to aim for the enemy warbot's sensors. A visual or infrared sensor smeared with gooey red gunk from a jelly round would effectively put a warbot out of action. With his warbots emitting ECM to provide a plethora of targets where none existed, the enemy would waste ammo and time. Lew Pagan was a pro; he knew his stuff. He wasn't spectacular or heroic; he was simply very good, the sort of platoon commander you could count on, absolutely and positively, in any fire fight.

Puma Alpha One is out of action, was the call of the umpire, declaring Pagan's Jeep killed by enemy fire. Captain Ollie Graham of the 7th R.I. Regiment (S.C.) enjoyed his role of umpire, especially because the Greys had trounced the Cottonbalers more than once in war games like this.

Adonica, what the hell are you up to? Kitsy broke her own call for proper tacomm protocol when she saw what Captain Adonica Sweet was doing with her warbots and Sierra Charlies.

Countering their robot rush with the Motega maneuver, was her quick reply. Adonica Sweet was an enigma. The petite blonde was a real beauty. She could have had an outstanding career making lots of money as a petite fashion model. Instead, she'd chosen to follow family tradition by serving in the Washington Greys. And she was far more aggressive than any of the other ladies of the Greys.

A robot rush was a standard assault tactic worked out by the Greys. Ordinary warbots advanced by leap-frogging, half the force standing fast while the other half moved through the forward line in the assault, then stopping a few hundred meters out, depending on terrain and cover, to concentrate fire and cover the leap-frogging advance of the rest of the warbots. When the Greys developed the Sierra Charlie combat doctrine, they'd modified this. The voice-commanded warbots of a Sierra Charlie unit would move forward ahead of the human soldiers, providing armored targets while the Sierra Charlies maneuvered behind them and closed the gap between them, whereupon the warbots, with their superior speed, would again move out.

But Adonica Sweet was doing something else that morning. Kitsy Clinton had never seen it before.

It looked like a bastardized version of the leap-frog tactic with Mary Anns being on element and Sierra Charlies the other. The Mary Anns were providing fire cover while the Sierra Charlies of Sweet's Scorpions advanced through their line and out ahead of them, exposing themselves to whatever fire could be directed at them by the enemy Sierra Charlie troops' M33A2 Ranger assault rifles, known to the Greys by the original Mexican designation Novia, or sweetheart.

Then as the Sierra Charlies pinned down the opposition with assault rifle fire, the Mary Anns would close the gap and proceed ahead of them.

It was dangerous as all hell. It meant that the Mary Anns had to suppress fire from the opposing warbots while the Sierra Charlies advanced. A 25-millimeter round from a Mary Ann would, under real combat, completely waste any human it hit. On the other hand, the Sierra Charlie's body armor would stop nearly any assault rifle or small arms round up to and including calibers of 9-millimeter.

Where the hell had Adonica gotten the idea of this tactic? She'd called it the "Montega maneuver." Did this mean that it had been something worked out by Captain Dyani Motega, whose ancestors had been Crow Indian scouts for the 3rd Regiment during the Great Plains Wars? Kitsy suspected that was the case. Dyani Motega had made astounding progress in the Greys since Kitsy had been injured in Iraq. And Kitsy didn't exactly like some of that progress, either.

Damn! Damn! Damn! Captain Kitsy Clinton swore. She'd been away from combat for two years and thus had inadvertently neglected to shield her inner thoughts from tacomm transmission.

Cougar Leader, the Pumas will cover the Scorpions.

How the hell are you going to do that and keep the Wolf Pack pinned down? Kitsy wanted to know.

Superior fire control, Lew snapped back.

That was too late. *Medic! Medic!* came the hurried call from Charlie Koslowski, Sweet's platoon sergeant. *Ginny, make it fast! Captain Sweet's taken a twenty-five jelly round in the chest!*

The jelly rounds used in the field war games were low-velocity high-drag projectiles designed to splatter on impact and spread gooey red dye all over the target. They were far more realistic than the laser guns formerly used which just put a red spot of light on the target. The jelly rounds not only marked the hit target, but if someone was unlucky enough to take one of the large caliber rounds from a 15-millimeter or 25-millimeter warbot gun, it also hurt like hell.

That was the chance that Captain Adonica Sweet had taken...and lost. But she was an aggressive type, and Kitsy should have expected that she'd do what she did. Kitsy also realized that she should have specifically ordered Adonica to be a little less aggressive. But if Adonica Sweet learned something that July morning on the rolling grasslands of southern Arizona near Fort Huachuca, Kitsy Clinton also learned something about company command.

Kitsy had been hit before. She knew what it was like, and she had a little trouble right then trying to be less empathetic with Adonica Sweet and getting the fire fight under control. Kitsy managed to do neither.

So, she did what she should do. She called for air support. *Hawk Leader, this is Cougar Leader! We're engaging a Wolfhound company here, and we need you to lay some ordnance for us!*

Ident your beacon, then designate what you want us to hit, Cougar Leader, came the reply from the new commander of the Tactical Air Support Company, Paul Hands. *Clancy, this one is yours.*

Reading the beacons. Give me thirty seconds to get there.

Kitsy didn't get thirty seconds of time for help to arrive in the form of air support. Bright flashes of 75-millimeter Saucy Cans air-burst rounds appeared over Sweet's Scorpions out in the field. The sprayed red dye just as they would scatter shrapnel if this had been for real.

Wolfhounds have us targeted! Kitsy called. *Take cover! Take cover! Alleycat Leader, I need some help here!*

I'm not going down into that mess of Saucy Cans fire, Clancy Thomas called from his AD-40C Harpy which had just rolled inverted into attack mode.

Scorpions are declared out of action, Captain Graham called. That was an official umpire ruling.

Aw, Ollie! All of us didn't get splattered! Adonica replied.

Umpire's ruling stands, Graham snapped back. And Adonica would have to abide by it. *You've taken fifty percent human casualties and lost eight of your Mary Anns. That's grounds for an out-of-action call.*

The Saucy Cans barrage didn't last very long. It was quickly followed by the main assault from the Wolfhound company as both enemy Mary Anns and Sierra Charlies erupted from cover and advanced with marching fire.

Kitsy had to keep her head down or be hit. *Alleycat Leader, this is Cougar Leader! We're pinned down and under assault! I need some help! Give me some Saucy Cans fire support! The Wolfers are out in the open now and very vulnerable!*

Cougar Leader, this is Alleycat Major! It was Battalion Sergeant Major

Nick Gerard who replied. *Alleycat Leader has his hands full as temporary regimental commander. Hand in there because the Wolfhound assault on your position has opened its flank to attack...and that's where Alleycat Leader is concentrating the regimental effort at the moment.*

Dammit, Gerard, we're getting creamed here! Kitsy complained.

All I can tell you, Captain, is to hold your ground Alleycat can't support you right now.

Basically, Kitsy Clinton knew she'd just been assigned as the company commander who'd take it in the chops in this battle. *Shit! Okay , if that's the way the major wants it, we'll give 'em hell! Puma Leader stay in stealth and increase your rate of fire.*

Cougar Leader, the Pumas are being overrun at the moment! But not before we got a bunch of those Wolfers!

Kitsy turned to her first sergeant and said aloud over the roar of battle, "Carol, if we're going to be wasted, we'll go down fighting!"

Master Sergeant Carol Head was an old hand, and he'd been through many real fights with live ammo. "Captain, we might as well. We have nothing left to lose."

Chapter Two

"Major Boswell, why is it that the United States is building a new ballistic missile silo and a very large missile inside it?"

The expression on the face of Major Boris Fedorovich Bugayev in the holographic video set and the tone of the Soviet officer's voice, much less his deliberate formal mode of conversation, immediately tipped off Major Arthur H. Boswell to the fact that something big had come catastrophically unbonded somewhere. "Comrade Boris, what the hell are you talking about?"

"Did you think that our Soviet surveillance satellites would not detect such a blatant breaking of the SMART-Three treaty?" the Soviet officer's image replied. The two of them conversed in a strange mixture of English and Russian they called Russlish, which was understandable to both of them.

"As I asked, Boris, what's got your back up?" Boswell told him. "What missile silo? Where?" He'd known Boris Fedorivich Bugayev for many years. They'd even taken the time and trouble to meet face-to-face in Berlin when the two of them had managed to wrangle two-week leaves at the same time - by prearrangement. They both served their respective defense establishments on their ends of a hot line that stretched between Tiff any, the big computer and space monitoring complex somewhere deep underground near Washington DC, and the Kaliningrad Space Defense Complex, the Soviet counterpart of Tiffany, which the two of them called Raisa, located deep underground somewhere on the outskirts of Moskva.

"You know of it! Do not attempt to evade the issue! It is not up to the Soviet Union to tell you about your own military activities!"

"Dammit, Boris!" Boswell exploded. "If you're going to make a fucking big deal out of something Zhigarev happened to see on some surveillance display at Zahvohd, at least let me know what that paranoid nut thinks he saw and where he thinks he saw it. We can get in a heap of trouble withholding information from each other!"

It quickly became apparent to Boswell that Bugayev was being watched by one or more people - probably KGB or GPU types - out of view of the holographic pickup. Boswell got the signals: a quick flick of Bugayev's eyes, the flip of the Soviet officer's pen back and forth, the uncomfortable movement of the man's arms and hands. Body language. Thank God that holographic teleconferencing allowed that element of interpersonal communication to come through.

So, this was serious red telephone stuff.

Someone over there was very nervous about something they'd seen from a Soviet surveillance satellite and had maybe even checked more closely with a high-resolution reconnaissance satellite. Boswell knew the Soviets had requested no hypersonic overflights in the past several months, but one might be expected very quickly if the Sovs were indeed super antsy about whatever the hell they'd seen.

Boswell didn't want to alert his colonel until he had a better handle on this bit of Soviet heartburn. So, he persisted, "Give me latitude and longitude coordinates. In fact, it would help if you could squirt me a fax or even a digitized graphics data stream. Degrade it to Level Four if you feel nervous about letting me know how good your resolution is." Boswell already knew that the Soviet military surveillance satellites could see the pimple on his ass if he wanted to show it to them. Most of the sensors came from US factories in a sort of accepted tech transfer. The US knew what the Soviets were stealing or buying through a complex chain of international purchasers. Better to know what your potential adversary is getting from you than to guess.

"It is more than just a missile silo. It may also be a high-energy ground-based laser weapon," Bugayev suddenly admitted. "It is not only a mere missile silo. It is an entire complex of buildings with extensive power lines leading to it and a new network of roads-"

"Comrade Boris, quit shitting me," Boswell snapped. "Where is it?"

"It is an area of many square kilometers. It is centered at latitude forty degrees thirty minutes north and longitude one-one-seven degrees thirteen minutes west," the Soviet officer's image finally admitted.

"Let me pull up some aerials of that area," Boswell said quickly, punching another keypad at his right. "Then I'll show you what I've got, and we'll see if it matches what you've got. Agreed?"

It didn't bother Boswell to show aerial views of part of the United States to his Soviet counterparts. Anyone could buy maps anywhere in the USA, and the Soviet surveillance satellites could check the maps against the satellite data. If the United States wanted to hide something in this era of twenty-first century open skies doctrine, it could be done using the same techniques the Soviets used. But Boswell wasn't aware of anything being deep under at this point. Soviet-American relations weren't lovey-dovey, but each side had a far less suspicious attitude about things that couldn't be hidden from one another.

"Agreed."

Where the hell was this place the Sovs had spotted? Boswell didn't know. Sounded like it was somewhere out west. Utah. Or maybe Nevada. "Tiffany," he told his computer complex so that Bugayev could hear, "show me the latest high-resolution aerial view of an area twenty-five kilometers around latitude four-zero degrees three-zero minutes north by longitude one-seven-zero degrees one-three minutes west."

Almost at once, an aerial photograph popped onto the screen before Boswell.

He didn't know where the hell it was.

But Bugayev was right.

An enormous complex of buildings, roads, and power lines covered the area. And there was something that looked like a very large and very deep excavation. The excavated earth was piled up on the sides of a mountain to the north; it looked like a deep mine with a tailings pile.

A careful look showed that several other mines were in the area; but they were far older, and their tailings piles were eroded.

"Tiffany, tell me the quadrangle map of this area published by the United States Geological Survey."

"Winnemucca, Nevada."

Boswell pointed at a large mountain, a huge white alkali flat, and a small town with a major highway and a railroad going through it. "Identify these locations I have touched on the screen."

"The high ground is Battle Mountain. The alkali flat has no name. The small town is Battle Mountain, Nevada," the computer's female voice replied earnestly.

"What is that apparent excavation I am pointing at?"

"Unknown."

"Tiffany, do you recognize my voice?"

"Affirmative."

"Who am I?"

"Major Arthur H. Boswell, United States Aerospace Force."

"I am placing my hand on the identification plate now. Confirm my identity."

"Identity confirmed. You are confirmed as Major Arthur H. Boswell, United States Aerospace Force."

The big megacomputer had not only reconfirmed what it already knew to be true, but also knew that Boswell was cleared for access to and release of whatever classified information he wanted. So, it didn't even hesitate for a picosecond when Boswell told it, "Tiffany, I want a verbal report on any - repeat, any - United States military activity occurring within the area displayed. What's going on there?"

"No military activity of the United States is being conducted in the area displayed on the screen."

"So, what does this picture show? What do you know about

anything that's going on there?"

"No information in data banks. Do you wish a search of other data banks?"

"It looks like a mining activity. Check the data bases of the Department of the Interior, the Bureau of Mines, the Social Security Administration, and the Occupational Safety and Health Administration," Boswell told Tiffany.

Tiffany went busily to work. It logged into those data bases accessed mining permits, ran searches on OSHA inspection reports, and looked for input of FICA funds coming from people in the area around Battle Mountain - and there weren't very many of those. In 645 milliseconds, Tiffany reported verbally, "No record of mining permits. No record of land leases on government properties in the area. No special increase m FICA funds from the area. No OSHA inspection reports."

"Tiffany, access the database of land records for the State of Nevada."

"Those records are not available to me."

"Get online with the State of Nevada computers in Carson City. Find out who owns that land."

"That networking is not available to me."

"Try the IRS database."

"That connection is not available to me."

Major Art Boswell sighed and turned to his counterpart's image in the holo tank. "Comrade Boris," he told Bugayev, using the familiar term of their everyday intercommunication, "there we are! You want our pictures?"

"*Da!*"

"Coming at you in Channel Niner-Romeo," Boswell told him. "Tiffany, transmit the aerial visual to Raisa in Kaliningrad at once, highest possible resolution baud rate, Channel Niner-Romeo."

"Information transmitted. Receipt confirmed by Raisa."

"So, Boris, what the hell do you want me to do that I haven't done?" Boswell asked his Soviet counterpart.

"Your visual information tends to confirm ours. But that could have been prearranged. We cannot gain access to the national data bases you appear to have queried. Therefore, we cannot be absolutely certain. We must know what is going on there. If you do not find out and tell us, we will invoke the SMART-Three treaty and send in an inspection team as it is our right."

Boswell didn't want the Soviets snooping around in Nevada. Neither did anyone in the Department of Defense. The National Security Council would have fits if the Soviets tried to use this as an excuse to get near some of the activities going on out in America's "Empty Quarter." Battle Mountain wasn't that far away from "things" a few hundred kilometers to the south. Site 51 was still a very black place. Boswell himself didn't know what was happening there, but he knew it was stealthed and camouflaged. It was carefully hidden from the surveillance, reconnaissance, ELINT, and other snooping spacecraft of other nations. Its electromagnetic and gravito-inertial radiations were carefully shielded by technologies that made the old Tempest facilities seem crude. Rumor Control occasionally passed a snippet of information that implied the development of a faster-than-light starship propulsion system. Or gravito-inertial tractor and repulsor beams. Or highly classified bio-electronic research that could make the U.S. Army's neuroelectronic warbots totally obsolete. Furthermore, the McCarthy Proving Ground for joint service robotics and bio-electronics was just northwest of Las Vegas.

He didn't want to be the one who would be nailed for giving the Soviets any excuse for sending an inspection team in there. Such an outfit could wander afield. The major threat of general war wasn't what it had been, but that was because American technology was the only thing that had held the dogs of war at bay for a hundred years. Truly advanced technology had to be kept under wraps - or at least its military applications.

But Boswell also knew the Soviets could get nasty in their tiresome way if something wasn't done to check out this anomaly in Nevada.

"I think we can get you the answers you want, Boris. We want them, too," Boswell admitted. "Can you live with it for a few days while we get someone like the FBI to check into what the hell's going on out there and who's making a hole in the ground that looks like a silo or beam weapon facility?"

"We expect a report within seventy-two hours. Then we will exercise our right to send in an inspection team," Bugayev stated, looking at a scrap of paper someone had passed to him from out of the holo pickup's field of view.

"We'll keep you advised, Boris." *That's for certain*, he told himself. He was glad he'd taped this. Although he hadn't wanted the colonel to joggle his elbow while this holo-conference was going on - the colonel had a tendency to be testy when called from his quarters at 0230 in the dark - Boswell now had to get the tapes on the hooter to higher command ASAP.

Who the hell was screwing around digging up the godforsaken Nevada desert? If it wasn't a mining operation, what the hell was it? One thing he did know, whoever was doing it sure as hell wasn't advertising it.

Boswell was wrong. He just wasn't watching the proper video channels.

Chapter Three

"Dammit, Captain Sweet, why did you have to pull that goddamned non-doctrinaire stunt in the middle of a war game?" To say that Major Jerry P. Allen was upset was to put it mildly. He was royally pissed off. He was probably as angry with himself as he was with Captains Kitsy Clinton and Adonica Sweet, who stood before the desk in the office of the regimental commander of the 3rd Robot Infantry Regiment (Special Combat), the Washington Greys, at Fort Huachuca, Arizona.

"What do you mean, non-doctrinaire, Jerry?" Adonica snapped back. "It was the Motega maneuver. Dyani has used it several times in recent war games."

Jerry Allen didn't reply at once. Then he said quietly, "I called you into this office, Captain Sweet, to chew you out personally and officially. Following Colonel Carson's example and procedure, I don't like to dress down an officer in front of the whole regiment. Captain Clinton, you're here because you're Captain Sweet's company commander. Therefore, you're responsible for her actions in the war games this morning."

Kitsy Clinton caught on right away. Formally, she replied, "Yes, sir! I know that, sir! Captain Sweet's use of the unorthodox Motega maneuver should have been obvious to me at once. However, I wasn't familiar with that tactical action, sir. And Captain Sweet was already doing it before I could order it stopped."

"No excuse, Captain," Jerry reminded her. He had to be stern with her, just as he had to be formal with Adonica. He liked Kitsy Clinton and always had. And he was glad that she'd been released from Walter Reed and had been cleared for active duty again. When her neck had been broken in Iraq and everyone thought she'd bought the farm, he'd been as gloomy as the rest of the Greys. Now Kitsy was back. And to have this happen on her first buck out of the chute was unfortunate. On the other hand, Kitsy had to get up to speed again, and she'd make mistakes at first. Kitsy hadn't been on a battlefield for two years...

Being format with Adonica was something else. Ever since the two of them had met during Operation Steel Band on Trinidad, they'd been deeply in love with one another. Thus, Jerry's emotions threatened to get in the way of his responsibilities as temporary regimental commander.

"I felt no compunction about using the Motega maneuver, Jerry," Adonica put in. But she did feel strange standing at attention in front of his desk. She'd rarely stood at attention for Jerry Allen. "It seemed to be called for at the moment. As far as I was concerned, if it worked for Dyani, it would work for me."

Again, Jerry Allen didn't reply at once. When he did, his voice was even more stern. "Captain Sweet, understand something right here and now. You're standing in the presence of your acting regimental commander until Colonel Carson returns from leave."

"Jerry, no one is here but the three of us!" Adonica objected. "We're all more than just close friends. You got a bitch? Lay it on the line! Let's talk it out as we usually do."

Adonica hadn't picked up on the signals Jerry was sending. Kitsy, being a West Pointer like Jerry, spotted it at once. She decided it was time to do something about it. "Major, with your permission, sir, may I speak with Captain Sweet right now? Right here?"

Jerry nodded. He didn't know exactly what else to do. He was afraid that something like this would happen some day. He didn't know exactly how he'd handle it when he found himself commanding the person he loved and being forced to reprimand her, even in private, for making a mistake that could have been deadly. The personal problem associated with the intimate relationship between Adonica and him was the sort of thing higher and wiser officers had worried about ever since the Washington Greys had allowed women into field combat alongside men and warbots.

"Captain Sweet," Kitsy told her platoon officer, "personal feelings have been left at the door of this office. I'm your immediate superior officer, and I'm making a request of you - and I'm sure you're aware that a 'request' is equivalent to a direct order. Please exhibit a respectful demeanor to your regimental commander...and to me. This is *not* a personal matter. It's official. Do you understand me?"

Adonica Sweet's pretty face suddenly lost its expression of friendly aggression and became profoundly serious. "Yes, Captain. I understand, ma'am. My apologies..."

"Accepted." Kitsy turned to Jerry. "Major, I believe I've straightened out some confusion on the part of my subordinate."

"Thank you, Captain Clinton." Jerry was momentarily relieved. He'd crossed the first difficult hurdle. Looking directly at Adonica, he reverted to his West Point First Class persona. That helped. Now he realized that the stratified class organization of West Point did indeed have practical use out in the Real World of the United States Army. "Captain Sweet, the Motega maneuver isn't part of our tactical doctrine. It was unknown and unanticipated by your company commander, who's been back for only a week," Jerry went on. He tried to handle this situation the way he thought Lieutenant Colonel Curt Carson would have done had he been here instead of on a well-earned thirty-day leave.

"Sir, it works for Captain Motega," Adonica pointed out stiffly.

"Captain Motega is an outstanding scout. That's why she commands the scouting platoon," Jerry reminded her. "She's *not* the commander of an assault platoon as you are. Although as commander of TACBATT I encourage everyone to exhibit initiative and independent thinking, I also demand that they communicate their intentions to their immediate superiors if possible. Sometimes it isn't possible. But it was today. The last thing any commander wants is the Big Surprise from his own people."

"I'm sorry you weren't prepared for it, Captain. And, Major," Adonica replied, her face expressionless, "next time, I'll let Captain Clinton know what I intend to do."

"Captain Sweet, I'll tell you what I didn't get the chance to tell you today," Kitsy said with equal simplicity. "When I saw what you did against an equal force of Sierra Charlies and warbots, I knew you'd get creamed by a twenty-five from a Wolfhound Mary Ann."

"That shouldn't have happened. Lieutenant Pagan was supposed to maintain suppressive fire," Adonica pointed out.

"You forgot one of several things our venerable regimental sergeant major has been trying to teach us," Kitsy told her flatly, referring to Henry Kester's whimsical but tested Code of Combat. "'Suppressive fire doesn't.'"

"The Motega maneuver was intended for scouting and patrolling under fire," Jerry reminded her. "It isn't an assault technique."

"When you made your frontal assault using it, you also gave away the basic position of the Cougars," Kitsy added. "The Wolfers already knew where Pagan was. It was his job as fire base to also attract enemy fire. It was your job to maneuver and hit the Wolfers where they didn't expect it, not to mount a frontal assault on them." Kitsy knew from experience that the pretty little blond captain had a violently aggressive streak in her contrast to Lew Pagan's solid, professional approach.

"And when the Wolfhounds clobbered you, that opened a weak point in our defensive offense," Jerry pointed out to her, then added, "Remember Killer Kelly?"

"No, sir. He was transferred out before I came aboard from OCS."

"He was too aggressive for the Greys," Jerry explained. "Ask Major Frazier about the details. Now Kelly is Gee-three for the Wolfhounds. We weren't dealing with an opponent without the same excellent cee-cubed-eye as we're supposed to have. Kelly apparently saw the umpire put the Cougars out of action. So, he obviously told Colonel Salley to move fast and exploit the weak point. That screwed up my whole wheeling maneuver."

"Wheeling maneuver? Major Allen, speaking of cee-cubed-eye, you said nothing in your Oscar brief about a wheeling maneuver!" Adonica reminded him.

Kitsy said nothing. Adonica was right. This was the first she'd heard of a planned wheeling maneuver on Jerry Allen's part. She suddenly knew what the big problem was and why the Greys had lost the war game that morning.

They were friends. Close friends. Too close in some cases. They assumed the other persons could anticipate the plans and actions of their friends based on familiarity and close association. They'd failed to fully communicate. They'd taken things for granted.

Captain Kitsy Clinton knew that Major Jerry Allen was just as much at fault for the defeat as Adonica was.

And as she was.

At that moment, all three of them knew what the problem really was.

An awkward silence pervaded the room.

It was at that point that Jerry Allen looked to his role model, Curt Carson. *What would Curt do?* Jerry asked himself. The answer was obvious.

Curt Carson never hesitated to admit he was wrong, even to subordinates. Then the colonel would entertain a frank and open critique so that the same problem wouldn't occur again. It took a very positive self-assured leader to do these things. Jerry was learning, just as Curt had learned from now-General Belinda Hetterick, who had learned from a predecessor long retired. Leadership wasn't all in the books. As Curt had once told Jerry, "Leadership is like sex; until you do it; you don't know a damned thing about it...and no one can really teach you beforehand."

"Ladies," Major Jerry Allen said quietly, "I need to apologize. Mostly to you, Captain Sweet. But to Captain Clinton as well. I wasn't imprecise in my Oscar briefing, but I did fail to communicate to you my change in tactical plan as the war game progressed. It became clear to me when the Wolfhounds began their advance that Colonel Salley decided to take advantage of two factors. The first was his knowledge that Captain Clinton had just returned from two years of medical treatment. The second smacks of Major Kelly's thinking because the Wolfhound attack was directed at the Cougars. He counted on your company, Captain Clinton, as being the weak link in our T-O and E..."

Kitsy bristled at the interference. "Major, are you implying that the Wolfhounds thought my company was weak because the Cougars have two women officers and a woman NCO whereas the Ferrets are an all-male outfit?"

Jerry shook his head. "Not the Wolfhounds. Major Marty 'Kill-em-all' Kelly did. I served with him while he was still in the Greys. He's one of those chauvinistic sons-of-bitches who thinks women shouldn't be on the battlefield because combat is a man's job..."

"Sir, with all dur respect, I request permission to-" Adonica began.

Jerry held up his hand to interrupt her. "Never mind what you think you'd like to do to him, Captain, but permission denied. He outranks you, and I don't want you to get into trouble for striking a superior officer."

"That's not exactly what I had in mind for him, Major," Adonica Sweet replied in a low voice, although the fire was still in her eyes.

"Whatever. Forget it." Jerry's face was impassive as he went on, "We all made mistakes out there today. I neglected to communicate my intentions to you, Captain Clinton, and you didn't blow the whistle on Captain Sweet quickly enough. Captain Sweet, you didn't communicate your intentions to Captain Clinton. But-" he shrugged-"that's what war games are for. Better we make dumb mistakes with jelly rounds going past than on an actual battlefield..."

"...and we'll make plenty of mistakes there, too," Kitsy added.

"As long as we don't repeat the same dumb ones we made in war games," Jerry corrected her. "I'm scheduling a critique, a Charlie briefing, for fifteen hundred hours. I'll bring up the dumb mistakes I made, but I'll say nothing about the dumb ones both of you made. I expect you to do that yourselves."

Adonica looked at Kitsy as Kitsy looked at Adonica. Both of them said in unison, "Yes, sir!"

"And consider that you've both been unofficially chewed-out by your temporary regimental commander, who's also discovered, as a result, that he probably rates an ass-chewing from the division commander..." Jerry paused for a moment to reflect on that. Then he grinned. "And I'm damned glad General Hettrick and the Seventeenth Iron Fist Division weren't involved today. I've seen Colonel Carson get it in the chops from General Hettrick. That's why I'm glad she wasn't there. Okay, you're dismissed! Let's get to the Charlie session..."

Both saluted and left. Adonica said nothing more and didn't break the official attitude she'd assumed as a result of having her nose rubbed in her familiarity by Kitsy. But Kitsy did pause at the door and turn back to Jerry. In a quiet voice, she said, "Major, considering the relationship between you and Captain Sweet, I want to say that you handled that very well indeed, sir."

"I wonder, Captain. I wonder."

And wonder Jerry Allen did. He'd been able to institute and maintain official military discipline during the confrontation over what was a trivial matter, the loss of a war game. No lives had been lost. No one had been injured (although for a week or so Adonica would have a nasty bruise on her torso where the 25-millimeter jelly round had hit and knocked her down). No equipment had been damaged or destroyed. Only the pride of the Washington Greys had been hurt. Jerry had had to eat a little crow because he'd been at fault, too.

But what really worried him was whether or not he'd be able to maintain that same sort of discipline if Adonica had been seriously wounded or even killed. Combat was a deadly game to play. It was bad enough that close friends were occasionally wounded or killed. He wasn't quite so sure how he'd handle it if the woman he loved was ever killed on the battlefield because of a dumb mistake she'd made. Or, even worse, as a result of a dumb mistake he'd made.

Kitsy thought she knew what was troubling him. So, she tried to give it some perspective and make light humor in her perky way. "All's fair in love and war, Major."

"Depends on the definition of 'fair,' Captain."

Chapter Four

Wyatt Bloomington didn't look like an FBI agent.

For that matter, Battle Mountain, Nevada, didn't look much like a town, either.

The FBI man would have looked more at home monitoring a bank computer's display screen. Actually, he'd been hired by the FBI because of his background as a CPA dealing with the casinos in Laughlin and Tahoe. The FBI didn't need detectivelike agents as much as they needed those who could monitor and mentor computers in the constant job of tracking down the money-mining activities of underworld figures. The sovereign state of Nevada was still a haven for individualists, outcasts, lost souls, entrepreneurs, gangsters, people with money to hide, people with money to lose, frontier types, people who thought the damned world was already too crowded, and people engaged in the classical activities of pioneers who were running from irate husbands, bitchy wives, bill collectors, possible litigators, criminal prosecutors, or lethal lovers. If Phoenix was the financial hub of the western Pacific rim, then Nevada was its Switzerland with far more liberal laws of all sorts, including banking laws. Most inhabitants firmly believed that "N-E-V-A-D-A" spelled "freedom."

Wyatt Bloomington had been sent out from the Vegas office simply because he was available, not because he was a sleuth. He was a money-mining expert, a man who was very good at tracing money from clandestine sources, foreign and domestic, that appeared to be "mined" in Nevada and was subsequently deposited in various Nevada banks. Some of this money came from legitimate real estate deals, some from casino winnings, some from various high-tech activities. But some of it came north across the now-open Mexican border from activities that were definitely illegal in the United States (but not in Nevada, which had laws that were much looser). Wyatt Bloomington was very good at the nit-picky and intense poring through computer files and data bases looking for illegal money mines. He'd never carried a gun in his life. He was not an outdoorsman. He was definitely not the kind of FBI agent to handle this scouting job.

As for the "city" of Battle Mountain, it wasn't a ghost town quite yet. It refused to die as it always had. Basically, a crossroads for stagecoaches, railroads, and interstate truckers, in that sequence, Battle Mountain was a place where you got off the train or the bus if you already had a job there. But the gold, copper, and barite mines were closed now, their lodes exhausted and their smelters crumbling back into the tailing piles. Battle Mountain had reverted to a wide place on Interstate 80, with one off-ramp to the east and another to the west of the "business district" with a refueling station at each exit. Long 150-car freight trains of the Western-Central Pacific Railroad still rumbled regularly through as they had for nearly two centuries, but they rarely stopped except to drop off or pick up freight cars on the siding. One lonely motel remained, more as a concession to those who had to come to Battle Mountain because it was the Lander County seat; the land, business, tax, marriage, divorce, birth, and death records were there. Truckers often stopped to eat at Don's Diner which boasted a sixteen-page menu. Other truckers stopped at the Calico Club because the girls were licensed, clean, and gave value received. Ranchers and a few prospectors came into Battle Mountain to visit Lemaire's general store, which had once been owned for two centuries by the town's founding family.

The only thing that kept Battle Mountain really alive was the huge and growing religious commune fifty kilometers to the southwest. But no one in Battle Mountain really knew a lot about it. "A bunch of religious nuts" was the general appellation the Battle Mountaineers used among themselves but never in front of those religious nuts. The strange people from the Galactic Tabernacle of the Human Future spent some money in Battle Mountain for supplies, but just enough to keep the town alive; they apparently needed Battle Mountain as a connection point to the American transportation system. The railroad delivered most of what went into whatever was going on back there on the alkali flats and in the hills-Bloomington had seen the satellite photos, and the activity was extensive. The Galactic Tabernacle of the Human Future must have a lot of money, he decided, because they'd built a rail spur down to their commune, laying the initial tracks along the abandoned right-of-way of the old Nevada Central.

All of this puzzled Wyatt Bloomington as he stood on the banks of the flowing Reese River and gazed southward along the tracks and the remarkably good two-lane hard-surfaced road. State Route 305 had gone to seed because hardly anyone used it except ranchers with four-wheel drives when they didn't fly their aerodynes into town. But the new road was right next to the old one and had lighter gradients. If Bloomington had had a military background - which he didn't - he would have spotted the fact that the new road had been designed for heavy trucking where shallow grades allowed higher vehicle speeds with heavier loads.

Bloomington paid little attention to the nonprofits that had proliferated in Nevada. The IRS rode herd on those 50l(c) outfits, and the FBI couldn't touch them unless someone suspected that something illegal was going on outside of the tax turf of the IRS. But he suspected that there was one hell of a lot of money involved here.

The people of Battle Mountain - less than a thousand of them now - were strangely silent about whatever was going on over the slight rise between the mass of Battle Mountain itself and the tilted rocks of the Fish Creek Mountains. In a way, they acted a little embarrassed, as if those religious nuts were somehow bringing a bad name to their town.

"We don't mess around out there," the county sheriff had admitted to Bloomington earlier in the afternoon. "Those people keep their noses clean. They don't come into town much. Don't hear nothin' about 'em or from 'em. The head honcho of their security people told us five years ago when they moved in that they'd keep their own camp clean and lawful...and they have."

A similar but stranger story had come from Bloomington's brief conversation with the owner of the Shellexxo station where he'd refueled the plain grey four-door government sedan. "Used to hunt over on the south side of Battle Mountain until the religious nuts bought the land. Can't get there now. Strongest, sharpest fence you've ever seen. Kids don't even get into any trouble out there no more now that the school closed down here, and we send them seventy klicks over to Winnemucca...and that there's a one-hour ride on the bus each way every day. So they's pretty bushed each night when they get home. Anyway, nobody screws around up on Battle Mountain anymore anyhow - especially since them two boys flat disappeared up in Galena Canyon 'bout two years ago."

That was of passing interest to the FBI man; The service station owner didn't have much more information, but he wasn't reluctant to repeat what he knew, which wasn't much. The man rambled on, probably because he didn't often get to talk to a stranger and impress him with local know-how. "Coulda fallen down one of them old mine shafts, but we didn't bother to look very long. You don't last very long if you fall a hundred meters down one of them shafts and get busted up at the bottom. The commune's security people wouldn't let us inside the fence. Promised to search for them. Never reported back to the sheriff, of course. But that sheriff lost the next election, and the kids' parents left town afterward. Sort of a closed book now. Besides, we got lots of hunting space elsewhere. And if the religious nuts want privacy for whatever they do out there, that's their privilege. This here's a free state. So damned much room that near everyone can do what he wants without botherin' his neighbor. Too many people comin' out here because of that. Funny we still call it the 'Empty Quarter.' Hell, any more you can't go a hundred klicks without seeing someone. Twelve-fifty-seven for the gas. Uh, yeah, I guess the company will honor that government credit card for your gas. Don't see many of them around here. You with the Department of the Interior, huh?"

Fortunately, someone in the Las Vegas office had provided a little cover for this FBI fishing expedition. Not that it did much good in the long run...

***

Bloomington studied the satellite photo again and recalled his supervisor's orders. "Wyatt, try to find out what the hell's going on south of Battle Mountain. Lot of digging. I hope it's just a new mine, but nobody seems to have any records of it. The Russkies saw it with one of their, satellites and threaten to send in an inspection team if the Bureau doesn't check it out as clean under thw SMART-Three treaty. And the boss sure as hell doesn't want a bunch of KGB types snooping around up there on our turf. Go in and talk to them. Find out who the hell they are and what they're doing. Get some photos if you can. Yeah, you can flash your ID, but tell them this is no official investigation, just checking up so State can get the Russkies off our ass."

Bloomington hadn't relished the thought of a long trip into the Empty Quarter, but at least it was a chance to get out of Vegas after a couple of long, hard, grinding months of tracking mined money.

It was Thursday, and he didn't have to be back until Monday morning. Might as well get it over as quickly as possible, then get to Reno for a little relaxation. Bloomington was a straight arrow as all FBI types were; the kind of relaxation he wanted was nothing more than eating good food, lounging by a pool looking at pretty girls he was far too shy to talk to, and getting lots of sleep…alone. If it was just a big religious commune, he'd get some photos of people with shaved heads and saffron robes and rice bowls…and go on to Reno that evening.

The Far Outers of the twenty-first century's romantic, anti-technology, back-to-nature movement bothered him a little. He didn't like surprises and living in his world of discipline and social restraint insured no surprises. The Far Outers, on the other hand, acted as if there were no restraints on human behavior. They acted as they damned well wished. Like the hippies of the 1960's and the back-to-sheepherding romanticists of the nineteenth century, to Wyatt Bloomington they were just another weird aberration of human behavior. Insofar as he was concerned, these people were off the track; the rest of the world would forge ahead and leave them behind as it had done before.

But in the meantime, it looked like he was going to have to handle an exceptionally well-heeled group of them around Battle Mountain.

The new road paralleled the new railway spur and turned west from old State Route 305. It went through a narrow defile between the 2,500-meter mass of Battle Mountain and a clump of rocks. As Bloomington drove the sedan into the gap, he noticed that a stout cyclone fence began to closely follow on both sides of the road. Finally, the road branched into a median-divided highway, and fences appeared on the median as well. Furthermore, the fences were so close to the road that no shoulder was available for turning around.

A stout steel barrier closed the road ahead of him, so he pulled up to it and stopped the car.

A large robot rolled up to the car. Another robot came up on the other side, and yet a third robot pulled in behind the car. None of the robots appeared armed, but Bloomington was aware that some police robots had weapons that could be hidden in a retracted position. He was surrounded. So, he rolled the window down and called to the robot that came right up to the left front window. "Good afternoon. I would like to speak to someone in charge, please."

"I am Captain David West of the Host of Michael, Galactic Tabernacle of the Human Future. I am in charge of this security shift. What is your business here, sir?" was the polite reply in a male voice.

Bloomington suddenly realized that he was confronted with neuroelectronically controlled robots. This surprised him because only the Department of Defense was supposed to have that highly classified technology.

Could this be a super-black DoD operation? he asked himself.

But he didn't raise the question. Instead, he pulled out his credential case and flipped it open to reveal his ID to the robot's visual sensor.

"I'm Agent Wyatt Bloomington of the FBI. I want to ask a few questions of someone in authority here."

The massive steel gate, strong enough to stop a light armored vehicle, suddenly swung open in front of the car. "Please proceed, Mr. Bloomington," the robot told him.

The three robots accompanied the car through the gate which closed securely behind them. But the road ahead was then blocked by yet another robot, this one far larger and obviously designed to stop a large motor vehicle. There was no way around the new robot because the heavy fence came up on both sides of the road, leaving no room to get past or even to turn a car around.

"You will be provided with transportation from this point, Mr. Bloomington. Please leave the car," the robot ordered as a large vehicle appeared behind the robot blocking the road ahead.

The security is tight indeed, Bloomington told himself as he got out of the sedan. It *had* to be a super-secure defense installation, even with a cover name like the Galactic Tabernacle of the Human Future. So, Bloomington relaxed a bit. He thought he was now dealing with yet another organization of the Department of Defense. Who else would be able to afford such strict security measures? Such stringent procedures and equipment were very expensive. And who else would have robots that were obviously controlled by classified neuroelectronic technology?

It did seem a bit strange to him that DOD hadn't informed the Las Vegas field office of this Battle Mountain activity. They'd certainly done so with the hyper-secure Site 51 complex on the Nellis Air Force Base Gunnery Range. Yet, as he recalled, the request to check Battle Mountain had apparently come to the Department of Justice from the Department of State because of the concern about possible SMART-III treaty violation. But why hadn't State contacted DOD?

Maybe they had. "You seem to be expecting me," he said to the robot.

"We've been expecting you for a long time," the voice of the remote robot operator replied. "The Prophet Mathys has warned us for years that the forces of evil would eventually learn of our quest and begin to harass us. We expected that people from the FBI would come first. So, we are ready for you, and we can defend ourselves against you!"

Wyatt Bloomington wasn't a trained field agent who could handle violence. So, he hadn't guarded his minus-x. He never saw the robot that knocked him unconscious by the simple, low-tech method of hitting him in the head with a blackjack from behind.

Chapter Five

"The Tabernacle of *what?*"

"The Galactic Tabernacle of the Human Future, Mr. President," General Albert W. Murray, USAF (Ret), the head of the National Intelligence Agency, told his boss, handing him the yellow-bound document. The fact that it was yellow-bound was a discreet signal to those who knew that the document bore the highest possible national security classification. Classified documents that sensitive weren't advertised with rubber stamps; the color of the binding was the code. "Here's the NIA report we found." (See Appendix II.)

"What is NIA doing with a report on a domestic religious group?" the President wanted to know. Only the two of them were in the Oval Office. Murray had requested a private palaver in spite of the fact that State, Defense, and Justice, and Interior probably should be involved and would be involved eventually.

Murray had anticipated this question. "We were concerned about the possibility that it might be a cover."

"For what?"

"We didn't know. We still don't know," Murray admitted. One of the reasons he wanted, a private conference with The Man was the fact that the NIA had blown this pretty badly thus far. "But we were also concerned about possible international connections to their prophet, Dr. Clark Jeremy Mathys."

"The television astronomer? My kids used to watch him. So did I. I wish my TV persona was that good. Plus, he's a good science teacher," the President admitted, riffling the few pages of the report but not attempting to read it then; he'd get to it this coming weekend at Camp David.

"He used to be," Murray agreed. "He also used to be a very good planetary astronomer before he apparently blew his neural circuits. According to the report, he's a genuine case. He's been 'talking' to extraterrestrials by neuroelectronic linkage with his personal computer."

"Al, all the nuts aren't up in the trees. By the way, this report is almost two years old," the President remarked, noticing the covered title page.

"Yes, sir. In spite of Dr. Mathys' extensive involvement with the international scientific community before he went ballistic, we found nothing to concern us from the national security standpoint. The analysis you're holding got flagged as a Priority Charlie Three mainly because some of my analysts believed the Tabernacle might become dangerous. It's a loose cannon that we don't worry about unless something like the Soviet heartburn surfaces."

The President tapped the bound report with his finger. "Did the FBI get a copy of this?"

"No, sir."

"Why not?" The President was the former CEO of a Fortune 500 company. He was known for being able to ask both piercing and embarrassing questions.

"We found no evidence of activities that would be of interest to any other federal agency...with the possible exception of the IRS. But they run their own show, and frankly, I don't want to step on their turf if I can help it, sir," Murray explained. "Mr. President, the activities of the Tabernacle are a domestic matter. You'd be more than a little upset with me if I'd gone any farther than I did." He didn't want to poach on the FBI's turf, either. Staying alive in a sensitive Washington position involved many factors, and Murray had held his job through several administrations by keeping his nose clean and giving no one an excuse to "request his resignation." True, he'd always known of fascinating skeletons in White House, FBI, and other agency closets that weren't legally part of his turf, and that helped a little. Sometim6 intelligence work revealed all sorts of seemingly disconnected threads.

"Well, it's become something more than a domestic matter now. Somebody out there in the wilds of Nevada seems to be building one hell of a big facility that Mosco thinks is a silo for a damned big missile," the President reminded him. "I need to respond in a believable manner to the Premier in the next day or so. This report of yours helps, but it's inconclusive and not supported by on-the-spot reconnaissance. Crittenden just reported they haven't heard from the agent they sent in there," the man admitted, thinking back to the telephone call he'd made to his attorney general a few hours ago.

Murray knew that, but he wasn't supposed to. So, he said nothing.

The President sensed this, so he went on, "Al, I don't ask where you get your information. But you've been dead-nuts right on target every time I've called for you inputs. What do you think is going on here? And I'll listen to any advice you might have on what the next move should be."

"Lots of stuff being transported into that place. Lot of stuff coming out, too…and we can't figure that one out. Judging from the rail and road transport activity we've seen on satellite images, the Tabernacle is indeed building a space-ship out there as the report indicates," Murray ventured to say. "That's part of their creed: The followers of Mathys will go to the stars, contact the extraterrestrials, and come back to save the human race from unimaginable evil about to be perpetrated by extraterrestrial enemies who've placed agents even in the White House."

The President shook his head. "Some of those nuts have fallen to the ground. I'd better read this tonight."

"Better read it in the morning, Mr. President," Murray advised him. "In view of what's happening, you might not sleep very well otherwise. These Tabernacle people seem to be even more paranoid than the Soviets. And they're prepared to defend themselves against anything we might try to do to investigate them. When you read that, you'll discover that we're considered by them to be their nemesis."

The President glanced again at the folder of satellite photos. He shook his head. "I know what it takes to build facilities like this," he remarked. Indeed he did. He'd helped plan, design, finance, and bring on-line dozens of large factories all over North America. He'd been one of those twenty-first century capitalists who'd moved to ensure that the United States remained on the leading edge of the world's economy by incorporating high tech into products and processes as quickly as possible. "Where the hell are they getting the money?"

"You haven't been watching the satellite channels used by various religions, Mr. President. Neither have I. Some of those religious people passing the collection plate on the tube always struck me as being among the most fraudulent con artists in the world. But it's a free country, and I don't have to watch them. My wife likes to watch Mathys every once in a while. She says he's got a fantastic pair of bedroom eyes. I guess that helps him raise money." He smiled slightly. "Anyway, the best data I can get out of the IRS is that they take in billions, all of it tax deductible. And most of it because of Mathys' tube appeal."

"So, what do you think my next step should be, Al?"

"Give Jim Floyd a call at the Pentagon and have him send in some troops for a reconnaissance in force."

This caused the President to start. "Dammit, Al, do you want to get me impeached? Send military forces into a domestic matter just because the Soviets put a little pressure on me? Hell, even Len Spencer couldn't make that sound palatable to the media!"

"You've got precedent, sir."

"This isn't two hundred years ago, Al. I can't send in troops to bust up strikes or chase Indians back to their reservations!"

"Yes, sir, I think you can."

"Explain!"

"Provo, Utah, is my hometown."

"What's that got to do with this?"

"We learned some things in school out there that they don't teach anywhere else," Murray explained.

"Such as?"

"There's a very old federal statute whose citation I don't remember, but Joan Crittenden can quickly find out, I'm sure. It was passed by Congress and signed by President Polk. It was first used by President Buchanan during the Utah Expedition of eighteen fifty-seven. I think President Cleveland also used it during the labor unrests of the late nineteenth century. It permits the President to use federal military units in situations where state authority cannot or will not act to provide for public safety under the Constitution."

The President passed his hand over his telephone and called, "Mary, get Attorney General Crittenden on the secure line right away, please." He turned back to his intelligence chief, who he knew had stood Number Four in his class from the Aerospace Force Academy. The President was reaching for straws here, and he had to cover his anatomy. Murray knew it, too, which was why he'd made the reference to the AG. "Governor Hopkins owes me a few. If Crittenden thinks this will work..."

"Mr. President, I suggest you also call the governor of Nevada right away and ask him to send a couple of state troopers in to see what's happening. I'll script the telephone request for you if you want," Murray offered.

"I'd appreciate that, Al." The President had no compunctions about using helpful associates whether they were on his actual staff or not. For the moment, he wanted to keep this matter totally under wraps. The usual leak from a "reliable White House source" could set off a media feeding frenzy that would quickly spread from Battle Mountain, Nevada, to Moscow. And it would only make things a great deal worse. "Your suggestion about the state troopers is a good idea. If they don't clear this up, I'll ask the governor to check it out with some Nevada National Guard troops. And if Hopkms balks at any point and Crittenden has the citation on that statute, I'll send in federal troops to find out what's going on. But we've got to keep it quiet. Very quiet."

"Yes, sir. I realize that. The idea that a bunch of rich religious nuts are building a 'missile silo' out in Nevada and that the Soviets might try to nuke it even with the Strategic Defense Forces on alert - well, I don't like the possible scenarios."

The President sighed. "Neither do I."

Actually, Murray was thinking that he didn't want the Soviets to know about some ultra-black Super Cosmic Magic Top Secret activities that were going on couple of hundred kilometers to the south of there, nor did he want the news media to even get wind of some of it.

The President knew about those, too, of course, even though he didn't fully understand the new bio-electronic technology involved. Or the details of the new energy systems. Or even the principles behind the gravito-inertial radiation research and development. He only knew that the scientists and engineers were delving as deeply inward through the universe of the human mind as they were also opening possibilities for the outward expansion of the human race. If the human mmd and the stars were to be conquered, he and others wanted it to be done by free human beings, not by those whose history was one of exerting total control over human beings.

While the President was talking to the attorney general, Murray took out his pocket processor and worked up a script for the telephone call to the governor of Nevada. By the time the President's telephone call was completed, Murray had finished, and the pocket processor had spit out a hard copy.

"She's checking," the President reported. "May take a couple of hours. Data that old usually hasn't been put in the data base."

"Yes, sir. So calling the governor of Nevada and asking him the favor of checking it out not only buys you the time you need but also covers you in a dozen different ways," Murray pointed out, handing him the hard copy. "But, if I were you, sir, I'd adjourn this conversation and call a meeting that involves me, Turner of FBI, the attorney general, and the secretary of defense. Then convene National Security Council immediately thereafter."

Murray was slick, the President decided. He also reconfirmed his suspicions that he should never get on the brown downwind side of the intelligence chief. The man could become a formidable enemy in the jungles of the Potomac.

Fortunately, General Albert W. Murray was an honorable person.

Not all the graduates of the service academies turned out that way. But when an impressionable young person has been subjected to four intense years surrounded by an honor code plus the motivators of duty, honor, and country, a very large percentage of those who survive to graduate place those intangibles even above their own lives.

"Thanks for the advice, General. But I want to add generals Barnitz and Carlisle as well as Admiral Spencer to that list," the President advised him. "I suspect we're going to have to ask our armed services to put the lives of their people on the line again, and I won't do that without having them involved in the situation as soon as feasible."

Chapter Six

"Curt, you can't afford this!"

Lieutenant Dyani Motega was both stunned and upset with the opulence that surrounded them. That was apparent to Lieutenant Colonel Curt Carson because Dyani had used his given name rather than her private, personal nickname for him.

"But I can, Deer Arrow," he replied, deliberately using the Anglicized version of her Crow Indian name that was his nickname for her - and also her tacomm code when she was in the field leading her SCOUT platoon. "Don't forget how the take in these casino hotels is set up. Room and board are usually at less than cost. The establishment makes it up in the casino because of the house percentage."

She shook her head in bewilderment, but her expression betrayed the fact that she approved and intended to enjoy this. The room was huge, and three walls could be made transparent to give one the feeling of being out in the forest beyond; or they could be made opaque for total privacy. Holographic projections could be ordered up for any of the three walls so that the room would seem to be in any part of the world the occupants desired...or nowhere at all. Two bathrooms were available, each with all the sybaritic amenities. Two "dressing rooms" the size of Curt's office back at Fort Huachuca had adjoining closets that were enormous. A holographic projector could turn any wall of the room, the bathrooms, or the dressing rooms into a three-dimensional theater capable of running programs ranging from instant news to the latest erotic fantasies from the flesh pots of the world.

"I really don't understand how they make this available for any price we could afford," Dyani argued.

"And the people who own and operate the Tahoe Grande don't understand how you can lead a scouting platoon where you can be shot at," Curt reminded her. "This is the sort of thing we fight to protect, Deer Arrow. So it's here for us to enjoy when we want to."

She looked directly at him and smiled. "I only want us to enjoy each other."

Curt grinned. "Well, I'll fight to protect that, too!"

"Now."

"In the middle of the afternoon?"

"We're on leave. Throw away your watch. Yes."

Dyani was one of few words. She made up for this in other ways.

Although Curt Carson had enjoyed the company of many ladies of the Washington Greys and had rated several of them as "first among equals" from time to time, he was more than enjoying the company of Dyani Motega. He didn't know why, and he didn't give a damn. For some reason, the happiness of Dyani Motega was essential to his own. This was totally irrational to him. He couldn't think straight about it, and he didn't care whether he could or not. Dyani had entered his life when she'd entered the Washington Greys, and then she'd slowly and inexorably grown on him until she dominated his off-duty thoughts day and night. This had never before happened to Curt Carson, professional man of arms, West Pointer, officer, gentleman, leader, tactician, fighter, man of affairs, combat hero, and target of many women.

Older men such as his father, had he still been alive, could have told him what was happening to him. And several superior officers could have warned him about the dangers, because he was a combat officer who was also Dyani's commander. And she, too, was a combat soldier.

He'd warned Jerry Allen about the dangers of his subordinate's relationship with Adonica Sweet. But Jerry was someone else, not him.

In fact, the whole situation was new to the twenty-first century United States Army. The ability of humans to direct warbots by neuroelectronic linkage in a remote location safe from the hazards of the battlefield had allowed women into what were formerly forbidden combat assignments. What had started in Panama simply grew from there.

The infamous Rule Ten, Army Regulation 601-10, had been adequate to ensure discipline because it prohibited physical contact between men and women while on duty. But when the Washington Greys had pioneered the new Special Combat doctrines where human beings had to go back onto the battlefield alongside directly commanded warbots, the ladies of the Washington Greys simply shucked their linkage harnesses, picked up Novia assault rifles, and brought to reality the ultimate in gender equality: the ability to place themselves "between their dear homes and the war's devastation." By the time the highest of the high brass discovered what was going on - the low brass in the form of General Belinda Hettrick actually took part in it - the Sierra Charlies were a reality, and the ladies of the Greys had distinguished themselves in combat alongside the men.

The Washington Greys had literally and proudly written the book on this.

And they were continuing to do so.

Much later, Carson and Motega decided to go down for dinner. Since the Tahoe Grand had a gourmet restaurant that was the ritziest of the ritz, they dressed for the occasion. All soldiers liked to put on pretty clothes now and then, just as academics did. Curt wore his white mess uniform while Dyani decided to continue being provocative in a skin-tight, iridescent, white thigh-length sheath that was really designed for a woman who'd been artificially enhanced by biocosmetics. Dyani didn't need biocosmetics; she was small, physically fit, and had learned from her close friend Adonica Sweet how to project feminine beauty. She'd let her heavy, sensuous black hair fall freely down her back. Since Army dress codes had been relaxed in competition with the Aerospace Force, Dyani wore no jewelry except a miniature version of her Distinguished Service Cross.

When the tall, handsome colonel and, his lady entered the restaurant from the busy, surrounding casino, they quietly and without fuss suddenly dominated the lavish room filled with beautiful men and women, most of whom were wealthy enough to have availed themselves of the most advanced biocosmetic technology. Many of them looked like Greek gods and goddesses while others had taken biocosmetics to its limits, their bodies deformed in ways that many people would have considered bizarre. In the twenty-first century, a person could have for real what formerly had been achieved with greasepaint and padding...but for a price which was often more than money and was sometimes painful in the case of the more exaggerated forms.

The beautiful and often grotesque women looked at Curt while fire welled up in their startling bosoms; in Dyani's case, their emotions were envy and jealousy. They wondered how a woman could be so beautiful and yet so natural. Except for some men whose proclivities were such that their feelings matched those of the women present with respect to Curt, every male in the room lusted for Dyani as she walked in her fluid, catlike, natural manner beside the tall colonel.

The table at which the human waiter seated them had a transparent top so that patrons could see the lower half of their guests and partners. It was indeed a posh eatery; service was provided not by robots, but by human beings, a very expensive luxury. Curt ordered for both of them because Dyani's choice of foods was usually very simple and she wanted Curt to teach her more about the sophisticated world with which she'd had little contact before joining the Greys.

"I spoke with Pappy Gratton earlier," Curt told her with a smile. As the regimental commander, he felt it necessary to keep his adjutant informed of his whereabouts and to keep himself informed of any unusual happenings in the regiment.

Dyani rebuked him gently. "Kida, we're on leave. Both of us needed it. If you can't get your mind off the regiment, I'm doing something wrong."

"The regiment will always be with us while we're Greys," he reminded her.

"And while you're the regiment commander."

"Part of the job, Deer Arrow, part of the job. Captain Kitsy Clinton has reported back-"

"How wonderful for Kitsy! That means I'll have to redouble my efforts." Dyani was genuine in her enthusiasm about Kitsy's return, and Curt didn't know whether or not her budding sense of humor was making itself evident in her remark.

"Do I detect a hint of green brass?" Curt asked, chiding her that she'd expressed a smidgen of jealousy for the first time. "Don't you understand that all ladies of the Greys are equal but that some are more equal than others?"

"Kitsy outranks me."

"So do Belinda Hettrick, Willa Lovell, and Joan Ward. But at the rate you're going, not for long. That was something else I had to check with Pappy about." He reached into his pocket and retrieved a pair of metallic objects in his closed hand. He took Dyani's right hand in his and pressed these objects into her palm. "The latest make sheet came through. I anticipated it. Congratulations, Captain Motega." He took his hand away from hers.

She looked down to see a set of captain's bars in her palm. From the heft of them, they were not silver-plated but of solid silver. She was usually happy and appreciative when Curt gave her silver jewelry, which she liked. But at the moment, all she could do was stare at her new insignia.

Curt thought she was going to cry for the first time since he'd known her.

But she didn't. She called up the incredible internal discipline that was part of her. "My father was a captain," she said very slowly in a low voice.

"I know. When we were at Fort Ord last week, I told him you might be promoted soon and asked him not to tell you."

"And you didn't tell me! But I'll forgive you because my father likes you very much. He would never betray the confidence of a friend."

"Well, I like him. And your mother."

"I'm sorry my sister was away at school."

"You have a sister?"

"Yes. She's two years younger than I am. She wants to follow in our father's footsteps, too. She's at ROTC summer camp."

"Well, Deer Arrow, these bars were your father's," Curt told her. "Captain John Tatoga Motega wanted to pin these on you himself, but the make sheet wasn't out at that time. He asked me to do it for him with all his love."

Dyani was suddenly deadly serious again as she looked at Curt. "I'm no longer hungry for food. Let's go where you can do your duty properly."

But they never got the chance to get up from the table.

"By God, if it isn't Curt Carson!" a voice boomed out. And suddenly a very tall, very lean, almost skinny man with a cleanly shaved head was standing by their table.

Curt looked up. He recognized the man immediately because he'd been a second classman in Curt's batt when the commander of the Washington Greys had graduated from West Point. He'd also known him for three years prior to that. Curt didn't want to be interrupted at a moment like this, but what the hell could he do when greeted by an old comrade and a former member of the Washington Greys? Curt forced a smile to his face and slowly rose to his feet, extending his hand to the man as he did so. "Steve Calder! Haven't seen you since the Zahedan hostage rescue mission!"

The man took Curt's hand in his own thin, scrawny one. "General Steven B. Calder now, thank you! And I see you got your silver oak leaf!"

"And the Washington Greys," Curt added. "General, eh? In whose army? Anyway, please meet one of my officers. Dyani, this is Stephen Calder, former Grey. Steve, may I present Captain Dyani Motega?"

Dyani extended her hand but did not rise, even if the man was a general. She was not in uniform, although Curt had introduced her by her rank. "How do you do, General Calder?"

"A pleasure, Captain!" Calder said smoothly, taking her hand. "A lovely name. Spanish?"

"No, sir. Crow Indian."

Calder hesitated for a fraction of a second before recovering and responding, "Really! Well, the Washington Greys are still favored with lovely young ladies, I see. And you have a DSC!" Calder noticed Diani's miniature decoration and his tone of voice suddenly became respectful. He knew of no other woman who'd earned a combat decoration second only to the Congressional Medal of Honor. Calder decided that Dyani was not only beautiful - Carson still knew how to pick 'em! - but also an outstanding officer. Crow Indian or not, he begrudged no one a decoration that was given only for extraordinary heroism in combat. He turned to Curt. "Did I interrupt?"

"No, we were about to finish and leave." Curt smoothly told the social lie. He didn't quite know at this point whether to spend a few minutes greeting an old comrade or to put off this man. Calder had been a warbot brainy with the 4th Company, Marty Kelly's "Killers," during the botched Zahedan hostage rescue when the Greys almost bought the farm and learned that NE warbots couldn't hack it against swarms of poorly armed Mongol-like hordes. Afterward, when the Greys began to develop the Sierra Charlie doctrines where people fought in the field alongside warbots, Calder had opted to transfer to a regular robot infantry regiment, the 506th "Currahee" regiment of the 26th "R.U.R." Division. Later, Curt had learned that Calder had resigned his commission once his service contract was up. Curt had lost track of the man thereafter.

But now Calder was standing before him claiming to hold general officer rank. Thus, in spite of the fact that Calder had broken into a very private moment for Curt, he was curious. Curt tossed a quick glance at Dyani, one that would tell him whether to brush this guy off or continue Old Home Week.

Dyani indicated one of the empty chairs and gave Curt his answer. "General Calder, will you join us for a moment? I'm sure Curt would like to learn where you've been and what you're doing now."

Can this woman really read my mind? Curt asked himself again because he'd wondered about this before.

"Thank you!" Calder took the chair Dyani indicated. "I gather you're taking some leave. You always went with one of the girls. I'm on a week's R and R here myself. So, you've got the Washington Greys now, eh?"

Curt replied as he resumed his seat, "Took a while."

"You don't sound enthusiastic about it. Too much bot flush involved with regimental command in the good old Army of the United States with all its computers and forms and reports and justifications, huh?"

"Well, Steve, like a lot of things, higher command often seems to be a pretty good thing until you get it. I'm having to learn how to be a regimental commander instead of a combat soldier. And you're right. The Army is still a lot of paperwork in spite of data processing and computers and AI."

"Aw, not all outfits are that way, Curt!" Calder said expansively. "I've helped a couple of Asian outfits try to get semi-roboticized. Even got to command a regiment myself in one of them. It's a lot easier to operate in armies that aren't bogged down by their own size and complex T-O-and-Es."

"So you went merc, huh?" Curt asked.

"Got to pay the rent somehow. Running industrial NE bots after being a warbot brainy is no kind of job for me," Calder admitted. Then, as when he was in the Greys, Calder began to brag. This had been a sore spot with Curt in earlier days when the Greys were full RI. Calder liked to boast to reinforce his own self-importance and lack of self-confidence. There had been times when the man had stood on the very brink of compromising classified warbot information. Curt and the other Greys had stepped in to save his ass because he was then a Washington Grey. This time, Curt let the man go on, hoping that he'd reveal what the hell he was doing as a mercenary trying to crank up operational warbot forces that were not those of the USA.

"But I'm with a good outfit now," Calder went on. "Pays well and regularly. Easy work. Lots of good mercenaries under me. Warbots probably not as good as yours, but good enough is the enemy of the best, as they say. And I'm a full general, no less! The man in charge!"

"In charge of what, Steve?" Curt wanted to know who would hire a man who couldn't cut it as a Sierra Charlie, who hadn't even tried but had run instead, and who'd then opted out of U.S. military service because it seemed that the 26th R.U.R. might become one of the Sierra Charlie divisions several years ago. Now the man was a mercenary with a warbot outfit. Who had warbots and would hire mercenaries? Curt had to find out.

Steve Calder looked quickly around the room, his eyes flicking over the lavish surroundings. "Well, we don't broadcast the fact that my security force has warbots and could act as a little more than a guard force. Might stir up trouble. Lots of enemies out there just waiting for an excuse to try and stop us. So, the Prophet wanted the very latest and the very best security force for Sanctuary in preparation for the Departure and the sure and certain attempt to stop him before he can get the Archangel Gabriel out of the hole. I was the guy who was able to give him what he wanted. I'm now the commanding general of the Host of Michael of the Galactic Tabernacle of the Human Future."

Chapter Seven

"What the hell, Steve, a religious cult with an *army?*" Curt Carson suppressed an urge to laugh because the name of the religion sounded so ridiculous. But Curt knew that religious groups *did* have armies. He'd fought some of them. But what sort of religious organization would have a "security force" that required even surplus non-classified industrial robots and the services of a former warbot brainy to run it? He was curious. Dyani sat impassively and listened; Curt knew that if he happened to miss anything, her perfect memory would pick it up.

The answer that Steve Calder gave him was partly anticipated. "Sure, why not? Onward, Christian soldiers. Remember the Mormon Battalion? Or our former foes, the Iman Abdul Madjid Rahman's Jerhorkin Muslims at Zahedan?" Calder asked rhetorically. "And it's a perfectly respectable church, not a cult."

Curt decided to begrudge the man his beliefs, but he also noticed that Calder couldn't keep his eyes off Dyani. Although he could understand why - other men in the restaurant were also having the same problem - it bothered him nonetheless because Calder had had the reputation in the Greys of occasionally stretching Rule Ten almost to the breaking point. From the stories that had circulated in Rumor Control, former Lieutenant Steve Calder had the powerful sexual drive of an Assyrian warrior with not one iota of affection in his soul. That was just Calder; he knew it, admitted it, and lived with it. Sometimes, it was difficult for the ladies of the Greys to do so.

"Yeah, that was a real sheep screw," Curt recalled. "Caused the Army to have another look at the soldier in the field, the ultimate weapon of World War Four."

"So, I understand. I don't know too much about the Sierra Charlie doctrine, but I read about it in *The Infantry Journal*."

"That was a couple of years ago," Curt reminded him, knowing that the piece Calder had referred to was a quick overlook based on the initial success of the Namibian mission. A lot had changed since then, but Curt wasn't about to follow Calder's lead and brag about it. If the man was heading up a religious mercenary force, Curt wanted to find out more about this Host of Michael Calder was commanding. Where was it? What kind of warbots did it have? If it was the ZI, it might cause trouble someday, trouble that maybe the FBI couldn't handle and the National Guard was ill-equipped to fight. Which meant, in Curt's mind, the Fort Fumble on the Potomac would probably send in the Washington Greys. In fact, the standard response in the Club was brewing trouble anywhere in the world was portrayed on the evening television news was a cry in unison, "Send in the Washington Greys!" If anything hit the impeller anywhere in the world, the Greys knew there was better than a point-five probability that they'd be sent out to piss bullets on a brush fire. That's what came from being damned good, they told themselves. And they were right.

"You'll have to tell me about it sometime. Sounds like a situation with a high pucker factor. Me, I've got a Sierra Hotel warbot outfit under my command," Calder boasted waving for the waiter and indicating he wanted another drink. "The Prophet wants me to keep nosies and enemies out of Sanctuary. So, the mission of the Host of Michael involves mostly patrol and perimeter security."

Sounds like an optimum application for warbots," Curt agreed, continuing to try to draw this braggart out and learn what was going on. The commander of the Washington Greys sensed that something wasn't right about whatever Calder was doing. In the first place, Curt really didn't like mercenaries; he couldn't understand why someone would fight for anyone who merely paid him. He knew that people like that existed in the world, and he knew that some people simply liked to fight. Curt Carson had to have a reason to fight. And his reasons were duty, honor, and country. Fighting, killing, and possibly being killed for any two of those three reasons seemed deplorable to him. So, he continued his gentle, conversational probing, although he really wanted to brush this guy off and enjoy the rest of the evening with Dyani. Duty before pleasure, and this was suddenly duty to Curt. "But last I heard linkage technology is still classified two steps above 'Destroy Before Reading.' What kind of up/down links are you using?"

Calder grinned engagingly. "Well, now, that information is restricted under *my* system of classification, Colonel!" He noted a moment of hostility on Curt's part, and quickly went on, "Oh, don't worry! I didn't break my American security oath or compromise any classified American Army warbot technology! In the first place, as you recall, none of us warbot brainies were privy to the actual linkage technology just in case we might be captured and wrung dry by the enemy using neuroelectronic mind-reading techniques. And please allow me to remind you of what Rudyard Kipling wrote." Calder was an avid Kipling fan who was fond of quoting from *Barracks Room Ballads* and other of the author's military-based works.

> *"There are nine and sixty ways*
> *Of constructing tribal lays*
> *And every single one of them is right!"*

"I don't follow you, General," Dyani spoke up, deliberately using the man's apparently self-given rank because she recognized what Curt was up to. She'd read Kipling, of course; nearly everyone in the Greys had done so. But Calder's use of the Kipling quote in reference to warbot technology was something Dyani didn't catch.

"The Brits use a different linkage system than we do," Calder pointed out, accepting a fresh drink from the waiter and signing the chit. "Same with the French and the Germans. Brazilians, too. Warbots work for all of them. Maybe their linkage systems are even better than the American one."

Curt shook his head. "I've fought alongside British and French warbot units. Their warbots are no better than ours. They've got their own little operational glitches, Steve," he added.

"But industrial robot linkage doesn't," Calder pointed out. Curt knew he was right. Indybots weren't prevalent in those parts of the pre-industrial world where a lot of eager hands and feet were available and needed the work to feed themselves and build their expanding economies. On the other hand, in most of the ultra-industrialized economies of the world where brains rather than willing hands and feet were necessary, a lot of indybots were used on production lines and in other places where the work was highly labor intensive. Only a indybot with pico-manipulators could handle the growing and stacking of pico-electronic modules or the manufacture of molecule-sized nano-machines.

"So I take it you've procured modified indybots working on the General Electric Telebot system or the Phillips RoboSkill?" Curt ventured.

"Something like that, but I shouldn't discuss it," Calder suddenly broke off, and action that gave Curt a clue as to what the Galactic Tabernacle of the Human Future was using to network the warbots of the Host of Michael. It really didn't help Curt; he knew little about actual linkage technology for the reason that Calder had earlier expressed. Curt and the rest of the people in the Robot

Infantry just used the technology and weren't expected to know or understand it. But if the American military ever had to come nose-to-nose with Calder's warbots, that little snippet of information might help. GE and Philips and others could be persuaded by one of their best customers, the United Stated government, to send in their knowledgeable techies for WCM - Warbot Counter Measures.

"And it's a nice job," Calder went on expansively. "Pays well. And I get to write the rules. Taking a two week leave here myself right now, which I am glad I did because I happened to run into you, Curt."

"Well, it's nice to see you again, Steve," Curt responded lamely, trying to send the man signals that the chance meeting had been grand, but...

Calder thought for a moment, then gave Curt the pitch. It surprised Curt. The way it was done by Calder showed that the man had forgotten a lot about both Curt and the Washington Greys. "Matter of fact, Curt, you might find the Host of Michael an interesting military job right here in the USA if you get tired of getting shot at by nasties or hassled by the goddamned rules. Let's see, if I figure it right since I graduated the year after you did. You'll be coming up for twenty in a few years, won't you? I can find a cushy, well-paid slot for you. Hell, I'd make one for you! And Sanctuary is a damned good place to raise kids. Lots of solid discipline. Good school. Wholesome environment. The Prophet places a very high priority on giving the Tabernacle kids the very best scientific and technical education possible. He knows what he's talking about."

Curt didn't reply at once because the waiter busied himself around their table. Even Calder kept quiet while this stranger was around them. This told Curt a lot. What Steve Calder was doing wasn't something he really wanted the world at large to know about right then. Curt immediately went to yellow alert; anyone who didn't want to talk about what he was doing around strangers was either doing something clandestine or was paranoid about it all. In any event, Calder couldn't really be proud of his command of the Host of Michael, or he was afraid that some of his remarks might end up in his boss's ear after going through a filter or two that would distort their meaning. But Curt decided he'd try to learn as much as he could about the Host of Michael and the Prophet.

"Uh, Steve, you'll have to excuse me if I appear to be stupid, but I don't have a lot of time to follow all the religions out there today," Curt said after the waiter had served Dyani and him their appetizer course and left. Calder had waved off the waiter's query about eating and merely ordered another bourbon and branch. "Who's this Prophet you think so highly of? Most religious leaders I've heard about certainly weren't into heavy science and technology education."

"Oh, I'm sure you've heard about the Prophet. His name is Dr. Clark Jeremy Mathys," Calder announced proudly.

"The astronomer and television personality?" Dyani asked.

"Same guy."

Curt nodded. "I watched some of his TV shows. He's good, all right. Seems like kind of an elitist snob the way he always looks down his nose at the camera. Sort of like a Soviet sentry giving you the once-over."

"That's just his way," Calder tried to explain.

"So what's he doing being the head honcho of a religion?"

"Well, according to what he told me personally," the mercenary general said proudly, "he got deeply into a study of some anomalies on the surface of Mars-"

"Not the old 'Fortress on Mars' thing again? Didn't the scientists put that to bed a hell of a long time ago?" recalled.

"Dr. Mathys says no because no one has ever there to take a look. Only unmanned probes have ever visited Mars. But Dr. Mathys went over most of the high-resolution spectral data from the *Wotan* Mars probe. He was one of the few who had the private wherewithal to spend the time doing it. He used his TV earnings to self-finance his own study. Hell of a lot of data there, he told me. Used some new neuroelectronic image enhancement techniques where you can build up a visual image in your head and thus concentrate on whatever aspect of it you want." Calder paused as if he was somewhat reluctant to discuss what came next. It sounded like he really wasn't sure he believed his Prophet. "Dr. Mathys told me that when he was in neuroelectronic linkage working on the Mars data, he was contacted through the computer by a group of extraterrestrials."

Dyani had a dubious expression in her eyes as she looked at Curt, who was trying to remain impassive at this revelation. Initially, this seemed to be an impossible happening.

Both Curt and Dyani were trained warbot brainies who'd been in linkage many times. A person didn't even become a Sierra Charlie until first going through the Army's rigorous warbot training regimen.

One of the first steps in the process of making a warbot soldier was to ensure that most of one's serious psychopathological hang-ups were faced and accounted for by that person. Some people couldn't do that. A lot of would-be warbot brainies couldn't hack it facing themselves and who they really were or what they really thought. Running a robot in intimate neuro linkage with your mind required that you have a clear, highly disciplined mind. If you had hang-ups you didn't know about, were unwilling to accept, or were not able to keep under control, you ran the high risk of blowing a few neural fuses if you happened to meet your Big Nemesis in linkage. Some people would go catatonic very quickly if that happened. It was easy to withdraw into the happy universe inside one's own skull, or get thrown into the living hell that might be there in a lot of instances.

Therefore, warbot brainies spent a long time in training at Fort Benning. When they graduated, as all the Washington Greys had, they were probably the sanest human beings ever to live on Planet Earth. This didn't make them super-people, however. Warbot training didn't strip them of their individual personalities, so individual differences remained. An example of that was Calder's basic all-warrior personality that would permit him to fight for pay as a mercenary with no ideological underpinnings except his own. However, the Washington Greys were certainly adults in the way they accepted total responsibility for themselves.

Dr. Clark Jeremy Mathys hadn't had that sort of intense soul-searching training.

Curt bad often wondered when something like this was going to happen. Neuroelectronic technology wasn't especially dangerous except to an individual, but there could always be that unique person who could accept the consequences of the technology and make it dangerous to others. Maybe Mathys was one of those. Curt didn't know the man and was aware of him only through television presentations.

"But, just between you and me, Curt, you wouldn't have to actually believe in any of the doctrines of the Tabernacle," Calder went on in covert tones with a low voice. "A lot of people in Sanctuary don't. I'm not in charge of the thought police. The Reverend Alastair Gillespie is the Keeper of the Faith. I buffer my Host against him. We have an understanding. I think you can understand why." Calder quaffed the rest of his drink in one mighty swallow and slammed his empty glass down on the table. He checked his watch. "But, hey, I'm not on a recruiting trip. Got an appointment with a lovely young thing in ten minutes up in her room. I'm serious, Curt. You need a place to land after twenty-and-out, give me a call. I'd like to see more of you while you're here, so buzz me through the hotel operator tomorrow…but not real early, you know. And just in case, here's my card." He stood up, reached into the pocket of his sternly cut military-like civilian suit, and flipped out a white card which he handed to Curt. "Now, if you'll excuse me, time is money, if you know what I mean! Dyani, a real pleasure to meet you! If you're with the Greys, let me add that my offer extends to you, too. We're an equal opportunity religion."

Curt looked down at Calder's business card which featured a logo that was a circle with an oblique arrow through it. It had a telephone number where Calder could be reached. The only address was a mail drop in Battle Mountain, Nevada. Then he looked up at Dyani. She was nicer to look at.

"Well, Deer Arrow, how about that?" he said with a slight smile playing around the corners of his mouth.

Dyani wasn't smiling. "Kida, that man may have his shortcomings as a military officer, but I don't think I like the sound of the outfit he's working for." She didn't have to say much more than that. She'd just voiced not only her dislike of Calder and the Tabernacle but something of her fear of what was involved.

"Fortunately, we can forget him," Curt told her.

"For right now, yes. I can. I will. Now I've got to get him out of your mind tonight. I'll try very hard to do that. I don't think it will be difficult." She tossed her hair over her shoulder and smiled at him. "Better chow-down, soldier. You'll need all the energy you can muster."

"Maybe I should have ordered the oysters," Curt remarked.

Chapter Eight

Sergeant Pete Cooker of the Nevada State Police, Badge Number 954 and the driver of patrol car India Seven Lima, was pissed. Payday was yesterday, and it wasn't just his paycheck that was burning a hole in his pants. If it hadn't been for the goddamned stupid captain, Cooker would have been supposedly patrolling his beat - Interstate 80 between Elko and Winnemucca. Actually, he would have been in the Calico Club in Battle Mountain. He'd wanted Lucinda all week. She was affordable to him only once in each pay period, but she was worth it. Pete Cooker liked his piece of tail as regularly as he could get it, more often if he could manage it. Legalized prostitution with mandatory state health inspection was among the reasons he'd applied for a slot with the Nevada State Police. Pete Cooker had served faithfully in the 538th Aerospace Security Police Wing, rising to the rank of staff sergeant and guarding gates at various bases of the United States Aerospace Force. But he hadn't guarded his own ass while he trifled with a buxom second lieutenant. Even in the so-called liberal Aerospace Force, the gulf between commissioned and noncommissioned officers still existed as it had fifty years before. When Cooker and the lieutenant got caught shacking in a guard shack on duty, he almost bought a dishonorable discharge. The only thing that saved his butt was his knowledge of the proclivities of the wing commander. He was banished to the back gate for the remainder of his tour and allowed out with an honorable if he kept his mouth shut.

Officer James Burkhardt, Badge Number 907, was out of the Winnemucca office as the man in charge of the fugitive detail. It would have been his day off to spend with his wife and family. But his boss in Carson City had called with this weird assignment to find a lost FBI man out in that religious commune southwest of Battle Mountain. Burkhardt didn't really know how to handle it if the FBI couldn't take care of its own. He had an Associate's degree in both criminology and electronic sensor technology, and he'd become very adept at using both of his educational training specialties in locating fugitives. Problem was, no fugitives were involved here - at least, none that he knew of - only an FBI man who'd failed to report back. This was a missing persons job.

Both men were newcomers to the force in comparison to Officer Harrison Corvis, who'd come out from Carson City to lead this look-see. However, the only think Corvis was qualified to lead was an unexciting, safe, risk-free life. At best, he was fit to command only the reasonably simple AI circuits of his office desk.

One should not get the impression that the Nevada State Police was staffed with incompetents, bureaucrats, and rakes. The driver of Patrol Car Echo Four Foxtrot with Sergeant Stan Smith, a very intelligent young man whose only failing was his inability to complete his degree in robotics engineering at the University of Nevada in Las Vegas. He'd blown the pittance of his hard-earned financial reserves in the casinos while trying to make a killing using a "system" generated by the UNLV megacomputer. He'd accounted for every variable except the human one. A part-time student who was also a casino pit-boss stumped onto Smith's program one night while running one of his own...and promptly sabotaged it by discreetly changing a few variables deep in the base code.

This rump contingent of the Nevada State Police had been sent out on orders of the governor as a result of a request from the Oval Office. Its only problem was that it was ill-equipped to handle the task it had been assigned. And that wasn't the fault of the four men, or of incompetency in the state government. It was simply a matter of expediency, of getting the only people available in a short time, or proceeding with limited intelligence data, and of considerable political pressure all the way up and down the line.

"So, what's the plan, Harry?" asked Officer James Burkhardt. "Or are we gonna stand around out here in the boondocks and play with ourselves?" Burkhardt had very little respect for Corvis, and it was apparent that it was reciprocal.

"Speak for yourself, Jim," Harrison Corvis snapped, looking at the map that was blowing in the breeze and therefore hard to read.

"What did you and Cooker find out in town?"

"The FBI dude was seen at the fueling stop on the west side of town, and he isn't holed up in the Calico Club," Sergeant Pete Cooker reported.

"I figured you'd check out the red-light district," Corvis muttered.

"The sheriff talked to him and told him a little bit about what's going on over on the other side of the mountain," Burkhardt added. "Told me the same thing, he says. Basically, we oughta keep our noses out of there. Couple of kids vanished up on the side of Battle Mountain itself a couple of years ago. This religious commune seems to maintain its own strong security force."

"The place has been surrounded by razor-wire barrier fencing for about three years," Stan Smith added. "The people in Battle Mountain itself didn't much care; those who were hunting on the mountain proper just shifted their hunting activities elsewhere."

"Stan and I have seen a lot of trucks and freight cars going in and out of the commune for a couple of years, too," Cooker put in his two-cents' worth. "Whatever this commune is doing back on the alkali flat, they're not real hospitable about it."

"So, as I asked, Harry, what's the plan?" Burkhardt repeated. He wanted to go home. Cooker wanted to go back to the Calico Club. Smith was worried that he wouldn't get back from this operation before he was scheduled to go on shift, and Joe would be pissed if Stan wasn't there to relieve him.

"I think," Corvis said slowly, "That we've got so many possibilities here that we've got to take the most obvious one first. The FBI agent might have been kidnapped by the commune's security guards. They might have caught him snooping around the perimeter fence."

"So, what do we do? Go up to the commune's main gate and ask them if they've seen this guy?" Burkhardt was slightly sarcastic. Corvis had had hours to review the data - which he had, and Burkhardt didn't - and yet no plan of action was being put forth.

"As a matter of fact, that's just exactly what we're going to do," Corvis finally said after apparently thinking about that for a moment and deciding that the sarcastic suggestion maybe wasn't so sarcastic after all. At any rate, it was a plan of action.

"And get clobbered ourselves?" Burkhardt wanted to know.

"Not likely, Jim. There's four of us, not just a lone agent snooping around. We're the law, remember? We got a right to go up to their gate, ask to see the guy in charge, and ask a few questions. Routine investigation, remember? And we've got authorization all the way from the governor's office on down."

"Uh, Chief," Smith ventured, using a safe and respectful title for a man whose police rank he really wasn't sure of, although he thought it might be captain, "why don't Pete and I set up communications with our watch office…just in case?"

"Yeah," Cooker added, "if these nuts did kidnap an FBI man, we oughta make damned sure that the whole fucking world knows what happens to us if they try the same thing."

"I'll plant my portable relay unit on that hill over there so that we can stay in touch with the Carlin remote communications outlet," Smith volunteered.

"Set it to send an emergency message code if either of our vehicle or brick transceivers stop sending a regular ID code to it," Cooker continued, recalling some of the procedure he'd used on aerospace force base perimeter patrol when he might be out of line-of-sight of the gatehouse or a lasercom station.

"I'm not sure the remote will do that," Smith objected.

"Give me five minutes with a pair of tweezers and it will," Cooker assured him.

"Just don't fuck it up, Pete," Burkhardt pleaded. The comm idea was a good one, but it still didn't prevent all kinds of shit from hitting the fan if the religious nuts were unfriendly. Burkhardt occasionally cornered a dangerous fugitive, put most of the time his job did not involve putting his life on the line. Corvis never worried about it behind his desk.

"Okay, go do it," Corvis snapped. "Christ, if someone starts shooting at us, I haven't been requalified on the range in about four years."

"Point the damned thing and pull the trigger until you have to reload, Harry," Burkhardt told him. "Pete, Stan, and I will nail those bastards cold if they start shooting."

"So, what the hell good is it going to do for me to shoot at them, too?"

"I figure you'll help keep their heads down while we blow their lips off."

"Hold it! We're not going in there shooting!" Corvis didn't like the idea of any possibility of shooting.

"Who said we were, Harry? But we'd better be ready in case we have to, right?"

"Right!"

Ten minutes later, Stan Smith and Pete Cooker had emplaced and checked the relay. The two-vehicle convoy started down the road toward the main gate of the commune.

They discovered what Wyatt Bloomington had. The road was suddenly surrounded by razor-wire fencing that would withstand the assault of a light tank. There was no turning around once they got within sight of the main gate.

Smith pulled the vehicle up to where the robot guard was standing. Smith had his 9-millimeter handgun on the seat next to his right arm while Corvis had nervously unsnapped the holster holding his own pistol. Cooker remained about twenty meters behind with Burkhardt in the second vehicle; both were ready to cover the lead vehicle with automatic handguns, assault rifles, and even a riot-control shotgun if necessary.

It didn't look like a friendly reception.

When Stan rolled down the left window of the vehicle the robot asked, "Please identify yourselves and state your business."

Stan held up his badge and ID. "Nevada State Police. I'm Sergeant Stan Smith. This is Officer Harrison Corvis. Just a routine check.

We'd like to talk to your security chief, please."

"And those two men in the vehicle behind you?"

"Also Nevada State Police. Officer James Burkhardt and Sergeant Pete Cooker."

"This is private property. Access is denied to those not affiliated with the Galactic Tabernacle of the Human Future," the robot announced in the voice of its remote operator.

"It's also in the state of Nevada and under our jurisdiction," Corvis snapped. "We'd like to speak directly with your security chief or other official of your group."

"That is not possible."

This was trying Harrison Corvis's patience. "Look, robot and whoever's running you, pass my request along to your boss! We are indeed state police, and we may indeed have business that must be discussed with your supervisors."

"State your business!"

"We're looking for a man who disappeared in this vicinity two days ago."

"We saw him. He's not here now."

"Well, that's just not good enough for me, robot! I want to talk with the security chief!"

"That is not possible."

Corvis reached into the pocket of his jacket and withdrew a hard copy. "I've got a writ of *habeas corpus* here, plus a search warrant. I'd rather not use either of them if I can get some cooperation instead. It could get messy." The search warrant was a boilerplate that Corvis had obtained in Carson City to cover most contingencies he figured he might encounter; such things were not hard to get if the state attorney general made a personal telephone call to a local judge.

"We are prepared for such legalistic attempts by the enemies of the Tabernacle to stop our activities here. You are the enemy. You are not welcome here. Return where you came from. Leave us in peace." The robot's weapon slowly emerged from its stowage compartment.

Four other robots appeared, all armed.

"I warn you! Don't threaten us with weapons!" Corvis snapped. "If anything happens to us, the rest of the state police organization will know."

"Yes, we have already determined that both of your vehicles are transmitting on an open mike and sending regular identification signals to some remote relay station. Your voice signals are being interrupted now. We are transmitting your ID sign al to your relay station. No one will know what happens now. You will not be allowed to depart because of your deceitful actions! Put away your weapons, tell your companions in the other vehicle to do the same, then get out of your vehicles! Now!"

The robots were now leveling their heavy guns on both cars.

"Holy shit! They mean it!" Stan Smith growled and decided he wouldn't give up without a fight.

In one movement, he grabbed his M101 Hellcat army surplus assault rifle from beneath the front seat, opened the vehicle door, and rolled out on the ground. "Bail out, Chief!" he yelled to his companion.

Burkhardt and Cooker saw and heard what happened. They were out of their vehicle almost simultaneously.

When the first guard robot fired, it wasn't a 15-milllimeter automatic that was used. A 100-millimeter tube rocket blasted out of its storage container on the robot's side and went for the hot engine of Smith's vehicle. The warhead blew on contact, but both Corvis and Smith were on the ground and shielded from the flying pieces of vehicle that mostly went over their heads.

When Cooker saw that, he lobbed a grenade out of his M101 Hellcat, then opened fire with the 7.62-millimeter side of the gun. He got off ten rounds before it jammed and stopped firing.

Burkhardt was also on the ground and firing a grenade against one of the other robots.

The grenades did their job. Two of the robots went out of action.

This didn't keep the other three robots from opening up with 15-millimeters. The ground around the burning first vehicle was a maelstrom of bullet impacts that sent spurts of sand and dirt flying into the air.

"God, they must have gotten Smith and Corvis!" Burkhardt yelled.

Another robot tube rocket found the second police vehicle.

"Shit! We can't hold out against robots!" Cooker yelled back to Burkhardt. "Damned seven mike-mike stuff just bounces off them!"

"And we don't even have body armor! Christ Almighty, they sent a soft team here when we really needed a warbot SWAT group!"

Sand from 15-millimeter impacts kicked up around them.

"Can we crawl out of here?" Burkhardt wondered, venturing to look over his shoulder from where he was lying on the road.

"Jim, them's indybots what have been modified into warbots like old Hairy Foxes!" Cooker advised him. "Goddamned warbots don't miss once they've gotten a target. They're firing all around us because our ID signatures are masked by the burning car and all the dust in the air! If we get away from this burning car, they'll have nifty targets even if we're glued to the fucking ground! We've had it, Jim!"

"You suggest we surrender?"

"I don't see what the hell else we can do!" the police sergeant said as three rounds popped over his head and went into the embankment behind him.

"How about Corvis and Smith?"

The firing suddenly stopped. Through the pall of dust, Cooker saw Smith slowly get to his feet, his hands in the air. The other sergeant yelled, "Jim! Pete! We've got no choice! They got Corvis!"

Burkhardt took a chance that the robots might locate him by his voice, but he yelled back, "Corvis hurt?"

"He's dead, Jim!"

Cooker swore.

Burkhardt left his Hellcat on the ground and slowly stood up, his hands in the air. "It's all over, Pete, unless you want to collect on your life insurance right now. Me, I'm finished for today. Maybe I'll get through this alive and be able to spend the rest of my life with my family…"

Cooker followed suit. Better alive and a hostage than a dead police officer. One dead police officer already meant that the Nevada State Police wouldn't rest until Corvis, inept and bungling as he was, had been revenged. He only hoped that the word had somehow gotten back to the relay station and that someone now knew that everything had gone to slime out here on the side of Battle Mountain.

"I knew I shoulda called in sick from the Calico Club this morning," Pete Cooker remarked as he stood there with his hands in the air.

Chapter Nine

"Dammit, Dmitri, listen to me and listen well!" The President of the United States rarely became frustrated, but he was at that moment. He turned from the holographic three-dimensional image of the Soviet Premier "sitting" across the table from him. The Soviet Leader was actually in a room in the Kremlin that had been fitted out as full holographic conference facility by the Soviet subsidiary of AT&T. The President said clearly to the young man seated next to him, "Vasilyi, make sure you get the translation dead-nuts, even though the Premier supposedly understands English."

The young man nodded.

A young woman was "seated" next to the Soviet Premier. She was his translator. She remarked to her boss in Russian what the President had told his personal translator in Washington.

"I want to thank the Soviet Union for bringing to our attention a serious problem in Nevada," the President went on, speaking to his Soviet counterpart. "It's an internal problem. You know about that sort of thing."

"*Da!* But we seem to take more effective action!" the Premier replied in Russian. It was a given that Americans would speak only English and Soviets would speak only Russian when international communications at a cabinet or ministry level or above were necessary between governments. At lower levels, verbal communication went on in Russlish.

"I've sent in our Federal Bureau of Investigation which was as much as I could legally do at first," the President explained again. "I don't know what happened to the FBI agent. No one does. In order to keep the news media from going into their usual frenzy because your people claim we're building a secret missile silo in Nevada, I've had to move very quietly. I asked the governor of the state of Nevada to send in his state police to have a look. They were ambushed by security robots."

"How can this be, Mr. President? Do you not know what is going on in your own country? Can you not send in your secret police, the NIA?"

"You know we don't work that way here, Dmitri. And we don't keep track of people the way you do in the Soviet Union. But we've learned that this so-called missile silo your satellite spotted is in a fenced-off area owned by a religious group, the-uh-the Galactic Tabernacle of the Human Future. It couldn't be a missile silo, Dmitri. Religious groups don't build ballistic missiles."

"You forget the Muslims in Iran and the Zionists," the Soviet Premier reminded him.

"No, no, no! Maybe there, but not here. Believe me!"

"I do not. The Soviet Union is sending in a team to investigate."

"I can't let you do that, Dmitri."

"What do you mean, you cannot allow me to do that? It is specifically written into the SMART-Three treaty!"

"Under the terms of that treaty, we jointly agreed to provide for the safety of one another's inspection teams if they were required," the President explained. This was a tough call, but he had to make it. "I cannot guarantee the safety of your inspection team. I'm going to have to send in armed troops to find out what's going on there. Shooting could start. Shooting has already taken place. The Nevada State Police group that Governor Hopkins sent there was taken prisoner, and one man was killed. So I'm requesting that Governor Hopkins send in the Nevada state militia. Dmitri, you must understand that I'm as concerned about this as you are. That's private property, and the police jurisdiction is under the control of the state governor. I can't touch it unless the state governor can't handle it. I've got to give Governor Hopkins the opportunity to do what he has to do, and I'm doing everything that I can possibly do under our laws. Is that clear?"

The Soviet Premier nodded. He, too, was under pressure from his security advisors and the defense minister. Only his control of both the Politburo and the KGB was keeping the Red Army and the generals under control at the moment. The Politburo was a hodgepodge of different political "parties," but the Premier had made sure that every member was nonetheless a communist or, at worst, a socialist. He could hold the wolves at bay a little longer. And he didn't want to risk having a Soviet inspection team hurt; that could be a major political set-back for him in the Kremlin.

"I think it is," the Premier replied.

The President decided to take a very unusual step without even consulting his advisors, the National Security Council, or congressional leaders. This was one of those things where the Top Man had to make the decision and stand by the consequences. He'd done that many times before as the CEO of a Fortune 500 company, a state governor, a senator, and finally as holder of the highest political office in the land. "Dmitri, to assure you of my honest intentions, I invite you to have your ambassador contact me at once. I will arrange for him to attend any National Security Council meeting concerning this Nevada matter, and I'll even clear him for entry into the Situation Room during times when we're dealing with the issue. Fair enough?"

The Soviet Premier honestly believed that the offer was real, but he also believed that the President would invite the Soviet ambassador only when the NSC meetings had been carefully orchestrated for Soviet benefit or when the Situation Room had been set up in advance for the benefit of the Soviet diplomat. He was too deeply steeped in the Russian paranoia and the principle that, in his country, foreigners saw only that which was for the benefit of the Motherland. But he couldn't refuse the invitation.

"I will withhold my inspection team for a while longer," the Premier promised. That didn't mean he wouldn't order the KGB to intensify its own investigation in Nevada.

When the holographic conference ended, the President immediately went back to the Oval Office and called the Honorable Walter Van Tilberg Hopkins, governor of the state of Nevada, on the ordinary telephone.

His meeting with the Soviet Premier went better than his telecon with the governor.

"I'm sorry, Mr. President, but I decline to send in the Nevada National Guard," the man declared. "This has escalated into a serious situation, and national security is at stake, not just the domestic tranquility of the state of Nevada. I have already lost four state troopers. I will cooperate with you in all respects, Mr. President, but please do not ask me to do your job for you." Hopkins could be a stuffed shirt on occasions - and this was one of those - and he was also a consummately cautious politician. He knew he'd just lost more than a few points with the Chief Executive, but the President still owed him more than a few IOUs. The loss of the state troopers had merely raised the count a little.

"Very well, Governor, but I'll have to move federal troops into your state."

"I realize that, sir."

"I'll keep you advised of what I'm doing," the President told him while at the same time telling himself the hell he would. The governor would learn after the fact. Damned if the Commander in Chief of the armed forces of the United States wanted news leaks from Hopkins' office. This had to remain under wraps for as long as possible lest the news media go ballistic and revert to their usual feeding frenzy. This one had all the elements of a juicy news story that could be pumped for weeks - at the expense of getting the problem solved.

So, his next call was to his attorney general. "Joan, I need the answer to that question I tossed at you the other day. Can I do it? Is that federal law still valid?"

"I found the law, Mr. President. I don't think it's been revoked or sundowned," the nation's top lawyer told him - cautiously. "It hasn't been invoked for over a century, so I don't know whether or not it's still valid. I'm searching for precedents."

"To hell with the precedents! I have to move! Governor Hopkins just declined to take action to preserve the safety and security of the citizens of the United States. He refused to send in the Nevada

National Guard. So: Yes or no? I'm about to call the secretary of defense and the Chairman of the Joint Chiefs. I need to send in our military forces. Can I or can't I?"

"The federal law is still on the books, Mr. President," she told him flatly.

"Thank you, Joan. Keep working on the precedent angle. We may need that information to save our hides if this situation gets farther into the slime."

Appropriate people were notified by the President, and the word went down the line in the chain of command.

Consequently, Major Jerry Allen was suddenly and rudely interrupted by the chiming of his comm terminal while spending a quiet but active evening with Captain Adonica Sweet in quarters. He knew this had happened to Colonel Curt Carson more than once, and he sighed and figured it was now his turn in the barrel.

It was as he anticipated, Major General Belinda Hettrick, commander of the 17th Iron Fist Division of which the Washington Greys were a part.

"Sorry to interrupt you, Major," Hettrick told him. It wasn't as much of an apology as it was a statement of regret on her part. She knew what Jerry had been up to when she called, and it was a lonely night for her that had been interrupted only by a DOD Execute Order. "I want to see you in my office in thirty minutes. So, duck into the shower and shag over here. In the meantime, where's Colonel Carson?"

"Yes, ma'am, I'll do that, and I'll be there! But I don't exactly know where Colonel Carson is," Jerry replied, running his hand through his hair to straighten it a little bit.

"You're the temporary regimental commander. You're the second in command. Why don't you know where your regimental commander is?" she wanted to know. Things were bad enough tonight. Subordinates who didn't know answers to simple questions irked her now when they normally wouldn't.

"General, he's on a thirty-day leave. I have his itinerary in the office.

I haven't dogged his steps because he needs this time off. He's never bothered me when I've gone on leave," Jerry started to explain.

"I get it. He doesn't bother you when you're on leave or pass with Captain Sweet, and you don't bother him when he's out with Captain Motega or Captain Clinton..."

"No, ma'am. That isn't it at all. If you want to talk to Colonel Carson, I have a staff man who's very good at tracking down people on leave when things hit the impeller. Please give me five minutes and I'll contact my adjutant. I guarantee Major Gratton will have the information you want on Colonel Carson's whereabouts tonight."

"Okay, Jerry, you call Pappy Gratton. Have him find Carson and tell Carson to call me ASAP. Now get dressed and get over here!" Hettrick was indeed upset tonight. Jerry knew she couldn't talk about whatever the problem was because she hadn't done so. Belinda Hettrick wasn't one to withhold information from her subordinates unless the circumstances made it difficult or impossible for her to talk - like on an unmonitored land telephone. *Hell,* Jerry told himself, *the Soviets can monitor telephone calls with their satellites just like we can.* But they had more trouble doing that than the American intelligence people because of the sheer volume of telephone communication that went on in the United States compared to the Soviet Union.

After Hettrick switched off, Jerry turned to Adonica. He unconsciously used the same phrase as Curt to signal that he was back on duty and Rule Ten again. "Okay, duty calls. Captain, put on a uniform. Find Kitsy, Russ, Ellie, and Bill Ritscher. I want ASSAULTCO ready for anything. Have Kitsy alert Henry Kester to get the regiment on Yellow Alert. I don't know what the hell has happened, but it looks like we're going to go somewhere and do something nasty to someone again..."

The blond, beautiful little combat officer reacted like the other ladies of the Greys when the balloon went up. She snapped immediately out of her romantic mood and quickly became all professional, gung-ho, and tactical. "Yes, sir! Uh, by the way, nice recovery just now. You're doing a fine job as temporary regimental commander.

Keep it up!"

"I'm not so sure I want the job if this evening is typical of the responsibilities and the consequences," Jerry Allen muttered. "It's more fun being a line officer. Even batt command has its drawbacks."

"You're doing okay on all fronts," Adonica told him. "Even when you have to break off contact and call a cease-fire."

As he pulled on his shirt, tucked it in, and fastened his collar, Jerry replied quickly, "You may think I'm pretty good, but you're more than just slightly biased." He picked up his waist-length field jacket, something like the old Ike jacket but with a modern cut, and remarked, "I know I'm not ready to command a regiment yet. Curt Carson's our regimental commander and leader, not me. So I'll be damned glad when Pappy gets the colonel back here and I get this monkey off my back."

Major Jerry Allen didn't know that he was going to have to keep that monkey clinging tightly to his back for quite a while this time, even when his colonel got back.

Chapter Ten

"I don't want you to take this the wrong way, Dyani, but..." Curt started to say as he steered the wind-jammer, driven by the action of the light breeze on its sail-foil, over the incredibly blue waters of Lake Tahoe.

Dyani turned her head from where she lay sunning herself on the cabin roof. In a tanning maillot, Dyani was someone to behold. The skin-tight Tandex material was transparent to ultraviolet light and only semi-transparent in the visible portion of the spectrum. A girl in a Tandex suit could soak up all the UV and Vitamin A she desired without worrying about shadow lines. When Curt didn't immediately continue, she asked, "Take what the wrong way?"

"I'm getting downright bored with all this relaxation," Curt confessed, then quickly added, "but not because of you."

Dyani sat up and moved closer to him so that she wouldn't have to raise her voice over the sound of the breeze. "That's good," she told him frankly. It was obvious that her statement had several meanings. A Dyani Motega phrase often did.

"I don't think so. Three weeks of catching up on sleep when I could and enjoying the luxuries of the Outside World that we fight to protect - well, I've had about all I can stand in one lump." Colonel Curt Carson was basically a man of action, but when he vacationed, he didn't want to do the things he did as a combat officer. Some of his colleagues went hunting, camping, skiing, or engaged in other strenuous outdoor activities. Curt figured he got more than a normal share of those in the Army. He did enjoy sailing and flying where he wasn't just at the mercy of the forces of nature as he was in the field but actually using them to do what he wanted. Then he joked, "Besides, it isn't easy keeping Superwoman satisfied."

Dyani's sense of humor had evolved since she'd been in the Washington Greys. "Do you think it's easy dealing with a superman?"

"You're doing just fine."

"You weren't. You haven't had more than a week's leave since I joined the Greys. You need this. You don't realize how much you've unwound. I do." She gave a little laugh.

Curt was surprised at Dyani's laugh. "This must be good for you, too. I've never heard you giggle before."

Dyani reflected a moment, then replied, "I haven't giggled since I left high school. Girls giggle."

"Was it a happy laugh, then?"

"Yes. I'm very happy."

"So am I," Curt admitted freely. "But I'm bored imbibing all this opulence."

"You can't spend all your time defending the free world," she continued to joke with him. "You'd become a fanatic."

"Well, I can't spend too much time wallowing in conspicuous consumption, either, especially with you."

"Nor can I. But let's enjoy it while we can. I once told you that we must keep our priorities straight. Something could happen to either one of us in our profession."

Curt knew that one of the wonderful things about Dyani was her total and forthright honesty with him and with herself. This both attracted him and made her different from many other women he'd known. But she'd brought up a subject that bothered him. "Yeah," he said and grimaced. "And I might be the one who gives the order."

"You'd give the order, and I'd carry it out," Dyani said simply.

"I hope I never have to," Curt replied with all the honesty Dyani had exhibited. "But you're right. I really shouldn't worry about it. We'll handle it if we need to." Curt wasn't ducking a tough problem, He'd learned that when he didn't have enough data to make a noncritical decision, his best course of action was to wait until more data came in. "But I'm worried about Jerry and Adonica. *That* situation's a river of fire whose course I can't predict, much less attempt to divert or control."

Dyani shrugged. "So don't. They adore one another, and they both do their jobs very well. They'll work it out. Trust them."

"I have to. But if Jerry can't hack it, his command career could come to a screeching halt. And he's too aggressive to be only a good staff man." Curt had learned that a good commander always trained his own replacement, preferably two. Jerry was one of those he had in mind. He hadn't quite decided on the other one yet.

An insistent chiming came from the cabin below deck.

"I should have left that damned thing at the hotel!" Curt muttered darkly. "Or given instructions that I'd accept calls only from our Commander in Chief to go out and save the free world from annihilation."

"You can't. You're a regimental commander," Dyani reminded him, moving quickly and smoothly with her typical liquid motion down into the cabin and reappearing with a commercial cellular comm brick which she handed to him.

He'd given explicit instructions to the hotel's robo-receptionist that he wasn't to be disturbed except for an emergency call. "Well, whoever it is picked a reasonable time of day to call when we weren't otherwise occupied," Curt observed.

"Reason has nothing to do with it. Why do you think I wore this tanning suit? Is the morning an unreasonable time?" Dyani never needed to use a lot of words.

"Maybe it's just a routine emergency," Curt muttered hopefully. "If it is, I'll have Pappy's hide when we get back to Fort Hoochy-coocha."

But it wasn't Major Pappy Gratton, his regimental adjutant, on the line. "Grey Head, Battleaxe here," came the voice of Major General Belinda Hettrick, commander of the 17th Iron Fist Division at Fort Huachuca, Arizona.

Curt sat up and snapped to. "Grey Head here, Battleaxe. Go ahead."

Hettrick's voice told Curt she was worried. "You're damned tough to reach, Grey Head! Pappy couldn't get through the robo-receptionist at your hotel. I had to pull rank and declare an emergency. Obviously, you don't want your sybaritic holiday interrupted. I don't blame you. Can you find a fiber optic land line phone ASAP?"

"Yes, ma'am. On my way. If we can catch a flight out of Reno, I can report for duty later this evening," Curt estimated. The vacation was over, he decided.

"Don't anticipate me, Grey Head! This isn't a panic deploy," the general told him. "Contact the San Francisco Presidio on land line using Code Tango. I'm having them set up a Charlie comm to me. Have them set up a Foxtrot Oscar circuit back to you. Then stand by to punch up a scramble code when I give it to you."

Whatever was going on, it was hot, Curt decided. Hettrick didn't even want to talk about it on the cellular brick. The Soviets and anyone else with ELINT equipment nearby or on a satellite could pick up ordinary land line, cellular, or satellite communications. Not so with the lasercomm links and fiber optics lines of the Department of Defense. And Hettrick was calling for a crypto scramble as well as ultra-secure Uniform Sierra procedures, which meant that the Pentagon was either intent upon keeping information from the Big Red Tide or the news media's Bohemian Brigade. Or both.

"Grey Head is on the way, Battleaxe," he told his commanding general. After Hettrick switched off, he looked up at Dyani and asked, "You heard?"

"Yes." She was deadly serious now. She knew something was in the wind.

"So we're heading back to shore," he said and sighed. With a smile, he added, "Dyani, put on something else or you'll start a riot when we land."

She couldn't suppress a little smile at the compliment. So, she struck a provocative pose for him and swept her long black hair off her shoulders. "So that's why men fight!"

"You'd better believe it! And knock it off or I'll willfully disobey that ASAP order from Battleaxe!"

By the time they'd tied the boat up at the dock, Curt was in a foul mood. Dyani couldn't help but notice it and guessed the cause. "Who was sniveling about getting bored on this long leave?" she remonstrated gently.

"That call could have come at a worse time...like it usually does in the middle of the night. As it was, I was heading for that secluded little cove where we could drop anchor for a while," he admitted.

"That's what I thought. Patience, my colonel. Another time will come," Dyani promised.

"Not likely on a warm summer day."

"But I can put on the tanning suit any time...if you want me to put on anything at all." When she spoke to him, it was always in her low, quiet voice.

They found a public phone outside the boat rental place next to a hamburger joint on the road. It was an old phone booth, but it had a modern fiber optics set in it. The phone booth was quiet. It wasn't very roomy for the two of them, but neither one minded the closeness. Curt wanted Dyani to hear what transpired. That was insurance against one of them forgetting something or, God forbid, one of them not getting back from there. When something nasty was brewing, security procedures such as this went into effect. They had to be prepared for the worst. "Duty calls, but this is official business," he remarked, indicating that Rule Ten was in effect but that Dyani was engaged in official business even sitting on his lap.

It took a minute to contact the San Francisco Presidio and to reach their communications center. Curt didn't identify himself until he was on-line with them then he said, "S-F-O Presidio, this is Code Nosrac requesting call back with a Foxtrot Oscar. Verify with Foxtrot Hotel Alpha Zulu, Code Adnil."

"Password?" was the only comment from the Presidio

megacomputer.

Curt searched his memory for the password he'd been given when he'd left Fort Huachuca at the beginning of the leave. It to be right the first time to protect comm security against another megacomputer running permutations and combinations of thirty-two-character passwords. So, it was an aphorism. "When gossip grows old, it becomes myth," Curt intoned.

"Repeat password for verification." The tone of the computer voice was one of suspicion and questioning. It was deliberately intended to imply that a wrong password had been given. But Curt knew he was right and repeated the phrase.

"Please disconnect at once," the Presidio magacomputer instructed him. But the tone of the voice was more of a command than an instruction. Again, it was to discourage hackers and others.

Curt hung up and relaxed. He looked at Dyani seated on his lap. Jeans and a plaid cotton shirt hadn't diminished her natural sensuality. "Damn Rule Ten! You're still an incitement to riot," he told her.

"Sir, we're on duty," she reminded him in a whisper. "However, it's nice to know that the colonel hasn't gotten too laid-back-"

The phone rang. Curt took the handset off the hook and was all military again. "Headquarters, Carson's Companions, Colonel Carson speaking."

"This is Presidio communications control," the computer voice replied, this time mimicking a female voice. Confirm the only operation in the last one hundred years in which the Washington Greys did not take part."

Quiz time again, Curt thought and answered without a pause. "Operation Just Cause."

Without a pause, the megacomputer instructed, "Identity the person who is with you."

"I am accompanied by Captain Dyani Motega, SCOUT Platoon, RECONCO, TACBATT, Washington Greys."

"Captain Motega, please identify yourself for voice print check."

"I am Captain Dyani Motega."

"Identity of Colonel Carson confirmed. Identity of Captain Motega confirmed."

"How did it know I was here?" Dyani wondered aloud.

"The sounds of your heart and breathing were evident," the megacomputer replied flatly. It was a good circuit.

Again, without a pause, Major General Belinda Hettrick's voice came through quite clearly. "Grey Head, Battleaxe here."

"Battleaxe, Grey Head here," Curt replied.

"Go now to Code Quebec Niner Foxtrot. Confirm receipt."

"Going now to Code Quebec Niner Foxtrot," Curt told her, and punched the memorized tacomm scramble code into the telephone unit. It was a standard tacomm frequency jump code programming sequence, but it required additional button pushing to scramble a twelve-button telephone.

Someone who really knew Army comm procedures might have been able to duplicate the scramble, given thirty seconds to look up the conversion in a current code data base. But the scramble system allowed only ten seconds to start entering the code before it locked out any additional attempts. The megacomputers would allow only a single login from either end of the connection and no more. This was a tightly closed and controlled secure channel.

"The two of you cosy in that telephone booth?" Hettrick asked in opening the conversation.

"Yes, ma'am, and getting hot too," Curt admitted as sweat started to bead up on the two of them. He didn't care; Dyani smelled good. He knew the general wasn't chiding him. It was standard procedure in such circumstances to have two listeners on either end.

"Colonel Salley is with me here. Never mind the salutations. Here's a quick briefing on what's happening: The Soviets are in a dither about something they've spotted on their surveillance satellites."

Hettrick spent the next five minutes bringing Curt and Dyani up to speed on what had taken place thus far. "So, we've been tapped by Fort Fumble on the Potomac to be prepared to go in with force if necessary. Once the White House turns us loose, our mission will probably be to find out exactly what's going on southwest of Battle Mountain and rescue the four kidnapped men, if they're still alive. Colonel Salley and Major Allen both recommend we don't even turn a wheel on a warbot here until we have better Gee-two. We've got only sat photos and spectrum analyses, plus the audio transmitted by the Nevada state troopers before their radios went dead. You're about four hundred kilometers by highway from Battle Mountain. Grab a rental heap and do a little recce around the place. Keep in mind that an FBI agent and four Nevada state troopers tried it and failed. So, don't go barging up to the main gate like those idiots did. See what the two of you can find out by wandering around outside the perimeter fence. You've got the best scout in the regiment with you and-"

"Excuse me, General," Curt interrupted her for the first time, "but would you repeat the name of the organization that's under suspicion at Battle Mountain?"

"The Galactic Tabernacle of the Human Future."

Curt looked at Dyani, who looked back knowingly. "General, I think we can do better than that. Do you remember an old comrade in the Washington Greys, Lieutenant Stephen B. Calder?"

"Sure! He transferred out after Zahedan when we started going Sierra Charlie. A braggy but pure warbot brainy, as I remember."

"He ran into us at the Tahoe Grande last night. He's turned merc."

"I knew that. He went to Africa, I believe. What's he doing back in the States?"

"He's the commanding general in charge of the security forces guarding the Sanctuary of the Galactic Tabernacle of the Human Future," Curt revealed. "I didn't know where the Sanctuary was, but you've just told me it's at Battle Mountain."

"Sierra Hotel!" Hettrick breathed. "Our first real break in this sheep screw! Did you get any good Gee-two from him?"

"Better than that. He offered the two of us jobs in his Host of Michael if we ever got weary of the Army," Curt said. "Want some real good recce? I think we can get it for you. Maybe from inside this Sanctuary place."

"What do you have in mind?"

"Calder was still checked in at the Tahoe Grande this morning. He's on leave playing with the bio-bimbos. He may still be here unless he's been called back to Battle Mountain by his boss. I'm going to find out. And with your permission, I'd like to look into the possibility of taking Calder up on his offer. But we're going to insist on the guided tour of Sanctuary before we make up our minds."

Hettrick paused for many seconds, thinking about this. "Curt, in view of the paranoid way the Nevada state troopers were greeted by those nuts and their warbots, you'd be going on a very dangerous mission."

"General, that's what we get paid to do."

Chapter Eleven

"Kida, I don't like this," Dyani told him. She was obviously distressed by what the two of them were doing. Otherwise, she wouldn't have broken her own strict internal discipline by referring to him by his nickname when, insofar as she was concerned, they were on official business. Dyani Motega had very strong personal convictions, and she adhered very closely to an equally strong set of behavior traits.

Curt decided he had to be strict with her in order to break through to her. "Captain Motega, this is a direct order. Although we're now on official business, please act as if we weren't," So saying, he relaxed in the chair and put his elbows on the table, watching the reflected lights from the swimming pool shift over her face. "Dyani, we're on a scouting mission."

He could see that she was trying. But she told him, "I was taught not to lie."

So that was it! Curt addressed her by what was both her combat and her nickname as he told her, "Deer Arrow, don't think of it as lying. Think of it as camouflage. When you're scouting the enemy, you don't reveal exactly what you're doing or what intentions you have in mind. Right?"

"Yes, sir. I mean: Yes, Kida." She paused for a moment, then added, "You're getting priorities confused."

He shook his head. "Not at all. If you have a problem with this, you can always remain silent." That was part of her image anyway. Dyani never really said much, preferring to remain silent even during the totally relaxed recreational periods of regimental Stand-to in the Club at Fort Huachuca.

He checked his watch. "Calder's late."

"Does he suspect?"

Curt shook his head. "I don't think so. Probably just finishing off his bimbo," he guessed.

He was partly right. At that moment, Steve Calder stepped out of the Tahoe Grade into the pool patio. With him was a stunning blonde. It was apparent that his companion had had a lot of biocosmetic work done on her. She was wearing the sort of clothes that enhanced her already exaggerated form. Curt knew that some military men were fetishists. Calder's fetish was more the obvious from the incredible woman who accompanied him - heavy-breasted, broad-shouldered, wasp-waisted, and slim-hipped with attire that smacked of S&M. Biocosmetics, the latest development of plastic surgery, could now give anyone who wanted it any appearance desired...for real. Some people took full advantage of this twenty-first century biotechnology.

Curt liked people as they were. But he also knew that it was his profession to protect the right of everyone to do as they damned well pleased as long as they didn't harm someone else or make others live for them. In the new millennium, one had to accept full responsibility for one's self or remain forever a child with all the restrictions that entailed. As far as he was concerned, everyone was free to choose their own form of poison and to live their lives the way they wanted. If that included voluntarily screwing up their own bodies, so be it. He knew he couldn't be the judge; he'd chosen to defend freedom, and that included defending *all* that was entailed in the concept.

The bimbo was also taller than Calder, and Calder was a long, skinny ectomorph.

Curt stood up and waved his hand in the circular arm signal that all West Pointers recognized as "assemble on me."

"Hi! Sorry we're a little late," Calder apologized when they came up to the table. He introduced his companion. "Javanna, this is Dyani Motega and Colonel Curt Carson. Folks, meet Javanna from Hollywood.

"Excuse me," Curt said, taking the woman's slender hand, "but I didn't get your last name..."

"I don't have one. I'm just Javanna," she replied in a little, childlike voice.

Curt suspected that Javanna was operating with less than a full magazine of ammo. But he'd assume otherwise until he found out for sure what this bio-bimbo was doing with Calder. If Curt had ever met a total airhead, Javanna seemed to be Number One in that category.

As they seated themselves, Calder explained, "Javanna's a spear carrier in phallus flicks when she's not up here at Tahoe between studio jobs. Obviously, she's no genius," he added crudely and cruelly to Dyani and Curt. "Just about enough brains to run the body. But she's got what she needs otherwise. And plenty of that, I assure you! A tiger in the sack."

Curt was used to the company of ladies who were smart and highly motivated, who served honorably and with courage in combat alongside men, and who had therefore achieved the ultimate in gender equality through their own efforts. They'd gone through personal battles that no man would understand. He always treated military women not only as he would any man, but with slightly more respect because of what they'd accomplished. If he'd made a remark like that about any of the ladies of the Washington Greys, he would have had his gonads handed to him shortly thereafter…if he lived that long. So Curt expected Javanna to take it personally and retaliate. She didn't.

"Oh, Steve, you're such a tease!" Javanna said coyly.

"So we can talk," Calder went on. "Javanna doesn't know anything about the military-"

"But you said you'd explain it all to me, Stevie!" Javanna reminded him.

"I will-"

"You men! Always with your toys." She didn't realize she was one of them.

"You bet!" Calder said, because he did.

"Diane," Javanna said to Dyani, mispronouncing her name because that's what it had sounded like to her childish mind, "does Curt explain to you the things he's doing?"

Dyani was nonplussed. She'd never run up against a woman like this. She replied, "No. He doesn't have to. I know."

"Oh, how nice for you!"

Dyani couldn't help but smile a little. "Yes, it is." The gap was too wide for her to even try to bridge. They had absolutely nothing in common.

"Well, you can certainly pick 'em, Steve. You always could, even at West Point," Curt tried to steer the conversation and butter up this man he was trying to spook.

"Thanks. You don't do too badly yourself." He glanced at Dyani.

She said nothing in reply, but Curt was glad Dyani wasn't carrying her combat knife. If she was, Curt hadn't seen it that evening and knew she was doing an admirable job of self-control.

Once they'd ordered drinks, Calder went on, "You said on the phone that you wanted to discuss something we'd talked about earlier? What's the hot skinny, Mister?"

Curt played with his drink glass and finally said without looking up, "Make sheet came out today. My Gee-one called me."

"And?"

"I wasn't on the list," Curt said. That was true. However, he wasn't scheduled to be on the list.

"So?" Calder was obviously trying to draw him in.

"So I've got nineteen years." Curt reached over the table and took Dyani's hand. She tried not to act surprised. "If I count all my unused leave time, it's probably over twenty. Besides, I'm not getting any younger, and new factors have entered the equation..."

Curt paused, but Calder didn't say anything, waiting for Curt to continue.

"I've never gotten married, you know." Curt went on, looking at

Dyani. Then he turned to Calder. "Not that I haven't wanted to. But being married and having kids doesn't mix with being a combat officer. Maybe it's time I got out and did the sort of thing I should also be doing, which is raising a family so my sons and daughters will carry on a very old tradition. So, right at the moment, I'm sort of reviewing the options open to me. Which is why I remembered our conversation and decided to call you."

Calder brightened. When he'd spoken to Curt earlier, it had never occurred to him that he'd ever have the slightest chance of co-opting a successful combat officer like Curt Carson. Curt had been one class ahead of him at West Point and had been a company commander already by the time Calder joined the Washington Greys. He'd always looked up to Curt a little bit because the man was a leader and a tactical genius. Now Calder was being given the opportunity to recruit Curt as a subordinate. The glory of being able to do this was overwhelming. Calder knew his general officer's rank was conferred on him by a religious zealot as part of the contract between himself and Dr. Clark Jeremy Mathys. Deep down inside, Calder considered Mathys to be a fraud, a jerk, and a real nut. But Calder also knew who signed the checks...and they were big checks, because Calder didn't work for standard U.S. Army military pay. And Calder got nearly everything he wanted - within reason. He wasn't about to probe too deeply at the edge of *that* envelope.

Calder flicked his eyes to look at Dyani. He could understand why Curt mentioned marriage and family. In spite of the fact that Dyani was just Dyani with no biocosmetic enhancement, she raised the fire in his loins because she was so natural and therefore so sensual.

He was internally elated at this golden opportunity that he rationalized what would otherwise have been serious concerns. He halfway anticipated some sort of covert attempt on the part of the United States government to pick up where the state of Nevada had left off, especially since he'd been briefed by telephone about the kidnapping of the Nevada state troopers. But nothing had been drained from the minds of either the troopers or the FBI man. So, he'd decided he was damned if he was going to break off an exciting leave with Javanna. But then when Curt called him earlier today, he'd had initial doubts about Curt's intentions. These were now gone, overridden by the fantasy of a dream come true: the potential of getting Curt Carson to come to work for him and serve under him.

It was a failure of judgement on Calder's part that was typical of the man. Calder wouldn't have lasted as a Sierra Charlie; he'd known that inwardly, half-admitting it to himself. Sooner or later, even if he'd remained in the regular Robot Infantry, he too would have been passed over twice and eliminated with an honorable discharge. The Tabernacle was the first good thing that had happened to him since resigning his Army commission. And his good luck had continued as he gave his mercenary loyalty to the Prophet of the Galactic Tabernacle of the Human Future. He dismissed the possibility that the Prophet might indeed have a direct line to the screwy gods of the Tabernacle's doctrine, but he figured maybe his luck had finally changed for the better. Now Curt Carson was broaching the subject of a job.

"What do you know about us?" Calder suddenly asked, trying to be businesslike and conceal his excitement.

Curt shrugged. "Not much. Just what you told me the other night."

"On that basis, why are we talking?"

"Because I'm beginning to evaluate options. And you're one of them. I need more information. If I make a change, it's a major decision in my life," Curt told him as sincerely as he could. "I won't make it lightly. Or on less than very solid information."

"So?" Calder tried to act with the sort of severe intent that he'd seen several real generals exhibit when being presented with something.

"So let me ask if you were serious about offering me a slot in your outfit?"

"Yeah, I was."

"That's what I thought. Well, I'm telling you now that I'm interested in learning more about it."

"What about the captain? Will she come with you?"

"Yes. Do you think I'd come without her? The deal has got to include her."

Calder turned to Dyani. "How about it, Dyani? Let me hear it from you. Are you interested in serving in my Host of Michael?"

When Dyani replied, she did so very carefully. "Where Curt goes, I go." She wasn't lying.

"You have an unusual name," Calder observed. "Wha''s your background?"

"As I said yesterday, I'm full-blooded Crow Indian. My ancestor, White Man Runs Him, served with the United States Army as a scout in the nineteenth century. My family has a tradition of military service ever since."

Calder laughed. "Born with mercenary blood in your veins!"

Dyani kept herself under rigid control.

Calder turned back to Curt. "Okay, I'm interested in hiring you. You're interested in working for me. What do you think is the next step?" He was fishing. He'd never before hired a mercenary who'd been a superior officer.

"I told you just now. If I make a change, I've got to have as much good information as I can get. I won't jump without knowing what I'm getting into. I want to see your operation."

Calder suddenly thought that this could indeed be an attempt to covertly infiltrate Sanctuary. The Prophet had warned him about allowing entry of those enemies who were everywhere out there in the world and brainwashed to slow down, stop, or even destroy the work of the Prophet before the S.S. *Archangel Gabriel* was completed and launched toward its rendezvous with the extraterrestrials in the asteroid belt. But the techies were so close to completing the space ship that it was unlikely any quick look at this point could provide information that might allow anyone to breach the defenses of Sanctuary.

He *knew* Curt Carson and had known him for nearly twenty years, Calder rationalized. Curt Carson was a man of honor. Curt could indeed be trusted. But Calder hadn't asked the right questions or listened very carefully to what Curt had said. Like most people, Calder heard what he wanted to hear, and he wanted to hear that Curt Carson could be a subordinate in the Host of Michael under the command of General Stephen Calder.

"When do you have to report back?" Calder suddenly asked.

"We've got another week," Curt replied.

Calder made a snap decision. It wasn't a good decision; he hadn't checked out all the elements. Unlike Curt, he'd never commanded any unit larger than a platoon of Robot Infantry consisting of himself and a platoon sergeant running a bunch of warbots. Calder had never had any staff training that would have required him to check out all elements of a situation before committing to a plan or operation. "You said you want to see what you're getting into. Okay, I want you to see what can be done by a West Pointer without the nit-picking regulations of the United States Army and with enough funding to get what's needed to create an impregnable defensive system. Would a personally guided tour of Sanctuary fill the bill?"

"Yeah, but I didn't think I'd get it if I asked for it," Curt admitted.

"Remember what old Colonel Creeping Jesus Blake used to warn us about in leadership class?" Calder said with a grin. "You'll never know unless you ask. And be careful what you ask for because you'll get it."

"So we've got it?"

"You've got it. I make the security rules for Sanctuary, and I can damned well give a guided tour to an old buddy who's thinking of joining me. Let me make a few calls." He looked at Javanna, who hadn't understood a word of what was going on. But she oozed lascivious sexuality when she returned his eager lustful gaze. That she *did* know something about. And what to do about it. Furthermore, it was something she enjoyed because it was one of the few things she could do.

"But not tonight, buddy," Calder said almost absently to Curt,

ignoring Dyani entirely as he rose and pulled Javanna to her feet. H
began to walk away, saying over his shoulder to Curt, "Have them
put the bar chit on my room tab. Stick around, you two. I'll touch
base with you tomorrow morning. We'll probably be in Battle
Mountain tomorrow night, so I might as well enjoy what's left of
my own leave!"

Chapter Twelve

"Let's get aboard. We travel in style," General Stephen B. Calder said expansively as he waved his hand toward the Starjet Express parked on the Tahoe airport ramp. The large corporate HSCT was painted flat white overall and bore only its registration number, the name *Mercury*, and a strange but simple symbol consisting of a circle with a diagonal arrow through it.

"Generals are supposed to" was Curt's comment as he lifted his bag and prepared to accompany Dyani and Calder across the ramp.

A young man in a powder-blue uniform wearing the same arrow-and-circle insigne on his collar table quickly stepped up. "I'll take your baggage, sir," he said in a strange, flat voice. "And yours, too, ma'am." Without a word, he hoisted the baggage of both Curt and Dyani and walked off toward the corporate jet.

"Generals and their guests don't carry their own bags, either," Calder pointed out.

"Your private jet?"

Calder shook his head and led the way to the aircraft. "Several of us high acolytes use *Mercury* here. We've got our own air lift capability. We're so isolated at Sanctuary that we have to. Not to worry," he assured them. "The Tabernacle has lots of money. The Prophet is good at shaking dollars out of the religious freaks and space dreamers. But he doesn't squander it on equipment we won't be using here on Earth much longer. I'll tell you all about the Plan. I can brief you about the Tabernacle during the thirty-minute flight over. Dyani, if you please," he lent her his hand as they reached the boarding stairs to the aircraft's cabin.

Dyani had said nothing since arriving at the airport. Curt knew she didn't really like this covert scouting mission. But she was a disciplined warrior. Dyani would put aside her fears and reservations when the colonel said, "March!" Once she had marching orders, she'd march and do the best marching she could. Of the two of them, Dyani had much better command of her emotions and far stronger personal discipline. Once when Curt had commented about this, she'd told him, "Men believe they're rational. They're really romantics. Women believe just the opposite." Curt doubted that, but he couldn't find a hook on which to hang an argument. Dyani often saw things quite differently.

The cabin was as sumptuous as any corporate Jet and dominated by the circle-and-arrow symbol on the forward and aft bulkheads. Conforming to Aerospace Force practice, the seats faced aft, telling Curt that this particular Starjet Express was a surplus VC-237, the sort of aircraft that could be picked up on the surplus market for a fraction of its original cost. Maybe th.e Tabernacle wasn't so flush after all, he thought. But then he recalled the strange comment from Calder that the Tabernacle didn't waste money on things that wouldn't be of much use on Earth. Whatever was going on here was definitely weird and somewhat spooky, he told himself.

Definitely spooky and also potentially dangerous. Five men had already disappeared. How many others had become missing once they'd stumbled onto whatever the Tabernacle was doing?

He and Dyani were therefore very much on guard. They might be walking right into an enemy camp, which was a fortuitous thing if they wanted to get good G-2 but risky as all hell if the enemy found out and turned out to be nasty as a result. All signs pointed to the fact that this Tabernacle group was slightly paranoid and just wanted to be left alone. Whether this was part of the psychopathology of the group or because they were indeed up to something they needed to hide, Curt didn't know but figured he was going to find out.

The two pilots seemed distant and rather robotic in their actions. They weren't talkative. They sequestered themselves on the flight deck, and that was the last that was seen of them on this flight.

A Starjet Express wasn't renowned for its short field takeoff characteristics; the Aerospace Force hadn't required STOL capabilities because they used it as a VIP transport off the four-thousand-meter runways of their old but venerated air force bases.

On takeoff from Tahoe's twenty-six-hundred-meter runway at nineteen hundred meters elevation that warm July morning, it rolled and rolled and rolled and rolled before sticking its nose up and breaking ground just as the runway end whipped underneath. But, like other old turbofan ships, once it got out of ground effect and the pilots cleaned it up, it climbed steeply to cruising altitude.

Dyani was white-knuckled, and even Curt was bothered enough to remark to Calder, "Takeoff had a high pucker factor. I was telling myself, 'To hell with science; today it isn't going to make it!'"

Calder grinned. "Good pilots. They fly by the book and by the numbers. Always keep the needles centered."

"Yeah, I was worried about them, too," Curt admitted. "What's with them? They both seemed sort of robotic."

With a shrug, Calder explained, "They've been programmed."

"What?"

"With the exception of us high acolytes, all our people who have a lot of contact with the outside world and who are in a position to know or learn certain things are programmed as a security measure."

Curt didn't like the sound of that. "Programmed? What the hell, Steve?"

"So? A little neuroelectronic patterning, that's all."

"That's sort of unlawful, isn't it?" With neuro-electronics, it was possible to know what was going on inside a person's mind, provided no training had been given to allow them to set up blocks. Warbot brainies learned how to segment and compartment1ze their thoughts so the neuroelectronics circuits of a warbot wouldn't be confused by stream-of-consciousness thinking. It was also possible with NE techniques to feed back into the human nervous system commands that would, in essence, reprogram that nervous system at high levels. Under international treaty and federal statute, it was unlawful to do such things unless a certified neuro-electronic-trained psychiatrist did it under a court order. Under very strict guidelines, it was allowed to be used for psychotherapy and, in some cases, for criminal rehab. But, by and large, the NE technology for doing so was comparable to a guild secret known only to the psych people. The controls were tight, tough, and unambiguous, and the penalties for misuse were severe, amounting almost to an eye for an eye.

Calder shrugged again. "Maybe. Religions have used non-NE versions of it for a hell of a long time. The Tabernacle is a modern, twenty-first century religion."

"You were going to brief us," Curt reminded him.

"Well, I'm going to let the Prophet himself do most of that," Calder remarked offhandedly.

"Dr. Clark Jeremy Mathys?"

"Right! He's much better at it than I am. I'm just an old Warbot brainy," Calder admitted. "I'm not up to speed on all the latest doctrine. The Prophet may have received more messages than Anunnaki about changes in strategy against the Nibiruans. We're pretty close to war again, you know."

"Steven excuse me," Curt interrupted him, "but I can't follow you at all. Anunnaki? Nibiruans? Strategy? War again? Explain please."

"If I can. The Prophet has a channel directly to the Anunnaki by using NE linkage with the megacomputer at Sanctuary," Calder tried to explain. "His channel to the Anunnaki originally opened up while he was in NE linage with a computer doing analysis of the images of the surface of Marks taken by the old *Wotan* space probe. At least, that's what the Prophet says, and who am I to dispute him? I'm just an old warbot brainy who protects him and advises the Tabernacle leaders about the forthcoming war."

When the tall, lanky, mercenary paused, Curt prompted him for further data because this was an unbelievable and crazy story unfolding in the cabin of the bizjet. "I've been around the world a few times since Zahedan, Steve, and I don't know of any country called Anunnaki or Nibirua. And if these outfits are getting ready for war and Americans in Sanctuary are going to be involved, isn't that something we'd damned well better know about?"

Calder smiled. "Oh, yeah, I keep forgetting that you're not fully briefed yet. Well, the Anunnaki and Nibiruans aren't from this planet. They're extraterrestrials from somewhere out in the stars," Calder explained earnestly. "They've been fighting each other for a long time. The Prophet claims the Anunnaki seeded this planet with our ancestors. They meddled with the germ plasm of Earth apes in a biotechnology lab they'd set up on Mars. This started a couple of million years ago, by the way. Seems the Anunnaki needed both the gold from Earth plus help in the form of cannon fodder, a new warrior species developed from apelike organisms on Earth. Well, the Anunnaki got whupped when the Nibruans discovered what they were doing here. The Anunnaki bio lab on Mars got creamed, so the experiment was never completed. The Prophet says it all ties in with ancient records like the Dead Sea scrolls as well as the recent close-up photos of Mars. The reason the Prophet formed the Tabernacle and set up Sanctuary was because the Anunnaki got in touch with him, told him they were again strong enough to take on the Nibiruans, and needed human warriors, imperfect as we are. The spaceship *Archangel Gabriel* is just about ready to launch the Prophet along with sixty-five people and a sperm-ova bank to the asteroid belt where the Anunnaki will pick him up...he hopes."

Curt couldn't believe what he'd heard. He was amazed that someone like Steve Calder would believe it. Or that Dr. Clark Jeremy Mathys, charismatic as the man was on television, could get other people to believe it. Curt decided these people were indeed nutty as a pecan orchard. But he couldn't help saying, "Steve, that's the most fantastic story I've ever heard! Is that what you believe?"

Calder looked around. The flight deck door was shut tight. The rumble of the jets and the rushing boundary layer created a noise level in the cabin that allowed conversation to proceed without shouting, and perhaps high enough to muddle any recording, he decided. Then he grinned and said, "Me? Hell, I'm just a soldier, not a philosopher. And sure as hell not a religious leader! I'm doing a specific job. I get paid for doing it. And I'm an honest merc. When I'm bought, I stay bought. Who knows who I might be working for ten years from now? So my reputation had better not be tarnished. I don't have to believe the Prophet to protect him; I just have to do my job." He got up, went to the bar, and poured himself a stiff shot of good bourbon whiskey, asking, "How about it? A little reveille bot lube?"

"Too early in the morning for Stand-to, Steve. I don't need lubrications yet," Curt begged off; then he added, "but I may if this story gets any wilder and I have to believe it in order to qualify for the job."

"Aw, don't worry. I've got a couple of long-handled shovels." Calder sat down again across from Curt, eyeing Dyani as he did so. She hadn't said a word, and her face remained impassive. Curt could tell that Dyani excited the man. "Besides, I won't demand that you believe the doctrines of the Tabernacle, just that you'll defend them and the people who pay you. Provided you've had enough of the old shit of believing in what you're protecting. I'm a realist, Curt. I found out I had to be if I was going to survive in the real world."

"So why does the Prophet need a warbot security force if this war is going to take place somewhere off this planet?" Curt wanted to know. "What the hell is he worried about?"

"The Prophet needs protection for himself, the acolytes, and all the people in Sanctuary," Calder explained. "He says that the Nibiruans, the evil ones, are here on Earth along with the Anunnaki, the good guys. Some kind of treaty or something keeps the Nibiruans and the Anunnaki from screwing around with Earth's life forms any longer, but the Nibiruans want to keep the Anunnaki from co-opting us for their on-going war. It seems that the Prophet has been told by the Anunnaki through his computer that the Nibiruans have infiltrated all the governments and businesses on Earth and will do their best to stop the Anunnaki and the Prophet...without making a big thing of it and tipping off all the other humans about what's really going on in the galaxy. Hell, it makes sense."

"May make sense, but it's paranoid as hell, Steve."

Calder shrugged again. "If the Prophet didn't think that way, I wouldn't have a job. Besides, you studied history at West Point. You know that all new religious movements in history have been persecuted. The Christians and the lions. The Anabaptists at Munster. The Mormons. And even some of the evangelical religions of the last hundred years or so." The mercenary leaned back, looked out the window for a moment at the Great Basin sliding by ten kilometers below, than added, "But if the Prophet's right, we're going to have a hell of a fight on our hands in the next couple of months when the Powers That Be discover what's going on at Sanctuary and try to stop the Prophet from launching the *Archangel Gabriel*. It may have already started. Which is why I'm glad you're interested in joining the Host of Michael."

It was apparent that Calder was waiting for some sort of affirmative reply from Curt because the man paused in anticipation. So Curt said, "That's why we're here. The more I find out, the more fascinating this is." He wasn't lying, although he was grossly understating his inner feelings. "I think my combat and leadership experience might be helpful. And Dyani is my top scout-"

Calder shook his head. "I can use you, but not Dyani...although I suspect the Prophet will allow her to join you if he marries you...which is something I take it you've planned anyway."

"Why not me?" Dyani suddenly asked.

"Tabernacle doctrine, my dear," Calder told her. "Even though the Host of Michael is an all-robot force, I can't take on any women. According to the Prophet, it isn't part of a woman's role to fight."

"What does he think a woman's role is?" Dyani wanted to know. She was being very self-controlled. Curt couldn't even see an inkling of disbelief on her face. But he did detect a flash of resentment because of the Tabernacle's chauvinism.

"Sort of like your Indian beliefs. 'Men do men's work; women do women's work.'" Calder quoted an old but largely untrue shibboleth.

"Certainly not my beliefs. Or the Crow Indian beliefs. At least, not today. And what does the Prophet think 'women's work' is?"

"I'll let him explain that," Calder begged off, sensing a rising hostility on Dyani's part. Calder had been a warbot brainy in the Washington Greys. He knew very well the extremely strong opinions of the ladies of the Greys. "I'll just tell you that he has six wives - officially only one. And women outnumber the men in Sanctuary. The Prophet doesn't go along with gender equality. He believes women are precious and must not be put at risk. That's because he says that women bear the future of the Tabernacle and even the human future, too. So, we men are expendable because we can service many women, but we can't bear children." Sensing an even stronger hostility welling up in Dyani, Calder quickly added, "But don't worry! I run the Host of Michael. If you and Curt want to keep it between just the two of you, fine by me! I can protect the two of you and let you stretch church doctrine. I just can't go so far as to let you serve in the Host of Michael...which is not to say that I sure wouldn't reject any advice or critique you might have on the basis of your own experience, Dyani. Anyone with a DSC knows something about being shot at."

As the sound of the engines changed, Calder looked out the window. "Okay, they've started the let-down. Sorry that there wasn't more time for a more detailed briefing, but we'll be in Sanctuary in minutes. Then you'll see for yourself what a sweet deal this could be for the both of you! And I've arranged for you to meet the Prophet himself this afternoon!"

Chapter Thirteen

The landing of the Starjet Express was surprisingly rough. Dust was kicked up past the cabin windows when the turbofans were put into reverse thrust position. When Curt could see out a little better, it appeared that the bizjet had landed in the middle of a desert.

"Sorry that it's a little rough," Steve Calder apologized as the plane rolled slowly to a crawl and made a turn. "We landed on our alkali flat."

"Seems to me that you people have to do a lot of maintenance on landing gear and engine filters," Curt remarked. "Wouldn't it be simple to lay down some asphalt?"

"Nope. It's a good natural airfield. We're making enough of a mess around here anyway. No sense in attracting more attention by putting in a jet-sized airport. And the Prophet doesn't want to waste money on things that won't be of much use to the Departure or the Return. He says the Anunnaki can put down a beamship nearly anywhere without a prepared landing area." Calder unsnapped his seat belt and stood up as he added, "But it hasn't rained lately, and the flat is starting to get a little rutted. Don't worry. This old Starjet is plenty rugged. But it's a high pucker factor for those who land here the first time."

The Starjet taxied right into what was apparently a large metal taxi-through hangar, and the pilots shut down the engines. "Keeps the ship cool and the snow off it in the wintertime. And keeps prying eyes from knowing when our planes are here and when they aren't," Calder went on, waiting for the cabin door to unseal and swing open.

"You've got more than one?" Curt asked, getting to his feet. Dyani also did so and stood in front of him while they waited for the door to be opened from the outside. She hadn't said much. But Curt knew she was acting in her proven role as a scout, looking carefully at everything, listening to everything, sensing patterns in what she saw and heard, and remembering all of it.

"Several," was all that Calder would admit to right then. "The acolytes do a lot of

travel. But I don't want an airport that would be a prime target when the shooting starts. Which it will when the balloon goes up and the Nibiruan mercenaries try to stop the Prophet. As you'll see, my big security and defense job is preparing for that, and I'm real short-handed on the personnel side of it. Which is one reason why I made you the offer. You know a lot about non-warbot tactics. Hell, you wrote the book, Curt! On the other hand, Sanctuary security is strictly a warbot-type patrol mission, and that can be handled easily by ex-brainies."

The cabin door swung open, its upper half hanging up to provide a cover while the lower half swung down to deploy loading stairs.

Two people waited at the bottom, accompanied by a long white limo and four av-service bots which were already busily at work securing the aircraft and hooking up fuel and consumable replenishment lines.

Curt and Dyani followed Calder down the steps.

Calder was greeted with general officer protocol by two large men in uniform with silver oak leaves on their collar tabs. Both men had shaved heads. Both were hard, wiry, and mean-looking.

"Colonel Carson, Captain Motega, may I present my aides, Colonel Helmuth von Kampf and Colonel Louis DeVille?" Calder made the formal introductions. "Colonel von Kampf served with the *Robotschutzgruppe* and Colonel DeVille with the *Legion Robotique*. Gentlemen, as I informed you earlier today, both Colonel Carson and Captain Motega are currently serving with the Washington Greys but want to join the Host of Michael."

Von Kampf looked and acted Teutonic while DeV1lle was suave in a Gallic manner. Curt realized that these two men were also mercs with backgrounds that included lots of fighting in very elite robot infantry outfits. As Curt shook hands with von Kampf, he remarked, "Were you near Munsterlagen during the Reunification, Colonel?"

"*Nein, mein herr,* I vas at Stettin." That was a tight fur ball, Curt knew.

"And you, Colonel Carson, were at Stridjom," DeVille put in. "I was also there and in Windhoek.

"We have much in common," Curt told them. But not as much as he wanted the three mercs to think.

They greeted Dyani as a lady, not as a soldier, in a formal European manner. "In some ways," DeVille remarked as he kissed her hand, "it is unfortunate that the Prophet does not permit ladies to serve in the Host of Michael."

Von Kampf said nothing about that. Curt knew the typical German policy of strict gender separation. The *Bundeswehr* didn't want Valkyries. *Der Faderlnd* wanted its women to build its population base. Period. The Washington Greys (and other mixed-gender American warbot outfits) always had trouble with the *Bundeswehr* troops in Germany because of this. Curt never figured out whether the Germans were jealous or resentful. Germany was still a male-dominated nation, and German thinking hadn't really changed over the centuries since the break-up of Charlemagne's empire created the country. Of all the nations of the world, Germany was the most closely watched lest it start troubles brewing as it always had done every time it had reunified in the past.

The limo was robo-controlled, but DeVille rode in the left front seat while Calder took the right front with Curt and Dyani in the back. When they rolled out of the hangar, Curt was stunned.

The were surrounded by a modern air base set in the midst of a green, grassy, Great Basin valley. Curt knew from his quick look at maps of the area before he'd come that Battle Mountain itself reared up as a massive series of granite blocks and cliffs to the north while the valley itself was hemmed by the ridge of the Fish Creek Mountains to the east and the Tobin Range to the west. He'd expected to see barren desert, but the mountains were covered with juniper and pinon and the valley with long, green grasses. The only barren part was the alkali flat where they'd landed.

"The techies found lots of underground water when they started to burrow for the Sanctuary Test Outpost," Calder explained. "That plus the cooling trend over the past couple of decades brought us more rainfall and a change in vegetation. Not a bad place these days."

Curt had to admit that the man was right. It was a beautiful valley.

And it was full of buildings and hard-surfaced roads. All blended in with the surroundings. The road itself was surfaced in sand-colored material, and the buildings were either painted in earth colors or partially buried. To the north, Curt could see what appeared to be a large excavation on the valley floor just north of the lakebed; this had to be the "missile silo" reported by the Soviets. Curt had guessed that it really contained the Prophet's spaceship, the *Archangel Gabriel*. What better way to build a tall ship under concealment than in a hole in the ground? The silo would permit ready access to any level of the ship, eliminating the need for gantry cranes and towers which would be a dead giveaway that the paranoid Tabernacle was indeed doing something out here. A silo could be passed off as a mine shaft.

Why, then, hadn't the Prophet and his security chief developed a reasonable story to this effect in order to pacify the FBI and the Nevada State Police? And set up a suitable decoy installation to allow first-hand inspection of a "mine"? Curt guessed that it was probably sheer paranoia on someone's part. Those who thought the world was out to get them usually weren't smart enough to set up such decoys.

"This looks like quite a spread, Steve," Curt remarked as he peered out the window of the limo speeding along the road under robot control. "How many people live out here in Sanctuary?"

"Oh, a couple of thousand," Calder replied, brushing off Curt's inquiry in such a way that important security information wasn't compromised.

"Doesn't that pose a logistics problem for you out here in the middle of nowhere?"

Calder shook his head. "Nope! It did at first until the Prophet and his techie minions tapped the hot springs to get both water and energy. We generate most of our own power from geothermal sources. So, we use the Nevada power grid only as emergency backup. Big fusion power station about fifty klicks north of here at Valmy, and we got a drop off the main east-west power feeders out of there. We've also got cold fusion capabilities." Calder turned in his seat to make conversation easier. "You know how it is out here in the American West, Curt. With water and electrical power, you can build a city. Vegas, Reno, Phoenix, they'd all cease to exist without water and energy."

"How about food?"

"We imported most of it from the Battle Mountain railhead, using our own rail spur until we got Sub-Sanctuary up and running. Now we're nearly self-sufficient."

"Sub-Sanctuary?"

Calder grinned. "You obviously haven't been watching the Prophet's television ministries. The Anunnaki told him through his computer to build a ship capable of going to the asteroid belt, then wait for them to come and pick him up. Since that could take a few years, he had the techies build a prototype underground asteroid base underneath Battle Mountain proper. It's been completed for over a year, and the techies have been growing most of our food in its hydroponic farms underground. When he gets the *Archangel Gabriel* to the asteroids, he and his Acolytes know exactly what to do and how to build an outpost where they can wait for the Anunnaki."

"So, when the ship leaves, your job is over and you just abandon Sanctuary, huh?"

"Not on your life! This is Earth base central, and we've got to hold it against all comers until the Prophet and the Anunnaki return. They'll set the prophet up as commander in chief of the planet. They've also promised to complete the 'experiment' on the human race that got interrupted by the Nibiruan attack on Mars. All of us have been promised biotechnical redesign. Of course, the Prophet and some of the acolytes get immortality out of the deal. But I'm not sure I want to live forever anyway. Otherwise, I wouldn't have opted for the military life."

Calder shifted back to his favorite subject: Sanctuary security. "So, it's more than the simple matter of keeping snoops and accidental incursions out of our land. Razor-wire fences, bot patrols, and a neat multi-spectral sensor suite take care of that. Boring as hell, but that's what the bots are for. My biggest challenge now is to design the long-term defenses, which involves Sub-sanctuary as a redoubt. We want to be able to withstand any weapon anyone on this planet can toss at us. Sub-Sanctuary is already hardened against as much as fifty megaton subsurface detonation! But that would take out most of this valley, of course. And to keep out any snoops after we've been nuked, I want to set up some heavy radiation sources that would be triggered by any such event. A couple of thousand rads in this valley would tend to keep out most invaders, including even hardened warbots."

Curt declined to comment. He knew that regular warbots were hardened against the type and level of radiation they might encounter if the battlefield went tactical nuke.

"Of course, if that happened, we're prepared to hit back, too. In fact, we're already prepared," the mercenary general commented darkly, then changed the subject. "But this valley is a pretty place to live, and I sure hope that our counterforce threat means we won't have to resort to those draconian measures. This is a warbot brainy's dreamland, Curt. Lots of room to tear around. No worry about the high brass because I am the high brass! Tight, lean, mean, and efficient force. Clean neat planning to handle all the scenarios. Exactly the weapons we need matched to the missions we're called upon to perform. And-"

"You've got missiles of your own?" Curt wondered.

Calder again shook his head. "Nice guess, but those plans are highly classified, Curt. You'd gain access to that compartmentalized security information only after you've signed the paper. And only to the extent you'd need to know about them. Which wouldn't be much, by the way. The slot I have in mind for you is strictly centered Sanctuary. I want to buck von Kampf up to the man in charge of the external counterforce missions because he's got just the background and personal profile for that sort of thing. So, von Kampf's robot security command would become yours. Not only the perimeter defenses we have now, but also the prime robot defenses against external attack and armed incursions. You'd get to set those up. A piece of cake for you because you know exactly how warbot brainies and even Sierra Charlies would try to attack Sanctuary. So, you're just the man to do that job!"

"Uh, what's in it for me? And Dyani?" Curt ventured to ask.

"How about double your current pay?"

"Where the hell am I going to spend it around here? Or if the Prophet takes off and we end up not being able to leave Sanctuary? Or if the Prophet comes back and changes the world?" Curt asked the difficult questions.

"Money is only for external uses, Curt. Like my leave in Tahoe. I didn't tell you about the internal perks," Calder explained. "We don't use money in Sanctuary."

"A commune?"

"Would I work for a commune? Not only no, but hell no! Neither would DeVille here. We've got perks. The best housing...free. The top choice of food...free. We've got our own biotech capability, and that's free, too."

"So, what are you offering over what I've already got in the United States Army?"

Calder looked at him and said with a straight face and a solemn tone, "When the Prophet returns with the Anunnaki, immortality is part of the deal for all those who served the Prophet. The Big Man admits that not all of us, especially his Host of Michael, can be expected to totally support his religious doctrines because of the kind of personalities we have for the sort of work we do. Frankly, as you may have suspected, I think the teachings of the Tabernacle are just a bunch of bot flush the Prophet uses to squeeze money out of the true believers, anyway."

Yet you believe you're going to get immortality out of this deal and you expect Dyani and me to ascribe to that part of the Prophet's doctrine? Curt asked himself. Calder was grabbing at dreams of glory, but that was part of his makeup.

"I know what you're probably thinking," Calder went on. "Hell, if the Prophet doesn't make it or doesn't return, we've got a neat place to live and a couple of billion dollars to use as we see fit. But I'm not willing to totally second-guess the Prophet, Curt. He's been absolutely good on the promises he's made to me, and he's delivered on all his promises to his Acolytes. If the Prophet does come through, you and your lady would be among those blessed by him. The two of you would be able to live as long as you want. And never get old. Right now, you're both combat soldiers who could be killed in any fracas. Think about that!"

Chapter Fourteen

"Well, that sounds like a very attractive perk. And I agree, this is a pretty valley," Curt remarked, but he didn't really think so. He was a man of action, a person who'd been around the world and back again several times. He knew prettier places and a lot of different types of people. He enjoyed freedom of travel and action, even if it was restricted somewhat by the Army. So, he had difficulty with Calder's carrot and told him so. "It seems to me that accepting this position means I'd be unable to leave this place. I'm not so sure immortality won't bore me out of my skull…"

Curt couldn't tell what Dyani was thinking because she remained impassive and very alert to what she saw and heard.

"We won't be here forever. We're going to win," Calder assured him.

"And that means that the Prophet and his Acolytes will run this planet…and perhaps the entire solar system," Colonel Louis DeVille added. "We will have no restrictions on our ability to travel. Or do anything else, for that matter."

"Provided the Prophet isn't conning you and does indeed come back, if he gets off the ground in the first place," Curt pointed out.

"The *Archangel Gabriel* will get off all right," Calder insisted. "The Prophet has some of the best engineers in the world working on it. And we've got the world's biggest terawatt laser to drive it. That laser will be converted to defensive weapon use once it propels the *Gabriel* out of the silo to escape velocity."

"This valley is not an unpleasant place in which to spend a few years waiting for the Prophet to return with the Anunnaki," the former French warbot brainy observed. "With a surplus of lovely women, it is even more romantic than Paris these days."

"As I told you, Curt," Calder went on quickly, "you don't have to believe the religious doctrine. As to the Prophet's intentions about

113

keeping his word, you'll quickly find out for yourself because we have an audience with him in thirty minutes. You and your lady will be able to get the measure of the man first-hand."

"Good!" Curt replied with as much earnest conviction as he could muster at the moment. That would certainly round out the recon mission he and Dyani were on to gather inside G-2. Meeting the Prophet might give them some new information. "When you told me that a spaceship was being built here and was almost ready to go, I guessed it was being built underground in a vertical shaft or silo over there by the lakebed."

"I should have known you'd be pretty damned perceptive, Curt," Calder said with a laugh, then confirmed Curt's guesstimate. "Actually, the best place to do it. Sub-Sanctuary runs from the launcher back northward under Battle Mountain. Over on the right here is where the above-ground living and working quarters of Sanctuary are located. Complete community, Curt. And every damned bit of it bought and paid for from the Prophet's television ministry which is unique in the annals of evangelism. See those antennas atop Battle Mountain? The Prophet can broadcast directly from Sanctuary over his satellite network. Our programming is received directly from the Tabernacle's own geosynchronous satellite and covers the entire western hemisphere. Two months ago, he got his second relay satellite in place, so now we've got complete worldwide coverage. The Prophet's TV ministry's take has more than quadrupled since the space link was completed."

"I've only seen his space colonization television series he made-when, ten years ago?"

"Nine. Man, you're missing a treat. The Prophet can really fire up the faithful here, and it seems to spread like magic to all those out there in the world with satellite dishes," Calder bragged. "The Prophet has given religious people who need some sort of godhead a cause that promises salvation and an end to all their troubles and boring lives. The religious types get to come here for retreats on a scheduled basis. They get their fervor pumped up again, but they can't stay. The Prophet wants them out in the world proselytizing others to the faith. As for the space advocates, he's also given them something to live and work for. They come here in droves to work for free just because the Prophet is doing something and promising that everyone who helps him will get into space in their lifetimes. He started out with just one big hangar building out by the alkali flat with a lot of sleeping bags on the floor and a chili pot simmering on a hot plate. Now the space techies come here with their wives and kids. They have those nice prefabbed bungalows to live in for free. They get their food free. The Prophet has set up a school for the kids - teaching them *his* religious doctrine, by the way, so someone will carry it on. All the techies have to do is build Sanctuary, Sub-Sanctuary, and the *Gabriel*. As for the acolytes such as myself and Louis here, we're the leaders who get a few extra perks, of course. So, will you."

"Perks like what?"

"Your habitat can either be up in the trees in Battle Mountain or down in Sub-Sanctuary, whichever way you decide you'd like to live."

"And we get the best food from the outside, including wines - although they are merely domestic California vintages," DeVille added. "There is more to life than just working, after all. One must have the opportunity to enjoy the finer things..."

Curt decided that Steve Calder and his mercenaries were indeed milking this situation for all it was worth. And their security services and counterforce plans must be worth a great deal to the Prophet.

It was a pretty soft merc job if you didn't care who you worked for or where your paycheck came from. Curt often felt a little bit guilty over the fact that his pay came from taxes collected from both the rich and the poor. But he'd sworn to defend those taxpayers with his life. Getting paid for defending the Tabernacle and its religious leaders with money donated by religious zealots against a promise that they might someday be lifted from their life of boredom and fear - well, that was something else. If the gods were indeed truly great and omniscient and omnibenevolent, why try to buy them off? Salvation should be available whether or not one paid for it. At least, that's what Curt was brought up to believe.

Sanctuary was indeed a small town spread out north and south and leading upward into the pinons and junipers of Battle Mountain to the north. The place was busy. Vehicles were on the roads. The people of Sanctuary were hard at work building and maintaining and operating their Sanctuary commune. From what Calder had said, many of them were also underground in Sub-Sanctuary.

The knowledge that Sub-Sanctuary existed was an important piece of intelligence information that Curt was certain General Hettrick or any of those above her didn't know about. Curt was observing and committing to memory everything he saw: the street layout, the location of buildings, and the centers of activity. In his own mind, Curt was beginning to formulate plans for how the Washington Greys might be able to move in on Sanctuary and take it from the Host of Michael if that should be necessary.

But he still lacked some critical intelligence data on Sanctuary defenses: Where were those defenses, what sort of weapons were involved, and how strong was Calder's Host of Michael?

The leader of the Host of Michael had also alluded to other measures that had been taken or were planned, because Calder wanted Curt's services to cover Colonel von Kampf's reassignment to those additional tasks.

What would I do, Curt asked himself, *if I were ordered to set up some sort of external operation above and beyond the actual Maginot Line sort of defenses of Sanctuary?*

He didn't know. He didn't have enough information yet.

So, he tried to get it. "Seems to me that Sanctuary security is something more than the razor-wire security fence, the intruder sensor suite, and the jackleg warbot guard force. You've got to have some sort of leverage on the outside. Otherwise, you'd get bottled up in here under siege for years. The government would simply keep the squeeze on and make it tighter and tighter until you had to give in."

"Oh, yes, as I told you, we've got other plans," Calder admitted.

"They're going to have to be damned clever to hold off the strongest nation on Earth."

"They are. We're continually planning and revising and coming up with new approaches."

"So as commander of the Sanctuary security forces, will I have any say-so in the overall defense policies and doctrines of Sanctuary? What's the full scope of authority and responsibility of the job you have in mind for me?" Curt wanted to know.

"Later, Curt, after you've met with the Prophet and he's given you the thumbs-up." Calder revealed something Curt had already guessed at. Calder had been in touch with his boss since yesterday. The merc's neck was out a mile on this one. It was apparent that Mathys wanted to check out this man whom Calder thought so highly of that he'd given him an offer practically without checking into Curt's sad tale of grief and woe in the United States Army - unless the checks were already under way. Curt hoped that Hettrick had been able to get the fake data into the computers before the checks went through.

"But I can and will give you and your lady a tour of our Sanctuary Security Central," Calder remarked with suddenness. "You won't learn anything you couldn't find out in an intense recon mission around the perimeter and from the air. And, as you might expect, I won't reveal some of the critical details."

The tour of SSC (Sanctuary Security Central) was just about as Curt would expect. They stopped at an unmarked building that was ostensibly and really a security vehicle garage. The command post was only one or two floors underground, and it looked like the old Titan missile silo museum near Tucson - clean, well-maintained, crisp, efficient. The control room itself reminded Curt of a similar center in that Mexican drug lord's citidal, Casa Fantasma, down in the Sierra Madres where years ago the Washington Greys had breached the defenses by stealth and wiped it out.

"No warbot brainies?" Curt asked, recalling that Calder had bragged about using converted industrial robots which would have required unclassified NE linkage techniques and robot operators.

"Sure, but you don't think I'd let you see those yet, do you? The

United States Army keeps the critical portions of its warbot linkage technology highly classified to prevent countermeasures. Don't you think I learned something from that and wouldn't do the same thing here?"

Calder was right about the reason for compartmentalized security classification of army warbot linkage technology. Over the years, Curt had gained enough information about it to make a good guess about the reason for it. One was simply to keep potential enemies from facing you with your own weapons technology. Another was that warbot linkage technology had to be susceptible to some countermeasures, so why broadcast that weakness? Calder's reluctance to let Curt and Dyani even see his robot operators at work told Curt that the Sanctuary's security robot system could be overly sensitive to known countermeasures technologies.

However, Curt didn't think these Host of Michael robot technologies were very much different from industrial robot techniques. In the control room, he knew what to look for, and he saw several perimeter control robots being operated from ordinary visual command terminals. Unless Calder had something better up his sleeve, his robot command procedures were crude and primitive to the extreme.

When they came up from below and returned to the vehicle, Calder suddenly instructed the vehicle's robot circuitry. "Limo, stop in Beamship Square." Turning to Curt and Dyani, he explained, "We're on our way to see the Prophet, but we have a few minutes to spare, and I want you to see the central focus of what you'll be defending. The techies may not believe all or even part of it, but their emotions often run away with them when they see it. As for the religious types on their retreats, some of them go ballistic and freak out. Fall to the ground. Wail and scream. Froth at the mouth. Speak in strange tongues. It's impressive..."

The limo proceeded down a broad street and into a circular plaza. When it stopped, Calder and DeVille got out. Curt and Dyani did too.

They found themselves in a circular central plaza where a surging, pulsing fountain threw walls of water up and around something gleaming atop a pyramid shaped pedestal. The object thirty meters up in the air was a gleaming, silver flying saucer of no particular specific design. Curt recalled having seen its generic shape in some of the UFO tapes he'd watched with fascination as a child.

A halo seemed to surround the flying saucer atop the pyramid. At irregular intervals, a blue electric spark snapped out of it into the surging water of the surrounding fountain.

Around the base of the fountain was a wall to keep people from getting into the pool of water surrounding the pyramid. Deeply engraved in the granite of this wall were symbols that looked like Egyptian hieroglyphics or Sumerian cuneiform writing.

"This is the Beamship Monument," Calder explained, and Curt thought for a moment that the man actually believed in this bullshit more than he'd let on to Curt and Dyani. Calder was almost reverent in his tone of voice. "The Prophet had it built to constantly remind everyone in Sanctuary that the Anunnaki have come to Earth many times in beamships like the one atop the pyramid. The symbols on the granite walls are direct copies of the Egyptian, Sumerian, and Aryan writings that go back more than fifty centuries. Where the writing can be de-ciphered, the translation tells the story of the interstellar war between the Anunnaki and the Nibiruans. The writings also forecast that the Anunnaki will return to utilize the human race as their warrior class. Over on the other side of the fountain are the inscriptions in ancient Greek telling of the Titans and the Olympian gods who were really the Anunnaki. The Prophet uses the ancient writings as justification for his religious doctrines."

He directed their attention up a long, broad avenue leading northward up a valley on the south slopes of Battle Mountain. Silhouetted against the sky at the north end of the valley was a building with a tall spire. "The Prime Tabernacle," Calder explained. "At night, the tip of the spire just touches the star Polaris when viewed from the base of the fountain here. The Prophet points out that the pole star doesn't move in the sky and the Tabernacle spire doesn't move either, a sign that the Tabernacle is as constant and true as the star that guided ancient mariners over the seas of

Earth. Neat trick. I guess it took an astronomer to dream it up. And an hour after sunset every night of the year, rain or shine, lazer beams point up from both the Beamship Monument and the Tabernacle spire. The Prophet tells his followers that the laser beams will help the Anunnaki beamships find Sanctuary. Hell, my guess is that if the Anunnaki exist at all, they know damned good and well we're here."

"He's built a very visceral religion here, hasn't he?" Curt had to admit.

"It's the only real Space Age religion. All the others predate the Space Age and do not take our modern knowledge of the universe into account at all," DeVille added, the admitted, "and I'm afraid that even I, a born and confirmed Roman Catholic must admit that."

"The Prophet is a very powerful human being," Calder added as he looked at his watch, sensing that the moment and the Tabernacle spire had about as much impact on these two military officers as they did on him. It was indeed spectacular, Curt decided, but he realized it was merely part of the idea and concept Calder and DeVille were paid to protect. "And it's time to get up to the Prophet's Domain. We don't want to keep him waiting…"

Chapter Fifteen

The main hall of the Prime Tabernacle was a planetarium.

But Curt and Dyani didn't see that at first. Their eyes were accustomed to the bright Nevada sunlight outside, and it took a moment to readjust to nearly total darkness.

Then the stars slowly came out.

As if suspended in mid-air, high in the Tabernacle hall by some strange anti-gravity device, a dimly-lit flying saucer slowly became evident to their readjusting eyes.

The hall was shaped something like the bow of a huge starship; it was possible to see the edges of the "deck" and the point where the "windows" began.

Low-intensity music filled the air. It was just on the edge of the hearing threshold.

The total effect was as if they had suddenly stepped onto the bridge of a hypothetical starship out in the void.

Curt felt uneasy. Dyani did, too. In fact, she took hold of his arm. That was the first time Dyani had ever intimated that she was afraid of anything. But Curt spotted it at once. "Don't worry," he told her quietly. "The place is full of subsonics in the background music."

Knowing the cause of their malaise didn't make him feel any better, and Dyani didn't relax her grip on his arm. Actually, her touch was reassuring to Curt. Dyani never resorted to a PDA (public display of affection), he knew her grasp was not one that asked for Curt's protection but a need to touch and hold someone else in this strange environment.

Steve Calder's low voice came to them through the gloom. "Yeah, it has much the same effect on everyone who enters. Here, follow my light. I'll lead you to the Prophet's chambers."

A small, dull red spot of light appeared from the tiny flashlight in Calder's hand. The deep red color wouldn't disturb their slowly adapting eyes.

Off to one side of the hall, Calder and DeVille led them into an elevator whose doors whooshed closed behind them. The effect was one of the elevators ascending, but the soft popping in Curt's ears told him it was descending instead into the bowels of what must be Sub-Sanctuary.

What they were seeing and experiencing had cost money - a lot of money. Dr. Clark Jeremy Mathys must have raised millions of dollars to create not only what they'd seen above ground in Sanctuary itself, but also in the Prime Tabernacle and Sub-Sanctuary.

The walls of the elevator cage suddenly became transparent, and it appeared that the lift had ascended through a cloud deck and was heading toward outer space. Again, the stars came out around them, and the Earth below seemed to fall away as its curvature became more apparent.

It was a damned good holo image, Curt decided, and one that had cost a great deal of money.

Religions from the dawn of the human race had always used the very best available technology to create impressive, mind-bending, highly emotional, magical illusions for their believers and recruits. A sense of wonder was essential for true believers.

Mathys had apparently used special effects to the maximum extent possible.

Over their heads, a strange space station appeared, and the elevator seemed to move in for a docking. Again, Curt knew it was SFX and that they were really deep below Battle Mountain in Sub-Sanctuary. No one had yet built an elevator to orbit; the materials to make the cables weren't available.

When they debouched from the elevator, the air in the room was cool to the point where it was vaguely uncomfortable. In the gloom, it wasn't possible to see very much, even though Curt's eyes had adapted. Dyani must have had better eyes and quicker adaptation, because she tightened her grip on his arm and gave a little gasp. She had seen something in what was to Curt only a shadow ahead of them.

The room of indeterminate size suddenly blazed with light bright enough to temporarily blind them for a second or so but not enough to cause real damage to their dark-adapted eyes. The light came from behind someone sitting in a chair in a relaxed fashion. The light level reduced quickly to reveal that five chairs were grouped around a low table. Seated in one of the chairs was a man. The light came from behind him but slowly dimmed as the cluster of chairs was illuminated.

"Good afternoon, Curt and Dyani! Welcome to the Galactic Tabernacle of the Human Future!"

It was a familiar voice. Curt had heard it before many times on television.

The short, spare, almost acerbic form of the man rose to its feet. It was Dr. Clark Jeremy Mathys. The man's round face and wide-set, dark, piercing eyes were also familiar. Those eyes were riveting. They appeared to hold Curt in an unwavering and unemotional gaze. Mathys extended his hand toward Curt. "Come sit down, Colonel Carson. I want to get to know you and your lovely lady. I've been told a great deal about you." Mathys' hand was firm and dry in Curt's, but Curt got the impression that it was a diffident handshake as if the man were greeting someone who really didn't matter too much to him. It was the impression Mathys had projected over television, the feeling that he was somehow slightly superior, much more intelligent, and talking to you because it was something he had to do, although he'd rather be elsewhere doing what pleased him.

But Mathys was obviously impressed by Dyani. He kissed her hand in continental fashion and told her in his low voice with just a little less disinterest in its tone, "I'm especially pleased to welcome you to Sanctuary, Dyani. You're a lovely young woman. If you join the Tabernacle, I'm certain that you will quickly ascend to a high position among the ladies who are already here."

123

"Dr. Mathys, I already have an excellent position among the men and women of the United States Army," Dyani, said in her typical straightforward manner.

This bothered Curt. They were literally in the camp of a potential enemy, one who was strong with a lot of money and a lot of people, both ready to do his bidding. It was not the time for Dyani's honesty. Curt was on high alert. He knew very well that the two of them were in great danger at the moment. From what Curt had been told by Hettrick on the comm link and by Calder, Curt believed that the man Mathys was unpredictable, a loose cannon, one who had stepped over the edge, a paranoid who might switch instantly from being friendly in an aloof way to being vindictive and arbitrary. Mathys was accountable only to himself.

Curt had met others like Mathys from time to time. Most had been adversaries. All had been people who'd had no accountability to others. Curt knew that absolute immunity would quickly lead to both absolute power and the random use of same.

Mathys was answerable only to the phantoms of unreality that somehow had been brought to the surface of his mind by some sort of uncontrolled use of neuroelectronic linkage with a computer. Perhaps it had been brought about by chronic depression. Mathys had apparently withdrawn from the real world for several years after all his attempts to promote additional government funding for space exploration had failed. Curt felt that the man was probably a prime candidate for psychiatric therapy utilizing NE mind probe techniques, a draconian measure that was used only as a last resort.

Mathys seemed to be twenty or thirty centimeters above them when seated. Some sort of clever design of the chairs or the floor placed the Prophet just a little bit above those with whom he spoke in this relaxed environment that was just *slightly* discomforting because of the lighting, the temperature, and perhaps even the ion balance of the air.

"I'm informed that you expressed to General Calder an interest to join me," Mathys began. "Why would you want to do this? You have a successful career in the American Army."

"Sometimes success is only illusion - like many of your special effects in the Tabernacle and here in Sub-Sanctuary," Curt replied levelly, informing his host that he did indeed know exactly what was going on and wasn't being fooled by any of it.

"I should have expected such an unemotional reaction to the Tabernacle as well as a careful evaluation of your surroundings," Mathys replied without a trace of warmth in his voice. But in spite of his lack of personal warmth, he was somehow nonthreatening and projected a trustworthy, believe-in-me image. Curt knew the man was very good at illusions. "You military men have been trained to think that way. You all tend to be nonbelievers who are ultra-rational in your world views. But, because you're all rationalists, you find certain aspects of the Tabernacle's doctrine also highly rational, even though you never become zealots."

"You're right, Doctor," Curt told him flatly. "Those army recruits who become zealots are quickly discharged. The sort of physical power a military person has under command absolutely demands personal discipline. And being a warbot soldier requires a mind that's rational with itself.

"Ah, yes, of course. The ultimate expression of the fact that man is not a rational being but a rationalizing being!" Mathys' attitude was one of an all-knowing snobbish sonofabitch.

Curt had encountered such people before at West Point; most of them hadn't lasted very long. However, in spite of the system, some had managed to fake their way into high command from time to time.

"But tell me: Why do you apparently want to end your professional career?" That was a direct question, and Curt knew the man wasn't a friend but one who was searching carefully in an almost paranoid fashion for cracks or gaps in a story.

"I don't believe I ever told Steve or anyone else that I wanted to leave the military profession," Curt snapped back, trying to control his irritation with the man's attitude. He guessed that maybe Mathys was deliberately attempting to bait him to find out what he was really like inside. If so, Mathys was good at it. But Curt felt he was the Prophet's equal. "I'll be a professional soldier all my life, just as Steve is. If my current employer, the United States Army, doesn't want me to continue to serve, it has ways of letting me know. Why am I apparently looking around? Because my name wasn't on the current promotion list. That means I've probably been passed over. If I'm not on the next list, that's a signal for me to retire gracefully before I'm honorably discharged for the good of the service. So, I'd damned well better start looking around right away."

"Were you looking for General Calder?"

"Not at all. I was on a thirty-day leave. We just happened to run into one another. General Calder and I were once comrades in the army. When he told me what he was doing, it seemed to me that I should investigate the matter. I want to have personal options."

Without comment, Mathys turned to Dyani. "And you? Why do you wish to resign your commission? You certainly worked hard enough to get it."

"Sometimes what we want turns out not to be as good as we had hoped." As usual, Dyani didn't waste words.

"Ay, yes, 'Be careful what you ask for because you'll get it!' But I'm skeptical. You're not married to Colonel Carson. Why?"

"Is it necessary to be married in order to enjoy one another's company?"

"In some circumstances, yes."

"We're both combat officers," Dyani went on when Mathys fell silent, waiting for her further explanation. "We must keep our priorities straight. Marriage and raising a family don't work well when both people are at possible combat risk."

"So, you would resign your military career to be with Colonel Carson?"

"I will go where Colonel Carson goes. I hope it won't be necessary to leave the military to do so."

"If Colonel Carson joins the Host of Michael and you come with him, there's no place for you in the Host."

"I've been told about your policy. But I wouldn't have to become an official member of the Host of Michael to influence it. And if Sanctuary is attacked, General Calder will need all the help he can get. Everyone in Sanctuary will become a soldier. Such things have happened before in history, and history repeats itself."

"Perhaps, but history repeats itself because we don't pay attention the first time," Mathys pontificated. Then he looked at both of them for a moment before continuing, "General Calder has expressed a desire to offer you a position in the Host of Michael, Colonel Carson. It's a high position with great responsibilities. Of course, it pays well; I pay all my people well. It also comes with certain prerequisites and honors - if earned by loyal service. However, I would also be placing great trust in you. Why should I do that?"

It was about as straightforward a challenge as Curt had had thrown at him in this meeting thus far. "Because nearly twenty years of service to the United States of America clearly shows that I can be trusted by those who not only want my trust but also reward me in a suitable manner."

"So, you're telling me that you'll sell out your trustworthiness for a better deal?"

"If you were being sent clear signals that you were no longer wanted or desirable, wouldn't you?"

"I'm not in a position where I must make such a decision," Mathys snapped back in an irritated tone. "I make the rules on the basis of what the Anunnaki tell me. No one comes into Sanctuary unless he is a believer and can prove it. We have too many enemies in the world. I wish I didn't need a security force, but I must face reality. My Tabernacle believers could be very good soldiers. But, like Muslims, they'd sacrifice themselves for their beliefs when they should be fighting to defend the faith. The Host of Michael must live for me, not die for me. Yet they must be willing to die if no alternative exists. This is one of the paradoxes faced by all great leaders throughout history. Another one is to ascertain that the leaders of the security forces are indeed loyal because they have the power of physical force to stage a coup. Fortunately, I have a way to check on belief and loyalty. Which I shall do before sending you to see Jasper Lyell, my financial officer, to discuss terms."

Mathys touched a sensitized location on the arm of his chair and said into a hidden comm pickup, "Reverend Gillespie, this is the Prophet."

"Gillespie here. Go ahead sir," a smooth, syrupy, disembodied voice echoed through the interview room.

"Please come at once to my conversation chamber prepared to carry out your duties as Keeper of the Faith. I need you to test two recruits. Therefore, please bring along Dr. Rosha Taisha."

Chapter Sixteen

At that moment, Curt knew he was in very deep trouble. He and Dyani had to get out of there immediately. Their very lives were at stake.

Dr. Rosha Taisha was an old enemy.

Very old.

He'd run into her more than seven years ago in the eastern Iranian backwater town of Zahedan. The beautiful Eurasian scientist was an expert in robotics and neuroelectronics. She'd been working with another religious leader, the fanatical Abdul Madjid Rahman, Imam of the Jehorkim Muslims, who'd hijacked a hypersonic airliner and taken 105 passengers and crew members hostage. The Washington Greys had been sent into Zahedan on a rescue mission, and Curt had been taken captive. Taisha had tried to break his mind to turn him into a follower of Imam...and failed. In the sheep screw of the second wave of the rescue mission, Taisha had escaped. Her whereabouts since had not been known, at least to Curt. However, he'd had the feeling that he'd meet up with her again at some time in the future.

This was that time.

But at that moment in that place, he couldn't do very much. He and Dyani were unarmed. Their immediate adversaries were three men, two of whom were mercenary warbot brainies. Maybe Curt and Dyani were in better physical condition and could overpower them...and maybe not. Mathys obviously had instant and immediate communication with others. Calder probably did, too. On top of that, the two of them were deep underground in the unknown labyrinth of Sub-Sanctuary which in turn was inside the heavily guarded Sanctuary compound that had already swallowed up five men, four of them armed.

This was not the time or the place to try a break-out.

Curt was going to have to fake it through and watch for the instant when he and Dyani could make a run for it. He knew they'd have to. They were already so deep into this that there was only a slim chance, in his mind, that they could simply walk out.

They'd been sucked in quickly. Curt believed that this was a standard practice for Mathys. People had already just disappeared around Battle Mountain, and no one had heard from them again. The Tabernacle had hundreds of square kilometers of Nevada rangeland in which to bury bodies.

One thought consoled Curt: Major General Belinda Hettrick knew that he and Dyani were here. If he didn't report back, Hettrick was a former Washington Grey and would move rapidly and decisively. So would the Washington Greys. Throughout all the years and all the tight spots he'd been in, one fact remained constant: *The Washington Greys never abandon their own!*

Sometimes they'd had to bend the rules real hard to carry on that tradition.

Dyani immediately sensed that Curt was upset about this announcement. She looked at him in inquiry, but he kept his cool and merely looked back at her. That look told Dyani a lot. Something had gone wrong. So, she was ready to fight her way out of here the split-second Curt decided to do so.

Curt barely saw the Reverend Alastair Gillespie come into the circle of chairs. The man was dressed in black. It wasn't unusual for a religious person to be dressed in black, but Gillespie didn't look like a Catholic priest. Not with the heavy black leather gauntlets, leather boots, and leather harness around his bloated torso. Furthermore, his leather glittered with silver spikes and buckles. What looked like a whip hung from his belt. He would have been overly dressed for a motorcycle gang, but not for an S&M parlor.

But the man's face didn't match the evil image of his costume. It was a mild, almost wimpish face with thin lips and tiny eyes behind old-fashioned, steel-rimmed circular eyeglasses. It was the face of a harmless schoolteacher - or bank clerk - except for the one silver earring that glittered in the light. It was pierced through his left earlobe. Curt was immediately reminded of the old photos of Reichsfuhrer Heinrich Himmler.

The person who accompanied the Keeper of the Faith was in direct contrast to him. She was attired in white slacks and a white lab coat that came up to her neck Nehru-style. Her hair and her almond-shaped eyes were as black as her lab coat and skin were white.

Curt's memory of Dr. Rosha Taisha was shattered by her appearance. Seven years before, she'd been a stunning, beautiful, exquisite Oriental doll in appearance. Now she was old, wrinkled, almost wizened. Something had apparently aged Taisha's appearance.

Could seven years make that much difference? Curt wondered. And what would cause such a drastic change?

"Did I interrupt something, Reverend?" Mathys asked his acolyte.

"Yes, but she isn't going anywhere," the man said in a small voice. "Ensuring continual fervor for doctrine is a never-ending job, Prophet. Who have we here?"

"A potential acolyte" - Mathys indicated Curt – "who is being considered for a high position in the Host of Michael under General Calder's command. He is Colonel Curt Carson of the United States Army. The general has spoken very highly of him. However, in light of the recent probings of the Sanctuary by federal and state police, I need to know if his visit here is a continuance of federal harassment and a possible precursor to an armed assault by the United States Army. If he's truly not here on a spying mission for our enemies the Nibiruans, the position under consideration for him is of such importance and sensitivity that I must in any event be assured of his intentions and potential loyalty."

Curt knew damned good and well that Mathys was insane at that point. Curt was dealing here with a very dangerous man. And his Keeper of the Faith was just as dangerous but could probably be handled a lot easier. Curt had handled sadists before.

"I'm sure we can determine that, Prophet." The man almost drooled in anticipation. "And the woman?"

"His fiancee. And I'm sorry to tell you that it is my desire that she not be tested," Mathys told him sternly.

"Oh, that's too bad, Prophet! The truth often comes much more easily and quickly to the lips of a person when a cherished companion is subjected to-"

"No!" Mathys' word was sharp and explosive. "I won't have physical harm done to women whose physical attributes will be important contributions to our gene pool. Or whose beauty will contribute to alleviating any possible boredom that might come while we await the Anunnaki Return either in Sub-Sanctuary or Star Base One."

"But, my Prophet, I am your Keeper of the Faith!" Gillespie objected.

"And you do a fine job maintaining discipline and fervor as the Keeper of the Faith, Reverend. But you occasionally overdo it. And I don't want that sort of thing to happen to such excellent potential recruit material as these two," Mathys lectured. Curt didn't know what sort of power Mathys had over this warped man, but it had to be substantial.

The situation was growing more bizarre by the moment. Curt wanted out, now! But he couldn't try. He and Dyani would certainly be either killed or captured quickly. Perhaps being killed would be the lesser evil; he didn't like to think what might happen to Dyani if they were captured alive in the hands of these truly insane people.

And he was angry with himself for making a whole series of mistakes that got the two of them into this sheep screw. He should have been more cautious. He should have tried to get better intelligence data. He should have evaluated his G-2 very carefully. He'd made the mistake of thinking that the Tabernacle was merely a typical American evangelical religious organization when he should have known from his own experience that religious fanatics were the most vicious people in the world.

Curt felt another sort of anger welling up within him. It was directed against Calder. The man had sold out to a bunch of evil gangsters, perhaps as depraved and obscene as the legendary Nazis. Calder had sullied the honor of the United States Army, his class at West Point, and the Washington Greys by associating himself with the Tabernacle run by these vile beasts. Personal honor was, in Curt's book, something that was beyond price, something that a West Pointer must never sully. Four years of intense immersion in a school where personal honor was valued above all else left a life-long impression on a young mind. Add to it the principles of service and duty reinforced by a tradition that a cadet was never permitted to forget during four long years. The result was a warrior who could be trusted to handle properly and only under direct orders the most awesome and awful machines of death and violence the human mind had conceived.

On the other hand, Curt wondered how Mathys had managed to convince intelligent people to design and build what he'd seen this morning in Sanctuary and Sub-Sanctuary. The sort of technological intellectuals who were responsible for all this couldn't be bought like Calder and his mercs, and they couldn't be intimidated or whipped into fervor by nontechnical religious ideology or even the mechanisms of a sadist. Unless, of course, Mathys had managed to put some spin on the typical techie ideology of wanting to do something because it was do-able, to hell with the cost or consequence.

Could it be that the Tabernacle had three legs supporting it - the religious zealots, the tech nerds, and the mercenaries - with Mathys appealing differently to each and acting as the central focus for the combined activity? If so, one of the three legs of the stable organization might be weakened. Curt knew how to approach the techies and the mercs to do this. If he got the chance.

So as he was mentally kicking himself in the ass for getting Dyani and himself into this situation, he was also thinking furiously about how he could get out of it and get back with information about who these Tabernacle people were, what their intentions were, and what they'd done to public safety officers and an FBI man. Or even how he could turn this whole thing himself and eliminate the need to send in the Washington Greys.

Mathys went on, addressing his subordinates, "Dr. Taisha, please check out these two people. I want the information by late today. General Calder, I want you and Colonel DeVille to ensure their security. I shall hold all three of you responsible for their well-being. Reverend, please join me; we have other matters to discuss." Mathys stood up, signifying that the interview was over and that his minions must now get to work following the orders he'd given. Mathys was imperious in the way he handled his people. Curt would never have given orders that way. There was no question in Curt's mind that Mathys was a totalitarian dictator. This didn't mean that the man couldn't command intelligent professionals and get obedience. Even Adolf Hitler had gotten the German techies and soldiers to do what he wanted by methods different than those used with other groups.

Calder and DeVille had arisen when the Prophet had done so. Now as Mathys walked away with his Keeper of the Faith and disappeared somewhere in the shadows of the echoing room, Calder looked at Curt and said quietly but firmly, "Colonel, will the two of you please follow me? DeVille, bring up the rear." The man had a touch of anger in his voice. Curt didn't know why, but he sensed that it might be due to the fact that the mercenary felt his judgement had been brought into question by his boss.

So Curt decided to make the most of that. He remained seated. "Where to, Steve?" he asked. He already knew. Dr. Rosha Taisha would take them to her lab and probably try an updated version of the neuroelectronic mind probing and imprinting that she'd once done unsuccessfully on Curt years ago in eastern Iran. Curt was both trying to buy time and to get some more information.

"To Dr. Taisha's lab," Calder replied, telling Curt nothing that he didn't already guess.

Curt held up his hand. "We're here as your guests, General," he said, deliberately using the man's paramilitary title conferred on him by the Prophet. "We came openly, expecting to be treated in a civil manner. Now I gather that the Prophet wants to subject Dyani and me to some sort of mind probing technique. We haven't agreed to allow this. What Mathys has ordered is against the law, as you damned well know!"

"Colonel," Calder replied, using Curt's title of rank in return, "I've been given orders. And Dr. Mathys is the law here."

Curt tried to be adamant. "I insist on knowing where you're taking us and what Dr. Taisha intends to do with us. Otherwise, you can forget this whole thing and take us at once to your main gate. We'll get back to civilization somehow…"

"Curt, you heard the Prophet. I'm sorry he decided to test you. I hadn't counted on that. I'm responsible for your security. I can't let you leave now." Calder was almost apologetic in his tone. He might have possibly suspected Curt's motives in coming here, but he also trusted a fellow West Pointer, officer, and former comrade in arms. He was a little embarrassed, which accounted for some of his anger. "I'm also responsible under direct orders for your well-being. I won't let anything happen to you. And I'll tell you where we're going. You're right in your guess that we're deep below ground. This is Sub-level Sixty-six, the most secure redoubt in Sub-Sanctuary. Dr. Taisha's lab is on Sub-level Two. Come along now!"

At least they'd be closer to the surface! Curt didn't relish the idea of having to bust out of an underground room 160 meters below ground. That was nearly an impossibility. On the other hand, he might be able to get out of Sub-level Two. So, he rose to his feet, took Dyani's hand, and silently signaled her with his touch and eyes that they should cooperate…for the moment.

"As for what Dr. Taisha intends to do," Calder went on, "she's our resident expert in robotics and neuroelectronics. I'm sorry. I should have introduced you-"

"I know the colonel," Taisha suddenly snapped. "I know him very well."

Curt suddenly realized that Calder's role in the Zahedan hostage rescue operation seven years ago was such that he, as a second lieutenant in another company at the time, was in another part of the fight and didn't know that Taisha had escaped from Curt in the final minutes of the skirmish.

"General, I will enjoy carrying out the Prophet's orders this time," the neuroelectronics scientist went on with a strange gleam in her eye.

Chapter Seventeen

Curt didn't panic. He and Dyani had to maintain their charade until the opportunity presented itself for a break. That opportunity would present itself when Calder and DeVille weren't expecting it because Curt would operate on the basic principle of Sun Tsu's art of war: All warfare is deception.

He wasn't afraid of Dr. Rosha Taisha's neuroelectronic mind probing. Any trained warbot brainy knew how to channel thoughts so that deep personal emotions and thinking were masked; it would be impossible to operate a warbot otherwise.

However, he knew from experience that Taisha had learned how to control a "test subject's" physical actions; she'd once stopped his breathing in Zahedan. And she could create the mental sensation of pain without causing physical damage. He could take the pain. Dyani was also well trained and extremely well disciplined, so she would be able to withstand it.

But he didn't know what Taisha had been able to do since he last saw her seven years ago.

As the five of them entered the elevator for the ride up to Sub-level Two, Curt tried to strike up a conversation with Taisha partly to find out some things he didn't know and partly to establish a diversion. He was ready to shift instantly from quasi-friendly chat to violent action if necessary, but he had to get his "hosts" relaxed and off their guards first.

"We haven't seen one another for a long time. A lot of things have changed, Doctor," he remarked to Taisha.

"You haven't," she replied sharply.

"But apparently you have. When did you leave Zahedan?"

"The same night your soldiers attacked, and I managed to get away from you," she said bitterly. "The Iranian government would come quickly to get the Imam. I did not want to be with him when that happened. Therefore, in the confusion, I walked out of Zahedan south to the Gulf of Arabia and made my way to Pakistan."

Curt couldn't help but shake his head in amazement. Most of that was real. "That must have been a hell of a tough journey!"

"Yes. I nearly died several times. I was rescued - if one can call it that - by Baluchi tribesmen and was held as their sexual captive for a long time before I escaped - twice. It was not easy. But I got out. And got to America by various means that I shall not discuss." Taisha was very reluctant to even discuss it, but Curt understood why she had appeared to age so much. The Gedrosian Desert between Pakistan and Iran just south of Afghanistan was probably the most terrible of all environments for a human being. Alexander of Macedon was the only one to have managed to get through it; he'd done it with an army. But even Alexander had returned westward by the sea, leaving his subordinate, Craterus, to bring the army back through the Gedrosian Desert. The people there lived short, brutal lives because it was a brutal environment in which no one had much of anything. They'd obviously captured Taisha and kept her as a slave. Such treatment along with barely adequate food did not tend to preserve female beauty.

"One tough trip," Curt admitted; then added, "I'm surprised you didn't write a book about it. An adventure like that would sell pretty well."

"With the Iranians looking for me? With your government probably also looking for me? No, Carson, I am not a fool!"

"The United States government never had any cause to want you, Doctor," Curt advised her. "You may have done some illegal NE probing of Colonel Lovell, Sergeant Sampson, and me, but that was in Iran, not here. And the statute of limitations has probably run out as well."

"You do not know everything about me," was all that Taisha would say to him.

This told Curt that she was probably wanted under warrant by Interpol or some other international police organization, or possibly by several governments as well. Curt suspected that Taisha had probably stepped over the line with her neuroelectronic experiments on human beings. He knew that she'd been obsessed with the concept of totally controlling other humans by feeding command signals to their minds and nervous systems through neuroelectronic means. Taisha wanted the ultimate power over people. She wanted to be able to get them to do exactly what she wanted. Someone must have really gotten to her as a child in order to warp a mind as brilliant as hers, Curt guessed. And, from what he'd seen of the Tabernacle's religious side just now, he knew why and how she had come here. Mathys and Gillespie would find her talents useful.

Curt tried to flatter her. "I know that you're an outstanding neuroelectronic scientist. I'm surprised you didn't go to work for Colonel Willa Lovell at McCarthy Proving Ground."

"I'm not wanted there. You Americans have restrictions that prevent me from doing the sort of research I've managed to conduct here, thanks to Dr. Mathys." Taisha's voice was still hard and sharp, but Curt detected that he'd managed to touch a sensitive and perhaps responsive nerve because she went on, "I'll run a check on the two of you because the Prophet ordered it. But I know that you have been trained as a war robot operator. I suspect that your woman has also been trained. I know your women warbot soldiers all too well. There is not too much that I can learn from your mind because it is trained. And I may have a problem going deeply anyway; you've both allowed your hair to grow out, which tells me that you may have become supervisors of warbot soldiers rather than operators. I was told not to harm you physically, so I cannot shave your heads to get better data."

She sighed. "However, I shall do what I can and make my report. At least, the Reverend Gillespie won't have a chance to get his hands on you." It was apparent that she didn't like the Keeper of the Faith. But Curt remembered that he'd strongly objected to the physical torture of the hypersonic airliner hostages in Zahedan.

Maybe there was hope that he and Dyani could bluff their way through here and not have to break out of Sanctuary.

On the other hand, Curt felt now that the two of them were inside, they would probably have a hell of a time getting out again even if they came through Taisha's probing with squeaky-clean results.

He wasn't sure that Taisha wouldn't find something, that she wouldn't be able to break through his training. It had been several years since he'd worked in full linkage with a warbot. The same held true for Dyani. In their transition from intellectual, techie warbot brainies to physical, down-and-dirty Sierra Charlies, it was quite likely that some of their former warbot training had gotten very rusty indeed.

Could he take a chance?

He didn't think so.

Therefore, he remained primed to break as quickly as the opportunity presented itself.

He only hoped that Dyani could indeed read his mind. He'd joked with her about this in the past because she certainly seemed able to anticipate him in their personal lives.

Dyani was being her usual quiet public self. He knew she was scouting, taking in data, remembering it, and staying as alert as a scout should be on a dangerous patrol behind enemy lines. Because this mission into Sanctuary was exactly that. Curt had had his doubts prior to meeting Mathys and Gillespie, but he no longer thought the Tabernacle was another harmless evangelical religion of the twenty-first century. It had roots that went back long before that.

They got out of the elevator and began to walk down a long, narrow corridor that wasn't straight and apparently had not been hewn from the granite of Battle Mountain. It was barely wide enough for two people to walk abreast. The walls, floor, and ceiling were plastered, and the tube was lit wanly by old fluorescent lamps. It looked a lot older than the parts of Sub-Sanctuary Curt had seen thus far.

"Old mine tunnel?" Curt guessed.

"Roger that," Calder replied. "This was the first section of Sub-

Sanctuary. The techies started out by converting old mine shafts and then excavating rooms off of them. The newer parts of Sub-Sanctuary were built using the technologies Gordon Palmer and his techies have been developing for Star Base One." The general of the Host of Michael apparently had no reluctance to discuss such things with Curt and Dyani. This told Curt that the man was more than just a little pissed off at Mathys for doubting his judgement. Curt had apparently conned Calder into actually believing that he and Dyani were fully prepared to join the Host of Michael once this little unpleasantness with Taisha had been put behind them. At least, Calder acted that way.

"What's this Star Base One project?" Curt didn't expect an answer.

He was surprised when he got one. "That's the underground base Mathys and the others intend to build inside an asteroid once the *Gabriel* gets them out there," Calder explained without hesitation. "The Prophet has proclaimed that the Anunnaki may not pick them up right away. So, they'd better be prepared to live on the rock out there until the pickup is made - if it ever is. Part of the doctrine, by the way. Palmer and his techies have used Sub-Sanctuary to develop the technology they'll need to build Star Base One."

A door to a compartment off the main tunnel opened ahead of them. A young man and a pretty young woman came out. The man was tall, gangling, wore his hair in a crew cut, and had a pair of heavy horn-rimmed eyeglasses perched on his nose. He looked like a techie, one of those who was a confirmed rebel among the ranks of the tech nerds. The girl was just that: a young girl, nubile, fresh, pink, and pretty in a plain sort of way.

Calder and his party surprised them. "Oh, hi, General!" the young man called out with a wave. "Dr. Taisha, Monica and I were looking for you."

"When we didn't find you in your lab, we thought you might be in one of the detention rooms," the girl added.

"Really!" The young man seemed to be both embarrassed and a bit frightened about being discovered with the young woman. "We weren't-"

"Hey, Henry, we're Host of Michael. We don't work for Gillespie," Calder said jovially. "If you and the Prophet's secondary wife want to play games in a secluded place, that's your business. I didn't see you doing anything wrong. So, don't worry about me. How are you, Monica Elora?" It was apparent that Calder now had a gotcha on these two, one of whom was obviously high up in the Tabernacle hierarchy.

"Well, who have we got here?" the young man asked, seeing Curt and Dyani.

"Two recruits for the Host, Curt Carson and his lady, Dyani Motega," Calder replied. "Curt, Dyani, this is the Prophet's Number Two wife, Monica Elora. And her escort is Henry VanDerCamp, the chief techie computer wizard."

Curt and Dyani just waved. There wasn't room in the corridor to do much else. "Hi!" Curt called out.

The couple joined the procession walking down the narrow corridor, placing themselves behind Calder and thus between him and Curt. It was crowded.

"I need to borrow a couple of your control stacks until my order gets here tomorrow, Doctor," Henry VanDerCamp said. "I'm just about finished with the attitude control system on the Gabriel, and I'll be behind schedule if I don't get a couple of Tee-Em Model Forty-fours plugged in this afternoon so we can check the system."

"Henry, I'll be using everything I've got for the next few hours," Taisha replied cooly. "I have no spares to lend you."

"Since when do you probe Host recruits?" Monica Elora asked.

"Since the Prophet told me to," Taisha shot back.

"Clark told you to probe Host recruits? Doctor, does it seem to you that he's getting, you know, too up-tight now that we're within a week of launch?" Monica Elora Mathys wanted to know.

"He's up-tight, Monica Elora, because we're getting some attention from the outside world all of a sudden," Calder remarked.

"Oh, so that's who those men in the detention room were!" Monica said. "What are you going to do with them, Doctor? One of them looks in poor health."

"I was told to hold them," Taisha replied. "General Calder didn't want them to get into the Reverend's hands."

"Yeah, we may be able to use them as hostages if things get any rougher," Calder added. "And if that's the case, we wouldn't want them to be broken up by the Reverend if we have to exchange them for something we want."

"Beastly man! I'm glad he can't touch me!" Monica Elora Mathys muttered coldly.

"He could," Henry VanDerCamp told her. "Don't worry. None of us techies will let that happen, Monica. A lot of us think pretty highly of you..."

Curt slowly put his hand on Dyani's arm and squeezed it lightly in a signal.

The group had just passed a door labelled "Exit." It was ajar. Curt saw the brightness of daylight through the crack in the door.

Only Colonel Louis DeVille was behind the two of them. VanDerCamp and Monica Elora Mathys were between them and Calder.

The conversation in the crowded tunnel had gotten everyone reasonably relaxed. Curt noted that even Calder's guard was down now. And the man was also doing something he felt to be unnecessary as well as an assault on his honor and judgement as the commander of the Host of Michael. He made the mistake of believing that Curt and Dyani were indeed serious about defecting to the Host because of their cool, calm reception of what could possibly be a very dangerous activity on the part of Rosha Taisha.

No one in the group was armed.

Curt decided it was time to abort the recce mission.

Without a word, Curt whirled on his heel.

Dyani was primed for it.

Curt hit Louis DeVille hard with all his weight and strength. The former French warbot brainy, who wasn't in nearly as good condition as the two Sierra Charlies, went down instantly.

Dyani knocked Monica Elora Mathys to the floor, creating a momentary barrier for Calder to get over.

The two of them leaped over the prostrate and moaning DeVille, burst through the exit door, and surged up the long flight of wooden stairs towards daylight.

Confusion remained in the tunnel after their exit because Curt and Dyani had moved so quickly and decisively that even Calder didn't realize what was happening until it was too late. Then VanDerCamp was in the way because he quickly knelt down to make sure Monica Elora was all right. Taisha, leading the group, took six steps before she realized all hell had broken loose behind her.

When the Eurasian neuroelectronic scientist figured it out, she screamed. "You should never have trusted Carson. Calder, after them!"

Calder, on the other hand, merely stood still and tried to take stock of the situation. He was shocked that Curt had behaved as he did and had bolted. He also knew that if he didn't catch them, he was in very deep trouble with the Prophet. Calder had his Host of Michael to protect him if it came to that, but he didn't want to get on Mathys' bad side at the moment, the man being as touchy as he was just prior to the launch of his spaceship.

"Well, go after them!" Taisha yelled at him. Calder shook his head. "No need to be hasty, Doctor. They're inside Sanctuary. They've got a longways to go to get out...if they can get out. We'll get them in a few hours or sooner."

"Get him, Calder!" Taisha snapped. "I know that man! He's a ruthless fighter who stops at nothing. And he's smart! Besides, your security procedures aren't designed to keep people in!"

"How did you know that?" Calder asked her quickly.

"I've gone out several times," Taisha admitted. "And gotten back in easily because the robot operators recognized me."

Calder reached for the comm unit at his belt and realized he'd left it in the limo before going into Sub-Sanctuary to meet the Prophet. Mathys didn't like Calder to wear comm gear when the two of them were together. The Prophet didn't want his mercenary to be able to talk to his troops in such situations. Mathys was truly paranoid, among other things, and was constantly on guard against a coup.

Trying to keep his calm and ignoring his French subordinate writhing on the floor, he asked Taisha, "Where's your office? I've got to use your phone."

Chapter Eighteen

Curt and Dyani found themselves at the top of an old mine shaft that had been left in its former state as camouflage. In fact, a weathered sign told them it had been the Copper Canyon Mine. They were on the east side of a small valley with a juniper-covered slope rising behind them. The position of the sun told them it was early afternoon.

They were surrounded by old mine tailings and could barely see the spire of the Prime Tabernacle in the canyon south of their position. They were obviously beyond the limits of the Sanctuary main base, somewhere on the south side of Battle Mountain...but still inside the security fence.

"You okay?" Curt asked, not even breathing hard after running up those rickety wooden stairs of what apparently had become an emergency exit from Sub-Sanctuary.

Dyani nodded and remarked, "I see I kept you in good shape, too."

"You're my chief scout," Curt told her, ignoring her remark and looking around. "Where the hell are we, and which direction do we go to get out of here by the shortest route? Got any ideas?"

"Yes."

"Up the valley, right?"

"Negatory! This is cowboys and Indians for real. And I usually played on the Indian side," Dyani reminded him, looking around carefully. It was obvious she knew what she was doing and what to do next. In the Greys, she was the commander of the scouting platoon, Sierra Charlies all, Curt's eyes and ears on the battlefield. This was her element. She made up her mind and said, "So we don't go up the valley. We don't go where it's obvious. And we stay high on the ridges in terrain where their clunky robots can't move. The Host isn't an internal police force; it's used to keep people from getting in. Calder is going to have trouble playing Sierra Charlie; he doesn't know how. So, we go where he doesn't expect us. And where his robots can't go. So, up the hill to the ridge. Then we look around and get our bearings."

It was a steep climb. Years ago, Battle Mountain had been barren of trees except for short scrub; the slight change in the climate had brought a little more rain to this region in the past several decades. This, combined with the ongoing worldwide cooling trend, resulted in forests of junipers and pinon pines now growing on the slopes. They would provide cover if the Host ran an air recce for them. It also would serve to confuse the hell out of infrared sensors and trackers because the air temperature was nearly at body temperature. Later that night, it would be different; but the trees would tend to mask human IR signatures against all but the most sophisticated sensors - and Curt didn't think the Host had those yet because the Greys had gotten them only a year or so before.

On the ridge, they could see the mountain sloping away to the Reese River Valley in the east. Several canyons cut the east slope of Battle Mountain. In some places, Nevada State Route 305 heading south from the town of Battle Mountain was visible.

"We go north along this ridge," Dyani decided. "I don't think Calder is following us, but if he is, he won't expect us to do that."

"And it's just good tactical doctrine to move along the ridges," Curt added. "I can go a hell of a long time with-out food, Dyani, but we don't have any water with us. I'm okay now, but we'll both need water in a few hours."

"Bound to be a small stream somewhere. Or a spring. Trees mean water. And I know how to find it even if it's underground in these canyons," Dyani Motega said confidently. Curt believed her; she was speaking from the experience of generations in her genes. "In any event, I estimate we're not more than four klicks from the fence. If we have to, we can strike for the fence in an emergency she told him.

She was right. For about an hour, they moved north along the ridge, keeping a watchful eye out for any signs that the Host of Michael was either tracking them or following them. Dyani was careful not to leave too many telltale trail marks. It was going to be tough as hell for ex-warbot brainies to find two experienced Sierra Charlies, one of whom was only a few generations from a nomadic existence.

About two kilometers along the ridge, they crossed the head end of a canyon leading eastward. Dyani quickly moved to the bottom of the shallow draw and began turning over rocks. Then she began to dig with her hands. In a few moments, she had a pool of water in the sandy soil. "Here's our drink of water," she announced, then looked at the bottom of some of the rocks she'd overturned. "And something to eat if you're real hungry and not very picky..."

"Thanks, but I can get along without eating real natural food for a little while longer," Curt admitted.

"My sandals are giving out on me," Dyani said after taking a drink and removing her sandals. "Starting to get a blister. And I've got holes in both soles."

Curt finished cupping water from the little pool into his hands. "Jesus, Dyani, don't get a blister now!"

"Finish up," she told him. "I'm burying these sandals here when I cover up our watering hole."

"You're going barefoot!?!"

"Yes. It'll be difficult for the first klick or so. But I've been barefoot before. I'll harden to it pretty quickly."

"Wear my shoes," Curt offered.

"No. You're bigger and weigh more than I do. The soles of my feet have a lower weight per unit area than yours. So your feet will have more difficulty adapting to sharp rocks. I may bleed a little bit, but not for very long. Stop trying to be gallant; I know what I'm doing!"

Curt knew that when Dyani made up her mind to do something, she was the immovable object opposing any force, even the irresistible one. Early in their relationship, Curt discovered what happened when an irresistible force - Curt - encountered an immovable object - Dyani. Result: an inconceivable concussion. It took him several days to recover from it.

Together, they skirted the valley and started down the ridge on its north side, heading east. No matter how carefully Curt and Dyani looked or listened, they could see or hear no signs of pursuit or even action to stop them.

They reached the point near the mouth of the canyon where they were about five hundred meters west of the perimeter fence around the entire land area - more than five hundred square kilometers of it between Battle Mountain and the Fish Creek Mountains on the east and the Tobin Range on the west. There they seemed to run out of cover from the junipers and pinons. But ahead of them to the east was the fence.

It seemed to stretch to infinity north and south.

"Let's check it out from here," Curt told Dyani. "We should try to spot any sensor locations."

"We can probably walk up to any sensor pole," Dyani added, hunkering down underneath a large juniper to get some shade. It was cooling off a little now with the sun riding the top of Battle Mountain behind them. "Any sensors that Calder's got probably look outward and along the fence in each direction. I doubt that he'd go for three-sixty views. Those are awfully hard for warbot brainies to handle, and warbots don't respond very well to the small imaging that results."

"That's what I guessed, too," Curt replied, scanning the scene before him. "I wish I had some binoculars."

"Use your eagle-type eyeballs. Sensors can't be that hard to spot." Dyani rubbed her feet as she sat.

"You okay?"

"A couple of cuts. Not bad. We're almost out. That makes it easier to take."

Her feet were bleeding.

"Should have kept those sandals on."

She shook her head. "I was getting a blister, remember? I wouldn't have made it this far if I hadn't taken them off and buried them. I'll be all right. We're almost out."

"But we're not out yet. The last hundred meters may be the toughest."

"Not if we do it right. Remember: I'm supposed to be the type accustomed to using sneaky tactics."

"So what do you suggest?"

"Look." She pointed. "Up there about three hundred meters to the north. The fence makes a right angle turn to the east."

"Probably following a section line and the Prophet's property."

"I see a sensor pole there."

"You're right. That's the obvious place to put one. Right at a corner."

"Then, why didn't you see it first?"

"Because I was looking at your poor feet, Dyani."

"I'm okay," she insisted, but she wasn't.

"You aren't walking like you're okay."

"Okay, so my feet hurt. Now stop talking about them. You draw my attention to them, and that makes it worse," Dyani told him. "We work our way north along the tree line here toward that sensor pole at the fence corner. Then we can probably just walk right up on it without it sensing us."

"Probably," Curt replied, then warned, "but it's a good idea to have Plan B. It may see us. So, we're going to act like we've been spotted anyway and hope that we aren't. How do we get through that damned fence? Pull the sensor pole down – maybe - and use it to pole-vault over? Belay that! I didn't mean to be smart-mouthed. It's been a long day."

"See that big gate at the corner?"

"Uh, yeah. I couldn't see it from my angle. Right where the dirt track comes up to the fence from the outside."

"I'll bet it has a lock on it," Dyani guessed.

"And damned few locks will withstand a stout rock," Curt added.

"Some will. And do we take a chance that we can bust the lock?"

"No. Looks like we'll have to go over that fence. Or under it."

"We can climb it at the hinge or lock sides where there's enough of a purchase for our hands and feet. The razor wire is probably on the outside."

"Right! We may get a few cuts, but we can get through if we're quick."

"We'll be quick."

"Okay, let's get into position and do it," Curt decided.

Dyani shook her head. "Give it another thirty minutes. Then the sun angle will be such that any sensor looking westward along the fence will be sun blinded. That cuts the possibility that one sensor will pick us up. If the sensor at the corner doesn't, the sensor to the south along the fence may be out of range even if Calder was counting on a small amount of overlap at sensor range mid-point."

Trying to lighten up things a little bit and get them in a relaxed and ready mode for the breach of the fence, Curt asked, "How come you know so much about fences and locks?"

Dyani looked askance at him. "Obviously I had to break out of the reservation, right? How else would I have gotten here? Seriously, when you're a scout, you get to know a few things about fences and locks, especially around Fort Huachuca where we play war games."

"Woman, I'll be damned glad when we get out of here and I can show you how much I value your expertise...in many areas," Curt told her gently.

"Let's get out of here. Then we can start thinking about things like that," Dyani, always the realist, warned him. Then she added, "But we do make a pretty good team, don't we?"

"We got this far, didn't we?"

They spent the next thirty minutes working their way into positions for their final assault on the fence, continually watching for signs of the Host of Michael and reevaluating the situation with the fence as they moved and change their aspect to it.

"We'll go in low," Curt advised. "Sensors are probably looking for targets that are people-sized. Any target that looks like a coyote is probably ignored. Otherwise, the watch tenders would be responding to false alarms all the time."

Dyani shook her head. "Not necessarily. If they're looking for us to breech the fence at some point, they may have reset the scan pattern."

"I wish we knew more about the system," Curt muttered. "It would sure as hell help if we knew if it was just set up to keep outsiders outside."

"It probably is. People who work in Sanctuary aren't the type who'd try to break out."

"If they could. I suspect part of their indoctrination is a lecture on how deadly it could be to try it, something which could be a simple fabrication on Calder's part."

"We're about to find out. Time to move," Dyani point out, glancing over her shoulder at the sun angle.

"Grab a rock and bust a lock," Curt told her, picking up a fist-sized one himself.

Together, they headed directly toward the corner of the fence where the sensor pole stood. Out of habit, they ran a zigzag path crouched low.

"Halt! Identify yourselves!" came the call from a loudspeaker on the sensor pole.

Curt looked around. No robots or people were in sight. Then he saw a cloud of dust erupt from a cluster of old ranch buildings about two kilometers southwest of their position.

They had to move quickly.

"We can't bust the lock," Dyani observed after making a rapid inspection of the latch and massive lock device.

Curt was getting a close look at the fence. It was three meters high, and the razor wire was on the outside surface. "We climb it then. And jump from the top. The outer side is covered with razor wire to keep people out."

"We can get up at the hinge point," Dyani pointed out. "Or the latch side." She put her right foot into the fence and tried to climb. "I can't climb this in my bare feet! They're cut up too badly!"

Curt ripped the fastener strip on his shoes and peeled them off. "Take mine. Climb! If we have time, you can toss them back down to me from the top! Go!"

Dyani didn't need to be urged. Something was coming toward them from the southwest, raising a huge cloud of dust as it did so. She slipped her bleeding feet into Curt's shoes, pressed the fastener strips closed, and started to climb.

Curt heard the crack as a bullet snapped overhead. "For the second time, halt and identify yourselves!" snapped the sensor pole speaker.

The approaching dust cloud was being stirred up by a very fast industrial robot vehicle. It was now less than five hundred meters away.

"Don't bother throwing back my shoes! I'm climbing barefoot myself!" Curt yelled to Dyani and started to clamber up the other side of the gate. He went up fast, got to the top, and saw that Dyani with her painful feet was only about halfway up.

Another round snapped by overhead. It was a big one. Curt guessed it was at least a 15-millimeter round from the fast-approaching robot vehicle. Again the pole loudspeaker rapped, "For the third time, halt and identify yourselves or the patrol robot will detain you by force!"

The patrol robot was fast. It skidded to a stop at the base of the gate, stopped shooting because it was too close, and quickly unlimbered an arm to pick them off the fence.

"Curt, jump!" Dyani yelled.

He did. It was a long way down. He cleared the razor wire, hit, and rolled in the grassy, sandy soil.

When he turned to catch Dyani, he saw the robot arm pick her off the gate just as she reached the top. She twisted out of its grip but lost her own on the wire...

...and fell back inside the Sanctuary fence.

"*Curt! Go!*" she screamed at him.

Then the robot had her pinned to the ground with its jointed arm.

Chapter Nineteen

Curt wasn't in very good shape physically or emotionally when he reached the edge of Nevada State Route 305. The four kilometer trek hadn't been made under the best conditions.

At first, the patrol robot that had grabbed Dyani began shooting at him. He'd been lucky to find cover. The next few hours were spent dodging from bush to bush, staying low or in gullies where Calder's robots couldn't get enough of a target signature to shoot at him. They weren't real warbots, only converted industrial robots. Thus, they didn't have the ability to track their outgoing rounds and bring the trajectory into convergence with the intended target on the next shot. In short, they missed a lot. However, as the ground and air cooled off and Curt became a better IR target, the shots had gotten close. So he had to make like no target at all and put distance between himself and the robots.

It was dark by the time he reached the road. He was dehydrated. He didn't even want to look at his bleeding bare feet. Dyani had been right; physically fit as he was, he wasn't used to going barefoot. Few twenty-first century Americans were.

But it was Dyani that bothered him the most. He'd had absolutely no alternative except to leave her. He couldn't get back over that razor-wire fence to help her. Now she was a captive of the Tabernacle. He didn't know what they'd do to her...and he didn't like to think about it. Curt hoped that she'd remain as Calder's prisoner. Would Taisha try to experiment on her as she had on him those long years ago in Iran? Or would she be given over to the sadist, Reverend Gillespie? Or to the obvious lechery of the great Prophet, Dr. Clark Jeremy Mathys? Curt had seen the lust in Mathys' eyes.

Curt was angry, frustrated, and quite irrational about what had happened. His physical condition didn't help.

If he couldn't turn around and go back into Sanctuary to rescue Dyani, he had to figure out something else. The best thing he could possibly do for Dyani was to get the hell out of there, get the Washington Greys fired up and moving out of Fort Huachuca, and come back to Battle Mountain. He intended to crush these bastards who called themselves a religious movement. Curt had his own personal religion; most combat soldiers did. He didn't fight for it because he was committed to serving the United States of America. But he detested the crazy spin Mathys had put on the Judeo-Christian religions ascribed to by most Americans. The Galactic Tabernacle of the Human Future wasn't a user-friendly group. It had all the nasty and vicious elements of Judeo-Christianity that his remote ancestors had put behind them in Europe during the Reformation and Inquisition. And it had polluted the grandest of all human dreams of expansion: the human colonization of the cosmos.

Curt decided that if he didn't have orders to go back into Sanctuary and take care of Mathys and the rest of the bastards around him, including the dishonorable Calder, he'd do it himself. He still had a week of leave left. He'd call for volunteers from the Washington Greys. And he'd damned well assault Sanctuary himself if the wimps in Washington wouldn't move their asses for fear of exposing them. Dyani Motega was being held in Sanctuary. *And the Washington Greys never abandon their own!*

He didn't give a damn whether or not Calder's Host of Michael might be patrolling Route 305 looking for him. It was an old, nearly abandoned road now that the Tabernacle had put in the new highway leading to the main gate. But Curt knew it headed toward the town of Battle Mountain. The old highway would lead him to telephones, a doctor for his feet, and water. But mostly he could get in touch with Fort Huachuca from Battle Mountain.

The bright headlights heading south along Route 305 didn't make much impression on him at first until they got closer and winked out.

Curt was too tired, too dehydrated, and his bleeding feet were hurting too badly. He didn't even try, to duck into the shallow ditch on the west side of the road.

Besides, the vehicle was coming from the direction of the town of Battle Mountain, not from Sanctuary's main gate which was several kilometers behind him.

The vehicle that pulled to a gentle stop in front of him was an old 1999 Chevrolet S-10 pickup truck that had seen younger days. It was well used but obviously well taken care of. It sounded like a purring kitten.

Both front doors opened, and a familiar female voice called out to him, "Howdy, Colonel! Would you like a lift into town?"

Suddenly Sergeant Major Edie Sampson was on one side of him and Master Sergeant Henry Kester was on the other.

"Damn, Colonel, your feet are all cut to hell!" Kester remarked.

"Where's Captain Motega?" Edie wanted to know.

"She's in the Sanctuary. She was captured while we were climbing the fence to get out. Those bastards have her. God knows what they'll do to her," Curt said wearily. Then it occurred to him who these people were and where they were. So he suddenly asked, "What the hell are the two of you doing *here*? Are the rest of the Greys with you?"

"The regiment's in Crescent Valley just oveR that ridge to the east, Colonel," Henry explained. "We airlifted ASSAULTCO up there late this afternoon. The rest of the outfit's due around midnight."

"The Wolfhounds will be in Buena Vista Valley to the west by sunrise tomorrow morning, sir," Edie went on. "Damn, your feet are a mess, Colonel! What happened to your shoes? Come on, let me get you into the truck before you bleed all over the place. You're cut up damned bad, sir!"

"And why the pickup truck? I could use a Saucy Cans right now to blast the hell out of that main gate! And what the hell are the two of you doing out here?" Curt asked again, trying to get situational awareness. His mind really wasn't very clear. Exhaustion and dehydration had him in their insidious grip. He really didn't know if he was dreaming this. He wondered to himself if he'd gone completely ballistic fighting and crawling and walking barefoot across that godawful four klicks to the road.

Edie helped him into the cab of the truck. "Major Allen put out scout patrols as soon as we got to Crescent Valley. Major Aarts had birdbots over the new road when Emma Crawford's birdbot sensors detected the sound of firing to the west. By the time Lieutenant Brown got his birdbot over there, you were nowhere to be seen. But he reported the robot and a group of soldiers taking Captain Motega back to the south. Majors Ward and Allen figgered you had to be out here in the puckerbrush somewhere. But you were doing a fine job of being no target for anything, including our sensors. Henry and I got detailed to see if you might be lurking in the boonies…" She held up a pair of infrared night-vision binoculars.

Henry Kester climbed into the other side of the cab and slammed the door. "Detailed, hell!" he grumbled. "Sergeant Sampson volunteered the two of us!"

"*Who* volunteered us?" Edie countered. "Colonel, I had trouble keeping our regimental sergeant major from bringing the whole damned regiment out here in the dark of night with minimum recce and practically zero gee two."

Henry started the engine, eased it into gear - it was the first time Curt had seen a gear-shifting auto vehicle except in a museum - and started to turn the truck around on the narrow road without putting his lights on. "Well, let's just say that we're here. Came in by Chippie to the Lander County Airport."

"Henry, those bastards in Sanctuary may have damned good radar coverage!" Curt snapped. "They must have seen the Chippie come in. Radar. I-r. Whatever. They've probably got it. They must know you're here."

"Colonel, there's such a thing as ECM and stealth and such, you know," Henry reminded him gently. "And we came in N-O-E as well. Didn't even get painted by ground-based FAA traffic control radars. Didn't get painted with anything. We were passive-stealthed for IR, too. To keep up the spoof, we borrowed this old truck from the airport manager because we didn't exactly want to be a conspicuous moving target even if those bastards can't shoot for shit."

As Kester began to accelerate northward on the road, Curt said wearily, "Okay, I'm beginning to get the situational picture here. That's going to make my job a lot easier. Have you got comm with Major Ward?"

Edie held up a tacomm brick. "Yessir!"

Curt reached for it. "I don't care if we've only got ASSAULTCO here! I want them deployed from Crescent Valley ASAP! We're going to assault Sanctuary tonight! They've got Captain Motega!"

"Colonel, we're under orders not - repeat NOT - to assault that place until we get direct orders from the Oval Office itself. So, take a breath. Ain't nothing you or anyone in the Greys can do right now," Kester remarked as he steered the old truck with amazing agility, finally putting on the headlights now that he had it pointed away from Sanctuary. He was obviously enjoying what he was doing, for he remarked in an attempt to change the subject and get his colonel's mind off an irrational track, "Haven't driven an Ess-ten in years! They don't make 'em like this anymore!"

"What? We're under orders not to attack Sanctuary?" Curt was astounded. He thought maybe he wasn't hearing right.

"We're under orders that if by any chance we found you and Captain Motega, we're to get you back to Crescent Valley ASAP. And, orders or not, we weren't about to mount an assault knowing you were in there." Edie Sampson reached behind the seat and pulled up a canteen of water. "Colonel, you look like you could use a drink. When was the last time you got a swallow of water? Your lips are all swollen up and caked with salt. Here."

"I'm okay," Curt insisted but took the canteen anyway. "I'm not dehydrated. Haven't lost any water. Haven't taken a pee in the last six or seven hours or so..." He raised the canteen to his lips. The water tasted better than anything he'd had for a long time.

"Colonel, we don't know what the full story is," Henry Kester tried to explain as he wheeled the truck down the road and topped the slight rise, revealing the lights of the town of Battle Mountain to the north.

"Another damned mushroom mission," Edie Sampson bitched in a low voice. "Keep us in the dark and dump gobs of fertilizer all over us."

"But it's damned big!" Kester went on. "We've got more brass on our ass in Crescent Valley than you could guess or want. General Hettrick's there. So's General Carlisle. And some sonofabitch from the White House who's supposed to be a 'negotiator.' As if we was gonna negotiate with anyone holding Captain Motega hostage! Even the presidential press secretary is there."

"What, no Bohemian Brigade?" Curt muttered thickly. "Damn, I haven't seen any news all day. We were sort of incommunicado inside Sanctuary. So, what's showing up about this in the media?"

"Nothing, sir," Edie told him.

"Nothing?"

"Not a frigging word! It's being sat on real damned tight," she remarked, producing a first aid kit from under the seat. "Colonel, lemme see your feet, sir. I can get some of that bleeding stopped long enough to get you back to Crescent Valley. And Major Gydesen and her BIOTECO should be in about midnight if Worsham's Warhawks managed to get through that line of thunderstorms southeast of Las Vegas."

Kester reached over Curt and took the tacomm unit. Sticking the stubby antenna out the window as he drove, he toggled it and called, "Grey Chief, this is Grey Major."

"Grey Chief here," came Major Joan Ward's voice.

"Grey Major has Grey Head. Repeat, we have Grey Head in the vehicles. But only Grey Head. Deer Arrow is not with him. Grey Head reports Deer Arrow was detained in the target area as we suspected from the recce mission," Kester reported to the chief of staff of the Washington Greys.

"What's Grey Head's condition, Grey Major?"

"Let me talk to her!" Curt snapped and grabbed the brick out of

Kester's hand. He knew all he had to do was to explain the situation and report that Dyani was being held captive inside Sanctuary. Major Joan Ward, his chief of staff and old comrade from West Point days, would understand and get the Greys moving toward Battle Mountain at once. "Grey Chief, this is Grey Head! The bastards have Deer Arrow! I'm okay. Just some cut feet. Sampson's bandaging them. Now I want you to listen up and listen up good, Grey Chief! This is a direct order! I don't give a damned what orders you may have been given! I want you to move out ASAP with the Greys toward Battle Mountain with everything you've got! We're going into Sanctuary after Deer Arrow! *The Washington Greys never abandon their own!* And get me a patch to Battleaxe or Wolf Head. I'll take all the help I can get here."

"Colonel, I'm under specific orders from Battleaxe not to do what you've just requested. And she's standing right next to me," Joan Ward's voice replied.

After a slight pause, Major General Belinda Hettrick's voice came over the comm set. "Grey Head, this is Battleaxe. You aren't totally aware of the situation except from your viewpoint. Right this moment, we have ourselves one goddamn stinking, lousy situation that you don't know squat about. So I want you to unplug your gonads, hook up your brain, and start behaving like I trained you. Like a regimental commander. I'll need you on the job badly after we wring you dry of the gee-two you got inside Sanctuary. Now, let Major Ward talk to Sergeant Sampson!"

"General, you don't understand. Captain Motega is-" Curt began.

"I *do* understand! I understand much better than you do at this point! We're going in to get her. That I promise you!" Hettrick fired back sternly but with compassion in her voice. 'So this is a direct order. Sit back, shut up, and let Kester get you to Lander County Airport where a Warhawk Chippie aerodyne is waiting to shuttle you here. There's a helluva lot more at stake than Captain Motega. I can't talk more about it even over a secure freak-hop comm circuit like this! Battleaxe out!"

Curt leaned back in the seat and dosed his eyes. He vented a huge sigh of frustration and exhaustion. "Drive on, Henry," he told his regimental sergeant major as he handed the tacomm unit to Edie. "I guess I'll just have to wait a few minutes to get the scoop with the group."

"Yes sir," the old soldier replied.

"Rumor Control have anything in the wind about this?"

"Yessir."

"Well, dammit man, *what?*"

"Colonel, it's more than a rumble from Rumor Control," Kester admitted to him. "I was in on the Papa briefing and was sworn to security silence, so a damned panic doesn't get going. But I figger I can and should tell you since you're my regimental commander. And there ain't a whole hell of a lot of chance that someone can get a good audio snoop on this truck cab with this noise level." He looked at his watch. "About four hours ago or thereabouts, the Oval Office got a phone call from a guy named Mathys. He said he was going to launch a spaceship in the next day or so and warned everyone to keep clear of Battle Mountain. He bitched that he didn't like government cops and military people spying on him and trying to stop him. So, unless everyone stays absolutely clear of Battle Mountain and lets the ship depart, he says he'll nuke Reno, Vegas, and Salt Lake City."

Chapter Twenty

Lieutenant Nancy Roberts put the Chippie down in the dark without a bump. Its three passengers were met by three officers of the Washington Greys at the edge of the cargo doors when they came out.

Colonel Curt Carson wearily returned the salutes of Majors Joan Ward and Jerry Allen as well as Captain Kitsy Clinton.

"Glad you're back, Colonel," Jerry Allen greeted him with a note of serious concern in his voice.

"Major Gydesen and Captain Helen Devlin are waiting for you," Joan Ward said; then she added, "They landed five minutes ago, and Devlin wants to look at your feet ASAP."

Captain Kitsy Clinton merely said, "Colonel!" They hadn't seen one another since two years ago when Curt had put her on an evac aerodyne out of Mosul to Walter Reed. Kitsy's neck had been broken by a Kurdish Amazon during the Battle of Asi. But now she looked about the same as before except for being a little thinner. She wasn't a big woman in the first place, and the weight she'd lost in Walter Reed Army Hospital made her petite size seem even smaller. However, the flash in her eyes told Curt that Kitsy Clinton was still in there.

He was very glad to see her again.

"Thanks for coming to meet me," Curt told the three of them, returning their salutes. In a no-nonsense manner, he went on, "The medics can wait. My feet won't bleed much more than they already have. Sergeant Sampson did a good job in the truck. Joan, can someone rustle up a set of cammies and boots for me? And maybe some chow?"

"Yes, sir. Waiting for you in your OCV," his chief of staff snapped back. "But General Hettrick wants to see you as soon as you get presentable."

"I'm presentable now."

"Yes, sir," Joan Ward agreed while disagreeing, "but don't you think General Carlisle and General Hettrick might like to meet with a colonel rather than someone who looks like he's been out sporting around the boonies all day?"

Curt then recalled that he was in slacks and shirt, definitely out of uniform, with the stubble of a beard on his face and dirty as hell. "You're right, Major. Damned if I'll report to my division commander out of uniform. I need a shit, shine, shower, shave, and shampoo, but I'll settle for two or three out of five right now. And damned if I'll report to my division commander before I have a sit-rep on the status of my command." Curt started to walk away from the Chippie, limping because his feet did indeed hurt in spite of the dressings and analgesics administered by Edie. "So lead off, Major Ward. Let's get this dog and pony show on the road. Where's my OCV?"

"Colonel," Jerry said, stepping up to him and taking his right arm. He was quite formal and military in his speech. "I'm sorry, sir, and I understand your feelings at the moment, especially about Captain Motega. But you've got to have your feet looked at, sir."

"And we anticipated that you'd want a regimental status report," Joan added, taking his left arm. "So, we're here not only to see to it that you get the medical attention you need but to give you that status report while Ruth and Helen take care of you."

"And I've got an MRE hot and ready for you," Kitsy told him. "You can chow-down while they patch your feet and we give you your sit-rep."

Curt couldn't help but go where his three officers wanted. Jerry and Joan were both big people, and they were a hell of a lot stronger than he was at the moment. "You three think you've got this whole sheep screw pretty well organized, don't you?"

"Yes, sir. That's our job," Joan told him in no uncertain terms.

"Besides, we didn't want to make you feel indispensable, sir," Jerry added.

"The Greys are all here now, all ready for you to resume command," Kitsy put in.

"And we're good to go for Battle Mountain, whatever the hell is there," Joan finished.

Damn, these are good people! Subordinates he could count on.

"And I want you to especially realize, sir," Kitsy Clinton put in, "that it took more than a little doing to move the regiment a thousand klicks on a few hours' notice. But the Greys have always been hot to trot and good to go."

"Especially you," Curt observed as they began to walk him toward a hulking OCV.

Kitsy smiled. "Yes, sir! And still am, sir!" She was walking beside them and just slightly ahead. Curt noticed that her movements weren't quite as smooth as they'd once been. She walked a little like a mechanical robot. And her arm and head motions were somewhat jerky.

"Captain, did you sneak out of Walter Reed, or did the biotech people actually clear you for duty again?" Curt wanted to know.

"They cleared me for full combat duty, Colonel," Kitsy chirped and undertook to explain as they crossed the ground between the Chippie and the OCV, "Mind you, it took a little persuasion - which I did in my own typical and inimitable manner. They didn't think I was fully ambulatory yet. Which, of course, I am, as any fool can plainly see. And in case you're wondering, as you probably are, they jumpered my spinal column between my third and fourth cervical vertebrae. I've got a bunch of nanochips in there. Not as many circuits as my spinal column, so some motions aren't quite as smooth as others...yet. But I guarantee you, Colonel, that everything - and I do mean everything - from my neck down works. And getting better as my spinal column rejuvenates."

"I didn't think it could do that," Jerry broke in. Curt knew the man had an encyclopedic memory. Jerry Allen had always been a literal fount of information.

"The neurophysiologists didn't think so either, but I'm the guinea pig that's refusing to follow the rules," Kitsy pointed out.

"So, what's new about that? You never did like to follow some rules, Captain Clinton," Curt reminded her. "And you bent a few from time to time."

"And we had a lot of fun doing it, didn't we, sir?" She may have been a little thin and a little wan and a little hesitant in some of her movements, but she was the same old Kitsy Clinton, Curt decided. And he was damned glad to see her for a lot of reasons right then because he knew he was going to have to talk to somebody. It might be Joan or it might be Kitsy. They'd understand. He could talk to Jerry man to man, but he wasn't sure Jerry could really empathize with his situation. The regimental chaplain, Captain Nellie Crile, was supposed to take care of personal problems, and he was good at what he did. But Nellie Crile was a Roman Catholic chaplain. Although the man could and did minister to all the different faiths of the Washington Greys, Curt often wondered about Nellie's advice in matters of the heart. A chaplain who had to remain celibate and wasn't permitted to marry just didn't have some of the basic experiences, Curt believed, that would allow him to get the proper perspective on such personal problems.

But this wasn't the time for that sort of thing. There was duty to be done and some nasty business to take care of. Especially if Mathys and his Tabernacle acolytes did indeed have nukes and the capability to deliver and detonate them as threatened.

Both Major Ruth Gydesen and Captain Helen Devlin were properly attentive to Curt's wounds. "Thankfully, it's just your feet," the doctor remarked.

"Yes, some of the ladies get quite concerned that perhaps other parts might be damaged," the chief nurse added. Neither of the two biotechs were reluctant to make oblique references to physical functions. "Glad you didn't straddle that razor-wire fence, Colonel."

Their lighthearted attempts to be cheerful were typical, but Curt wasn't much in the mood for joviality, even the black humor that soldiers use to make very difficult things somewhat bearable. Or to maintain their perspective on life. Curt didn't realize it in his current condition, but he'd lost his perspective and with it some of the important factors that a combat leader had to have.

Joan Ward and Jerry Allen brought him up to speed on the regimental status. The whole Third Herd was present and accounted for. All warbots were up and running. Weapons and ammo status were right up to ops specs.

And the word about Dyani had spread very quickly through the regiment. She wasn't super-social like Kitsy Clinton, but Dyani was known and respected and cared about because she was a real person, a woman of proven bravery, audacious expertise in the field, high standards, and insistent refusal to compromise her personal standards.

On the way from Gydesen's Biotech Support Vehicle to Hettrick's divisional OCV, the group met Captain Adonica Sweet. It didn't surprise Curt to have Adonica tell him, "Colonel, I'm glad to see you, sir! Don't worry, we'll get Dyani out of there okay."

What did surprise him was First Sergeant Tracy Dillon of Dyani's RECONCO. Dillon was from Montana, and Curt had originally anticipated some problems because of Dillon's long family history in a region where the Crow Indians predominated. "Colonel, Rumor Control has it that Captain Motega's still in that religious commune. I want you to know, sir, that any son of a bitch who lays a finger on her is going to have to answer personally to me! And I guarantee I'll get pretty damned personal with the bastard!"

Curt thanked him, thinking that he'd have his own personal confrontation with a number of people, including "General" Stephen Calder.

But mostly the Greys that Curt encountered on his trek merely greeted him. They didn't need to say anything. He knew they knew. It was like an electric charge in the air. Various individuals and units of the Washington Greys had been in deep trouble in the past in many places around the world. Always, the attitude of the rest of the Greys had been simply one of hard work to get them out and back with the regiment again. Sometimes, Curt knew, only their bodies had come back, but their memories had remained always with the Greys.

It wouldn't happen that way this time, Curt vowed. It couldn't.

And he was feeling pretty strong about it when he entered Major General Belinda Hettrick's OCV.

General Jacob Carlisle was there along with Colonel Frederick Salley of the Wolfhounds regiment. And Curt saw another old familiar face: Len Spencer, who was now the White House press secretary. Carlisle introduced him to a self-important little man, Chester "Chet" Martinside, who said he was a trained hostage negotiator from the State Department. Curt ignored him after the introduction because the commander of the Washington Greys had absolutely no intention of negotiating with Mathys for Dyani.

Curt thought it was strange that no members of the Bohemian Brigade were present, only Len Spencer. But, if Mathys was indeed threatening to nuke three cities, Curt understood the role the nation's news media would have to play - and why he'd heard nothing about the threat. Washington was sitting on it, but a respected member of the media was in on the deal.

"How do you feel?" Hettrick asked him solicitously.

"Goddamned lousy, and excuse my language, ladies," Curt replied briefly; then added, "One hell of a way to end a thirty-day leave."

"Well, sit down, get off those feet, then let's see if we can get a handle on whether or not we can resolve this mess," Hettrick went on, unfolding an additional seat for Curt aloo side her.

The divisional OCV had no more space than an ordinary bus. Actually, it had less because of all the comm and AI equipment necessary to conduct planning and to handle C3I (command, control, communications, and intelligence).

"Colonel Carson," Chester Martinside began, "I presume you saw the NIA report on the Tabernacle before you went in there?"

"No, sir, I didn't even know there was one. Why wasn't I briefed on it before Captain Motega and I tried to penetrate the place?" Curt replied, surprised to learn that such a document existed.

"Call it a glitch in communications, Colonel," General Carlisle, the Army COS, replied. As former chief of the 17th Iron Fist Division and the Washington Greys, he knew Curt from many campaigns together. He was straightforward in his answer. Carlisle didn't play games with his subordinates. "I apologize for the fact that it didn't get to you. These things happen. Sometimes the big war is fought over bureaucratic turf. And the grubs in the field take it in the shorts."

"Yeah, we've been through that one before, General," Curt agreed. "I've learned to live with it. Hell, I've got to live with it. Part of the game."

"This is not very long," Chester Martinside interrupted, picking up four pages of hard copy from the table. "Colonel, please read it right now. Then tell us what's right in it and what isn't. And what else we should know about these people and their organization."

Curt sat down and took the hard copy. Hettrick brought him a welcome cup of coffee; she didn't have to, and Curt knew it was highly unusual for a major general to serve a cup of coffee to a mere lieutenant colonel. But military rank seemed to mean very little in the OCV right then. The job ahead of them was more important than strict adherence to rank protocol.

Curt started to read. He'd never had a document in his hands before whose cover sheet simply stated, "Cosmic Magic Top Secret, Eyes Only." That was about as high as classification got. Actually, there were layers above that, but Curt had never heard of them. He quickly speed-read "NIA Briefing Paper 35-B-N-007." (See Appendix II.)

Then he placed it down on the table and remarked, "It's all there. And there's more, of course. Whoever researched that was good, but it doesn't really get the flavor of that miserable outfit. They've not only taken a little bit from every known religion but also from every vicious and violent totalitarian ideology of the past. I didn't meet their business officer, Jasper Lyell. I would have if Mathys hadn't smelled a rat and demanded that Dr. Rosha Taisha mind-probe us."

"Didn't we run into her before?" Hettrick asked.

"Yes, ma'am. In Zahedan. And she's meaner and nastier than before because she went through hell after we withdrew from that Iranian hell hole," Curt explained briefly. "I don't know what she's got in the way of NE equipment now, but Mathys sure as hell has the money to buy her anything she wants. We broke out before she got us into her lab."

"Why didn't you wait until you'd gotten a look at what she was doing?" Chester Martinside suddenly asked.

"Sorry about that, Mr. Martinside. But Captain Motega and I saw a chance to break, and we took it. We might not have gotten another one." Curt wasn't really going to make big excuses. Ignorance of Taisha's capabilities might be a critical factor in the forthcoming assault, but Curt didn't see how. "I met Henry VanDerCamp and Mathys' Number Two Wife, Monica Elora. Mathys runs a male-dominated operation, and the report is right about its polygamous nature. Mathys strikes me as the sort of individual with great sexual appetite who gets into a position of totalitarian power like this."

"Lots of historical precedents," Len Spencer observed. "And a lot of people like that trying to lead nations today."

"Do you know where they're holding Captain Motega?" Hettrick asked.

"I think so…"

"How about the other four? The FBI agent and the three state troopers?" Len Spencer wanted to know.

Curt nodded. "Probably in the same place. I can get in there within thirty seconds of the time I hit the ground if I'm put down on the right spot. And I know the spot. General Hettrick, I formally and officially request to lead a picked assault team when we hit Sanctuary. And I hope it's going to happen just before dawn."

"It's not going to happen at all," Chester Martindale snapped irritably. "I'm in charge here, in case you don't know, Colonel

Carson. I'm authorized to negotiate for the hostages, give the Tabernacle people what they want, get them to disarm those nukes, and let them go out in to space if they want. You military people are here to back me up, not to go in there and kill American citizens."

Chapter Twenty-One

"Mr. Martinside, I hate to bust your bubble, but you aren't going to be able to negotiate with Dr. Clark Jeremy Mathys! I don't give a damn how good you are!" Curt growled.

"Look, Carson, I know that you gung-ho military types think that the application of force is the only answer in situations like this," Martinside fired back quickly, sensing at once that this was an assault on his turf and authority. "Your military training leaves you with no alternative but to go in there with guns blazing, wipe out the bastards who try to stop you, and rescue the helpless hostages. And you think the American public will venerate you as heroes for doing that! Hell, every SWAT team in America thinks that way, too. We'd have blood flowing in the streets all day every day if the kill-'em-all types had their way."

"With all due respects to your negotiating theories and expertise, Mr. Martinside," Curt told him, not exactly happy with the idea that he'd have to stand by and watch while this man attempted to cut deals with human lives...and especially Dyani's, "where the hell were you with your negotiating techniques when more than a hundred hostages were held in Zahedan and we had to go in and get them? And when more than a thousand people were trapped in the diplomatic compound during the Bastaard Rebellion? Or when the Shi'ite Dayaks held one of my battalions captive in Borneo? Or when-goddamnit, some people won't negotiate! They have to be smacked down and put away!"

"Colonel, you're undoubtedly a brave man who's seen a lot of combat," Martinside said coldly, trying valiantly to smooth feathers that he suddenly sensed he'd ruffled unnecessarily. "I'm delighted that you and Colonel Salley are at my back during these negotiations. Your reputation will help me talk the hostages out."

"You don't know this man Mathys!" Curt insisted.

"And after a few minutes of conversation with him, do you?" Martinside fired back.

Curt told him in a frustrated tone of voice, "Yes, especially after reading that NIA report - which I should have seen before we went into that hell hole! Mathys is a religious zealot. He's certifiably paranoid and obsessed. Probably manic-depressive as well."

"Are you a certified psychologist, Colonel?" Martinside persisted, now trying to get this insistent man off his back and get some cooperation from him willingly instead of under orders from his superiors.

"I'm a practical, practicing psychologist, Mr. Martinside," Curt replied levelly, not fully realizing how obsessed he himself was at the moment. "Otherwise, I couldn't lead troops into combat."

"Mr. Martinside, General Carlisle, if I may make a comment here," Colonel Rick Salley put in earnestly. "I'm from South Carolina, sir. I grew up around the sort of evangelical religious leaders that Dr. Mathys must be according to the NIA report and Colonel Carson's personal observations. They all talk to God, and they've got God on their side, sir. You can't reason with them. Maybe you remember the Salley Cult. I do because I'm a Salley. My ancestors colonized South Carolina, so a lot of Salleys are still there. I've had to live down what the Salley Cult did, sir. So, I had to learn a lot about it. Let me tell you that Jeremiah Salley couldn't be reasoned with, he wouldn't negotiate, and he brooked no dissension or opposition. He and his people would kill with no remorse because God told them to do it. Mr. Martinside, if you want the opinion of someone who does indeed know something about people like the Tabernacle tribe, you'll believe me when I also tell you I don't think you'll buy us anything but trouble by trying to negotiate with a madman."

Martinside raised his head and looked down his nose. "Colonel, I respect your profession and your eagerness to begin combat. But I suspect that's just what you and Colonel Carson want to do: take the easy way out and lead your troops into deadly combat. But this time you'll be killing American citizens in the process."

"No, sir, that's not the case, sir. Colonel Carson and I will likely be the first ones killed if we do. And we'll have to order our friends and comrades into deadly combat. Sir, if I honestly saw a workable alternative, I'd certainly back it to the hilt. It would make my job a whole hell of a lot easier, sir," the regimental commander of the Wolfhounds replied earnestly. Salley was always super-respectful, Curt knew. He had a tendency to end nearly every sentence with "sir" or "ma'am." It was part of his legacy from West Point.

"Gentlemen, if you will, let's back off a moment," General Carlisle broke in smoothly and diplomatically, having stayed in the background in order to give his two officers a chance to express themselves in a way that he couldn't, not to a man who'd been detailed by the White House to lead this mission. Carlisle believed the Army would have to move in on this one eventually. But he also knew that the man in the White House had to be able to cover himself by first attempting to achieve a non-lethal solution by negotiation. "Colonel Carson, you certainly have a great deal of information about the Tabernacle and its people. You've spent a difficult day in Sanctuary and barely escaped with your life. One of your valuable officers had to be left-behind. But other factors are involved in this operation. May I suggest that we proceed with an orderly plans session here?"

Martinside knew he was in a nest of those he considered to be bloodthirsty warriors. Therefore, he was silently and somewhat reluctantly glad that General Jacob Carlisle was such a diplomat. He'd wondered why the Army Chief of Staff and a member of the Joint Chiefs had elected to come on this mission in person rather than manage it from the Pentagon or the White House Situation Room. Now he knew. Carlisle had an enviable reputation as a military diplomat. This confused Martinside because he hadn't thought that military people could also be as diplomatic as Carlisle was turning out to be. Martinside hadn't studied history well enough to realize that some of the best diplomats of the past had been military leaders.

Having been handed back control of the meeting by this diplomatic general who could have taken it himself, Martinside decided to get right to the nub of the planning. He determined that perhaps it would be helpful to him if these military mavericks did indeed know some of the delicate issues involved. Maybe it would temper their gung-ho approach.

"Thanks, General. I think we have to keep in mind here what our real objective is: to get Mathys to back off his threat to nuke Reno, Vegas, and Salt Lake City and tell us where the bombs are. Once that's done, it's possible to negotiate for the release of the hostages…"

Curt knew about this from Rumor Control, of course. But he figured it was time to find out what was really going on. "Mr. Martinside, this is the first I've heard officially that nuclear weapons are involved."

"It's been going around Rumor Control, Curt," Colonel Rick Salley told him.

"Yeah, Rick, I know. I said 'officially.' I want to know the full story. We can't intelligently plan a critical operation like this on the basis of rumors," Curt told him. "Mr. Martinside, nukes put a whole new spin on this situation."

"That aspect isn't your concern, Colonel," Martinside snapped back. "It's being handled by the FBI."

"And the FBI screwed the pooch when they sent an agent into Sanctuary a few days ago without proper briefing and without adequate training," Curt told him, seeing here an opportunity to make an end run around this negotiator and mount a controlled assault on Sanctuary. The bomb threat made it mandatory to do it quickly, Curt knew. He also wanted to do it quickly because Dyani was in there. "If the rumor is true, it means we're dealing with totally irrational and completely insane people. Therefore, the Army shouldn't be considered a bunch of armed people who are here to make you feel more secure in dealing with a madman. As I've said before, I don't think you can deal with Mathys. However, I think Colonel Salley and I can manage to cut Sanctuary off from the outside world and thus prevent Mathys' people from triggering those bombs. And I'm not so sure Mathys isn't bluffing-"

"Curt, are you willing to take the chance that a couple of million innocent people might be killed?" Len Spencer suddenly put in.

"Len, I share your concern, but I want to make sure it's a real concern and not just a smoke screen put up by Mathys. The man is awfully good with special effects. He's an expert with blue smoke and mirrors," Curt explained. "Mr. Martinside, can you explain why you believe that Mathys has the capability to make good his threat?"

"No, I can't," Martinside admitted. "But, as Len just pointed out, we don't dare take the chance! We must assume that Mathys does indeed have nukes ready to go."

"From the standpoint of a military person who's been trained to evaluate threats, Mr. Martinside," Rick put in, "I'd like to know how the Tabernacle might have developed and deployed such a nuclear threat. Otherwise, it doesn't make sense to me, either."

"What do you mean, Colonel?" Martinside asked.

Hettrick joined the conversation for the first time, having been satisfied that Curt and Salley were handling the threat evaluation properly in spite of Curt's concern for Motega. Certainly, she suspected now that Martinside was no planner or organizer, even though he might have been a good and experienced negotiator. Martinside was going to need the expertise of his military subordinates or he might get himself into a negotiating position in which he would give away, the whole farm for nothing because he had no way to back up his side of the deal. The Iron Fist Division was Martinside's means to get things done as well as his security blanket. "Mr. Martinside, I also have strong doubts that the Tabernacle tribe has nukes. Nuclear explosives aren't as easy to make, deploy, or initiate as, say, TNT or Comp B, both ordinary chemical explosives. In the first place, fissile material isn't easy to get-"

"Nonsense! Tons of nuclear waste have been dumped over the past hundred years!"

Hettrick shook her head. "I'm sure General Carlisle will confirm what I'm telling you, sir. Nuclear waste material is *not* nuclear bomb material. Biologically messy if it's just been declared waste because of its short half-life and high radio activity. But useless in a bomb..."

"How can you say that in the face of evidence from the Soviet nuclear disaster at Kasli-?" Martinside began.

"Which was a chemical explosion that ruptured tanks of nuclear waste material," Carlisle reminded him. "No nuclear reaction was involved."

"To build a nuclear bomb, you have to get bomb-grade fissile material," Hettrick went on explaining. "That's not available in the United States, Canada, or Mexico. It would have to come from somewhere else. Mathys would have had to pay dearly for it. Getting it into the United States would pose another problem..."

"Maybe not if you've got personal jet aircraft, General," Martinside pointed out. "According to the FAA registration list, Mathys has several. Carson, does the Tabernacle have corporate aircraft?"

"Yes, sir. We rode in one of them," Curt admitted.

"So if he bought the hot stuff overseas, his people could have had it smuggled into the USA. Customs normally doesn't look for that sort of thing since it's such a long shot," Martinside hypothesized.

"All right, let's for the sake of discussion here say that Mathys could have bought fissile material overseas and smuggled it into Sanctuary," Hettrick admitted, believing that this was a useful discussion. If it led to a good guess as to the nature of the nukes, it might help either locate them or figure out a way to keep them from being triggered. Either one would be a long step toward solving the problem. "Making a Fat Man implosion bomb requires not only plutonium but a damned good knowledge of explosives and the ability to trigger them within microseconds. A Little Boy cannon bomb is easier to make and detonate, but it requires bomb-grade ninety-eight percent uranium..."

"In addition, of course, to having the critical neutron kernel for both types," Carlisle added.

"Sir, the kernel just increases the probability of a critical mass fission from perhaps twenty percent to better than ninety percent,"

Hettrick went on. "If the bomb doesn't go bang, it goes glop. Just melts down, and you've got a very messy and very radioactive situation on your hands."

"Both of which," Carlisle pointed out, "are perfectly useful outcomes for Mathys. If the bomb is under city hall, city hall goes, either way. Along with anyone in the building when the nuke goes bang or poof. Which leads me to think that's what we're dealing with. But if it's a cannon bomb, it's big and heavy. Carson, did you see any evidence that the Tabernacle has either an airborne or missile delivery system?"

"No, sir. If a Tabernacle nuke does indeed exist, it's got to be a ten-ton monster. Takes a big airplane to carry it. Or a big missile. I saw neither one," Curt replied, still not believing that Mathys had a nuke at all.

"So how the hell could they get a bomb that big and heavy into any of the three cities?" Martinside wanted to know. "Or do they have suitcase bombs?"

"Not very likely. Very unlikely. I know what it takes to make a suitcase nuke, and it takes a *lot* of very high technology indeed. Plus manufacturing capabilities and materials that are not readily available outside of highly classified weapons plants. Suitcase nukes are very sophisticated devices. And only about a dozen people in the United States know the actual details. The information is highly compartmentalized. So, I don't think the Tabernacle has suitcase nukes." Carlisle apparently knew what he was talking about. He and Hettrick were of the generation of officers who'd had the tail end of tactical nuke training. Curt had never received it since the hazard of tactical battlefield nukes had pretty much disappeared by the time he was commissioned. Nuclear explosives were general mass destruction weapons for general warfare, the ultimate expression of general warfare. The military professionals didn't like the idea of fighting with nukes because ultimate destruction had never been the real goal of the military forces with the exception of some of the historical Asiatic hordes who'd broken loose over the steppes of Asia and into eastern Europe. Someone had finally gotten smart about that sort of thing in the long and potentially deadly decades following World War II. It was possible to retreat with a scorched earth policy and still be able to grow wheat next summer; not so with tactical nukes which could spoil things for decades or more. Sane military leaders and planners finally realized that a battlefield nuke could make a battlefield untenable for their own troops. A battlefield tactical nuke was just about as sensible as the legendary nuclear hand grenade; you pulled the pin only if you didn't care about living.

"So, the Tabernacle nukes are likely to be very big and very heavy," Curt mused, beginning to get an idea of a plan here. He approached it like a War College study of the sort he'd recently done in order to graduate from that institution. "Several problems here. First: How do they get the materials into Sanctuary? Two: How do they process them into three nukes? Three: How do they transport them to three cities without being detected? Four: How do they trigger them remotely?"

"We've already discussed the first," Martinside broke in. "They could get the fissile material on the international market."

"You need some other stuff, too," Carlisle added. "The main weight of a nuke is the tamper. It has to be massive to contain the fission reaction. Otherwise, the bomb just sort of melts down without much of a bang at all. Two readily available materials make good tampers: steel and concrete."

"They brought plenty of both into Sanctuary to build what I saw there," Curt recalled.

"So how do you get a ten-ton mass of concrete and/or steel out of there?" Carlisle went on, asking rhetorical questions in the Aristotelian manner: Ask enough questions of the student, and the student eventually answers the question himself.

"Not by aircraft," Martinside replied. "The FAA list showed no aircraft that could lift a ten-ton payload."

"What did you see in Sanctuary that might give them some nuclear capability, Curt?" Hettrick asked.

"Good roads," Curt recalled.

"I don't know of a single truck that would carry a ten-ton load and still make it through the state line inspection stations without being questioned," Len Spencer put in.

"And a good railroad spur," Curt continued.

Everyone looked at one another.

Chapter Twenty-Two

"What kind of freight car could carry a ten-ton nuke?" Len Spencer suddenly asked, breaking the silence in the OCV.

"Almost any of them," Curt replied, remembering his recent War College work which had involved handling logistics problems using the old military support system, the railroad.

"What kind of freight cars would go in and out of Sanctuary so often that hardly anyone would pay attention except the railroad's computers?" Rick Salley added the question.

Chester Martinside turned around and grabbed the mobile telephone off the bulkhead beside him. "I'll get on this right away..."

"Stand at east, Mr. Martinside," Major General Belinda Hettrick advised him and keyed another comm set beside her. "Georgie, this is Battleaxe," she called the 17th Iron Fist Division's megacomputer, Georgie, located back in Arizona.

"Georgie here," came the male pseudo-voice of the computer that had been named after the legendary Lieutenant General George S. Patton.

"Georgie, make whatever links you need with other computers. Get into the traffic and car locator computer of Western-Central Railroad. Get data on the number and type of railway freight cars that have come in and gone out of the Tabernacle Sanctuary at Battle Mountain, Nevada. Report to me by hard copy a list of types, quantity of each type, and source of destination of the top quantity of cars."

"Working!" came the computerized reply. "Connection made with Crocker. Crocker demands defense security authorization to permit access to company data banks."

Hettrick pulled out a keypad and handed it to General Carlisle, who quickly typed in a series of key words and numbers.

"Access granted. Data being downloaded. Data being analyzed and collated. Requested hard copy being printed."

The hard copy printer on the wall whirred and spat out a strip of paper.

"Cement cars, hundreds of them," Hettrick remarked, scanning the print-out. "Flat cars with steel panels and re-bars. Hundreds of them, too. Eliminate the flats. Cement cars came in from Reno, Vegas, and Salt Lake. Major cement plants there, too."

"Any of those cars sitting on sidings in those three cities on demurrage?" Len Spencer wanted to know.

"That's a tough one!" Martinside guessed. "Hundreds of cement cars out there."

"Crocker tracks them, especially if it's networked with the other railroad traffic and car locator computers," Len told him. He turned to Belinda Hettrick whom he'd gotten to know so much better during the Sakhalin Island earthquake clean-up than during the Bastaard Rebellion in Namibia. "Belinda, if Crocker chokes on the request, check to see if the Tabernacle owns any railway cars. Sometimes it's cheaper to buy a railway car to carry something you're shipping a lot of. Otherwise, you pay demurrage if it sits on your siding while you're waiting to unload and use its contents. I get the feeling that the Tabernacle has lots of money but that they're also a business operation. Maybe this Jasper Lyell bought a bunch of cement cars and Mathys' techies converted some of them to hold his nukes."

"Georgie's already checking, Len, and thanks for the suggestion," Hettrick said absently, working the keypad rather than the voice command because it was faster for this sort of data entry. "I've also asked Georgie to see if he can find out whether or not any of them have been modified."

The hard-copy printer suddenly spewed more paper. Hettrick scanned it again.

"The Tabernacle owns fifty cement cars registered GTFX," she answered. "Georgie has located all fifty of them. Ten are in Sanctuary at this moment. Five are in Reno, eight in Vegas, four in Salt Lake, and the rest in the Los Angeles, Phoenix, San Francisco, Denver, and Albuquerque areas, sitting on sidings at cement plants. *Wup!* Here's about a dozen of them that were consigned by the Tabernacle to temporary storage in yards in those cities."

"That was too easy," Martinside muttered.

"Give us a difficult one sometime, Chet," Carlisle told him. "One of the things business firms such as railroads have to know is where their capital assets are. And we've got to have access to that information in case of emergency...which this sheep screw is. And we've got some excellent computers, too. When we can't recruit a big army, we use megacomputers to handle most of the necessary CYA paperwork that's required these days."

Some people, Curt thought, were still in the eighteenth century when it came to technology. Martinside was apparently one of those, which didn't surprise Curt. Social types never were comfortable around real technology anyway. Most of them thought of technology as creating only inhuman replacements for human beings.

"Let me have that print-out!" Martinside snapped, reaching for it. "I'll have the FBI all over those cars in less than an hour."

"I'd advise against trying to open them to get at any bomb triggering mechanisms, Chet," Carlisle added. "The Tabernacle techies may have booby-trapped them. At least, if I'd built them, I would have."

"Well, we can haul them out of the cities in a couple of hours," Martinside remarked. "And I'd like to alert the emergency civil defense teams and news media in those cities."

"Not only no, but hell no!" Len Spencer exploded. "I don't know a single person in the news media in any of those cities who wouldn't come absolutely unbonded at this news. They'll go ballistic on us if we even mention the word nuke. Then we've got the panic we don't want."

"Okay, okay! You're the expert in that area. But now that I've got this lever of knowing where his nukes are, he'll talk," Martinside said triumphantly.

"You don't know for sure yet. We don't know, either. We aren't omniscient. We were just speculating," Hettrick reminded him.

"I'll know for sure in an hour or so," Martinside promised her and picked the phone off the hook, dialed a number, and began to talk to someone in hushed tones.

Curt ignored the man. He broached the next question to the group. "I think I've got a handle on how he might try to trigger the nukes. He's got to communicate with them or with one of his henchmen in those cities. He's got to give the signal. Which means communications. General Hettrick, I'd like to get Sergeant Edie Sampson and some of my good communications people on the problem right away."

"My cee-cubed-eye people can also help," Rick Salley pointed out.

"Right, Rick! We'll need all the ECW and ECM capability we can muster."

"What do you have in mind?" Hettrick asked.

"Cut 'em off from the world! The telco knows where the hard-wire and fiber optics lines come into Sanctuary," Curt pointed out. "We can be on them in less than an hour. We can lay heavy electronic countermeasures over Sanctuary to keep him from getting any electromagnetic signals in or out except the ones we want."

"He's got an extensive satellite network for his Tabernacle broadcasting services," Len Spencer reminded them. "How the hell do you pull the plug on laser comm beams up to satellites?"

"Well, I might suggest some cooperation from the United States Aerospace Force," Curt ventured to suggest. "Seems to me they could get to those two satellites of his out in geosynch in a couple of hours with a couple of their space planes."

"Those satellites are private property, Colonel," Spencer pointed out.

"Who said anything about capturing his satellites?" Carlisle suddenly remarked. "General Bill Davis can just park a space plane next to one in between the bird and the ground. A space plane is pretty opaque to a laser comm beam, Len. And if nothing really happens, it can be a 'regrettable mistake' caused by an inspection of Mathys' comsats as potential weapons. Legal as can be, sir."

Spencer thought about this for a moment. The round-faced reporter had also changed a lot since Curt had met him in Namibia years before. The man had matured, but none of his pugnacious approach to life and love had disappeared. It had been modified because he'd gotten the Pulitzer he'd wanted, so he wasn't quite so aggressive in that area any longer. But he was still a dedicated man, and Curt felt Len Spencer wanted more out of life than being the top media man in the United States as the presidential press secretary. Other writers had from time to time in history achieved very high political office because their names became household words. That kind of public recognition was hard to discount.

"It's do-able," Spencer replied brusquely. "Jake, you get to Admiral Spencer and General Davis. I'll touch base with Al Murray and General Barnitz so they can brief The Man."

Curt suddenly saw he was winning. Tired and concerned as he was, he'd managed to swing the operation from one of passive negotiation on Martinside's part to a pro-active mission. Curt had effectively disarmed Mathys' nukes...if their speculations were indeed correct. With that restraint on an assault and hostage rescue operation inside Sanctuary removed from consideration, his next step was to get the wheels in motion to get in there and get Dyani out.

So, he turned to Hettrick and said, "General, Mathys isn't going to be very happy when he suddenly finds himself isolated from the world. And he still has the capability to launch that spaceship, maybe with the hostages on board as extra insurance against our ballistic missile defense system shooting it out of the sky. In any event, we've got our people in Sanctuary. We should be prepared to get them out if Martinside can't talk them free - and I don't believe he can. So, I'd like to get my staff together with Colonel Salley and his staff right away. We should be primed to move at once when negotiations fail."

"Colonel, I have direct orders that we are not to assault Sanctuary without specific, direct orders from the Commander in Chief," Carlisle reminded him.

"Yes, sir, I know that," Curt replied carefully. He didn't want to blow it now, not after having spent a lot of time and energy that evening maneuvering the situation. He was dog-tired, but he forced himself to put that aside. He still had work to do. Life-critical work. "But don't you think it would be a good idea if we were ready to do what is probably going to be necessary? Especially since the Greys and the Wolfhounds have already been called in on this one and rushed a thousand klicks to the site?"

The Army's Chief of Staff and member of the Joint Chiefs looked at Curt like a parent would view an eager but somewhat unruly teenager - with general approval but a warning to rein back the enthusiasm a little bit. He knew from experience that Colonel Curt Carson was always good to go, always a top-notch tactician, always a good leader. But Belinda Hettrick had also briefed General Jacob Carlisle on the fact that this was somewhat different. In spite of all the professionalism in the world, all the dedication to duty an officer was capable of, and all the order - following discipline a general officer would ever want from a field subordinate, Colonel Curt Carson had a very personal interest in this operation. His good judgment was probably warped as a result. The psychological pressures on Carson were extreme, as Carlisle now knew from watching Curt that evening.

So, instead of answering Curt directly, Carlisle turned to Hettrick and remarked, "General, I received no orders that would prevent our people from doing the necessary planning for a contingency operation if negotiations fail. Since the Joint Chiefs prevailed upon the Oval Office to move the available Iron Fist regiments up here on very short notice, it's prudent to engage in a bit of planning and even passive recon just in case you have to actually take some action."

Hettrick smiled. She knew what was going on in Carlisle's mind.

Having served under the man for a long time - first in the Washington Greys and later as the regimental commander under his 17th Iron Fist divisional command - she knew his suggestion had two purposes. The first was real; it was not a good idea to have two action-oriented regiments sitting on their ass waiting for something to happen, chomping at the bit to make it happen, and then be called on at the last minute to lash up an ops plan. The second was more subtle; Carlisle wanted to get one of her regimental commanders off everyone's back and put him to work doing something he would perceive as useful and meaningful lest he suddenly pull one of his typical stunts of doing what he wanted to do in spite of orders.

Both Carlisle and Hettrick knew Curt Carson.

But they didn't know how powerful the motivation was that was driving him this time. Furthermore, the man was suffering from fatigue. So, his superiors had decided they were going to be super-cautious about him.

And General Belinda Hettrick knew with sadness that if Curt Carson didn't get his ducks lined up personally, it could destroy his career.

Chapter Twenty-Three

"Ready on Camera Two! Stand by the Tabernacle opening title! Three...two...one...roll title! Stand by for fade in, Camera Two! Prophet, you're live! Camera Two...take!" The director in the control room was on his feet behind his desk, waving his arms and pointing his fingers in animated fashion, orchestrating the late-night Tabernacle show, *Frontier of Your Future*. The signal went out to the satellite ground station and then up to geosynchronous orbit as a pencil-thin beam of laser light. It also went into the quietly humming recorders for delayed broadcast to the Orient and then to Europe.

The Prophet of the Galactic Tabernacle of the Human Future, Dr. Clark Jeremy Mathys, looked into the camera lens and smiled. "Good evening, space people and my loyal followers. Tonight, I have a very special message to you. Many things happened today. As the Anunnaki have told me and as I've passed along to you, the evil Nibiruans have corrupted many humans here on Earth. These human opponents are intent on doing anything within their power - and some of their powers are awesome by our standards - to stop me and the Tabernacle from carrying out our God-given mission to rescue humanity and forge ahead into a glorious future here on Earth as well as throughout space. I have been given a vision of the future by the Anunnaki. It is my intention as their appointed representative on Earth and your leader to ensure that all humankind has its heavy burden of pain, misery, poverty, and guilt lifted from its shoulders so that everyone will be able to live as we were intended to live. And we will all live for a very long time, as long as the Anunnaki who made us. And without worry or travail. Without sickness and death. With plenty of everything for everyone. With a whole galaxy to live in alongside our extraterrestrial friends. With a sublime mission to conquer the evil Nibiruans as the Anunnaki's specially engineered warriors. For what better purpose can you dedicate your lives and fortunes than to save humankind, our planet, and the galaxy? What higher mission is there than to do what is necessary to permit humankind to venture freely outward to the stars in your very lifetime?"

Mathys waved his arm at the artificial star field projected behind him. It looked as real as if he were actually in space on the bridge of a starship and seeing all those stars through the clear vacuum of space. "There is our future! Out there is our destiny! Millions of stars await our colony ships. Billions of planets await our seed. Uncounted races of intelligent beings await our emergence from the cradle of Planet Earth to become valued and contributing members of the galactic neighborhood."

He dropped his voice into a more serious level and went on, "The Nibiruans, however, have begun their moves against us by using their agents here on Earth!" He slowly began to work up to a controlled fever pitch that caused his followers to hang on every televised word. Anyone who knew history or had listened to the great demagogues would have instantly recognized Mathys for what he was and for what he was doing. Most intelligent, thinking people would have spotted the inconsistencies and paradoxes in his doctrines, but those people weren't his targets. He went directly to those who wanted and needed strong leadership they could follow without thinking very much, a plausible but impossible goal that would make their dreams come true without working very hard for it, and a devil they could hate instead of hating their colleagues, friends, and family members whom they had to get along with. He'd also attracted the idealistic techies who'd become disenchanted with their jobs and frustrated at being unable to do what they knew could be done with their beloved technology. The techies didn't believe his doctrine; he didn't care as long as they worked for him in his communal base and gave their all to what he wanted to do.

"Now, I have told you again and again that Sanctuary is the very place from which we will go forth to the stars. Sanctuary is the very place where all of you can find your own sanctuary against the troubles of the world. With your help, I have built Sanctuary to do all these things and more. But our beloved and sacrosanct Sanctuary has now been violated by the evil mercenaries of the Nibiruans! Three times in past weeks, the soldiers of the loyal Host of Michael have been forced to defend Sanctuary. We now hold in Sanctuary those who attempted to enter and destroy us. They will be treated well. If they accept the doctrines of the Tabernacle, they will be allowed to join us."

Mathys walked slowly across the "bridge deck" in front of the view windows showing the star fields. Then he looked again at the camera with an intent expression. "Great danger is imminent for all of us. Including those of you outside Sanctuary. The Host of Michael can protect Sanctuary. But perhaps not those of you in the outside world. Therefore, I call upon all of you who live in the great cities to go as quickly as you can to the open, natural countryside. Why? Because the cities themselves may become subject to the wrath of the Nibiruans. Do not panic. Do not rush. But leave. Return to your roots in the land, in the natural environment of our despoiled planet. Be ready for the Return. Because I have been told by the Anunnaki that the time has come!" He was stealing from the Bible and the Koran and other sacred texts. But he knew them all. And he felt a bit like Hosea exhorting the Israelites to leave the cities and dwell again in tents.

He gazed benevolently at the camera lens with its winking red light. "I am delighted to announce that my acolytes and I will soon leave in the spaceship *Archangel Gabriel* for the asteroids where we'll build Star Base One and await the Anunnaki beam ships. I have announced our intentions to the leaders of the world and asked them to make sure that people remain clear of Sanctuary. I have told the authorities to be alert for the launch. We intend to operate with the safety of everyone in mind because we mean no harm to anyone."

He paused for effect, then said with dismay and disappointment in his voice, "But my announcement has been met by disbelief and by outright opposition from the Nibiruan mercenaries among you. They are taking steps even as I speak to stop me. And they will try everything they can to keep us from joining our Anunnaki allies and bringing to you and the rest of humankind the hopeful future we all so desperately desire. My friends, it will be a wondrous time when the Anunnaki come among us again and give us the technology and understanding we need to conquer our enemies and the forces of nature. And to bring again to everyone peace and prosperity of the Golden Age of our human youth."

The floor director made a rolling motion with his two hands and held up two fingers, signifying that Mathys' time was running short.

"We are approaching the time of the final battle, my friends. It is as the Anunnaki have told me it would be. And the outcome of that final battle still depends on all of you continuing to believe in and support me. I may not be able to speak to you again. I may be departing with sixty-five acolytes in the *Archangel Gabriel* as quickly as the ship is completed and made ready for launch. And that time is growing close, my friends. You may see the *Archangel Gabriel* rising on its trail of fire to the stars sooner than you think. And when you see it, I know your prayers for safety will be with all of us because we go outward to bring you the wonderful, hopeful future that was promised to us millennia ago. When I'm gone, I charge you with maintaining the faith so that we may return to an Earth that will welcome us and our Anunnaki allies. So, this may be farewell for a time. But you will be with me always in my heart, and I ask that you keep me in your hearts and minds until the glorious Return from the stars!"

A woman's voice suddenly echoed throughout the studio. It was loud and clear. "I'm all right, Curt!" The shout was followed by the muffled sounds of a struggle.

Mathys was one smooth character. He ignored the interruption. Turning his back to the camera, he put his hands behind his back and appeared to look benevolently out the "starship" windows toward the stars. Camera Four picked up his far-seeing visage.

"Fade Camera Four!...Bring up rolling credits!...Feed up closing music volume!...Cue Harold for final voice-over...Stand by Camera Six credit roll...Take!...Go to Tape Five with money appeal message and address...Take!...Okay, Prophet, you're off! Sorry about the shout. It went out live, but we'll edit it from the tapes."

Mathys didn't even bother to say thanks to his director or the technical staff that had made the broadcast possible. In fact, he never even acknowledged they were there at all. He quickly walked off the starship bridge set because General Steve Calder, Reverend Gillespie, Tabernacle technology director Gordon Palmer, Number One wife Sarah Carmichael Mathys, and business manager Jasper Lyell were waiting for him off-set and indicating to him that they wanted to talk with him at once.

With them was Captain Dyani Motega. She was filthy, and her slacks and shirt were torn. Her bare feet were dirty and bleeding. Her wrists had been cruelly strapped together behind her with a nylon wire tie, and her mouth was stuffed with a handkerchief.

"Sorry, Prophet," Steve Calder tried to apologize. "That was the first thing she's said since we captured her."

"With your permission, Prophet," the Reverend Gillespie added smoothly, "I have some heavy leather cuffs that will immobilize her without physically damaging her...and I can certainly improve upon that crude gag General Calder was forced to use on the spur of the moment."

Mathys didn't look at him but gazed at Dyani with heavy-lidded eyes. He ignored Gillespie's suggestion. "Well, General, you made good on half your promise. Or maybe it's more than half. You didn't capture the man."

"We may have killed him outside the fence, Prophet," Calder hypothesized. "Our warbots had him in range for a long time before they lost the target."

"Never mind. We have another very valuable hostage. Actually, she's far more than hostage," the Prophet remarked. Everyone knew what he meant. Some of them had seen his glances at Dyani Motega earlier.

"Prophet, I know you don't wish to harm her," Gillespie broke in instantly, "but I have ways of restraint that-"

Mathys glanced at his Keeper of the Faith with a hard look in his eyes. "This one isn't yours, Reverend. You're an excellent Keeper of the Faith. You've rescued and convinced many who would have otherwise bolted the faith. But we don't need to reeducate this one. I don't want her physically harmed. Taisha has been pestering me for fresh, new subjects for her accelerated neuroelectronic reprogramming techniques-"

"Uh, Prophet," Gillespie broke in again, "it is not that I want her. She's just shown that she's very strong and extremely violent. She's not a good subject for my methods." He really wanted to try, but he was a typical sadist. He wanted only helpless victims who wouldn't fight back. Sadists abhorred actual physical violence; they really wanted willing victims. There was much truth to the old psychiatrist's joke that a sadist was a person who did nice things to a masochist. Modern neuroelectronic psychiatry had revealed much in this area. But Gillespie also had a streak of voyeurism in his perverted psychological makeup. The Keeper of the Faith and henchmen and henchwomen who were a little different, far more vicious, and didn't really give a damn about their "subjects." He thought it might be pleasurable to watch them at work on this woman.

"Reverend, we don't have time for primitive methods," Mathys reminded him. "We're very close to Departure. And the enemy is at the gates. I want to take this woman with us. She'll be a valuable addition to our gene pool."

"That means someone is going to get bumped," Calder reminded him. "Sixty-six people is all the *Gabriel* will handle."

"General, I'm putting you in charge of this matter," Mathys told him. He wasn't worried that Steve Calder might attempt to claim this woman for himself. In Sanctuary, such a thing as gender equality and women's rights didn't exist; the Prophet had built his space movement around the classical religious doctrine of male supremacy. Still, many women joined the Tabernacle, and the outside joke about this space religion existing for the psycho-sexual gratification of its advocates had more than a bit of truth to it. The Prophet knew that Steve Calder liked his women very much but liked them far more kinky than the Prophet's taste. For that reason, Calder had been told a long time ago that there would be no room on the *Archangel Gabriel* for any women except those who were strong and natural. Women who'd been altered or artificially enhanced with biocosmetics were too great a risk because no one had any baseline data on the long-term effects of many biocosmetic processes that were commonly used to exaggerate physical attributes.

So, Calder had opted to remain in Sanctuary, ostensibly because its long-term security was "his job" but really because he'd recruited sufficient enhanced women to form what the Soviets would call a social battalion.

Dyani Motega's primitive natural characteristics were, Mathys had decided, something that should be introduced in the Tabernacle's off-world genetic base. He believed in his twisted mind that it could be a long time before the Anunnaki arrived to take them off Star Base One. And the Anunnaki rescue mission might be intercepted by the Nibiruans before it had the chance to get through. Mathys was secretly prepared for the long haul. In the back of his mind, the scientist that he'd once been kept nagging at him in a small voice that this could all be just a bunch of bullshit. So, he tried to quietly prepare options.

"Prophet, I'm going to be extremely busy defending Sanctuary against outside invasion," Calder suddenly said. He didn't want this hot potato on his hands. He didn't want to be responsible for bumping one of the women from the ship. He was slated to stay in Sanctuary, and he'd have to get along with that angry woman, whomever she turned out to be. "And since I'm not going in the *Gabriel*, I shouldn't have any connection with the passenger manifest."

"I'll take care of the bumping decision," Mathys told him, knowing that this would provide him with a lot of leverage to bring some of his recalcitrant and cheating wives into line very quickly. Promiscuity wasn't officially condoned in Sanctuary, but it wasn't exactly prohibited either...except with the Prophet's wives if you were stupid enough to get caught. Mathys considered the consequences to be "evolution in action." So, he gave a specific order to Calder, who was used to getting and following specific orders. It was one way to ensure that Calder did as he was told. "General, get with Todd Cartwright and give him this woman's weight, sizes, and other specifications for clothing and quarters on the *Gabriel*. Then I want you to turn her over to Dr. Taisha and make sure that her retention facilities are secure against a breakout. This woman has shown herself to be opportunistic; she'll try to bolt the instant she sees any crack in your security measures. And I want you to see to it that she's cleaned up and made presentable. You shouldn't have to do it yourself; that's why I authorized you to hire sufficient staff and subordinates. I expect you to do what's needed, but I also expect you to delegate." He turned to the others present, signifying that he considered the subordinates listened to, the imperial decision made, and the orders given that must be followed without further concern on his part.

"Very well, what did all of you want to see me about?" he asked the rest of the retinue.

"Prophet, I'm not going to continue to take abuse from the technical people or from your immediate acolytes!" Jasper Lyell told him with about as much vehemence as the financial wizard could ever bring into a discussion.

"You wouldn't catch hell from me if you'd pay the bills so our vendors would deliver the stuff we have on order!" Gordon Palmer spat out. He was an intense middle-aged techie who was considered an "old, retreaded engineer" by the younger Tabernacle technies with both affection and disgust, depending on the circumstances. "VanDerCamp tells me he's having to scrounge parts from Taisha because vendors won't deliver until their previous invoices are paid. Cartwright reports that some critical parts failed to meet specs but that the vendors won't make good on warranties until the bills are paid..."

"We've had a little trouble in the last few days," Lyell admitted. "The federal government has frozen some of our assets and bank accounts. So, I've had some checks and bank drafts bounce. But I have other accounts they haven't found yet, and I'll take care of it as soon as I can."

"That could delay the Departure," Palmer pointed out. "We won't go until the ship's ready-"

"And that's what I want to talk to you about!" Sarah Carmichael Mathys told her husband. "Our quarters aboard the *Gabriel* are terrible! None of what I specified as absolute necessities have been installed! Now I learn that you're hot to take along another woman I haven't checked out yet! When this new girl gets in Taisha's lab, I want to inspect her. And interrogate her. Thoroughly. Very thoroughly!"

"She won't talk," Calder reminded her.

"She will when Taisha and I get through with her!" Sarah Mathys promised.

Chapter Twenty-Four

"Rick, let's get our staffs together and start planning this goddamned operation," Curt said to Colonel Frederick Salley of the Wolfhounds regiment as they left Hettrick's OCV. "I want to be ready to move the instant we get the word. Matter of fact, we may want to put out a few patrols to test the Sanctuary defenses..."

Salley looked up at him querulously, noticing Curt's limp and his bandaged feet covered by slippers from the Biotech unit. "Do I hear you correctly, Curt? You sure you're the same guy who always used to tell the rest of your classmates that a commander should never try to plan a hazardous mission except on a full belly and after a full night's sleep?"

"Yeah, but those were different circumstances back in the days when our mission was to capture the Bear Mountain Bridge and forge on to Peekskill," Curt replied testily, referring to the little tactical war games the cadets at West Point had to carry out under the watchful and jaundiced eyes of the military faculty. Then he reminded his classmate, "This is the real world."

"Yeah, and in the real world things never happen fast...except when we don't believe they'll happen fast at all and they do. Look, it's going to take Carlisle and that negotiator a few hours to get Sanctuary cut off from the world," the other regimental commander remarked. "And to find out if our WAG about the nukes is correct. And to let Martinside fall on his face when his negotiations fail. And then maybe to convince the Oval Office to let us do the job we know we're going to have to do eventually anyway."

"I've got people being held in Sanctuary" was all that Curt would say after a short pause.

"And she's a very fine woman and officer, too," Salley pointed out. "She can take care of herself while we plan a good mission to get her out. Remember that I've been up against her scouting unit in our Arizona war games. She's disciplined and tougher than hell down inside. She knows we'll be coming. And if she's being held by their General Calder and his mercs, she'll be all right. She's military and so are they. Is this guy Calder the same cadet who was one of your plebes?"

"No, he was one of Joan Ward's rats," Curt said wearily.

"Okay, I remember him now. The class braggart."

"He still is."

"And horny as hell. He'd chase anything with boobs."

"Yeah, but his tastes have gotten sort of bizarre, what with all the bio-enhanced sex toys around these days."

"He isn't likely to go after Dyani," Salley tried to console him.

"Maybe yes, probably no. But I don't know if he can keep her away from Mathys' perverted Keeper of the Faith. Or Mathys himself." Curt paused and stopped walking. His feet hurt him pretty badly right then. "That isn't really it, Rick. I don't trust Calder. The sonofabitch has sold out. He's become a merc. And if he's the one responsible for those nukes being scattered around among innocent civilians, he's a terrorist! So, the bastard has sullied the honor of his school...our honor, Rick. And the honor of my regiment - which, unfortunately, he once served in. I not only want to get Captain Motega out of there alive and well, but I want to get Calder, put him in the guardhouse, and see him in the federal court where I can testify against him. War and armed conflict is one thing; that's our profession, and we're proud of being able to serve and defend our country. But terrorism is an abomination that targets innocent women and children. I won't tolerate it if I can do anything at all about it. I may order my regimental sergeant major to cause a black burgee to fly from our regimental colors until the sonofabitch is caught. Bastard!" Curt usually didn't use some of those epithets, and he'd used fewer and fewer of the more common ones since he'd assumed regimental command. Taking his cue from both Belinda Hettrick and Wild Bill Bellamack, former regimental commanders under whom he'd served, he felt that it demeaned a regimental commander to talk like a basic training drill sergeant except in very special conditions. Curt was like Patton in many ways except that one.

"Sounds like you're nursing a real blood feud, old buddy."

"Call it what you want," Curt growled.

"That sort of outlook can kind of cloud a commander's objectivity, Curt," Salley warned him gently. "It could make this siege pretty drawn out for you."

"There's going to be no blood unless Calder wants to spill it," Curt promised in bitter tones. And in his fatigue and worry, he went on using words and phrases he hadn't spoken since his days as a platoon leader. "And he'd fucking well better be careful whose blood he spills, too. And where the hell he spills it. There's going to be no siege, either. I'm sure as hell not going to sit around on my ass keeping Sanctuary isolated from the world and waiting for Calder to take the initiative. If we're ordered to besiege Sanctuary, I'll provoke a fight with the sonofabitch and his Host of Michael…and then be forced to defend myself by going in and shoving a Saucy Cans up his asshole. That's why we've got to be ready to push off the instant we get the good-to-go signal."

"Okay, I agree we ought to get cracking on an ops plan. But I can't get my staff here for another six or seven hours," Salley explained. "They're busy setting up the temporary ops base over in Grass Valley. In fact, I've got to get back over there and check in. My chief aerodyne driver dropped me off here on his way up with a belly full of Sierra Charlies and Mary Anns."

"Okay, okay, if that's the way it has to be. Oh-seven-hundred tomorrow," Curt replied with frustration. The goddamned world just wasn't responding like he thought it should.

"Oh-eight-hundred. Your OCV or mine?"

"I don't much give a damn one way or the other."

"We'll come here. Hettrick's here. So's Carlisle. We may need one or both them to pull some strings for us. Now go get some sleep, dammit. You look like you've just walked twenty tours and done a hundred snap-ups after getting your ass beaten with a coat hanger."

After Salley left in one of the Warhawk's aerodynes for his own regimental headquarters a couple of valleys to the west, Curt stumbled into his OCV and sat down, thankful to be able to get off his feet. The clock on the wall said 2319 local time. "Kester?" he bellowed.

No answer.

He slapped the switch on the wall tacomm and called for Major Joan Ward, his chief of staff. "Grey Chief, this is Grey Head in Grey Can. Report ASAP!"

No answer.

Curt resolved to chew out both Major Joan Ward and Regimental Sergeant Major Henry Kester for not being on duty.

"Okay, where's the godamned OOD?" Curt growled and snapped the tacomm switch again. He wasn't in shape to exercise any sort of command right then, but he didn't realize it, and no one was there to tell him so. "Officer of the Day, report to the regimental headquarters vehicle!"

The rear hatch cracked, then opened, and Captain Kitsy Clinton stepped in. She was wearing the OOD brassard, clean cammies, and a field cap on her dark curls. She saluted. "Good evening, Colonel."

"Where the hell is everyone?" Curt wanted to know.

"Major Ward is taking five. So's Sergeant Kester. Nearly everyone's been up and at work for more than thirty-six hours now, Colonel," Kitsy explained. She consulted the ops board which Curt, in his fatigued condition, hadn't bothered to read. "Hal Clock's Cavaliers are on picket duty until oh-four-hundred. Hassan's Assassins are getting ready to relieve them then. Brown's Black Hawks are partially operational; Lieutenant Brown has two birdbots up on recce over Battle Mountain massif. Captain Sweet's Scorpions are-"

"Okay, I'm sorry, I guess I should have read the board," Curt admitted, then, noting her appearance, asked her, "How long have you been up, Captain?"

"Oh, about forty-seven hours, sir. I'd be logging sack time myself if

I didn't have the duty," she admitted, not flagging a bit but trying to maintain a tactical, high-and-tight attitude.

He looked at her. Kitsy's eyes were like two burned holes in a blanket. Her face was drawn. She looked tired. "Are you okay, Captain?" he asked, strangely solicitous. He liked this sparky little officer. She'd made an astounding comeback from a combat-sustained injury that might have left her a paraplegic the rest of her life, paralyzed from the neck down. He knew she'd been so damned insistent about rejoining the Greys and had made such a bloody nuisance of herself at Walter Reed that the biotechs were delighted to release her for duty as quickly as they could just to get her off their backs.

"No, sir, I'm pretty tired. But I do have the duty. So…"

"I want you to call up your supernumerary and report in sick," he told her. "You've just gotten out of the hospital. You shouldn't be standing duty yet."

"Excuse me, sir, but that's bullshit! I may be tired, but I'm no goddamned gold brick! I was officially released for duty from Walter Reed, sir."

Curt put his elbows on the situation table and rubbed his eyes with tired hands. "Okay, have it your own way, Captain. So, go roust up my staff and get them over here. I'm calling a Papa Brief. I want to know the condition on Sanctuary."

"Yes, sir," Kitsy said but didn't move.

Curt just sat there, rubbing his eyes, then looking blankly out into space. His shoulders were hunched, and his head hung slightly forward. Kitsy knew the signs. She knew the man. And she knew what was bothering him. It was bothering her, too, but in a different way. She didn't like to see this man in this condition.

So she just stood there.

Finally, Curt growled in a low voice, "Get your sweet ass out of here and carry out my order, Captain!"

"Sir, if you insist, I will do so. But I will also ask Major Gydesen to come over here and pronounce you unfit for duty in your present condition."

"You do that, and I'll-"

"The OOD has that prerogative, Colonel. In fact, the OOD has that duty, too. I can't declare you temporarily unfit for duty, but the regiment's chief medical officer can and probably will," Kitsy told him adamantly, not moving from where she stood. She was playing with fire, but she knew her commanding officer.

Finally, Curt just couldn't hold on much longer. He put his face in his hands and, with utmost weariness in his voice, said, "Please sit down, Kitsy."

That was the signal she was waiting for. Rule Ten was in effect, but her commanding officer had signaled that he wanted to speak informally. She sat down next to him but did not touch him. She, too, was a West Pointer. She, too, had strong self-discipline when it was demanded. It was demanded right then. Otherwise, she would have behaved far more compassionately, far more like a woman whose man was tired and hurting.

Their disciplined and adult behavior would have absolutely astounded officers of a hundred years ago and been unimaginable to a Civil War soldier.

"Talk, Curt," she told him softly. Then she added, "Please."

He overcame the urge to hold her. It wasn't the time or the place.

"I'm glad to see you back," he told her honestly.

"I'm very happy to be back. But I'm not glad to see you in this condition," she admitted.

"It's my own damned fault, you know. I probably let things get too far out of control. Dyani used to warn me about keeping our priorities straight," he said, still with his face in his hands.

"I knew something like this might happen that day in the Mosul hospital when I could do nothing but just lie there in that iron frame...and Dyani walked in with the newly minted brown bar on her collar," Kitsy recalled, then added hastily, "Not that I wasn't delighted for her. I like Dyani. There isn't a woman in the Greys who doesn't like and respect her. But I knew what might happen, and it did."

Curt raised his head and looked at her. "You knew what I didn't know?"

"Come on, Curt! That woman has adored you from the moment she joined the Greys! Maybe before that. I talked with her from time to time before I got my neck busted. She's very disciplined. But I knew if she was ever commissioned I'd have another competitor," Kitsy blurted out, then shrugged. "So that's my world. Alexis Morgan resigns her commission and goes off to Brunei. In comes Dyani Motega. And Kitsy goes off to Walter Reed to grow a new spinal column. But let me tell you something that's dawned on me in the past few hours. You and Alexis had it under control. You and I had it under control. This time, it isn't. Or you wouldn't be sitting here in this condition tonight."

"How the hell do you know what I feel? I don't even really know myself how I feel!" Curt objected. "Or what I ought to be feeling. Except I screwed up and left a lovely lady of the Washington Greys in deadly jeopardy."

"It's more than that, Curt. If Alexis were here, she'd tell you the same thing. Hell, your very close buddy Joan Ward will tell you the same thing when she wakes up in a few hours. Or Belinda Hettrick, for that matter. You've worried and fretted about a similar situation in the case of Jerry and Adonica."

"Are you telling me that I'm letting an affair of the heart affect my professional life?" Curt suddenly wanted to know.

"When you put it in those quaint terms, yes. Remember, this is the first time you and I have had a little tete-a-tete since Mosul. Rumor Control was buzzing when it got the news that you and Dyani had gone into Sanctuary together as a recce team. When we got here and I found out you'd gotten out without Dyani, I knew when I saw you that you were suffering from more than fatigue and the hurt of bleeding feet. In quaint poetic terms, your heart was bleeding, too. But not with blood."

"You may be right, Kitsy...So have you got any bright ideas what I can do? Or should do?"

"Yes," Kitsy told him without hesitation; then asked in cadet terms, "Are you entertaining comment, criticism, and critique?"

"I am."

"Okay," she replied, took a deep breath, and told him bluntly, "First of all, realize that some of us care for you and Dyani both...a lot. Let me call Ruth Gydesen over here so she can give you something that will pull the plug and let you crap out totally unconscious until tomorrow morning. Oops, until later this morning now. And here's your order book. Give me an order to advise your staff to meet as soon as practical and put together a plan for your appraisal at a Papa briefing tomorrow morning at oh-eight-hundred."

Curt looked at her. The old Kitsy Clinton was indeed there. And more. She'd grown up while still keeping that childlike, impish, pixie quality. She was, Curt suddenly saw, maturing into one hell of an outstanding officer. He might have to revise his plans for training a successor.

"It's a damned shame you're on duty now, Kitsy," he told her.

"And so are you, Colonel Carson!" she quipped with a sparkle in her eyes, her deliberate use of the formal means of address signifying that she wanted to tell him something quite professionally. "But there will be other times. There always have been. Rule Ten, you know. Now maybe I shouldn't say this to you, and I probably have no right to, and you can probably court martial me and nail my tits to the wall; but...as a temporary regimental commander told me one night not very long ago in the jungles of Borneo: 'I'm going to be a brass-plated sonofabitch and tell you to shape up *now!*' Start acting like a regimental commander, sir! And we'll all get Dyani Motega out of purgatory a hell of a lot faster! Your personal situation aside, we have a tradition: *The Washington Greys never abandon their own!*"

Without waiting for his verbal answer because she saw from the expression on his face what it was, she stood up, patted Curt on the shoulder, and toggled the tacomm switch. "Grey Bio, this is Grey

Day. Please send the major to the colonel's OCV ASAP! Bring a sleepy pill, plus a baseball bat in case he won't swallow the pill. If you don't have a baseball bat handy, any nearby rock will serve to rock him to sleep so we can get some work done. And so he won't fret about it."

Chapter Twenty-Five

"My name is Dyani Motega. I am an American citizen. My service number is six-zero, two-eight-six, one-one-two, niner-five. I hold the rank of captain. My date of birth is seventeen-three-twelve."

"Yes, yes, you have told us that before," was the exasperated response of Captain Manuel Sebastian de Vargas e Morales, the officer of Calder's Host of Michael who'd been assigned to accompany the prisoner. He was a former remote-controlled airborne reconnaissance vehicle officer who'd been cashiered from the Forca Aerea Brasileira for crashing a multi-million dollar airbot into a general's latrine while on maneuvers just after said general officer left hurriedly with his pants down. His two Host of Michael airbots were down for maintenance at the moment, the grimy landings on the alkali flat having destroyed their old, nonsealed wheel bearings. Unhappily, the replacement bearings hadn't arrived yet. He didn't know why, but the vendor had said something about holding the shipment until the Tabernacle made good on the last check that just bounced. Vargas didn't understand these things; he was a mil techie, a warbot brainy. Therefore, he was somewhat ill at ease with his assignment to ensure the safety and security of this American warbot officer who'd been captured. The FAB had no women, nor did the Host of Michael. Vargas didn't really know how to behave or to treat Dyani. "Reverend, I'm sorry, but I can't get anything out of her except the information that's required by the Geneva Convention."

"Too bad," the sadist growled unhappily. "But the Prophet has given specific orders that don't permit me to use my proven methods for getting people to speak quite freely." The Reverend Alastair Gillespie was present out of avaricious voyeurism. Besides, there was always the chance that this violent American officer might really become quite meek and submissive under Taisha's ministrations. He was ready to step in and exert his authority the moment that happened.

This was why the Prophet, knowing how his Keeper of the Faith thought and acted, had told his secondary wife, Monica Elora, to be on hand. "Reverend, let's see what Dr. Taisha can accomplish first," Monica Elora Mathys suggested quietly and meekly. "Your 'proven' methods can get your victims to babble quite freely. But there's usually no truth behind their words. They'll say anything that might bring the sessions to an end." She'd had to witness one such session as an object lesson on what happens to those who fall from grace. She'd had nightmares for weeks. All it had done was convince her not to get caught, to lie if necessary to keep out of Gillespie's hands, and to do her best as a Prophet's wife to keep others out of his grip. She didn't like Gillespie. Most of the Sanctuary women - and there were far more women in Sanctuary than men - disliked the Reverend with great intensity. Furthermore, Monica Elora didn't have to kow-tow to the Reverend. As a wife of the Prophet, she was effectively above him in the pecking order. She wanted to make sure that both Gillespie and Taisha didn't physically harm this woman captive; the existing wives of the Prophet would take care of putting her in her proper place when the time came. Thus, Monica Elora didn't want to see the captive's mind totally destroyed, either; when that had happened with someone else a few months ago, the poor thing had become like a three-year-old child and thus totally unable to care for herself.

Dyani was as uncooperative as she could get away with. The men of the Host of Michael had quickly learned that they'd better not get close to her unless she was fettered and hobbled. Dyani had scratched, bit, and shown no reluctance to render a very swift knee to a man's groin. Two Host of Michael soldiers were in the hospital that night. Monica Elora and three other women had succeeded in giving Dyani a shower and dressing her in clean clothes, but they'd had to be a little rough with her. Monica Elora had had to stoop to borrowing some of Gillespie's S&M equipment to keep this strong, violent captive from wordlessly and suddenly lashing out against her captors. Dyani Motega simply wasn't making life very pleasant for those who held her.

Dyani was scared but only because she didn't know whether or not she'd be able to hold out against the torture and mind probing these people might be able to carry out. Otherwise, she activated her extremely strong self-discipline to keep her alert and on top of the situation to the extent she was able. She knew who she was and what she wanted and what was important to her beyond everything else. Thus, she had her own self-respect at stake in her external behavior as well as the honor and tradition of both her family and her regiment. Again, and again in the Greys, she'd seen the truth of the tradition: *The Washington Greys never abandon their own.* Furthermore, she'd seen other ladies of the Greys take the initiative even while being held captive, kill their jailers, break for freedom, and become a positive, active force in their own rescue. She knew she could do nothing less now as well as when the time came to kill. Dyani thought of it in those terms. She was less than two centuries from a nomadic, barbarian background. She would cause blood to flow with no second thoughts and no regrets. These people - with the possible exception of Monica Elora Mathys - were savages, beasts, and people who, in her opinion, were better off dead anyway.

She was ready for whatever they tried to do to, or with, her. And she was ready to kill instantly without torture or lingering pain. Or to put them so badly out of action that dozens of their companions would be required to succor them as wounded.

Dyani Motega was not a passive woman. She made things happen the way she wanted them to happen when she could; she didn't wait for others unless she had a reason. But these people really didn't know the full meaning of that yet. She knew she was still being looked upon as just another woman by this crazy, polygamous, male-dominated cult.

Dr. Rosha Taisha finally turned from her banks of laboratory equipment. "I won't be able to do the sort of thorough job I'd like," she complained, but to Monica Elora and Captain Vargas, not to Gillespie, whom she deliberately ignored. Dyani knew there was high tension and great dislike among these people; she'd try to exacerbate it when the time came. "VanDerCamp and Cartwright cannibalized some of my circuitry for the *Archangel Gabriel.*"

"I could probably get it back for you if you really need it," Monica

Elora Mathys remarked.

"It would help," Taisha admitted, "but I don't need it in order to get started. If you could ask them to return it in an hour or so, it would be very useful then."

"Tell me what you need, and I'll call Cartwright. I'll never be able to get it out of VanDerCamp. He's such a nerd techie that he'd consider the world to be coming to an end if he couldn't continue to use it." Monica Elora might have thought of him as a tech nerd but also knew he was a refreshing change from the Prophet's treatment of her as an object for his pleasure.

"I need the AI modules and stacks he borrowed from me earlier today just after Carson and this woman escaped," Taisha explained. "I don't have enough computer memory or correlation power to do everything I'd like to do with this woman. She's a total outsider and a complete unknown. It will take me about an hour of probing to find her weak points. That I can do easily with what I've got. Going deeper and exaggerating her personal hell in order to loosen up her securely held memories will take the additional AI equipment."

The Prophet's second wife reached for the telephone on the wall and punched numbers into it. "Consider it done, Doctor."

Taisha turned to Dyani and ordered brusquely, "Up on the table!"

Dyani just sat there.

The neuroelectronic scientist turned to the two men. "Well, lift her up on the table and strap her down!"

Vargas was somewhat hesitant. In his culture and at his class level in Brazil, one did not lay violent hands on a woman.

Gillespie, on the other hand, held back with what Taisha suddenly saw was fear.

"I, uh, would suggest you administer a strong dose of sedative first, Doctor," Gillespie ventured. "She's a very violent woman."

"Huh! Trussed up as she is in your equipment, Reverend, I don't see that she could move enough to harm anyone," Taisha observed. "Besides, the use of mind-altering drugs complicates the

209

neuroelectronic techniques and can render some of them useless. I prefer to work with undrugged minds."

The two men looked at one another and finally picked Dyani up and laid her facedown on the table. This was not without retaliation on Dyani's part. Gillespie made the mistake of getting his hand too close to her face. With a sudden motion, Dyani bit him, creating a wound deep enough to draw blood.

Gillespie recoiled in panic, holding his blood-covered hand. "You bitch!" he shouted, quickly withdrawing from her to search for a bandage or another way to stop the bleeding.

That gave Dyani the chance to lash out with hobbled legs at Vargas; but he was primed for her to try something now, and she missed.

Monica Elora dropped the phone while she and Taisha completed installing Dyani on the table and ensuring that she wouldn't be able to move. Gillespie, in near-shock, left the laboratory room. Getting hurt was not to his liking. As the Keeper of the Faith, he had other work he could do that was more to his pleasure. So he abandoned for the time being any plans to acquire Dyani Motega as a subject.

"I really don't like this," Monica Elora complained , with distaste. "I'm not into S-and-M and bondage at all. Doctor, this is just like something out of those old science-fiction Frankenstein horror movies."

"Did people believe that some scientists wouldn't make those old movies come true some day?" Taisha snorted in derision. She looked down at Dyani prostrate on her stomach on the table. "Now I can get to work. Too bad she has such a thick mane of hair; I probably won't be able to get good neuroelectrode contact on her skull unless I shave her head." She turned to pick up the electric clippers she kept for just such a purpose.

"Doctor, I wouldn't shave her head if I were you. The Prophet told me that she was not to be harmed or changed physically," Monica Elora reiterated the instructions from her husband. If she hated Gillespie, she didn't like Taisha a lot more. Taisha had done things to people's minds comparable to what Gillespie had done to their bodies. In fact, Monica Elora Mathys really didn't want to be here at all. But she had no choice. She'd been given orders by the Prophet, and one did not disobey his orders. So, she had to be very careful to carry them out to the letter. If something happened, she and Vargas would be held responsible. And no one wanted to think what might happen in that case. Monica Elora was currently beyond the reach of Gillespie; that could be changed by a simple edict of her husband who, after all, had several other wives to enjoy.

"Oh, very well. I'll just have to do the best I can!" Taisha replied with irritation; then began to complain, "The Prophet told me when I joined him that I would be given everything I needed for my research. He told me I could do anything I wanted with certain people who were Nibiruan agents. Well, I can make do with the people I get. But not without my equipment! You have influence with the Prophet, Monica Elora. I hope you tell him about VanDerCamp and the other techies commandeering my equipment. All they think about is their toys!"

"I've done what I can for you right now," Monica Elora pointed out. "I hope you can work around your equipment difficulties and get this woman quieted down so she doesn't kill the Prophet the first night he's with her." Monica Elora didn't want to see that happen. It would throw the cult into an internal civil war. And she might end up on the wrong side and in the wrong hands. However, she was already plotting how she and some of the other wives might quietly get Dyani out of the way. They had their ways. Harem wives always did.

"It will take me a little more time than usual to break the hostility and self-discipline of this one and turn her into a very cooperative mate for the Prophet. But I can do it. A real challenge at last!" Taisha knew what the Prophet wanted. Some of her work had involved neuroelectronically preconditioning men so they experienced multiple or delayed orgasms or enhanced sexual fantasies during copulation. And she'd had more than one opportunity to test these with the Prophet himself. He didn't really want her as a wife because Taisha was no longer beautiful, and Taisha didn't relish becoming one of his harem, either. The unofficial relationships that existed between them suited both of them, and they kept it quiet.

But not so quiet that the wives didn't have some suspicions.

"If you break her mind too badly, you're in deep trouble, Doctor," Monica Elora warned.

Dr. Rosha Taisha shrugged. If things went badly and that happened, she had an excuse. The technies had taken some of her critical equipment. And a regrettable accident would occur as a result.

With expert skill, Dr. Rosha Taisha attached neuroelectronic electrodes to the base of Dyani's skull, sweeping aside the long dark hair in the process. Other electrode networks were affixed down her bare back. A maze of wires and cables led off to equipment along the wall. It took Taisha nearly half an hour to make sure all the cables were properly connected.

"Doctor, why don't you let me get you one of our robot NE harnesses?" Captain Vargas asked. "It might certainly simplify the hook-up and speed this process." He was not only embarrassed at having to watch this, but he also felt it slightly repugnant that Taisha was misusing technology this way. He was a real warbot brainy, which meant that he liked technology more than violence.

Taisha shook her head. "I'm not allowed to shave her head. Therefore, I couldn't get good scalp interfaces with the skull electrodes," she explained in a distracted manner as she checked and double-checked. "So I've had to revert to more primitive methods...which will, I assure you, work just as well even though they take longer to attach."

"I need to know," Monica Elora announced, "exactly what you're doing. If the Prophet later wants to know, I must report to him." She was worried that this crazy electronic lash-up might cause something to go wrong. If Dyani Motega was killed as a result, Monica Elora Mathys might be held responsible alongside Taisha.

"You wouldn't understand," Taisha snapped.

"Then it is up to you to explain it to me in terms I can understand, Doctor," the Prophet's wife told her. "I'm responsible for her well-being just as Captain Vargas is responsible for her security. If something goes wrong and this woman is killed, I'll need to know what went wrong."

Taisha drew herself up and bristled. She was unafraid of a wife of the Prophet. This wasn't the way most other women in Sanctuary viewed the highest of the high harems. The Prophet's wives wielded enormous behind-the-scenes power. Anyone familiar with the ancient history of the Middle East - as well as the more recent history of many Islamic countries where polygamy was still the way of life for kings and princes - knew the instabilities and intrigues that such a system produced. But the Prophet was no great student of such non-scientific history; he also had appetites and, now, a means to satisfy them.

"Do you doubt my expertise?" Taisha asked crisply.

"I only know what's happened in the past," Monica Elora told her bluntly. "And that I'm responsible with you for what happens tonight."

"Nothing will go wrong!" Taisha insisted. "If the Prophet wants this woman to be a willing wife, I will make it so! And, Captain, we will also learn the truth about why she and her colonel came here."

Facedown on the table with her chin resting in a padded cup so that she looked straight down, Dyani heard this and felt the cool electrodes down her back. And she braced herself for whatever was to come.

She didn't think it would be pleasant.

She was right.

Chapter Twenty-Six

"I will try to explain everything I'm doing as I do it," Dr. Rosha Taisha remarked in the distracted manner of a stuffed-shirt professor who's forced to explain the mystical processes of the arcane art of science to the unwashed and unlearned. "First, I will conduct a series of tests to determine whether or not I have control over this woman's central nervous system. I will do that by sending signals through the pads to the nerve trunks branching from her spinal column. Her nervous system will interpret and decipher these incoming signals as muscle commands and switch them through the lower centers of her brain to the appropriate outgoing command nerves, thence to the proper muscles which will then twitch or spasm, depending upon the level of stimulus that I'm required to use..."

"Strapped down as she is, couldn't that hurt her?" Monica Elora Mathys wanted to know.

"Only if she manages to resist. Then I'll be required to apply stronger command signals. Eventually, her own muscle commands will be overrridden by my commands, and the result will be a violent convulsive muscle movement," Taisha muttered, adjusting the settings on her equipment that would send the electronic signals to Dyani Motega's body.

"Remember: Don't harm her," Monica Elora warned. She didn't like this at all. She was a small young woman with softly rounded curves, made for bed, not violence. She was a baby-doll toy. And she really wasn't very smart. But the Prophet didn't like his wives to be too smart; they might try to control him. However, even though they weren't as brilliant as he with his doctorates in planetary astronomy and physics, his wives surreptitiously managed to exert some control over him anyway. This was because most of them knew the man was about ten RAMs short of an effective full processor at this point in his life. His chronic depression, paranoia, and manic-depressive behavior had taken the sharp edge, off an otherwise brilliant mind."

Dyani heard what Taisha said, of course, and gave silent thanks for Monica Elora's presence. Dyani would now know what was really going on and therefore could prepare herself for it. She'd had more than a year of neuroelectronic warbot training at Fort Benning before joining the Washington Greys. Although the Greys weren't a full warbot outfit but a Sierra Charlie unit, the qualifications for being posted to any RI regiment, including one that was Special Combat, demanded that all newcomers be warbot-trained. Thus far, the Greys had been successful in making the transition back to fighting in the field, and they'd done it with old warbot brainies. It was too early yet to begin a new procedure of training Sierra Charlies directly from Basic Training. The hallmark of any military service was simple: If it works, don't change anything unless you do it one step at a time. Too much hung in the balance otherwise. With people's lives at stake, it wasn't a good idea to experiment in an uncontrolled fashion.

So she completely relaxed her body as a first step. Then she began shifting her mental condition from the wide awake, talking, working beta state to the meditative alpha state, being careful to block any tendency to go into theta state which was predominant during learning. This was easy for her. Shifting brain wave patterns could be quickly learned, but she'd had some prior training as a child. Her modern family had retained useful vestiges of the Crow Indian heritage. Among them was the ability to shift attention to the 13-Hertz alpha brain activity from the 8-Hertz beta; this hadn't been understood by the ancient medicine men, but it was not necessary to understand a technology to be able to use it.

She prepared a trap, primed it, and set it to trigger.

Then Dyani began to set up blocks to keep neuroelectronics signals from sending information queries into her deep mind. She shifted to visual and audio modes, the very primitive areas of the brain. Amerindians had no written language until the awesome power of the white people convinced them to develop one; before that, they'd depended upon pictographs and verbal storytelling. So Dyani went deep and began to sing in her mind.

The song was an ancient chant for young warriors taught by her father to his children. Former Captain John Tatoga Motega had sired only two daughters to carry on a family warrior tradition. But in the new world where women could again become warriors, he could teach them the ancient lore and hope they might decide to follow family tradition. They did. Dyani silently recited the chant from memory, using the ancient words of the Crow language. (See Appendix III.)

Dyani also filled her mind with visual images. She saw as a Crow Indian would see. She visualized things as she knew them to be, not as they appeared to be. As the image of her sister rode a horse across her mental field of view, Dyani saw her sister's leg on the off-side of the horse as though in phantom view. For her to visualize it any other way would have been to see her sister with a leg cut off. Although the leg was hidden by the body of the horse, Dyani knew it was there. So, in her mind, she saw it. In her reality, she saw it.

Her arm twitched. She didn't cause it to twitch. Taisha had done so. Dyani allowed it to happen. She was enduring.

Both legs jerked against the bonds. She let them jerk. Her legs were strong, but the bleeding ribbons of her feet caused waves of pain to wash up her legs as the movements abraded them against the table.

"Excellent! Excellent!" Taisha remarked in what was a highly subdued cry of initial victory. "She is easily controllable! She does not fight me as Curt Carson once did. But, again, I have better technology and better equipment now..."

"So you can control her. So what?" Monica Elora asked. "What are you going to do? Put a receiver on her head and turn her into a radio-controlled human robot?"

"I could do so if I wished," Taisha stated. "But I do not have the technology of the American Army's warbots. I would have to spend all my time controlling her. One American warbot soldier can direct up to a dozen warbots. But they won't reveal the technology."

"So? You've got a warbot brainy here," the Prophet's Number Two observed. "Why not try to get that information from her?"

"Because I know the warbot operators are cannon fodder! They aren't told how their warbots operate. They are only trained to operate them," Taisha explained with aloof superiority. Then she appeared to get an idea and added, "But I have never before tried to probe a female warbot soldier. Female minds think differently from male ones. I'm going to try to go in and see what I can find in this woman soldier's mind…"

"Without the AI modules and stacks you said you needed earlier?"

"I will go as far as I can without them. It may not work. It may be dangerous. But I will withdraw before damage is done," Taisha stated. She didn't know what those limits might be, and she knew she might be pushing the edge of the envelope of her own expertise. But she decided to try because a scientist *should* try to go beyond the known into the unknown.

Taisha stripped to the waist and began to don a neuroelectronic linkage harness used to control Westinghouse industrial robots. It was the best available. It was the closest thing she could get to the highly classified General Electric military warbot harnesses used by the Robot Infantry.

She made the final connections to the rack of equipment, sat down, and clenched a pickle switch in her hand. "I'm going into her mind. I will give verbal reports as I do so. The signals in the linkage harness are being recorded. If something happens, this is a dead-man switch and will get me back out of linkage with the woman the instant I release it."

"Doctor, you told me this could be a dangerous thing to do!" Monica Elora recalled. "I don't think you should do it. You could harm either yourself or this woman. If that happens, I'm in very deep trouble with the Prophet!"

"Don't worry," Taisha attempted to reassure her. "I'm the expert here. I know what I'm doing. I've been inside dozens of minds. And in the end, I've controlled them, drained them, and returned the subjects to the real world with attitudes and outlooks acceptable to the group."

Taisha really wasn't a legitimate NE experimenter. And she wasn't totally honest with herself or with the Prophet's wife. In Iran, she'd first attempted to mindwash the Jehorkhim followers of the Imam; she'd succeeded only partially because she'd been able to learn their fears and devils. In the years since, going into a mind and imprinting it had given her only a fifty-fifty success rate. The failures had been spectacular; she'd gotten out with only minor mental damage and some physical trauma that had resulted in her premature aging.

Some warbot brainies had gone through a similar experience when they'd been rapidly de-linked from their warbots in combat, resulting in the traumatic mental shock of being KIA, "killed in action" in their slang. It usually took six months to rehab a KIA victim. In Taisha's case, she'd had no such help, and the results had taken their toll on both her physical appearance and her mental stability.

It had been worse for her victims. They'd died horrible deaths in the inner hell of their own minds, confronting their own personal devils and phobias...and losing. The only alternative to such a living hell was to turn it into a dying hell...and most victims had simply suicided by shutting off their own minds and thus also shutting off their bodies at the same time.

She didn't tell Monica Elora about this part of her background. She'd told no one. Taisha would have been hung or shot in seventeen countries if the word had ever leaked out. Physical murder was indeed murder most foul, but mental murder was more insidious and could never be totally proved.

It wasn't the dangerous technology; all technology was dangerous, including the ancient technology of fire. In the hands of compassionate neuroelectronic rehab professionals working with professional ethics and standards, NE rehab techniques had brought people back from mental hell. In the hands of a person like Rosha Taisha, it could be turned into a death machine capable of besieging a mind until a bloodless death occurred.

Taisha activated the linkage between her harness and that strapped to Dyani.

"Interesting! Interesting!" Taisha reported verbally, not only for her audio recorder, but also to reassure Monica Elora that all was well. "A strong mind! A disciplined mind. A strange mind. I see and hear symbols that I can recognize...but I cannot understand the verbal signals. I cannot even make pattern from them...No known language pattern...Almost a religious chant...Violent religious chant! Visual images make no sense. Surrealistic. Nomadic. Primitive. Barbaric."

Dyani "felt" Taisha's alien presence. She made no effort to block it or resist it.

Taisha didn't understand. She knew the verbal symbols held meaning, but she couldn't squeeze meaning out of them. And they were blocking her further probe into deeper recesses of Dyani's mind. She, saw images, but couldn't make sense of them.

Then, with no warning, everything changed. It all came down around her. Dyani's mind opened before her, and she was confronting a strange warrior that was woman yet man with alien thought patterns she couldn't fathom - except that she knew with sudden fear and terror that these were deadly.

Taisha realized too late that she'd been sucked inside a wily, cunning, vicious; violent, ruthless primitive mind in which the veneer of civilization had instantly and abruptly been stripped away, leaving her to confront the ego that was Dyani Motega. This time the concepts came through loudly and clearly in another chant, blocking out all of Taisha's own thoughts. This time, Dyani chanted the ancient ritual in English:

> *I am the meaning of all things here.*
> *I own this spirit.*
> *I am woman; I create.*
> *I am also warrior; I destroy invaders.*
> *I count coup upon you, invader!*

The weapon that was suddenly there slashed Taisha. She felt her skull open and her mind pour out. She saw a red haze of blood everywhere. She felt the fire of pain engulf her. When she tried to scream, only a vomit of blood came out. When she raised her hands to ward off the weapon, her hands disappeared, and her wrists became spouting fountains of blood.

Taisha knew all this had to be only in her mind, but it had been made so real! She was at the mercy of demons unleashed by this powerful, alien woman of such strength and power.

But Dyani was no demon. She'd become the controller of demons. She'd trapped the Eurasian woman and allowed Taisha's mind to touch her own. In that thought instant, Dyani had seen Taisha's demons of her own mental hell...and unleashed them. Taisha had been in Beijing and Manchuria, and her childhood memories of the blood and violence and death of Chinese soldiers raping, killing, and mutilating her American mother had been buried deep for thirty years but had never left her; she hadn't allowed them to the surface until suddenly they were now released. What she remembered about her mother's slow, painful torture and bloody, lingering death was now happening to her in her own mind.

And it was so long. It took so long. It happened over and over again, and yet Taisha was not permitted to die a bloody death as she was slashed and cut and brutalized. And she could not retreat. She was at the same time terrified and obsessed with what was happening in her mind.

Taisha thought she had no hands, yet she released the dead-man switch with an effort of will that overcame the demons. Self-preservation won out.

But it hadn't won much.

She was only dimly aware that she was in the chair in her laboratory and that both Monica Elora and Captain Vargas were standing anxiously beside her. A cold, wet cloth was on her face. Her hands and wrists were being massaged. And Monica Elora's voice was barely heard.

"Doctor! Doctor? Can you talk? Are you all right? You've been unconscious for six hours. We couldn't pry the dead-man switch from your hand. Captain Vargas finally pulled the plugs on your harness."

"I'm afraid I may have hurt her," the Brazilian mercenary's voice said. "I couldn't de-link her gently. She was catatonic. She was in trouble."

"She's still catatonic," Monica Elora said.

"Rapid de-linkage."

"Oh, my God! Can she be saved?"

"Don't know. Here, let me carry her to the biotech station down on Sub-level Ten. You stay here and release the woman. I'll be back shortly because we may have two casualties on our hands here."

Chapter Twenty-Seven

Curt came awake suddenly because the inside of his regimental OCV was beginning to get warm and he'd started to sweat. It took him a moment to remember where he was. Then he looked at the clock on the wall. It said 0713.

He then knew he was somewhere near Battle Mountain, Nevada. He remembered what had happened yesterday. And then everything suddenly cascaded down upon him. He had a horrible, sinking feeling inside.

"Oh, shit!" was all that he was able to mutter in a soft, bitter growl.

First Lieutenant Hassan Ben Mahmud was sitting quietly at the comm console. On his sleeve was the brassard of the OOD. "Good morning, Colonel. Glad to see you're awake at last," the dark-haired, dark-eyed, incredibly handsome young man said brightly. "The sun is up, the regiment is up, and we're good to go, sir."

"Lieutenant," Curt growled again, "did you read the order book when you came on duty?"

"Yes, sir!"

"Did you see the order that I was to be awakened at oh-five-hundred?" Curt wanted to know.

"Yes, sir!" Hassan didn't act a bit reluctant.

"Then, why the hell didn't you follow my orders, Lieutenant?"

"Because, Colonel, the regimental medical officer entered a countermanding order," Hassan told him and punched it up on the screen. "Major Gydesen wanted you to sleep until you awakened after she gave you that sleeping pill."

"Goddammit!" Curt exploded. "I can't even trust my own people! I told her I didn't want a sleeping pill! And her goddamned order caused me to lose more than two hours! And we won't have enough hours in this day anyway!"

"Yes, sir. But allow me to bring you up to date on the situation," Hassan told him. "Your officers have been up since oh-five-hundred. Your second in command has held a preliminary planning session. Colonel Salley and his Wolfhound staff will be here at oh-eight-hundred. We're ready in all respects for the Wolfhounds, sir. We're also ready to move when you get orders, sir. So, you didn't miss much, Colonel."

Curt thought that this was a hell of a way for a regimental commander to start the day - with his subordinates running the show and the regiment possibly within hours of having to go into a highly unusual combat situation. He got up - and was sorry he hadn't put something on his feet because the dull pain reminded him of their lacerated condition. But he managed to brush past Hassan and stick his head through the left aux hatch.

The sun was up. The day was incredibly bright. The Washington Greys were bivouacked in a grassy valley between two north-south mountain ranges. It reminded him of the valley of the Sanctuary. The regimental vehicles were parked carefully about, making use of cover and defilade.

"Sergeant Major Kester?" Curt yelled.

Someone clambered up the steep stirrups on the rear of the OCV. It was Major Jerry Allen, and he was attired in a full combat gear. "Good morning, Colonel. I'm having chow sent over for you. I can brief you while you're eating."

"To hell with chow! I-" Curt began but was interrupted by Sergeant Major Henry Kester coming up the front stirrup ramp.

"Good morning, sir," Kester said with a quick salute. "I have some hard copy dispatches here to bring you up to speed on the latest developments."

"As I was about to say, to hell with - what do you mean, Allen? Brief me on what? And what the hell dispatches are you talking about, Henry?" Curt started getting his wits together.

"Feeling better today, sir?" Kester asked solicitously. "I made sure the OCV has plenty of hot water so you can shave. If you want a hot shower, it's available over in the biotech area."

"Goddammit, what the hell's going on around here?" Curt wanted to know.

"I'm sure you'll find that we've done things to your satisfaction, Colonel. Why don't you let me brief you while you're shaving and having chow?" Jerry went on firmly.

"Chow can wait-"

"Sir, I'll be happy to shave you if you want," Kester told him. "You've got a pretty heavy stubble there, sir."

Henry had never shaved him in all the years the man had been Curt's right-hand NCO. Curt realized that his regimental sergeant major was tactfully telling him that he should shape up and look as sharp as his troops. And his designated second-in-command was informing him that his team hadn't been lazing around while their regimental commander got a good night's sleep in preparation for what was to come.

Curt looked at the two of them and reached out his hand to Kester. "Give me the hard copy, Henry. I'll read it during chow. Go do what you have to do to ensure that our warbots and equipment and ammo are hot to trot."

"They are, sir."

"That figures. But go do it anyway. Major, get me that chow and come on in. I need to find out what you idiots did while I was drugged by my own medical officer." Curt realized he was being very hard on his-two top men right then. He'd just arrived, so to speak, even after spending a long night in the interrogation session with Hettrick, Carlisle, and that wimp Martinside. Curt hadn't had the steam left afterward to crank himself back into his command.

Hassan hied himself over to Major Ward's staff OCV while Curt shaved, gave himself a sponge bath, and tackled the hot MRE that Sergeant Manny Sanchez brought over from the logistics vans. As he began by plugging in his razor and starting on his stubble, he remarked to Jerry Allen, "Okay, Mister, bring me up to speed fast.

What did you do? Take over the regiment for me?"

"Yes, sir, that's exactly what we did, Colonel. And exactly what my job was. And I don't mind telling you, I'm just happy as all shit to turn this sheep screw back over to you," Jerry told him. "Now I know why you used to bitch and moan when you had the regiment on a temporary basis. I'm not ready for it yet. TACBATT is all I can handle at the moment."

"So, what the hell's been going on? I sure as shit didn't expect to find the Greys here last night." He had to admit to himself that shaving made him feel a little better.

Jerry Allen knew from the way Curt was talking and the harsh soldier phrases he was using that the man was under considerable strain in spite of a good night's sleep. "General Hettrick passed along a Red Alert at oh-eight-ten yesterday, followed by an Oscar briefing at divisional level at oh-nine-hundred because of the receipt of DOD Execute Order Thirty-five dash seventeen dash two. With concurrence of the National Security Council and the Joint Chiefs, the Commander in Chief authorized the Iron Fist to deploy all available regiments to the Battle Mountain area under deep stealth. The Greys were airborne at eleven-ten, followed by the Wolfhounds. We were on the ground here by fifteen-thirty, and the entire regiment was here by nineteen-forty-five. The Cottonbalers are deploying from the Vee-Eye and will be in the Austin area by thirteen-hundred today, I am under strict orders from General Hettrick not to initiate any assault against Sanctuary. On returning command to you, I am instructed to inform you of the unambiguous nature of that order which still stands...damn it!"

Curt finished cleaning up and sat down for breakfast. He really didn't want it. He thought that Dyani sure as hell wasn't eating a good breakfast this morning in Sanctuary. And he caught Jerry's list remark. But he said nothing about it for the moment. "Very well, Mister, what the hell was the planning meeting that I missed out on this morning because my medical officer ordered all of you to let me sleep in?"

"Colonel, we have the latest stereo multi-spectral satellite images accompanied by aerial obliques. The most recent of these was made at oh-three-hundred today." Jerry keyed a terminal, and a series of vertical images of the landscape of Sanctuary came up on several screens. As he continued briefing his regimental commander, the views on the terminals changed at his command. "Our birdbots have scouted the Sanctuary perimeter fence, have identified the type, location, and signatures of all Sanctuary security sensors, and have determined the location of all security communications centers and relays. We have located and identified twenty-seven Sanctuary warbots. They are modified General Robotics and Westinghouse industrial security patrol robots now mounting twenty-five mike-mike and fifty mike-mike cannon. We have seen nothing comparable to our Jeeps or Saucy Cans. Before Sanctuary was isolated at oh-two-fifteen today, we located and identified all landline comm trunks, including optoelectronic cables. We have also located and identified all Sanctuary radar, laser, and infrared sensing and tracking stations which are now under heavy ECM by both the 28th Special Signal Corps Regiment from Wendover and the Aerospace Force.

"At this time, RECONCO is deployed and on watch, keeping the eastern side of Sanctuary under close surveillance," Jerry went on crisply. "ASSAULTCO is at Yellow Alert status and ready to move within fifteen minutes. AIRLIFTCO has all Chippewas fueled and ready to load warbots and Sierra Charlies for possible vertical envelopment. TACAIRCO has all Harpies fueled and armed-up on a ten-minute scramble basis. We can have ASSAULTCO on the ground inside Sanctuary thirty minutes after the go-word is given. TACAIRCO can provide air support of such an operation."

Curt was wolfing down his breakfast as he listened. Although he wouldn't admit to himself that he was hungry, he was. Jerry watched with some relief, recalling Curt's continual advice to him in the past that one should never go into combat without first having a good breakfast. "Okay, we're good to go. I expect that. What the hell was the planning meeting about, Jerry?"

Curt's use of the young major's first name for the first time also wasn't lost on Allen. "Sir, we wanted to get our staff work done so you wouldn't have to worry about it. We've evaluated the situation.

We've considered the defense situation at Sanctuary. We've allocated ordnance to specific targets. We've determined on the basis of surveillance and your verbal report where we want to insert various ASSAULTCO platoons for the maximum effect and the quickest possible resolution of the situation. Colonel Salley's staff has done the same, and we've kept in close communication with his people on this. Therefore, at this time, we have a consolidated and coordinated series of assault scenarios ready for your approval and forwarding to General Hettrick." Jerry smiled. "We've just been doing our homework, Colonel."

Curt glanced quickly at the hard copies Kester had given him.

"The FBI hasn't found the nukes yet," he noticed.

"No, sir, but if they were to be triggered by signals from Sanctuary, we've got ECM laid all over the place like a wet blanket," Jerry explained.

"No word of this has leaked to the press yet, has it?"

"No, sir. I guess some of the people in the town of Battle Mountain know something's going on. Same for Carlin, Winnemucca, and Austin. The official word is this is just another army maneuver. But the Battle Mountain folks aren't buying it. They know too much about Sanctuary, so they know something's up."

"Jesus, I hope they keep their mouths shut," Curt fervently hoped.

"They've got no choice, sir. We cut their communications links, too." Jerry brightened. "And Battleaxe told me to pass the good word along to you."

"The good word? We're going in?"

"Negatory, sir. Not yet, dammit. But Captain Motega is apparently all right. During a live video broadcast by the Prophet at twenty-one-hundred hours last night, her voice was clearly heard and identified in the background yelling that she was all right."

"Goddammit, Major Allen, you waited until now to tell me that?" Curt exploded, standing up suddenly and scattering the remains of the uneaten breakfast over the table and the floor.

"Yes, sir. And please sit down, sir," Jerry told him cooly. "Please, Colonel...Curt."

When Curt did so, Jerry went on, "You don't need to remind us that the Washington Greys never abandon their own. You taught me that. And I needed to let you know right up front today that the Washington Greys have busted their asses so that we're all high and tight, real tactical, and good to go. But will you please just listen to someone who's your student, your subordinate, your colleague, and your friend?"

"Major, this is no time for man to man-" Curt began.

"I think it is. Everyone in the regiment is more worried about you than about Dyani," Jerry told him frankly.

"What?"

"Dyani is a great lady, a brave and valiant soldier, and a damned strong person," Jerry said respectfully, knowing that he was walking on the edge of insubordination if his commanding officer was really too far stressed-out. But he believed he had to do this. "When Alexis Morgan resigned, Adonica found herself in the big sister position Alexis used to hold in their relationship. Dyani and Adonica have established that sister relationship. So, Adonica probably knows Dyani better than any other woman in the Greys."

"What the hell has this got to do with-?"

"Please, Curt, let me go on. The fact that Dyani is alive in Sanctuary means to Adonica that Dyani will not give in to those bastards. And Sergeant Edie Sampson knows that bitch Taisha, too," Jerry reminded him. "Both Adonica and Edie don't think Taisha can hurt Dyani. Maybe the Keeper of the Faith can, but Ruth Gydesen doesn't think a sado like him could possibly handle the sort of violence Dyani is capable of dishing out."

"Okay, I know the lady. I'll buy that," Curt admitted.

Jerry nodded. "Now, we've been through a lot of sheep screws where our ladies have been in deep shit...and they behaved much better than we did! And, as you know, you've lectured me loud and long about maintaining a very close personal relationship with a lady of the Greys. As a result, Adonica and I have worked out the snags and hitches that might come up when one of us finds ourselves in deep slime…or maybe even gone and gotten ourselves killed. It hasn't been easy. But you've goaded the living shit out of us about it, so we've done it." Jerry paused.

This gave Curt the opportunity to recover from the shock of being given a friendly lecture by a subordinate who was also a very close personal friend. "And are you telling me that I haven't? If you are, you're right."

"You haven't had a colonel on your back the way Adonica and I have," Jerry told him bluntly.

"As I just said, you're right, my friend."

"So you did."

"And you and Adonica have worked it through?"

"Yes."

"Care to give some solicited advice, then? To a friend?"

Jerry thought a moment, then went on. "That's what I set out to do just now when I put my head in the lion's mouth. First of all, Curt, don't blame yourself for anything that might happen. Realize this is part of the warrior's life that all of us voluntarily accepted and live with. Death may be involved, too. But also realize that you aren't Dyani's keeper any more than you're the keeper of the Washington Greys. Adonica knows Dyani, and Dyani doesn't do anything unwillingly…sometimes not even after a good fight."

"Tell me about it," Curt suddenly said, a flood of memories coming back to him.

"Gee, it's nice to realize that other people have spats, too."

"Like the one you and Adonica had on Sakhalin."

"Which required a direct order from our regimental commander so we could get it worked out," Jerry recalled. Then he sighed. "Look, no question exists in the minds of anyone in the Washington Greys about the nature of the relationship between you and Dyani. It's far deeper and stronger than the one that once existed between you and

Alexis Morgan."

"Yeah, Jerry, it is, and I don't know why," Curt said.

"As a man who's been there and is still there, I can sure as hell tell you. As cadets, we beanies chased the beanettes or the town girls, and we got our gonads in an uproar. But we never progressed to more than what I now know was puppy love."

"Hell, Jerry, you know that I had a hot one going with that nordic goddess, Frederica," Curt objected.

"And on the basis of what you know today, was it the real thing? I doubt it! Curt, you and Dyani found the real stuff! Want to know one of the reasons the high brass gets all bent out of shape about women in the military, especially in combat positions? You sure as hell know now, don't you? Or do I have to draw you a picture?"

"No, you don't. But I'm still damned well going to go into Sanctuary. I'm going to get Calder for selling out, using terrorism, and leading us into that mess. And I'm going to get Dyani out," Curt vowed.

"We all are. Only a direct order is keeping us out right now. But I agree with you; we'll have to go in there and do it. Probably, hopefully, today. We're ready. We've done the planning, as you'll see shortly." Jerry paused. "But I'm willing to bet we'll run into Dyani fighting her way out."

Chapter Twenty-Eight

Dr. Clark Jeremy Mathys was furious. "Gordon, you'd better have a very good reason for waking me up at this hour and interrupting my rest!" It was obvious that the Prophet hadn't been resting. Or sleeping. His Primary Wife, Sarah Carmichael Mathys, was with him, dressed in a flowing red silk peignoir with her long blond hair in disarray. The Prophet himself was hardly dressed for a full conference, even in the luxurious privacy of his own living quarters in Sub-Sanctuary. What the acolytes didn't know was that Mathys and his Number One Wife hadn't been alone. Two young proto-acolytes and Number Six Wife were still in the sleeping quarters. It had been a fine orgy, and Mathys had both enjoyed the erotic stimulation of voyeurism as well as a wide choice of partners and activities. He felt that the growing stress of the situation warranted his recreational excess.

"Prophet, you'll have to be your own judge of that," the Tabernacle's chief engineer and Director of Technology told the religious leader.
"I thought it was important enough to be of concern to you."

"Well?" Mathys asked when Gordon Palmer paused.

"Sanctuary has been cut off."

"What do you mean?" Sarah Carmichael Mathys snapped. She was vexed at having a very pleasurable early morning episode broken off at what she considered just the wrong time. These techies were beginning to get on her nerves. She really didn't understand them or what they did. She only knew that their services were vital to maintaining her comfort and achieving her husband's goals. Otherwise, she would have done without them.

"During the night, our landline and microwave communications links with the outside world were disrupted," Palmer explained. He was an older man who was nevertheless full of the frustrations of a brilliant engineer whose ideas, concepts, and proposals had fallen on too many overly conservative ears. He was a good technical man and an outstanding manager, but he'd never really been able to work on what he wanted. He believed he'd piddled away his career on mundane technical tasks that hadn't made a hill of beans difference in the world. Now he'd left his fiftieth birthday behind him and realized he was playing in the second and last half of his life. He'd always had the dream of making the world a better place; he'd joined Mathys Tabernacle only because Mathys had promised him the freedom Palmer desired. His arrangement with the Prophet meant that Palmer didn't have to be a true believer, only loyal to Mathys. As for the Prophet, Mathys knew that most techies of the sort he needed to do what he wanted wouldn't necessarily subscribe to the, Tabernacle's doctrines. (But he was surprised at the number who did; some techies apparently needed a religion in spite of their supposedly objective world view.)

"Furthermore, all our satellite links appear to be inoperable, even the jam-proof laser beams," Palmer continued in a frustrated tone. It was apparent that he'd tried to locate the source of the trouble and had been unable to do so. "We can't access our satellite transponders, and we're unable to pick up downlink signals. It's as if the beams were being blocked."

"Impossible!" Mathys snorted. He uncrossed his legs, arose from the pillowed couch, and began to pace the parlor of his quarters. Stopping at the wet bar, he poured himself a cup of coffee and laced it with Irish whiskey. "Laser beams can't be detected off-axis; no side lobes. And they can't be jammed."

"They can be and have been interrupted, Prophet," General Stephen Calder put in. This was a full Tabernacle staff meeting with all the acolytes present. It was rather unusual to hold such a meeting in the Prophet's palatial private digs, but this was an unusual situation. "My guess is that the Aerospace Force sortied Black Star deep space cutters from LaGrange Five and simply stationed them between our sats and the Earth. A laser comm beam is pencil-thin, so it wouldn't take a very large vehicle."

"I knew it! I prophesied this! The Nibiruans are behind this!

General, why didn't you take steps to defend and protect Tabernacle property and capabilities?" Mathys exploded, hoping to lay the blame on someone but not realizing at that instant that Calder was going to be one of his indispensable people in the hours and days to come.

"Prophet, I was given specific orders by you - and I have hard copies in secure places," Calder fired back without apparent rancor. It didn't pay to irritate the Prophet. On the other hand, Calder always knew he'd have to cover his ass by requesting, duping, and sequestering hard copy orders from the Prophet. Not that said orders would really cover *all* his anatomy if things went to slime, but the knowledge of their existence might create enough of a delay to allow him to get out and away from ground zero. "Those orders told me to concentrate on the defense of Sanctuary by organizing a purely defensive security force. I was told that any perceived offensive capability would cause premature triggering of Nibiruan retaliation. In short, we had to play the security game without drawing attention to ourselves. You told me that developing a military space capability would be perceived as an offensive act and that our satellite assets were protected by international law. So, the Host of Michael is organized exactly and precisely according to your directives, Prophet."

Before Mathys could react and perhaps retaliate against him, Calder went on, "But that's the least of our problems. We've got others that are very close to home. Sanctuary was put under a heavy lid of ECM during the night."

"Talk English!" Mathys snapped.

"Electromagnetic Counter Measures," Calder explained.

"What are those?"

"Let me put it this way, Prophet," Calder told his boss. "Our radar units send out a pulse and it disappears. Just seems to get sucked into nothingness. No return whatsoever, not even ground clutter beyond two clicks. We're even running with the AGC and gain wide open, and we see no returns. Same with lidar; no reflections. We send out laser illuminating signals and try to work secondary lidar, and we get no reflections beyond the fence. And our infrared sensors tell us that there's nothing beyond the fence but a black hole at absolute zero temperature."

"Man, that takes power and more high-tech than I'd like to think about," Gordon Palmer muttered.

"Yeah, Gordy, but it's do-able" was the remark of Todd Cartwright, chief engineer of the S.S. *Archangel Gabriel*, a technie who was no slouch himself when it came to the highest of high-tech know-how. "It would take a lot of hardware and software, but it's do-able."

"That's what I said," Palmer reiterated.

"Nibiruan technology?" Mathys suddenly wondered.

Palmer and Cartwright didn't hold with the Prophet's doctrines. To the two of them, there were no extraterrestrial Anunnaki or Nibiruans, no beam ships, no galactic civilization. Insofar as they were concerned, the highest of high-tech was human, not alien.

"Not likely," Palmer guessed.

"The technology is available," Cartwright added.

"Why didn't we buy it? Why don't we have it, too?" Mathys asked.

"We probably could have established effective counter-countermeasures, Prophet, but it would have been very expensive," said Jasper Lyell, the financial wizard who ran the Tabernacle's money machine. He stroked his short black beard away from his mouth and added, "I felt that the general and Gordon were probably right in their early assessment of the threat. However, I thought their recommendations were far too expensive for our resources and cash flow at the time. I'd planned to recommend acquiring the equipment when our financial position justified the expenditure."

"Dammit, Jasper, if more money was needed, you should have told me!" Mathys snarled. "I can raise money. I can raise any amount of money you want! All I have to do is get on camera and give the world my message. The money pours in when I ask for it. And you know damned good and well I can do it. You should have told me!"

Lyell didn't argue. It didn't pay. The CEO of the Galactic Tabernacle of the Human Future held the purse strings. He had the real power. And Lyell wasn't stupid enough to deny the Prophet pocket change for toys, whims, and women. Jasper Lyell wasn't about to shear the Golden Fleece or kill the goose that could lay golden eggs on demand. Lyell was no real believer in anything except "the long green stuff with the short future," as he joked about money from time to time with acolytes other than the Prophet. This didn't prevent him from having his own stash in the banks of Bahrain and Brunei - and in several dummy investment corporations. The fountain wouldn't flow freely forever, and Lyell knew that things change. So, he'd set up his Golden Landing Mat against the time that would happen. It looked to him as though this was the time. He wanted out and was looking for a way to do it. "Prophet, it's a matter of priorities. And the *Archangel Gabriel* was your first priority. A laser-powered spaceship hasn't been the cheapest thing in the world to develop. Would have been cheaper to go with ordinary chemical rockets, I'm told."

"Yes, but the requirements demanded a propellant source that couldn't be cut off," Cartwright reminded him. "Catalyst propellants are difficult to make, and we don't own or can't buy the only companies that can make them-"

Lyell held up his hand. "Spare me the sordid technical details again, Todd. We've been over that ground before."

Mathys came back, sat down, crossed his legs, and sipped his coffee. "Okay, let's stick to the immediate matters. Calder, are the Sanctuary perimeter defenses secure?"

"From the fence inward, yes. We just can't look out."

"Is this ECM action and communications isolation the preliminary to a military assault on Sanctuary?"

"I have to treat it that way, Prophet."

"Okay, seal Sanctuary. No one comes in or goes out without my specific approval in each case." Mathys paused and then asked, "Can you stop the attack if it occurs?"

"Yes, sir, we're configured for that. But as I've told you, the length of time we can hold out depends upon the level of the attack and how long it continues. Any defensive position can be overrun by any attacker willing to pay the price," Calder reminded him of a military verity. "But I'll make their first assault so expensive that they'll rethink their course of action. Their assault can't be kept secret once they unleash it. So, I'm counting on American public opinion to prevent them from destroying a religious center."

"Well, when they initiate their attack, I'll give you the signal to trigger the nukes," Mathys told his military chief.

Stephen Calder answered, "Prophet, with the outgoing comm links down and all the ECM laid on us, those cement cars will just sit on those sidings and maybe bubble down to the point where they can be opened in a couple of hundred years or so...and provide some entrepreneur with a Golconda of nuclear waste to reprocess."

"What? And you didn't work out an alternative plan to trigger them?" Mathys was astounded.

"Yes, sir," Calder put in. "But, as you know, it requires killing our own people to do it."

"And did you plan for such a contingency, General Calder?"

"Yes, yes. If I can get my standby kamikaze nuke triggering unit out of here and into position, they'll trigger them by hand."

"Do it," the Prophet ordered brusquely.

"Yes, sir." Calder really didn't trust his standby kamikaze force. It was manned by members of the Host of Michael who were also Tabernacle religious fanatics, willing to give their lives for The Cause. Such soldier fanatics were notoriously unreliable and had to be carefully watched and guarded because they were loose cannons in a military organization. And some of them wouldn't perform when it came time for the final act. Even when the Japanese used kamikaze pilots during World War II, some of them chickened out when they were airborne; the fact that they were locked in their bomb-laden airplanes and couldn't abort didn't deter some of them from heading for the Soviet Union where they would land and be interned. And live. The world never heard about them again, of course. "But at this point, Prophet, with our outgoing signals capability down, your threat may have lost its credibility."

"So? They think I can't trigger my nukes? Send one of your teams to Las Vegas right away. Get them there. If you can't fly them out, drive them out through Austin." Mathys snapped the order

Calder merely said, "Yes, sir." And tried to figure out a way to get a kamikaze bomb squad out under the command of someone he could trust, like Colonel Helmuth von Kampf. He couldn't really spare von Kampf. In fact, Calder was short of nearly everything, including time. He hadn't figured that the Host of Michael would be called upon for an all-out defense of Sanctuary for at least another two months. Todd Cartwright had kept him advised of the progress on the Gabriel, and the ship was at least sixty days from full completion. As a result, Calder's planning was behind the power curve. He wasn't up to what he considered to be a full capability to withstand a siege. But he didn't dare say so. Like many people, he had a tendency to put off until next week what he should have done today because there was no real pressure to get it done right away. And, like many military commanders in the past, he found himself suddenly facing combat action with a shortage of everything.

The Prophet of the Galactic Tabernacle of the Human Future then turned to his chief engineer. "Gordon, I want you to send the enemy a signal that I wish to deliver a message to them. When I can talk to them, I'll warn them to remove their ECM or Las Vegas will be nuked immediately as proof that we can do such a thing, communications blackout or not! If they won't talk right away, the Las Vegas bomb will be detonated as a show of force and intent. And then they'll talk for certain!"

Gordon Palmer reacted differently to Mathys orders. He'd known of the construction of the primitive U-235 gun bombs, and he'd opted out of any responsibilities for them by fobbing the job off on Calder and Cartwright. Regardless, he'd never really believed that Mathys would go through with his nuking threat. Palmer was unhappy working on weapons, especially weapons of mass destruction. So he said, "Yes, sir. I can try to get the word out. But, Prophet, I want to know something. If you nuke Las Vegas without warning, are you willing to live with the blood of a million people on your hands?"

"That's the concern of those evil minions of the Nibiruans who initiated the siege of Sanctuary today! If a million people in Las Vegas die in nuclear hell as a result, their real killers are those humans who chose the side of Nibiruan darkness rather than the Anunnaki way of the light! Nothing must stop me! And I will allow nothing or no one to stop me! The Anunnaki have told me to forge ahead on our holy mission in spite of all resistance to the truth!" Mathys eyes blazed. Palmer had seen that look before. The Prophet had gone over the edge again.

"I'll get the word out," Palmer promised. "I may have to tie the message to a rock and throw it over the fence to do it."

"Take it out yourself if you have to! Just get it out!" Mathys would later rue that order which he'd made in the heat of emotion. As a paranoid, the actions of the United States government had shoved him all the way over into near irrationality. Furthermore, he'd whipped himself up into a frenzy just as he did for the violent sermons he delivered to the innermost of his most dedicated acolytes to keep them fired up.

"Cartwright! How close are you to being able to launch the *Archangel Gabriel*?" Mathys wanted to know.

"Sir, we're doing final installation on the attitude and flight control systems now," the spaceship's engineer reported. "But several shipments of nanoelectronics haven't arrived. They were delayed in shipment because of extended nonpayment of prior invoices."

"Can we launch?"

Cartwright shook his head. "No, sir."

"You said that only minor control systems weren't completed. Can you cannibalize any equipment here in Sanctuary to complete the job?" Mathys background as a planetary astronomer had required him to know enough about control systems technology to be able to build or fix lash-up systems on telescopes and remote unmanned spacecraft. Mathys was not a techie, but as a former scientist he'd had to get his hands into the hardware when no one else was available to do it.

"I can try. Henry VanDerCamp has already gotten some stuff from Dr. Taisha's lab."

That reminded Mathys. "Where's that woman you captured yesterday, Calder?"

"I had Colonel DeVille take her to Dr. Taisha's lab last night, Prophet."

"Have you gotten a report back? Where is she? And where's Monica Elora?"

"Still there, probably."

Sarah Carmichael Mathys stood up. "I'll go look into the matter, Clark. You sent Monica Elora along to protect that woman, but I noticed that the Keeper of the Faith didn't show up for the meeting here. I think I'd better find out what's going on up there." She walked toward a door and was gone. She didn't ask for an armed escort. No one in Sanctuary would dare lay a hand on the Primary Wife of the Prophet...

Chapter Twenty-Nine

Colonel Curt Carson had to admit to himself that he was impressed.

Remembering his own principles of leadership, he voiced his opinion to his subordinates. "Damned good work! Very nice! But you haven't left a whole hell of a lot for me to do."

"Except convince Battleaxe, General Carlisle, and the White House to turn us loose, sir," Captain Kitsy Clinton said. "Which should be only an incidental task for you, considering what you've been able to accomplish in the past."

"Yeah, I'm Super-Colonel," Curt remarked bitterly, recalling the halcyon time a few days ago. He sighed and tried to regain his perspective by quipping, "Flattery will get you anything, Captain. Keep talking."

"In that case, Colonel, I-" Kitsy began.

Curt held up his hand. "I shouldn't have said that. Captain, you often take things literally."

"Sir, I was taught by you to obey orders to the letter."

"Yes, I know. And above and beyond, if necessary, in order to do what was required or desired," Curt remarked. "Did you coordinate this with the Wolfhounds?"

"Yes, sir," Jerry Allen replied smartly. "All done by telecommunications. And we even contacted the Cottonbalers CO and staff while they were airborne. They'll be on the ground in Austin a hundred and forty klicks south of here in a few hours."

"The Cottonbalers can put the plug into Sanctuary's south end at Dixie Valley and be prepared to move north into Sanctuary as a diversion or even to provide a reserve force," Major Russ Frazier added.

And Captain Bill Ritscher put in, "They're fresh from the Vee-Eye and eager as all hell to get their first action as Sierra Charlies after a long tour in Chad and subsequent rejuvenation and retraining in the Vee-Eye."

Curt liked the way his people worked together to organize the operation. It was a closely coordinated combined arms assault that involved two Sierra Charlie regiments with a third as a reserve. It was fast, simple, and surgical. He couldn't have done better himself if he'd tried. However, he'd been getting much needed rest last night when this was done, and now he didn't begrudge the fact that Major Ruth Gydesen had slipped the sleepy to him.

But even after a good night's rest without dreaming, Curt still felt empty inside in spite of the fact that Dyani Motega had been heard from however briefly.

"I like the way you've concentrated forces on the Host of Michael command center," Curt remarked, studying the ops plan displayed by Georgie on the tactical board of his OCV. "And on the airport facilities along the edge of the alkali flat. But why the hell are you leaving the silo to the Wolfhounds?"

"We're not, sir. And Colonel Salley's Wolfers want to stay clear of it, too," Major Joan Ward pointed out.

"Why?"

"We don't know what the ship uses for propellants," Jerry explained. "If it's one of the catalyst propellants, we don't have the hazmat equipment to get near that crap. So, we'd better stay clear."

"On the other hand, Colonel," said Major Ellie Aarts, commander of RECONCO, "I don't think they're using cat propellants. They've got a hell of a lot of electrical power coming into the valley from the north. They don't need all the kilowatt-hour capability inherent in the size and number of the incoming power lines. I think they may have a laser-powered rocket in that silo."

"Laser-powered?" Captain Bill Ritscher asked. "A laser just puts out a whoping powerful light beam-"

"Hell, Bill, think of a laser beam as beamed *energy*," Major Cal Worsham rasped, speaking as he normally did in sentences punctuated with explosively emphasized words. It was just Cal Worsham's way of talking. Some Greys thought the man had lost too much hearing from flying Aerodynes too long without ear protection. Others knew that Cal Worsham was just one rough sonofabitch who talked loud and mean but was really a teddy bear when you got to know him. At least, the ladies of the Greys said so. "The tech-weenies say they could *transmit* enough laser energy from ground-based stations to keep *any* aircraft aloft at multi-mach speeds...*Except* us pilots will *not* strap on a flying machine that's *dependent* upon a *continual* input of ground-based power. *Damned* if I want to suddenly find *myself* flat on my back at ten *thousand* meters, *nothing* between me and the *ground* but a thin Chippie and *no way* to get power back. *Thank you*, I'll fly things that have *self-contained* power! And it's my big pink body in the damned thing, after all!"

"If it's laser-powered," Jerry mused, calling upon his encyclopedic memory, "then they've got a humping big mother of a terawatt-plus laser in the bottom of that hole. The beam energy vaporizes solid propellant in the ass end of the ship, and that creates hot gas for thrust. Maybe that's why they put it all in the hole in the first place. Easier to include some laser-focusing equipment for use after the bird comes out of there..."

"We don't have to know how it works, Jerry," Kitsy reminded him. "It's not our job to romp all over Aerospace Force turf. If the Commander in Chief wants that spaceship shot down - and I don't know why he'd order that if it's got people aboard - then it's the sort of thing the Aerospace Force will have to wrestle with. I don't know a damned thing about stopping or shooting down spaceships. But we might be able to stop the launch real easy."

"I know," Jerry snapped. "You want to cut the power lines coming into Sanctuary."

"Damned right! Put the bastards in the dark, Jerry," Kitsy maintained. "Why give them any energy source they might be able to use against us somehow?"

"They're not supermen," Curt told all of them, calling on his experiences inside Sanctuary yesterday and recalling the people he'd met. "In fact, they're not even very well organized. Too much internal politics. Besides, Calder told me they've got their own internal power sources. Lots of hot springs around here; geothermal energy is for the asking. And he said they've got some cold fusion reactors. But I think the Wolfhounds ought to take out the power lines anyway."

"I could do the job real fast with one salvo from the Saucy Cans," Bill Ritscher announced. "Take out one set of towers. Ought to be a good fireworks show when we cut or short that much electrical energy."

"Better let them know up at the Valmy power plant and switching station," Sergeant Edie Sampson advised. "If our assault causes a major load to be dropped suddenly or some big short develops, the system could experience a ripple effect and black out the whole northern part of Nevada."

"Good idea, Sarge," Major Hensley Atkinson, the Greys' G-3, observed, making a note. "I'll take care of it."

"If they've got terawatts of electrical power available underground to use in launching that spaceship, all hell could break loose if something went wrong in that hole," Ellie Aarts guessed.

"Not our worry," Curt told her. "This is a good plan. We'll stay the hell away from that launch silo unless we absolutely have to go in there."

He leaned forward and looked carefully at the ops plan display. "But you missed something."

"What's that, Colonel?" Jerry wanted to know.

Curt stabbed his finger into the hologram at the location labelled "Copper Canyon Mine." He explained carefully, "Taisha's lab is within a hundred meters of the second level underneath that old mine. The shaft is being used as an emergency exit from Sub-Sanctuary. That's where Captain Motega and I came out. So that's where I go back in with a hand-picked force of Greys like we did at Casa Fantasma. Taisha has a detention facility near her lab down there. I don't know for sure, but I'll bet the FBI man and the Nevada state troopers are being held there. So, add Copper Canyon Companion Force to the ops plan, Major Allen. I'm going in there leading ten picked volunteers."

"Uh, sir, the regiment-" Jerry began.

"Major, we've been in enough lethal sheep screws together that you ought to know damned well by this time of the truth of Sergeant Kester's principle: *No tactical plan survives the first contact.* All of us know what has to be done and what to do, regardless of what happens. After the first mad minute, any fight takes on a flow of its own. That happened in Operation Iron Fist and on Sakhalin. I ended up just standing around watching it happen and cheering everyone on. So, this time I'm going to go into Sub-Sanctuary and get our people out. *Verstehen sie? Comprehende?*"

"Uh, Colonel," Jerry started to say, "if you recall our conversation earlier today-"

"I do, Major. I do indeed," Curt told him.

"Then you'll agree that Battleaxe may not buy off on that, Colonel," Jerry added.

"Battleaxe will buy off on it," Curt assured him. "Put it in the ops plan. And, by the way, what's the code for this plan?"

Curt sensed at once that his staff and officers had some reluctance to tell him. In fact, Kitsy stifled a snicker.

"Well?"

"Uh, Colonel," Sergeant Major Edie Sampson, the chief technical NCO for the regiment, replied, trying to keep a straight face, "as you know, we're strapped with the order to allow our divisional megacomputer to select random names for operations in order to maintain security-"

"Dammit, Sampson, what's either so goddamned funny or so stupid about what Georgie decided to call this operation?" Curt wanted to know.

"Sir, I tried to get him to change it, but Georgie has gotten damned stubborn since the upgrade a year or so ago," Edie explained. "He insists that this is Operation Blood Siege."

"Sounds like we're protecting the Red Cross against rampaging bands of anemia victims," Curt admitted, a bit amused himself. Computers often acted as though they had little minds of their own, and this was one of those times.

"Or those stupid damned shoot 'em up blood-and-guts war novels and comic books Nick Gerard reads," Kitsy added, then giggled. "Sorry, Colonel, but if this is the silicon logic that Georgie has fallen into, is our next mission going to be called Operation Glory Guts?"

Military humor was sometimes almost adolescent in nature and often didn't seem like humor to nonmilitary people. Often it was merely a way to release tension. Other times, it helped military people maintain their sense of perspective in a world of death and destruction that often seemed completely mad. As Curt knew, some of the funniest situations he'd ever encountered had occurred in the deadly melee of combat. In all cases, he knew that humor kept people from becoming self-important zealots. Like the humorless Dr. Clark Jeremy Mathys had become, Curt thought savagely.

"Well," Curt admitted, "in case you didn't spot it, there is indeed a bit of bad blood here. It's between me and 'General' Stephen B. Calder who used to be one of us. I can live with the fact that he went mercenary. But then he became a merc who took a job where it was probable he might have to fight his own regiment. Then I found out he'd stooped to terrorism. This operation isn't going to be a siege, but there's blood involved. Not the kind of blood that gets splattered all over the pages of Nick Gerard's war novels. The kind of blood that makes me want to order a black burgee to be flown from the regimental colors. This sonofabitch who turned terrorist was once one of us..."

Silence fell over the interior of Curt's ACV for a moment. Then Kitsy piped up seriously, "Why haven't you done so, Colonel?"

"Colonel, I believe I could find a piece of cloth that would make a temporary black burgee," Major Russ Frazier growled.

Second Lieutenant Larry Hall, a new platoon leader in Captain Bill Ritscher's GUNCO, piped up, "Sir, I don't know if a vote of your officers and lead NCOs would count here, but I'd like to call for such a vote and fly that black burgee. It will motivate all of us to perform so well and honorably in Operation Blood Siege that we can remove that stain from our regimental history."

Hall's first sergeant, Forrey Barnes, who'd earned his Purple Heart on Sakhalin, said quietly, "Lieutenant, I'm pleased they're still teaching the importance of honor and tradition at West Point."

His company commander, wounded in Brunei, spoke up, "So move!"

"Second," was the quite word from First Sergeant Tracy Dillon, who'd earned his Purple Heart the hard way in Namibia.

"Dammit, Dillon, I outrank you, so I get to second it!" Kitsy Clinton told him.

"Yes, ma'am, but I got my Purple Heart before you did, ma'am."

"Only because I wasn't there with you when you did, Sergeant."

"Colonel," Edie Sampson announced from her position by the comm consoles, "Colonel Salley and the Wolfhound staff have arrived. You and your staff are to report ASAP to the Battleaxe OCV."

Without further discussion, Curt said to his adjutant, "Affix the burgee at once, Major Gratton. Regimental staff, let's go. The rest of you, make sure you're good to go on this ops plan."

"One item, Colonel," Jerry remarked quickly. "Copper Canyon Companion Force. Who do you want to volunteer?"

"Dammit, Jerry, I meant it when I said volunteers. I never 'volunteer' anyone in the Washington Greys! That's for the chicken-shit warbot brainy outfits!" Curt exploded. "I want ten volunteers. Sort it out among yourselves. Jerry, you're in charge of giving me ten names for my approval when I get back from this headquarters bash."

"Yes, sir. Sorry, sir. Will do, sir." Jerry knew that his regimental commander was still up tight in spite of what they'd talked about earlier. He wondered how he'd act in a similar situation. He hoped that he'd never have to face it.

Major Jerry Allen knew better than anyone else in the Washington Greys just what Colonel Curt Carson was laboring under at the moment.

Chapter Thirty

"Monica Elora, would you please unstrap my restraints?" Dyani asked the Prophet's Number Two Wife.

"No. You're a violent woman. You're so strong you could do anything to me," Monica Elora Mathys replied. She wasn't a very large girl. And she was young, a soft-faced nubile teenager in appearance. "I'll wait until Captain Vargas comes back."

"Why would I want to hurt you? You haven't done anything to me," Dyani pointed out with cool logic. "I have to go to the bathroom. I don't want to make a mess on the table. We'll both have to live with it for a while if I do."

"I shouldn't set you loose." Monica Elora was deathly afraid of Dyani. But Monica Elora Mathys was afraid of nearly everyone.

"The Prophet told you to make sure I wasn't harmed. He told Captain Vargas to look out for my well-being," Dyani reminded her gently. "Captain Vargas isn't here, so his job is your responsibility now."

Monica Elora shook her head. "No, it isn't."

"Do you want to take the chance that your husband doesn't think so?"

The Prophet's young wife hesitated, then asked, "You promise you won't hurt me?"

"I'm an officer of the United States Army. I give you my word of honor that I won't hurt you," Dyani told her truthfully, fully intending to do as she promised. But she hadn't promised that she wouldn't try to escape.

Monica Elora was quite a naive young woman, and she really didn't understand about such things. But Dyani seemed sincere. So, she wordlessly began undoing the straps of the cuffs around Dyani's wrists and ankles. As she did so, she asked, "You're an officer in the

Army?"

"Yes, I am."

"I've never met a woman officer before. I always thought war was something that men do."

"It took women a long time to get combat assignments alongside men," Dyani pointed out as she rubbed her freed wrists. "It's the ultimate in sexual equality, Monica Elora. We have the right to fight. We have the right to do what it says in our national anthem: to place ourselves between our 'loved homes and the war's desolation.'"

Monica Elora seemed confused as she unstrapped Dyani's ankles. "But isn't the right to fight the right to win nothing? War isn't a triumph. War is failure. It's the ultimate wasteland."

Free at last as she slid off the table and stood up, Dyani asked, "Is that the bathroom over here?"

"Yes. Please keep the door open so I can make sure you aren't up to something that might hurt me."

"Monica Elora, I gave you my word. But let me ask you something: Would you fight to preserve what you believe in? To protect the Tabernacle and the Prophet?"

"I don't know. I've never thought about it. But it seems to me that the equal right to die is worthless compared to the right to share in life's glories."

Dyani had heard this philosophy before from school-mates who thought freedom and liberty were God-given rights that no one would take away from them, things they deserved because they were entitled to them. "Sometimes you have to fight because you have no other option, Monica Elora. Not everyone likes to fight. That's why our country has an army of people like me. I don't like to fight, but know I have to do it for everyone else."

"You're strange. Weird. What's your real name?"

"Dyani Motega."

"Mexican?"

"No. Crow Indian."

"Oh. You don't look like an Indian."

"What's an Indian supposed to look like?"

"I don't know, Diane. You don't look any different than me. Except you've got a beautiful suntan." Monica Elora was apparently kept indoors and out of the sun; her skin was fair and pasty white.

"I'm Dyani, not Diane. My name means 'deer.' I do indeed have a suntan. I got it at Lake Tahoe before I came here." Dyani knew that she was gaining the confidence of this young woman who had probably never experienced real freedom. Dyani somehow felt sorry for her, a poor little sex toy who'd never gotten an education and whose mind had been warped by the religious teachings of the mad Prophet.

While in the bathroom, Dyani took the opportunity to wash up and give herself a brief sponge bath with a damp towel as combat soldiers learned to do in the field, quickly cleaning specific nooks and crannies of her body in a minimum of time with the minimum of equipment and water. Her feet were caked with dried blood, and they still hurt; but she merely cleaned them up. She knew they'd heal.

Monica Elora watched with fascination. "I've never seen anyone wash up like that before. I love baths. When Dr. Taisha tells me it's all right to take you up to the Prophet's wives' quarters, I'll let you take a real bath."

"Thank you. But I don't think Dr. Taisha will be coming back," Dyani revealed.

"Oh? Why? What happened to her?"

"She tried her mindwashing technique on the wrong woman."

"What do you mean?"

"It backfired on her, Monica Elora," Dyani tried to explain but didn't go into details on how she'd lured Taisha into her trained bi-cultural warbot brainy's mind and then unleashed Taisha's own bi-cultural mind with all its buried horrors. Now Dyani was looking to escape, perhaps out the same route as before. This time, once she got out, she wouldn't get caught. She'd lie hidden on Battle Mountain until the Washington Greys showed up or an open opportunity to get out presented itself. So, she suggested, "All right, let's go up to your quarters. I'd like to see where you live."

"I haven't been ordered to take you there yet."

"Does the Prophet have, to order you to do everything?"

"Uh, no, but...but you'll try to escape. And the Prophet doesn't want you to escape. He told me he wants to take you with us on the *Archangel Gabriel* when we leave in a few weeks."

"Tell me about what the Prophet intends to do with this spaceship, Monica Elora." Dyani saw an opportunity to gather some intelligence data.

"We're going to fly out to the asteroid belt. We're going to build Star Base One. Then the Anunnaki will come to get us in their beam ships and take us to the stars with them. We'll help them fight the evil Nibiruans."

"You just told me that you think war is failure, the ultimate wasteland," Dyani reminded her, tidying up her shirt and jeans. She wouldn't be able to wash them, but at least she could get some of the dirt off them.

"Uh...but this isn't war between people. This is war against real evil. Besides, we're going to build a new civilization out there. All of us will have to have a lot of babies, and I love babies. I can't wait to have a baby. A lot of them!" Monica Elora suddenly bubbled. "We're taking sixty women and only six men, you know. And a very large sperm and ovum bank so we don't end up, like, you know, brothers and sisters having to mate..."

This crazy Prophet was going to take his licentious crew and their male-dominated doctrine along with him, Dyani surmised. And it was totally repugnant to her. It didn't fit with the strict code of morality that her father had so strongly impressed on her and her sister.

These people, Dyani suddenly realized, were modern anti-intellectuals. They were maybe one of the first groups of back-to-nature romantics of this century. Every century seemed to have them - the hippies of the twentieth century, the "shepherds and maidens" of the nineteenth, and probably others in earlier centuries that she didn't know about. They wanted out of the civilized world whose technology they claimed they despised, yet they demanded the technology that would support them in their "natural" lifestyles. Dyani saw that Mathys had put a unique high-technology space-oriented twist on it that had attracted not only the cult types but also the techies. The way he'd done it by creating a troika of religious types, techies, and military mercs was brilliant. And he'd created stability out of a potentially unstable situation. A troika arrangement was the most stable of all human organizations because each group tried to keep the other two from ganging up against them while at the same time trying to get the cooperation of one of the other two to become king of the hill.

Their tete-a-tete was interrupted by Sarah Carmichael Mathys barging in with another woman who was older, very big and brawny, and a lot more purposeful. "Proselytizing the newcomer, I see," the Number One Wife observed. "I'm glad you're doing that, Monica Elora. Perhaps our training has been successful after all."

"I try, Sarah."

"I know you do, child." She looked around. "Where's that techie doctor? And that Captain Vargas from the Host of Michael who's supposed to be guarding this prisoner?"

Dyani kept silent. This was Monica Elora's show. Dyani was looking for an opportunity, and she didn't want to miss it when it occurred. Besides, it wasn't up to her to report on the whereabouts of Taisha and Vargas.

"Something happened to Dr. Taisha when she was mind-linked with Dyani," Monica Elora reported. "Captain Vargas had to take her to see the biotechs."

"Dyani, eh? Unusual name," the Number One Wife observed briefly. "What's she doing unrestrained?"

"I let her loose. She had to go to the bathroom."

"You little idiot? This woman is strong enough to break you in little pieces!"

"She gave me her word as an officer of the United States Army that she wouldn't hurt me."

"Oh, an army officer, eh? Well, that explains her excellent physical condition." Sarah Mathys looked at Dyani. "You've got a beautiful body, woman. I've never seen the Prophet so smitten so quickly before. Too bad he isn't going to have the chance to enjoy you."

Monica Elora had apparently seen Sarah Carmichael Mathys' anger before because she almost recoiled from this statement. "What do you mean by that, Sarah?"

"I've worked very hard for over a year picking and training the sixty women who will go on the *Archangel Gabriel* when we leave," the Number One Wife explained in a low voice. "Now I've been told to get rid of one so we can take this outsider along. You don't know how that disrupts my plans, Monica Elora. I won't be able to control this Dyani. And it will get me into trouble with some of the six men on the crew; they've helped me select the sixty, and they each have their favorites."

"Yes, Henry VanDerCamp told me he'd convinced you to take me."

Sarah Carmichael Mathys had already decided to take Monica Elora, but by letting the ship's computer control technologist convince her anyway, Sarah Carmichael Mathys now held some of his IOUs. "But no matter how I choose, I'll make enemies of some of them if I carry out the Prophet's order. So, I don't intend to. If Dr. Taisha can't create an unfortunate accident, we'll just have to do what we can and report to the Prophet that this woman was irreconcilable, and we had to get her out of the way..."

"You're not going to hurt her," Monica Elora said. It was both a question and a statement. She really didn't like the malevolent power of the Number One Wife, and she was far more afraid of Sarah Carmichael Mathys than she was of Dyani at this moment.

"Of course not. I expected Dr. Taisha to have done the job in her usual bumbling, experimental way. But since I was afraid she'd bobble it again, I brought Bertha along just in case. Bertha can do the job quickly and painlessly. You know Bertha's an expert." There was no hiding the malignant, malicious, and hostile tone of her voice.

"You can't kill Dyani! That's murder!" Monica Elora objected.

"Child, I've had to get rid of a lot of women in the past few years. They made the mistake of challenging my position. I let you rise to Number Two Wife because I didn't think you had the brains or the gumption to ever oppose me," Sarah Carmichael Mathys admitted, then snarled. "If you get in the way, or if you don't help out here, I have a replacement for you on the *Archangel Gabriel*...and don't you ever forget it!"

"The Prophet won't allow it!"

"The Prophet will never know. He's never found out in the past. Bertha doesn't talk. And you'd better not talk, either, child."

But Bertha talked for the first time since she'd lumbered into the room. "Let her talk, Sarah! Let her talk! She'll soon say something that makes you angry. Then I'll get my hands on her, too!" Then she reached into the folds of her clothing with both hands and withdrew a sharp, shining, pointed knife in her right hand and a short leather whip in her left.

Dyani decided that the Galactic Tabernacle of the Human Future had certainly attracted some wholesome types right out of the psychological sewers of America. And she knew she'd have to act fast and very soon now. She'd been glancing around the laboratory. She'd already spotted several things within reach that could suddenly become deadly weapons. She poised herself for her opening. She knew she'd get only one chance and couldn't telegraph her moves by even the slightest twitch of a muscle.

Big Bertha had to be Dyani's Number One Target. Then Sarah Carmichael Mathys. Monica Elora was a null-person in this one, but Dyani hoped she wouldn't get hurt in what was coming.

"Bertha, take this woman into the bathroom. It will be easier to wash away the blood in there-" the Number One Wife began.

Dyani suddenly had to change her tactics. Bertha had moved around the room and behind the table. Dyani wouldn't be able to get to her first. So, the combat-hardened officer suddenly grabbed at a white steel equipment cabinet and pulled it over on top of Sarah Carmichael Mathys.

The Number One Wife hadn't been expecting that, and the instruments and surgical tools cascaded out and hit her just before the cabinet fell on her. It wasn't heavy enough to pin her, but the surprise was enough to flatten her.

Dyani grabbed a wire chair and swung it up just in time to have Bertha's knife blade glance off it as the big woman slashed at her.

The leather lash snaked out from its coil on Bertha's left hand. Dyani stepped forward and into it. It snapped around her waist, and she felt a momentary shock of pain as it connected with her. But then Dyani stepped back quickly, putting all her weight and strength behind pulling that whip. She yanked the huge Bertha right off her feet and toward her.

As Bertha's surprised face snapped forward, her jaw met the heel of one of Dyani's hands thrusting forward and upward as Dyani recoiled, putting all her mass and all her strength behind the thrust. The crunch of splinters of jawbone was clearly heard. It was followed by an even more sickly sound as Dyani's other hand caught Bertha's upper lip and nose, quickly and suddenly driving pieces of Bertha's facial bones up into her forebrain. Dyani's wrists and forearms were cushioned by the sudden eruption of soft red meat and liquid crimson blood from the big woman's shattered face.

Dyani didn't even watch as she stepped sideways and let Bertha continue falling forward onto the hard, white floor that was quickly becoming blood red. The whip wound round her waist pulled away from a suddenly limp hand while the long, gleaming knife clattered to the floor at Dyani's feet where she scooped it up in one quick motion.

Moaning, Sarah Carmichael Mathys rolled slowly out from under the pile of debris.

Dyani didn't waste time. She could have killed the Prophet's

Number One Wife right there, but she didn't. Her objective was to disable enough people to allow her to escape. She didn't even want to take Sarah Mathys as a hostage; the Prophet might not think twice about having his Host of Michael fire right into her, sacrificing her for the great good of the Tabernacle - which Dyani vowed to disrupt as much as possible if possible.

So she merely re-aimed the swing of her right leg as she began to head for the door. With her toes curled to keep from breaking them, she kicked Sarah Mathys hard in the side of the head where the woman's jaw joined her skull just below and in front of her ear. And Dyani didn't stop to survey the damage. She knew she'd kicked in a spot that probably broke the woman's jaw and destroyed several molars - and hopefully knocked her unconscious.

But before Dyani bolted out the door of the lab, she had the presence of mind to squat and peer around the doorjamb.

An armed robot of the Host of Michael was in the hall, guarding the door of the detention room where the FBI agent and the Nevada state troopers were being held.

Chapter Thirty-One

Dyani saw that the robot was a highly modified General Robotics industrial security bot, a type that used its infrared sensor to scan for movement except for objects moving slowly near the floor. No junkyard owner wanted to waste ammo on rats. But the robot would open fire with its 9-millimeter Magnum Man Stopper on any human-sized target whose closure rate was such that the target would reach the robot before anyone in the central security center could give the order to fire. The robot had no auditory sensors, and its visual spectrum sensor was usually operated in standby mode to save power. In short, it would see Dyani's infrared image if she moved quickly but not if she stayed below its vertical scan or moved at a normal walking speed.

As she was pondering this in the split second she had available to decide what to do, she heard a scream in the lab behind her. It was Monica Elora, who had been so shocked at the speed and violence of Dyani's attack that she hadn't moved or said a word. Now, seconds later, Monica Elora reacted blindly.

Dyani stepped back into the lab in the hope of keeping her quiet. But the highly agitated and terrorized young woman simply continued to scream. Even Dyani had to admit that the scene was pretty bloody. And so was she. But it was someone else's blood, not hers.

Monica Elora bolted past Dyani into the hall, running as hard as she could.

"Monica Elora! No! Stop!" Dyani yelled at her.

It was both useless and too late. The robot sensed her running toward it. That was the sort of movement it was programmed to act upon in self-defense.

Dyani drew herself fully back from the door because she knew what was going to happen.

The robot fired one round. The sound was deafening. No second shot was heard. A warbot or an industrial security robot only had to fire once to hit the target. A warbot shot to kill, but an industrial security bot shot low to disable an intruder in the legs.

Now Dyani had to move without hesitation, but not rapidly. She had to behave like a human security guard approaching the robot to find out what happened. When she stepped out of the door into the hall, she saw the robot's visual sensor flick on, and she knew she was being seen in the Host of Michael control center. Time to get out. Sorry about the other prisoners, she thought.

But voices came from the detention room as she sauntered slowly past, expecting at any moment to feel the impact of a bullet in her leg.

Monica Elora was on the floor, screaming and moaning, holding her wounded leg where a dark red stain was slowly spreading and discoloring her robe.

The robot continued to scan, but once its visual sensor swept over her and paused for a moment, it continued to swing back and forth, looking for other intruders.

For some reason, Dyani wasn't immediately tagged as an intruder. It was probably because the officer on watch didn't know who she was. Since she was moving like she owned the place anyway, the watch officer must have decided that she was some techie Tabernacle type. Dyani didn't care. She came to the emergency exit door and pulled the latch.

It was locked.

She decided that if she couldn't get out, she'd raise a little hell while she was in Sub-Sanctuary. As a trained scout with the genes of generations of scouts, she'd paid attention when she'd been escorted around Sub-Sanctuary both as a guest and as a prisoner. She knew the security control center wasn't very far away.

Time, too, to get the prisoners now and, if they were in any shape to fight, have them accompany her. Strength in numbers, she told herself.

So, she slowly walked up to the waiting robot, thinking any moment that it might quickly turn and fire its weapon at her. But it didn't. Its operator was probably confused by her.

She hefted the dagger she'd retrieved from the fallen Bertha. It was a fine piece with a good steel blade, not a modern composite one. With the pommel of the knife, she smashed the plastic lenses of the visual and IR sensors. That would probably bring more robots on the run, but it might also confuse the watch officer even more if the robot suddenly lost all sensors.

Stepping over Monica Elora's moaning form as she lay on the floor, Dyani went into the detention portion of Taisha's lab. Three doors lined each side of the short hallway at right angles to the main corridor. Each was locked, but the locks were designed not to be forcible from inside. With her knife blade, Dyani quickly pried each latch open and swung the door, then went on to the next.

Four men were there. They were primed for something because of the ruckus in the hallway, but all of them were amazed to see Dyani.

As they stood there looking at her, she told them, "I'm Captain Dyani Motega, United States Army. If you're in any shape to follow me, I'm going to break out of this underground maze and maybe even take command of their robot control center. Who's with me?"

One man wore bandages, and Dyani could see that those bandages covered two bullet wounds. "Sergeant Stan Smith, Nevada State Police," he introduced himself. "I can't shoot worth a damn with my right hand, ma'am, but I'm left-handed anyway. Let's go."

A big man walked up to her and told her gruffly in a voice of authority, "Officer James Burkhardt, Nevada State Police. I don't know where you came from, honey, but thanks for springing us. I'll take over from here, sweetie."

Dyani was smeared with Bertha's blood. Her shirt was spattered by it. Her jeans were covered with it. Even her hands were bloody. She simply looked up at Burkhardt, coiled the short whip in one hand, and felt the sharp tip of the dagger in her right hand. Looking straight into his piggy little eyes, she told him in a quiet voice,

"Officer Burkhardt, my name is Captain Motega. I fought my way in here to get you out. I have the only weapons in the group at the moment. If you'll follow me, we'll probably find some more. If you won't follow me, you can stay here and face the robot security forces that are probably on their way." She looked at each of them in turn. "I haven't got time to argue or engage in a stupid fight over leadership. Follow me. Or get out of my way and rot here if you want that."

And she turned on her heel and strode back out into the hall.

Sergeant Pete Cooker merely whistled and said, "Hell, man, I'll follow that broad anywhere for any reason. I'm sure as hell not going to fight. Not with her!"

"Well, Pete, you always were a lover, not a fighter," Smith told him.

They followed Dyani.

"Stand straight, walk proud, act purposeful," she instructed them. "The security watch officer will probably think we're just Tabernacle techies. Or he'll be confused."

"Hell, they'll know where we are every second. They'll send their robots after us," Burkhardt complained, a bit embarrassed and therefore pissed off at having been intimidated by someone he considered to be only a mere, pretty girl.

"Have you seen any robots or security sensors since we left your jail?" Dyani asked.

"No, but-"

"The Host of Michael is a security force designed to protect Sanctuary from outside intrusion. It isn't an internal police or spy outfit," she pointed out. "The only reason the robot was stationed in the hallway was to keep an eye out for anyone who was trying to free you. No one figured you could get out of those locked rooms. I didn't trip any alarms because no one suspected that a lone woman would do the trick..."

"I sure as hell didn't," Cooker agreed.

"So how about the woman who got shot?" Wyatt Bloomington

wanted to know.

"I don't know very much about industrial robots. I've been trained as an army warbot operator," Dyani admitted. "So, it was my guess that she moved in a way that triggered the robot's preprogrammed self-defense system. I must have guessed right because I didn't act that way…and I didn't get shot."

Some people had a built-in compass in their head; others had a mental map; others just had a sense about where they were. Dyani Motega had all three. She remembered corridors and doors and stairways. If she didn't really know where she was, she stopped for a split second while some unconscious guidance system in her mind kicked in.

She did stop quickly at a restroom to wash off the blood while her four followers stood quietly in the corridor and tried to act natural. A lot of techies went past, busily at work doing whatever it was they were doing. No one paid the slightest bit of attention to them for the simple reason that no one was ever in Sanctuary unless it was all right for them to be there in the first place. Even in their state police uniforms, the troopers got no more than occasional looks, then a shrug. What the hell, it wasn't anyone's business what three state troopers and a man in a rumpled business suit were doing standing around looking like they belonged there. "Not my job to worry about them" was the general reaction.

Dyani was pleased. "You're all pretty good. Come join the Army, and I'll be happy to have you serve in my scouting platoon. All of you managed to look like part of the furniture."

She led them directly to a side entrance to the central security control room. She'd been there before, of course. And the door was unlocked and unguarded. No one would ever want to break into the control room. After all, no one was in Sanctuary without clearance. "Now, when we get inside, you'll see six watch officers at their control posts and one senior watch officer. Move quickly but don't run. One of you on each watch officer. If someone yells or asks a question, just tell him you're here on orders of the Prophet to help with the emergency. Got it?"

Captain Dyani Motega was, of course, an expert at misdirection, stealth, and cunning. She knew how to take advantage of the average person's initial confused reaction to something unexpected or unusual.

"I'll be dipped!" was Burkhardt's quiet mutter as they simply walked into the control room.

Cooker was also sharp. He saw the rack of Mendoza M5 submachine guns on the wall. He grabbed one as he walked slowly by and threw another one to Sergeant Stan Smith in a smooth movement. Wyatt Bloomington picked one off the tack as he walked by.

The control room was a scene of quiet activity. Everyone was intent on watching their screens which presented the IR and visual sensor outputs of various security robots or perimeter fence sites.

"Lieutenant!" one watch-stander was complaining in bewildered tones, "I can't get squat out of that robot you had me station down on Sub-level Two next to the NE lab detention cells! I've lost sensor output, and all the circuitry and links check out perfectly! Even got good bot telemetry! I can't figure out what the hell is wrong!"

"Dammit, Art, do I gotta nursemaid you through everything you do on watch?" the senior watch officer fired back at him. "Someone must have taken out its sensors after it fired on that woman. Have you played the tape yet? Can you identify who she was?"

"No, but I got the biotech team on its way to check it out."

"Jesus, it's bad enough that we're blanketed with ECM to the point where we're in a goddamned black hole! I gotta run everything…Who the hell was it that clobbered the sensors?"

"Another woman. I didn't recognize her."

Dyani stepped up behind the senior watch officer. He suddenly found a very cold and very sharp knife at his throat. "That was me," Dyani said. "Now sit down very slowly. And don't yell. Or you won't have a throat to yell with again."

"The rest of you, *freeze!*" Pete Cooker snapped. "Nevada State

Police!" In all his years on the force, he'd patrolled the back roads of the state and had never made an arrest. So, he'd always wanted to do what he did just then.

"And the FBI." Wyatt Bloomington held the SMG with some trepidation. He hadn't handled a firearm since his initial agent training many years ago. But he felt a lot better with it in his hands, even if he thought he could do nothing with it but hose a lot of bullets around and scare the shit out of someone.

"And the United States Army," Dyani finished.

The senior watch officer made a move to reach out to a red switch.

Dyani merely nicked his throat, and blood started to drip. "Don't do that again," she told him in a voice that was sheer ice water. "Next time, the blade goes deep."

"Uh, you mean business, don't you, lady?"

"Yes."

"What do you want?"

"Out of Sanctuary. Armored vehicle. Fastest way through the main gate."

"Uh, Jesus, lady, I can't do that!" the watch officer complained. "The general could override from the standby center, and the robots will waste you before you go ten meters!"

"Not if you're with me."

"Uh, careful with that knife, lady! Uh, yeah, even if we're with you. You don't know the general. Or the Prophet!"

One of the watch officers panicked and bolted toward a door.

To his great surprise, Wyatt Bloomington pointed the SMG and squeezed the trigger. Rounds ricocheted around the room, and two of them found targets. The panicky watch officer went down as his head exploded. Another one took a round in the chest as he sat in front of his control station, jerked, and fell backward with a strange, raspy rattle in his throat.

"Lieutenant," another watch officer managed to say with a very dry throat, his eyes shifting from his consoles to the muzzle of the submachine gun that Stan Smith held pointed unwaveringly toward him, "got a request here from the Prophet's office for a robot to proceed out the main gate carrying a message."

"Do it," Dyani told him. "Now. And not a word about what's going on in here."

"I heard stories about you American women warbot brainies," the senior watch officer remarked. "But I didn't think you were this tough."

"I'm not a warbot brainy. I'm a Sierra Charlie," Dyani admitted proudly.

"Oh, shit!" was the gasp of dismay from the officer. The reputation of the Sierra Charlies had spread, but the officer had no idea that a woman Sierra Charlie could be this cold, this calm, and this ruthless. "Okay, I'm doing it, I'm doing it!"

"Burkhardt," Dyani snapped at the Nevada police supervisor, "go check the doors into this place. Make sure they're stoutly bolted. Then kick that dead watch officer out of the way and take over his watch station. Can you figure out how to run it?"

"I'll do my damndest, Captain!"

"That may not be good enough. Figure it out. Do it."

"You bet! Probably standard industrial security stuff. Looks like it." He had to admit to himself that this woman was one tough bitch. How the hell could such a beautiful woman be so cooly lethal? Maybe Kipling had been right about the female of the species.

"The general himself is delivering a hard copy note to the robot" came the report from one of the surviving watch officers who'd decided he'd better cooperate. He might have been a mercenary, but like most mercenaries, he tended to back away when his hide was at stake. This job had been a merc's paradise until just now. Nothing except collect pay, stand one watch in three, sit on your ass and run old robots, watch perimeter fence sensors, and enjoy the women of Sanctuary. Except it suddenly had gotten very deadly indeed. And there wasn't a whole hell of a lot to be done about it. No one had ever considered that Sanctuary might be penetrated and taken from inside.

"Another message from Prophet Prime! It's the chief techie himself. He wants us to watch for any opening in the ECM and report it. Seems the Prophet is going to send a radio message out when the ECM lifts."

"Hah!" another watch officer said joyfully. "Well, folks, your little game may be over pretty quick. The ECM may have knocked out our triggering center, but I'll betcha the Prophet's going to tell the world he's activated our kamikaze squads to detonate those nukes by hand!"

"Nukes?" This was the first Dyani had heard of such a thing.

"Yeah, probably Vegas or Reno first. You didn't think that the Prophet and the general were just going to sit here and let the world besiege Sanctuary, did you?"

Chapter Thirty-Two

"I don't know how you people did it, but you sure managed to put together one hell of an assault plan," Major General Belinda Hettrick observed when the staffs of the Washington Greys, the Wolfhounds, and the Cottonbalers finished their briefing.

"Just an all-nighter, General," was the response from Colonel Rick Salley of the Wolfhounds.

"Amazing what can be done with modern telecommunications, ma'am," commented Lieutenant Colonel Maxine Frances Cashier of the Cottonbalers. "Especially with Georgie's latest upgrade."

"That's more what I meant," Hettrick replied. "I'm amazed you could work around the heavy ECM being laid in here by the Signal Corps."

Maxie Cashier was more of a technie than Curt or Salley. "We got Georgie to network with the Signal Corps' megacomputer. Together they played a reverse version of frequency hop," she explained intensely. Like Belinda Hettrick, she'd come up to field command within her regiment. "When we used tacomm, Georgie and Samuel Eff-Bee recognized the skip code pattern, then cleared the ECM off the specific freak as we hopped to it."

"It was clean enough that we could feed high-bit rate graphics through it," Salley added. "So we're all good to go, ma'am."

"Except for one thing," Hettrick reminded them. "You're not going to get to go until I get the word. And, Colonel Carson, you will not - I repeat, NOT - engage in your standard tactic of carrying out a reconnaissance in force, thereby provoking the enemy to attack so you can counter-attack. Understand?"

"Frankly, General, it never entered my mind this time," Curt told her honestly. "My estimate is that Mathys and Calder will do something provocative on their own. My rationale for getting us up on the starting blocks anticipates we'll get orders from Sixteen-hundred Pennsylvania Avenue to move."

"I know. You want to get in there and get those hostages out," Hettrick interrupted. "Hell, I know the tradition, so don't waste time reminding me. By the way, I won't buy off on that part of the plan involving the Copper Canyon Companions strike unit. Colonel Carson, your job is to remain at your regimental command post and command your regiment."

Curt knew that Belinda Hettrick used to lead the Greys up front until she caught the poisoned Bushman arrow in Namibia. Now she was reluctant to allow her regimental commanders to operate "beyond the book." The field manuals said that battalion and regimental officers should exercise command "from the hill behind the battle" instead of down with the troops. But Curt's own combat experience told him that after the first mad minute, no one gave a rat's ass about the manuals. So, he didn't argue. He'd have his Copper Canyon Companions force picked and ready. If he succeeded, it wouldn't count against him. If he didn't...Well, he didn't figure on losing.

Deep down in the part of him that was the romantic in every professional military person, he had trouble thinking about any career future without a certain woman. But he had work to do that morning. He was a professional. Jerry Allen had been right in what he'd said to Curt at breakfast. A lot of people counted on him.

Hettrick turned to General Carlisle, Len Spencer, and Chester Martinside. "Gentlemen, the Iron Fist Division is ready to act."

"Thank you, General, but it's not going to be necessary," Martinside told her bluntly. "The Army is here to show we could use force if necessary. Your presence will indicate to the American public that the federal government was prudently covering all aspects of public safety...although we managed to negotiate a solution to the problem."

"Classic political stance in a stand-off," White House press secretary Len Spencer added. "Bring till the SWAT team J-I-C, then talk the crazy into coming out and giving up. Okay, Chet, I'll work the news media angles on that. But I hope you can get Mathys to talk before he sets off one of those nukes as a show of force."

"How's that coming, Len?" Carlisle wanted to know.

"We found the one in Salt Lake City. It's being hauled out to Dugway right now. But no score in Reno or Vegas yet."

"Did they learn how the Salt Lake nuke was to be triggered?"

Spencer shook his round head. "No way! Didn't want to take the chance it might be booby-trapped to go bang when someone started messing around with it. The first order of business was to get it the hell and gone away from things. When they get it to Dugway, the O-D teams will have a look at it."

Hettrick's aide de camp, Major Joanne Wilkinson, stepped in, smiled a silent greeting at Curt, and reported, "General, a scouting party of the Greys just intercepted a Sanctuary robot two klicks east of the main gate. It was carrying this message to you."

Quickly ripping open the paper enveloped, Hettrick unfolded the sheet of Tabernacle letterhead, read it, and handed it to Carlisle, who did the same and passed it at once to Martinside.

Chester Martinside's sallow face broke into a broad smile as he read it. He looked up and announced, "Dr. Clark Jeremy Mathys has just requested we clear UHF channel sixty-three so he can communicate with me!" He slammed it down on the table with gusto and gleefully said to the Army COS, "Jake, you can send your army home! Mathys wants to talk. That's the opening I need. Now I'll talk him out of this!"

"I didn't notice that Mathys said he wanted to negotiate, only that he wanted to communicate. And the President is the one who sends us home," Carlisle reminded him. He turned to Wilkinson, whom he'd snatched from potential twenty-and-out retirement to be his aide because she'd burned out as Curt's regimental COS. "Tell Signal to open that channel. But I want them to monitor it and shut it down fast if they detect any subcarrier modulation that might be a nuke trigger signal."

"Yes, sir," she replied and started to go.

Cashier's regimental G-2 whispered something in her ear and handed her a hard copy that had squirted out of his hand-held tacomm printer. She turned to the group and announced, "General, the Cottonbalers have apprehended six members of the Host of Michael travelling south out of Sanctuary in a truck near Little Antelope Spring. When my troopers were seen, they were fired upon. We returned fire and gave chase. The Host soldiers were halted when they overturned their vehicle in a dry wash. All but one of them fought to the death. They had with them written instructions for locating and triggering the Tabernacle nuke in Las Vegas. General Hettrick, you'll want to pass this information up the line to the proper authorities. The Cottonbalers will hold the wounded survivor, take charge of the remains, and step up patrols for other such groups coming out the south side of Sanctuary." She handed the hard copy to the Iron Fist Division commander.

Hettrick didn't bother to read it, but immediately passed it to Carlisle. "Thanks, Max. Good work. Mr. Martinside, do you still think you can negotiate with Mathys? The sonofabitch had a kamikaze team on its way to the Vegas nuke even while he was requesting to 'communicate' with you. I'll bet that he wanted to 'communicate' the fact that he was going to fire the Vegas nuke as a show of his intent to continue to be a bastard."

Martinside reached for the hard copy in Carlisle's hands. The Army COS let him look at it while he, too, studied it, then handed it to Wilkinson. "Joanne, get this to JCS right away. Landline FAX for greatest clarity. They'll have it in the hands of the FBI within minutes. Chet, do you want a copy in your hands when you're talking with Mathys?"

"I think that would be helpful, Jake." Martinside was somewhat more subdued now. He knew he was going to have to work very hard on this one. "But I'm not going to tell him I have it. Not at the start."

"I didn't think you would." To Hettrick, he remarked, "I think we may have to activate Operation Blood Siege. Do you want your regimental commanders to get back to their OCVs?"

Hettrick shook her head. "No, General, I'd like them to stay and hear what they're up against, if they don't already know. Their regiments are cocked. A tacomm call from them sets Blood Siege in motion."

"Sure you just don't want them here so you can mother-hen them, Belinda?"

She shook her head again. "Hell, no! A mother hen in combat breeds sitting ducks. They know what to do, and I never micromanage them."

Martinside glanced at his watch. "Let's take five, Jake. Mathys doesn't want to talk until the hour."

"Do you mind if my people continue to sit in on this, Chet?"

"Not at all, Jake. Maybe they'll learn something about how to win without fighting."

Curt had the sense to keep his mouth shut. Hettrick and Kester had taught him how to win without fighting, and he'd done it successfully many times.

Curt didn't leave the divisional OCV with the rest. He stood there, and finally Hettrick stepped up to him and said, "Colonel?"

"General?" he responded.

"You're doing an admirable job of getting things under control," she told him.

"Thank you, ma'am."

"Now do a *good job* of it."

"I'm sorry if I don't come, up to the general's expectations."

"The general has always expected a lot from you. And will continue to do so. The general expects the sort of professional motivation she's tried to imbue in you."

"You've always taught me to lead. That means never ordering subordinates to do something I wouldn't do."

"Your subordinates already know what you'd do. Otherwise, they wouldn't follow you. And they wouldn't have put together

Operation Blood Siege for you. Curt, you were in no rational condition to do so when you came out of Sanctuary last night," Hettrick pointed out. "But I have no problem with that. You were wounded...in more places than your feet. However, you're recovering today. You're letting your people help you."

"I'm supposed to be leading them," Curt objected.

"These days, military leadership is something more than mounting your white horse, waving your saber, and exhorting your minions to follow you into the breach. Leadership is mostly what you do off the battlefield," Hettrick confided. "I tried to tell you that when I was commanding the Greys. Guess I didn't succeed. Now I know I couldn't succeed. Regimental command is so different from company command that it's like sex. It can't be taught, and no one knows what it's like before they do it. And, my dear Colonel Carson, allow me to point out that love and war aren't very different in that regard. But one *must* keep them separated."

"I'm trying, Belinda."

"I know, Curt. Keep trying. You're winning."

"It's all fresh ground."

"Agreed. For you and for the military profession. An obvious but overlooked consequence of a mixed-gender army. But look to some of your people. Every one of them has managed to get his own separate handle on it. Education is always a two-way street. The teacher often learns from the students. And the leader often learns from the led."

Martinside came back in with Carlisle, followed by the three regimental staffs. The federal negotiation expert wasn't looking so cocky. Curt guessed that Carlisle had had a chat with him during the break. The COS was known for diplomatically speaking his mind in private. He had no fear of his career. He'd already put his career on the line for principle. He'd won. He was one of the few military leaders who'd done so.

When the UHF frequency was opened, Martinside announced, "Hello, Tabernacle. I'm Chester Martinside. I'm a representative of the President of the United States. I received your message that Dr. Mathys wishes to speak with me. The agreed channel is open. Go ahead, please."

The response came in the familiar voice of Dr. Clark Jeremy Mathys, known world-wide because of his award-winning space documentaries and known to millions of followers now as the Prophet of the Galactic Tabernacle of the Human Future. "I did not wish to speak *with* you, Mr. Martinside. I want to speak to you. Please see to it that this message gets to your president. Although I hold five of your people, including a woman, they are not my hostages. I know you think nothing of the lives of hostages because you will do everything in your power to stop me and the Tabernacle from completing our glorious mission. So, I will not threaten the hostages I hold. I intend to take one of them with me. Therefore, my Host of Michael will not release the others until after my departure."

Mathys paused, but Martinside didn't attempt to interrupt him at this natural break point. The negotiator wasn't there to argue. He was there to convince, to cajole, to negotiate. And he knew that the first step in negotiating with disturbed people such as Mathys was to let them talk as much and as long as they wished. Martinside wanted to keep Mathys talking.

Mathys had probably expected a reaction from Martinside at this point. When he didn't get one, he went on imperiously, "However, you have attempted to cut me off from the world. You have frozen my legitimate bank accounts. You have denied me what I need and can legitimately pay for in order to accomplish my mission on Earth. This is a serious matter and demands that I retaliate to show you that I cannot and will not be cowed or intimidated. This isolation began shortly after I informed you of my intention to destroy the cities that surround me if you persisted in attempting to breach my Sanctuary with your police and military forces. I now intend to go one step further because of your electromagnetic isolation of Sanctuary. I will detonate a nuclear device in Las Vegas today. It is not my desire to be a mindless killer, so I am warning you to evacuate the city before you have the blood of more than a million people on your hands. Therefore, you will be forced to inform the world of what you are doing to me and abide by the forum of public opinion. If you lift the isolation of Sanctuary, free my financial affairs, and withdraw your armed forces, I will not destroy another city. I wish to leave the Earth, and I will soon order the launch of the spaceship *Archangel Gabriel* from Sanctuary. My intentions are well known to anyone who reads the doctrine of the Galactic Tabernacle of the Human Future. So do not attempt to interfere with the realization of this doctrine, or yet another city will be destroyed. Do not attempt to breach Sanctuary or impose your will upon those I leave behind, because they have the power to destroy cities if you do. That is all I have to say to you."

"Well, now, Prophet, I think we ought to talk a little bit about this," Martinside began.

"I do not. I know who you are and what you do for a living. You have been very successful, Mr. Martinside, in talking hardened criminals and terrorists into giving up and turning themselves in so that your police can incarcerate and eventually send them into penal slavery for the rest of their lives. Therefore, I will not discuss anything with you. I have warned you. I will-"

Something or someone interrupted Mathys in Sanctuary. The Prophet was apparently talking on an ordinary telephone handset because his voice and several other voices suddenly were heard muffled and indistinguishable. Mathys had his hand over the transmitting mike.

Then he suddenly came back in full voice. "I have no further message to transmit to you. Goodbye." And the connection was cut from Mathys' end.

"What the hell?" Martinside had never been so abruptly cut off by anyone before.

Hettrick jumped in right away. "Georgie," she called verbally to her megacomputer back in Arizona, "did you get a good recording?"

"Yes, General."

"Can you reconstruct what the muffled voices were saying?"

"Yes, but a full-frequency reconstruct will require additional computer power from Tiffany and Old Hickory."

"Go get it! In the meantime, give me any brief synopsis you can construct."

Georgie paused for four seconds - a very long time for a computer of its power. That pause signified that Georgie was working very hard. Then the megacomputer's voice came back, "Someone informed him that his main robot security control center of the Host of Michael had been seized by Captain Motega and the previously captured public safety officers."

Curt, Salley, and Cashier all stood up at once. But it was Colonel Maxie Cashier who voiced the question for all of them, "General Hettrick?"

"You know my feelings," Hettrick answered and turned to her superior officer. "General Carlisle? American citizens and a member of the armed forces are in immediate jeopardy. How quickly can we initiate Operation Blood Siege?"

General Jacob O. Carlisle suddenly found himself in another situation where his career was on the line over a matter of following orders or acting on principle. "I'll call Washington right away. But I'm just covering my ass. If I get a strong negatory, I'll have to sound the recall. But in the meantime, General Hettrick, initiate Operation Blood Siege!"

Chapter Thirty-Three

"General Calder, you were responsible for that woman Motega! You were to ensure her security! Now I discover that she somehow drove Dr. Taisha insane. She injured my Primary Wife. She caused my Number Two Wife to be severely wounded. She killed one of the housemothers. Then she released the public safety officials we're holding in custody. On top of all that, she seized your central security and robot control center! Either your Host of Michael is incompetent or we're dealing with a superwoman! I suspect the former! I don't see how anyone could do all the damage she's done unless everyone else was completely incompetent! What have you got to say for yourself?"

Dr. Clark Jeremy Mathys was livid with rage now that he'd gotten a full report on what was happening inside Sanctuary. He'd hired this former army officer and West Point graduate because the Tabernacle – Mathys - needed armed security. He'd authorized millions of dollars for Calder's use in fencing the thousand-plus square kilometers of Sanctuary, buying and modifying industrial security robots, installing sophisticated sensor systems, and hiring several hundred men to fill out Calder's TO&E for the Host of Michael. Mathys knew it was a necessary business expense if the forces of the evil Nibiruans were to be held at bay. But at this moment, he was struck with the possibility that maybe he'd hired the wrong man or paid too little attention to something be really didn't want to worry about.

Calder himself knew that this wasn't just an ass-chew. He realized he hadn't covered all the bases. The Host of Michael was wanting in the area of internal self-defense because he'd concentrated on perimeter defense to keep out people like the FBI man and the Nevada state troopers. Calder was prepared for a siege. But he'd never counted on having to handle an internal security affair. Motega had broken loose and apparently ripped through his skimpy internal security procedures like they were soft, wet toilet paper. He found it almost impossible to believe that such a beautiful, quiet woman could have done what she had. The woman warbot brainies he'd known in the Washington Greys were tough-minded and could operate NE warbots with the best of the men. But except for the new officers just out of the rough physical environment of West Point and the major military academies, women warbot brainies weren't experts in deadly hand-to-hand combat. Nor could they have stood up to the bruising physical world of an old-time foot soldier in the poor, bloody infantry.

So, Calder tried to explain the situation as best he could from his viewpoint. "Prophet, Motega is a Crow Indian. How could I know she's also a savage with all the barbarism of her ancestors? And she's one of the Army's new Sierra Charlies trained in personal, hand-to-hand combat. Again, I had no way of knowing that the Sierra Charlies had been trained to fight so viciously. When I was a warbot officer, we never got down and dirty in combat the way we used to at West Point. The West Pointers such as myself were always the most physically fit members of the regiment...but Motega isn't a graduate of any military academy."

"Haven't you kept up with the literature in your own professional field, General?" Mathys would naturally ask this because, as a degreed scientist, he'd once had to spend nearly all his free time in the eternal paper chase of staying current with the literature.

"Yes, sir, but reading about the Sierra Charlies is a hell of a lot different than getting to know one the hard way...as we've just done."

Mathys was also in a difficult position. With Sanctuary surrounded and cut off from the world, and with an unknown number of armed units of the United States defense establishment poised beyond the perimeter fence, the Prophet couldn't sack his defense minister. In Mathys' opinion, the French mercenary Colonel De Ville just wasn't up to taking over; the man's Gallic ego might cause him to overreact to save his own personal honor at the Prophet's expense. And he didn't trust the Teutonic rigidity of Colonel von Kampf, either. Mathys knew at this point he should have paid more attention to the Host of Michael in recent months. But he'd had other things that had occupied his full attention. So, he glowered at Calder and said in a low voice, "General, discipline or punishment for the Host of Michael will have to wait. You and your men can redeem yourselves if you show yourselves capable of smashing this woman and taking control of Sanctuary's security once again. *If you're successful,* I can chalk up your command's performance to the learning curve. Let's get right to the heart of the matter. What are you going to do about the present situation?"

"Let her sit there and starve, Prophet."

"What? You don't intend to take back your security center?" Mathys was astounded at this plan.

"No, sir," Calder repeated, then explained, "Her colleagues cut us off from the world. I'll cut her off from the rest of Sanctuary. I'll switch control of security to the emergency center in the Prime Tabernacle. Within an hour, she'll discover she can't do anything at all where she is. Then I can concentrate on external security. Once the external threat is annulled, I'll go in and take her out of the game."

Mathys thought about this for a moment, then told him, "Save the Motega woman if you can. She's got true warrior genes. That makes it even more important that she accompany us on the *Archangel Gabriel*. The Anunnaki didn't fail completely in their ancient biotechnology experiment. I understand now that some humans turned out to be better warriors than others. She must be among the fortunate ones whose ancestors were the more advanced biotechnology experiments."

"Prophet, your other wives may not stand for it," the Keeper of the Faith advised. "This woman is too violent. She's harmed two wives thus far. Those two will likely harbor vengeance."

"Alastair, they wouldn't *dare!* I give the orders in my family! If I tell my wives not to harm this outstanding female warrior, they'll feel my wrath and your re-educational measures if they step out of line!"

"Thank you, Prophet. I shall be ready to do my best to reeducate them."

"As for the Motega woman, if she must be kept in fetters or endure the womanly wrath of my wives, that's her problem! If she decides to see the light and embrace the faith, the decision is hers to make. Alastair, I won't have you trying to convince her!"

"Prophet, I have my hands full with other poor victims of recidivism." The Reverend Gillespie didn't want anything to do with Dyani Motega. She fought back. Gillespie much preferred the meeker ones. Let the Prophet handle the hellcat himself if that's what he wanted. Gillespie knew Mathys was profoundly attracted to this woman who was so much different from the others who surrounded him. Perhaps the Prophet felt that the Motega woman was a challenge. But Gillespie didn't. He'd forego that sort of challenge.

"As for you, General, get out of here and get to work redeeming yourself and the Host of Michael!"

"Yes, Prophet," Calder snapped with brusque military professionalism, adding, "I'll have Motega sealed off very shortly and have full command again."

"And report to me when your team detonates the Las Vegas device. At that point, I will send another message to the government of the United States. By that time, they will know they aren't playing with a fool!"

Calder entered the lift to take him back up to Sub-level One right under the Prime Tabernacle where his emergency command post was located. But just as the lift reached Sub-level Two, it suddenly slowed to a stop, and its interior lights went out.

The electrical power had apparently died.

He punched the button that would cut in the emergency system deep within Sub-Sanctuary powered by hot springs beneath Battle Mountain. The dim emergency lights came on, but Calder had to slide the door open himself.

The corridor was lit with the dim red lights of emergency standby.

When he got to the CP, he found Colonel Louis DeVille and Captain Manuel Vargas already there along with a dozen of his other officers. DeVille saluted Calder as he came in and reported, "We're up and running, General, but just barely."

"What happened to the electrical power? Report!" Calder snapped.

"The main power line to Valmy is out. We don't know why yet. Our sensors along the north fence have gone out as well. I have a team of four men and two security robots in a personnel vehicle on the way there to give us sensor capability in the area," DeVille said.

Calder turned to Vargas. "Give me a report on the status of the women who were hurt in Taisha's NE lab."

"The doctor is presently catatonic. The biotechs are working on her but don't believe they have the ability to break her catatonic state," the young Brazilian told his commander, knowing full well that he'd probably get his ass royally reamed for screwing up and leaving the NE lab with Taisha. "I checked on the Prophet's wives when they were brought to the main hospital. Sarah Carmichael Mathys has suffered only fractured jaw and is even now on her way back to the Prophet's apartments. Monica Elora Mathys suffered a bullet wound in her left leg just above the knee; she is reported to be in stable condition."

"No one killed. Good."

"Not true, General. One Bertha Stutthof was murdered in the lab by being struck in the face with a very powerful weapon, perhaps a club."

Calder had known of her. She was a mild female version of the Reverend Gillespie but with slightly different proclivities. He considered her death to be no real loss. He was slightly worried that Sarah Carmichael Mathys might think differently because Big Bertha had been the Number One Wife's counterpart to the Reverend.

So, he didn't comment but asked DeVilie, "Report your progress in taking command and control back from the primary cee-pee and isolating it."

"We have practically all of its functions now transferred here, General," the French mere told him proudly.

"General!" came the call from one of the men at the consoles. "The heavy ECM blanket has suddenly disappeared! We're picking up spotty ECM on certain radar and comm frequencies we commonly use, but the overall interference is gone!"

"Can we work around it?"

"To some degree."

Calder grimaced. "They're attacking," he guessed. It was only a WAG, but even so he knew that a WAG on the conservative side here was far preferable to a flat dismissal of coincidental occurrences.

The main outside power lines were out, and Sanctuary was on back-up electrical power sources. That move was an attempt to deny the Host of Michael any surplus of available electrical power from outside sources, throwing them completely on the internal sources which the enemy hoped might eventually be over-taxed, destroyed, or captured. Calder wasn't worried. The geothermal energy available from the numerous hot springs in the area coupled with the cold fusion reactors in Sub-Sanctuary meant that he could carry on for a long time with ample power.

The ECM was gone. Its absence meant that it would be easier for American robot forces to communicate with their warbots and between themselves. Calder knew how the United States defense forces operated, and this was consistent with that know-how. Modern armed forces required a very high level of exceedingly intense C3I (command, control, communication, and intelligence) because of their heavy dependence on high technology for the operation of their weapons and the exploitation of their war-fighting doctrine.

The two things should not have happened so close to one another if there was any other logical reason than the initiation of the assault on Sanctuary.

"All right, keep the primary cee-pee isolated, and concentrate on Sanctuary defense! I want all security robots ready to move to the perimeter fence at points where we detect enemy forces moving in. I want all available air defense units out of their holes, on the ground, and Baby Sams ready! I suspect a combination of horizontal and vertical assault. Be prepared for possible Aerospace Force support in the way of tactical precision bombing…"

In the captured primary command post, Dyani Motega had seen the lifting of the ECM blanket and watched the slow isolation of the CP's incoming data streams. She suspected that Calder was isolating her preliminary to an attack on the CP by the Host of Michael.

But since the Host was primarily configured as an external security force, she didn't think that they could carry out a successful attack on the CP.

She also guessed that an external assault was under way. The sudden glitch in the electrical power, the automatic shift over to reduced emergency illumination, and the lifting of heavy ECM told her that the Greys were probably at the Gate and moving in.

Dyani didn't discuss this with her four companions. They might have been retired military, but they probably didn't have the recent combat experience she did. And their training might be rusty. She didn't have time to debate the situation. She knew what Curt Carson would do. So she did that. She led.

"All right, everyone, we're getting out of here," she announced loudly. "Grab any personal weapons you can and all the ammo you can carry. Pete, any grenades or tube rockets in that arms locker?"

"Yeah, both."

"Take them!"

"Hey, honey, we're safe in here! They can't get at us! Why the hell do you want us to bust out of here and expose our asses?" Burkhardt questioned her.

"Her name is Captain Motega," Smith reminded his colleague.

Dyani recalled one of Regimental Sergeant Major Henry Kester's aphorisms in his Code of Combat. "Because if it's difficult for the enemy to get to us, it's difficult for us to get out if it becomes necessary. So, we're getting out now. If you want to stay, that's your decision. But I'm going topside and see if I can't get out of Sanctuary. Or put up a good fight inside the fence because I believe the Army has started its assault. I think we can help them more upstairs than we can down here in an isolated hole. Grab a personal weapon and let's go!"

"What about these three watch officers?" Pete Cooker asked.

"Leave them! They've been isolated by their own command." She picked up a Mendoza and a dozen clips of ammo. As she started to move toward the door labelled "Exit Up," Pete Cooker handed her a bundle of surplus Army M10 stun grenades. He'd picked ug two old 50-millimeter self-guided shoulder-launched tube rockets. Smith had two SMGs and was loaded with ammo.

Dyani noticed that Burkhardt had shut up, grabbed an SMC and ammo, and gathered with the group. He started to open the exit door.

"No," Dyani told him. Kneeling down, she took one of the grenades off the bundle and slowly opened the door, peering around it from near the sill.

Anyone who might be in the exit way and shot when the door opened would shoot over her head.

No one shot.

She was through the door and moving quickly up the flight of stairs almost before her followers knew it.

At the top, she found herself in a little staircase kiosk inside a garagelike building. Through the windows, she could see dozens of trucks and robot carrier vehicles. Pete Cooker was alongside her with the others behind him.

"Standard industrial security vehicles," he remarked. "Some additional armor has been put on. Looks like they're moving out."

The garage was busy. Men armed with SMGs were boarding trucks or loading robots into carrier vehicles. Vehicles were moving out the open garage door. No one was paying any attention to the staircase kiosk.

"I can't believe this outfit," Smith muttered. "They didn't have this escape staircase guarded. They don't have guards anywhere! What the hell?"

"The high command figured they'd isolated us, dummy," Cooker told him. "They didn't think we'd try to get the hell out of the cee-pee."

"They act like they're used to following orders and not thinking for themselves," Smith observed.

"I think they're moving out to counter a more serious threat than we were down in that hole," Dyani said, carefully surveying the surroundings.

"Yeah, when the high brass in Reno orders you out of quarters on a possible shooting mission, you usually don't watch minus-x in your own garage!" Pete Cooker admitted. "You're too damned scared of what's going to happen. At least, I always was."

"Scared now?" Stan Smith asked.

"Yeah, but I ain't wet my pants yet," Cooker admitted.

"Pete, see that personnel vehicle about three meters to our left?" Dyani asked.

"The one with the circle-and-arrow and number one-seven on the door? Yeah."

"Can you drive it?"

"Damned right!"

"Listen," Dyani told her squad of irregulars, "we're going out this door acting like we belong here. We're going to walk toward that truck. Pete, you're going to climb into the left side of the cab. I'll get in the right door. The rest of you in back. If someone starts shooting at us, don't fall to the floor. Run while dodging and firing back from the hip. The chances of being hit by anyone with an SMG is very low. Especially if you're a moving target, which is hard to hit."

"You act like you've done this before," Burkhardt observed.

"Yes. I have. Many times. With real marksmen shooting assault rifles. And if I haven't gotten hit doing it, you probably won't," Dyani reassured him.

"Where we going?" Cooker wanted to know.

"Out that door with the rest of the vehicles. After that, we'll play it by ear. But our destination is the front gate and freedom."

"Yes, I believe I've had enough of this place," FBI Agent Bloomington remarked. He was deathly scared, but so was everyone else in the crowded little kiosk. He smelled a strange odor, the stink of scared people.

"Let's move out," Dyani said.

She opened the door and began walking toward the truck. The others followed.

They might have made it except for one thing.

Dyani was the only woman there.

"Hey!" came the call from somewhere! "What the hell are you doing in here, girlie?"

When the first round went over her head, Dyani was already on the run for the truck.

Chapter Thirty-Four

"Prophet, the assault has begun! What appears to be a full regiment in land vehicles is moving rapidly down Buffalo Valley from the north along the power line. The objective of this group appears to be the silo. I have dispatched a unit to ambush the enemy as it comes abreast of Timber Canyon and enters the mine field there. The enemy encounter with the mines will divert their attention and prevent them from continuing their southward movement toward the silo while we attack them from their left flank."

General Stephen B. Calder's report was clipped, concise, and professional sounding. But the leader of the Host of Michael was doing his best to disguise the panic in his voice. The approaching American army had broached the north perimeter fence as though it hadn't been there. It was an assault in force. He thought he was ready for it. But every military commander in history had always wondered whether or not his line would hold.

"Why are they coming in from the north?" Mathys wanted to know. "Why not from the east through the main gate?"

"Two possible reasons, Prophet. The main gate is the most obvious point for an assault. It's a military verity that one attacks where least expected. The second reason appears to be the objective of the attack itself: to capture and destroy your launching silo. That was the item that prompted the government's original attention to Sanctuary," Calder reminded him. "The silo was the object that bothered the Soviets. So it's my guess that the Soviet government has told Washington to either destroy the silo or they'll do it themselves."

"That's ridiculous! How could Soviet missiles possibly get through the space defense system? Everyone knows that the strategic defense shield is impenetrable!"

"Sir, then you've changed your mind about that?"

Mathys had once been a staunch detractor of such a system. "Yes, but that was before the Anunnaki told me they'd encouraged the deployment of the missile defense system to protect what I'm doing! They told me that was no easy task, General! The Nibiruans were solidly against it and did everything in their evil power to stop it."

"Yes, sir." Calder let it drop at that. He had enough trouble on his hands at the moment. "Here's another reason why the American army may be attacking from the north. The battle will be kept away from the above-ground homes and other civilian activities of Sanctuary. I suspect the White House has told the army commander not to attack the innocent men, women, and children who live here. Attacking from the north means they'll encounter only my Host of Michael, a paramilitary force." Calder knew the general policy of the United States. The news media would raise holy hell if the Army barged in on a religious enclave, slaughtering people right and left. The obvious safe way to do it was to attack Sanctuary in such a way that the civilians wouldn't be involved and that the overtly religious trappings of the group such as the Prime Tabernacle would remain untouched.

At least that's what Calder told himself. And he believed it.

But his analysis panicked the Prophet. "They can't be allowed to capture the silo! We are within days of being able to launch the *Archangel Gabriel!* I must get to the asteroids! I must prevent the Nibiruan henchmen from destroying mankind's last great hope of salvation!" He stopped ranting because it wasn't going to help him at this point. Instead, he looked levelly at his military commander and gave an order in a serious tone, "General, you are to defend the launch silo at all costs! Stay on this circuit. I'm calling an immediate general meeting of all acolytes."

Rapidly, Mathys punched the buttons that would summon the video images of his closest associates and display them on interactive screens in his underground office. Calder stayed in the circuit, of course. Quickly, the Reverend logged in, followed by Jasper Lyell and Gordon Palmer.

The Prophet was brief. "Gentlemen, at this instant the *Archangel*

Gabriel is at great risk. The American army units are moving on it from the north. I cannot take the chance that they won't shoot at it with artillery or ballistic rockets. General Calder and the Host of Michael will hold the enemy west of Timber Canyon. But the fact that the American army has broken through our perimeter and is heading directly toward the silo means that we can no longer delay. We will board the *Archangel Gabriel* at once and launch as soon as possible. Reverend Gillespie, your immediate task is to round up the women and get them aboard. Palmer, alert your technical people and prepare them for the launch."

The Reverend Gillespie merely nodded, but Gordon Palmer was agitated when he replied, "Prophet, the ship isn't ready to fly!"

"It must fly!"

"I told you: It's not ready."

"Why? What needs to be done?"

"The guidance and control systems are marginal," Palmer tried to explain. "VanDerCamp has had to make do with kludges, borrowing equipment where he can so that he can run tests. The equipment we ordered hasn't arrived yet."

"Cartwright told me about that. But we'll have to go with what we've got or with whatever can be put into service within the next few hours. The chances of that equipment being delivered now are slim to nothing," Mathys pointed out, reminding the techie that they were in a military situation now, that the good old days of doing it in the best techie style were over.

"Prophet, you don't understand! Guidance and control are critical!" Gordon Palmer objected.

"Is the propulsion system ready?"

"Yes, sir."

"Are the life support systems ready?"

"Yes, sir. Everything is reasonably well checked out except the guidance and control systems," Palmer admitted.

"What you're talking about is basically the automatic pilot, correct?

You designed a robotic helmsman for the ship, correct?"

"No, sir. Cartwright did with VanDerCamp's help. It's not my design."

"So, we go without the complete robot pilot. Anything a robot can do, a human being can do. Put a human operator at work to monitor the incomplete robot during flight. Human pilots did a very good job flying airplanes long before they had autopilots. Human pilots are still used in space planes." Mathys' experience with robotically controlled equipment was limited to telescopes. It was always possible for the astronomer or technician on site to override the robotic, automatic telescope positioning controls or even to take complete control from the robot. He didn't see that this was any different. He'd personally steered a big telescope to accuracies measured in small decimals of an arc-second. Surely, steering a spaceship couldn't require any greater accuracies.

"Prophet, this is a different matter. The degree of precision required as well as the microsecond response times-" the Tabernacle's chief engineer tried to explain.

"In short, you're saying you couldn't fly it, right?" Mathys tried to shame his chief engineer.

It didn't work. "I couldn't do what the guidance and control systems have to do, Prophet."

Mathys sighed and was forced to play his trump card. "Put Cartwright on the circuit."

"He's here, Prophet."

"I'm on, Prophet." The image of the brilliant young engineer came on the screen alongside Palmer's older, middle-aged features.

"Todd, you're going on the *Archangel Gabriel*, right?" Mathys asked an unnecessary question, but he was leading up to something. He was going to force Todd Cartwright to pilot the *Archangel Gabriel*.

"Yes, Prophet."

"Can you fly it?"

"No, sir. Not without a whole hell of a lot more computer power and AI capability than it now has." Cartwright was a techie and didn't know how to lie about technical matters, even when he was faced with the possibility of having one of his pet ideas fail to check out.

"Do you really want to go?" Again, that was an unnecessary question.

"Yes, Prophet, I do. I've wanted to go into deep space all my life. Not just to the Moon, but real deep space in the solar system. Even to the stars. You've given me the only chance I'll ever get to do it."

"I'm going to give you a clear choice, Todd: Fly the *Archangel Gabriel* or stay on the ground. Henry VanDerCamp can take your slot on the crew." Mathys put the knife in and twisted it hard. He might lose his spaceship engineer, but VanDerCamp was an acceptable alternate to Cartwright. VanDerCamp acted like he knew more about the spaceship than its chief engineer, and VanDerCamp was driven not only by a techie urge to get into deep space but also by the psycho-sexual gratification of being one of six men aboard with sixty women. VanDerCamp was a horny techie, much more so than Cartwright. Mathys began to play that strategic plan.

With only an instant's hesitation, Cartwright replied, "Uh, I'll fly it, Prophet."

Gordon Palmer suddenly put in, "Prophet, with all due respect, sir, I'm backing out. I'll stay on the ground." The Tabernacle's chief engineer obviously didn't want to trust his life to an incomplete spaceship.

"So stay, Palmer! Continue to draw your pay as my chief engineer if you want. You'll be the only big wheel techie running Sanctuary until I return. And, if you didn't realize it, you've just solved one of my problems," Mathys told him with some bitterness. "Now I don't have to bump one of the sixty women to take Motega: So we'll have five men and sixty-one women. General Calder, go into your captured command center and get her out...alive. And do it now."

Someone spoke off-screen to Gordon Palmer, who took a written note and nodded.

Calder decided he'd have to find some manpower to carry out the Prophet's direct order. "Yes, sir. I'll detach a platoon to do just that right away, sir."

"No, General, I won't let you delegate this one. You go get her yourself. If you don't succeed, I'm going to hold you directly responsible. You won't be able to fob off a failure on one of your subordinates. I want that woman! She's going to mother some outstanding warriors for the Anunnaki!"

"Excuse me, Prophet, but one of my engineers just handed me a note," Gordon Palmer interrupted. "Steve, one of your watch officers just came out of your primary command post and passed the news to a technician that this Motega woman and her irregulars have abandoned it."

"General, I think you'd better get down there right now!" Mathys snapped.

"Prophet, I'm supposed to be defending Sanctuary against an invasion at the moment," Calder tried to object. He didn't know what was going on, but he did know that Dyani Motega was showing herself to be cunning, ruthless, and unpredictable. He really didn't want to have to face her in real combat.

"What I just told Gordon holds for you, General. I gave you your rank, and I can also take it away and promote Colonel von Kampf-"

"Colonel von Kampf went south with the Las Vegas team, Prophet. In fact, he hasn't reported back since the ECM was lifted. He should have done so by now..." Calder tried to report.

"Then get Colonel DeVille on the screen if you're too much of a coward to go after that amazon!" Mathys snarled.

At that point, Calder came to the same conclusion, he'd surmised Gordon Palmer had figured out: Time to leave a sinking ship with a madman at the helm. Getting out of the emergency CP meant he'd have some flexibility. Maybe he could even manage to get out of Sanctuary. He was suddenly aware of the possibility that he, as commander of the Host of Michael, might be indicted for the robotic murder of the Nevada state trooper. No one had ever brought a case like that to trial before. Would a jury acquit or convict a security chief whose robots had killed an intruder on private property? He didn't know. And he didn't want to have to find out. So he started planning to abandon ship. "Yes, sir! I'll turn over command of the invasion resistance to Colonel De Ville, sir."

"I want you to bring Motega to the silo. We'll be loading as quickly as I can get there," Mathys pointed out. "I want to be aboard and have all systems up and running in case we have to lift out of the hole before the Americans get there."

"Yes, sir. I'll find her, capture her, and bring her to the silo," Calder promised, knowing full well that he might have a slim chance of doing so. But he'd try. And it would get him out of the immediate line of fire of the Prophet's growing irrational command style.

But if she'd left the main CP, where was she?

And was she armed? Probably, since the CP had a small arms locker.

Where could she go?

Up the emergency exit to the main vehicle garage, he knew.

"Prophet, I've got to sign off here. A lot of work to do very fast." Without further amenities, he cut the circuit from the emergency CP in the Prime Tabernacle.

Turning to Vargas, he snapped, "What's the situation in the main vehicle garage over the primary cee-pee?"

"No communication with anyone there at the moment, sir."

"Get it!" Why the hell did his command have such lousy communications when the crunch was on? His mercs in the Host of Michael were a strange mixture of foreign and domestic warbot brainies, plus some foreign infantry and tech troops. The old warbot brainies had a tendency to communicate all the time, of course, just as he'd done in the Washington Greys; but they tended to communicate between themselves, not with higher command. And he hadn't assigned a communications specialist to the unit he'd had DeVille deploy from the garage.

While Calder fretted and worried about the Prophet, about the onrushing northern invasion force, about the abilities of the Host to stop the thrust at Timber Canyon, about the Las Vegas nuke team, and about the possibility of yet another assault on Sanctuary from another direction, DeVille and Vargas worked to find somebody, anybody, who would answer their radio calls. They didn't care if the American army heard them; they were just happy to be able to work without ECM blanketing everything. They could work around the occasional bursts of interference. What they really needed was someone to answer their hails.

"Uh, General, we got through to someone in the primary cee-pee," DeVille suddenly reported. "They came down the emergency exit to get out of the fire fight in the garage. We've got wounded. But so does Motega and her crew."

"Where are they?"

"They fought their way out. Drove right over some of our men. Smashed a few vehicles in the process. But they got out the garage door with a vehicle. Right now, they're engaged in a moving fire fight with some of our troops on the main highway through Sanctuary."

"They're headed for the main gate! Barricade the inner road leading to the gate!"

"Yes, sir, it's being done, General."

"By God, she came out of the hole. She's in the open now. I'll get her!" Calder swore. "Vargas! Come with me! I want you to drive the command car we left upstairs in front of Prime Tabernacle! We'll head her off and trap her between three forces! If she won't surrender to me, I have no compunctions about shooting that bitch!"

Chapter Thirty-Five

Grey Head, this is Avenger Leader.

The neuroelectronic tacomm call came through Curt's battle helmet as he waited inside his regimental OCV, waited for the Battle of Battle Mountain to take shape and form, waited for the possible news that the President might call the whole thing off, waited for news of anything. This call from Major Ellie Aarts, commanding the RECONCO with its eyes and ears and sensors all over the skies and in its scouts on the ground, might be the one he was waiting for.

So, he thought back into his own NE tacomm helmet unit, *Grey Head here. Go ahead, Avenger Leader.*

In the heat of battle, neuroelectronic tacomm was the fastest possible means of communications between people other than direct linkage of their minds. But direct linkage meant you could do almost nothing else. NE tacomm was fast because people didn't have to vocalize their words, only to think them so that the NE sensors of their helmets would pick up the brain signals.

Black Hawk Four reports a fire fight in progress inside Sanctuary. It apparently began under cover in a building and has now erupted into a running fire fight on the roads of Sanctuary. We're seeing IR signatures of handgun discharges and grenade bursts. Building coordinates and current fighting unit coordinates are on the data bus. Grey Head, I don't know how or why, and I can't justify my guess, but I think it's Mustang Leader!

"Edie, put it on the display!" Curt verbalized to his chief tech sergeant, then went back into NE tacomm mode. *Avenger Leader, do you have a high-res visual from a birdbot?*

Affirmative! Coming down the pipeline now.

"Avenger report coordinates plotted. Birdbot visual on Screen Four," Edie Sampson reported back to Curt.

One look at the data plotted on the holo chart of Sanctuary told Curt that the garage was directly over the Host of Michael CP, because he'd been there. And the running fire fight was between a single vehicle and a group of four in pursuit.

This was confirmed by the high-resolution visual image picked up by a birdbot's "eyes," transmitted to RECONCO's OCV, and then massaged into a visual presentation. It showed a Tabernacle armored truck being pursued by four other armored trucks. The fire fight was proceeding northward on the main Sanctuary highway artery. Curt saw people in the truck firing what appeared to be submachine guns. He saw an indistinct image of someone leaning out of the truck cab and firing. The mane of black hair flying in the wind was enough for Curt to identify who it was.

Dyani Motega was fighting her way out of Sanctuary, not only in the tradition of the ladies of the Washington Greys, but true to her own personal beliefs. "The Guard dies but never surrenders." She was far from being dead. Or from surrendering.

Avenger Leader, any other activity within Sanctuary?

Affirmative. Lots of it! Major vehicular force heading cross country from the Sanctuary built-up area to where the Wolfhounds are coming around the mountain to the west. Small activity around the main gate where a vehicle is proceeding westbound in an apparent attempt to intercept the vehicle being chased from the garage area. And now I see what appears to be an ordinary staff car proceeding southward from the Prime Tabernacle, again appears to be on an intercept with the same chased vehicle.

Anything else?

Negatory! The civilian side of the house seems to be very quiet. In parking lots and the housing area, people have gone inside.

Thank you, Avenger Leader! And I think we've found your scout platoon leader. Curt knew Ellie would update him if anything changed and that she'd keep the info flow on the data bus. Major Ellie Aarts was the best reconnaissance company commander he'd ever seen. She'd been a warbot brainy, then a Sierra Charlie, and then had converted back to running the only NE warbots left in the Washington Greys because she'd gotten tired of being shot at. So, she knew what to look for and what it meant to a "poor bloody Sierra Charlie" down there on the ground taking incoming.

Curt punched up the link to Hettrick. *Battleaxe, this is Grey Head.*

Go ahead, Grey Head.

Reporting to you recon data that indicates the possibility that Mustang Leader may be active inside Sanctuary. On your data bus. Visual birdbot images as well. If Wolf Head concurs, may I initiate Thrust B For Blood?

Wait one, Grey Head...Roger, I see your data. I concur that it may be Mustang Leader. But I want you to wait and allow Wolf Head to make deeper penetration. I don't want that Host cross-country vehicle force to turn around and go after you as you come in.

Battleaxe, the Greys can handle that contingent! But Mustang Leader may need our assistance P-D-Q. Looks like the Host is trying to box her.

Dammit, Grey Head, hold your horses! Hettrick fired back at him. *Jumping Jake ordered Operation Blood Siege because Blue Maxie's people caught a kamikaze nuke team heading for Vegas and saw there was no room for Chet to negotiate with Mathys. And Jumping Jake hasn't got a go-ahead yet from Fort Fumble on the Potomac. So, we're all the hell and gone out on a limb here, merrily sawing it off behind us! Jumping Jake and Battleaxe are prepared to take it in the chops and survive because we know where bodies are buried all over Fort Fumble. But if you jump the gun without our green light, you're sucking for a general court if not a 'requested retirement.'*

Curt then knew he shouldn't have asked Battleaxe. She had no recourse but to tell him that, because tacomm was always recorded for post-mission debriefing, education, and possible rug-pulling if something really went to slime. Curt knew he should have fired up, gone into Sanctuary, and stood on the carpet later.

Battleaxe, I'm going to get airborne and ready.

This time, he didn't ask. He informed her of his intentions. Or at least part of them. As the Battle of Battle Mountain progressed and the haze of battle increased, he wanted to be ready to take advantage of the opportunity to move.

He didn't wait to hear what she said in reply. Instead, he toggled his regimental command tacomm frequency and called, *Greys all, this is Grey Head. Mount 'em up and move 'em out. Go right up to the eastern perimeter fence and be ready to penetrate.*

He'd made an educated guess, based on experience. Eight Chippies would hover just outside the Sanctuary main gate, fronted by eight armed Harpies ready to pound sand, blast gravel, and shake rocks with their ordnance. This airborne force would be either intimidating or provocative to the Host of Michael, who already had a going fight on their hands with Rick Salley's Wolfhounds in Buffalo Valley.

Then he gave the order that had not been authorized. *Copper Canyon Companions, report to Tiger Two and be hot to trot.*

He stood up, grabbed his Novia, and called, "Henry! Let's go!"

Edie Sampson also stood up.

Curt shook his head and told her, "No, Edie, I desperately need you here to keep our comm nets up and running."

"Colonel, I'm not about to stand here and let Captain Motega get wasted."

"She won't be," Curt promised.

"Damn! And I was spoiling for a good fracas, too."

"'They also serve who only stand and wait,'" Curt quoted. He was out the rear hatch of his OCV and sprinting toward the waiting Chippie before she could reply. He knew his redheaded chief tech sergeant didn't like the idea of standing on the sidelines, but her job in the regimental OCV was absolutely critical at this point. Without communications and readership command, a modern military force with its awesome weapons of terrible destructive power became a juggernaut capable of wasting lives unnecessarily.

As Curt walked up the loading ramp and into the cavernous Chippie hold with Kester, right behind him, he saw in the dim interior light that the Copper Canyon Companions were there.

But they weren't the right volunteers, the ones Curt had selected.

"Captain Clinton, what the hell is going on here? I selected Captain Frazier and Hassan's Assassins for the Copper Canyon

Companions," Curt sputtered in frustration, noticing that Kitsy was accompanied by her first sergeant, Carol Head. The big Bohemian NCO had both his Novia and Black Maria. Sweet's Scorpions were seated in the webbing. They'd been among the volunteers, but Curt had decided to pick Russ Frazier, whose company, the Ferrets, had the reputation of being very aggressive.

"Colonel, seems we got into a little poker game while we were sitting around this morning waiting for something to happen," Kitsy told him, trying to hide her grin. "The Ferrets and the Assassins lost. Gee, it's just too bad that Hassan hasn't learned not to draw to an inside straight, sir."

Captain Adonica Sweet stepped up behind her company commander in an effort to lend support. "Sir, we don't want Calder and his Hosts to get the idea that the rest of us can't fight as well as Captain Motega."

"And just because we've finally gotten the right to fight doesn't mean we don't have to work like hell to keep it," Kitsy added. "Already a lot of people have complained that too many women are in command positions in the Greys. So, we have to remind them from time to time that this twenty-first century army of ours is an equal-opportunity one or they're likely to send us back to our tatting, as the old southern saying goes."

"Tatting? What the hell is that?" Curt asked, knowing full well that he wasn't going to be able to switch forces and get the Ferrets and Assassins in here. The Chippie's cargo doors were already closing behind him. Time had run out. These ladies of the Greys had snookered him. He didn't like it, but there wasn't a whole hell of a lot he could do about it right then. Later, he'd have to do some reprimanding.

"Lace-making," Kitsy informed him. "Me, I'd rather wear it than make it...when the time is opportune for such a thing."

"Take your positions," Curt said with resignation. He wondered if Rick Salley had similar disciplinary problems with his ladies. "You been briefed? We're not going into the Copper Canyon mine."

"Yes, sir, we've downloaded the tactical information. We're going to take out about six or eight enemy trucks and do nasty things to any merc who has the balls to shoot at us," Kitsy replied seriously. "And even nastier things if Captain Motega has been harmed."

Curt made his way up to the Chippie's flight deck under the bubble. Lieutenant Ned Phillips and Flight Sergeant Barry Morris were there. Curt took the third seat, plugged his tacomm into the intercom jacks, and ordered, *Move it out, Mr. Phillips. Warhawk Leader, this is Grey Head. Come to airborne status. Remember, stay outside the fence until they shoot at you.*

Christ on a crutch, Grey Head! I spend my flying career trying to keep from taking the goddamned Golden BB, and now you want me to sit up here and beg for it! came the tacomm "voice" of Major Cal Worsham, who, for some reason, sounded just exactly like he did when he actually spoke.

Just don't let it hit you, Warhawk Leader, Curt advised him. *How are you set for fuel?*

Worsham's "voice" came back through the Chippie's tacomm system, *We can hack about two hours hovering in ground effect. After that, we'll have to drop you off and relay the Chippies back to Lander County Airport for refueling. The Harpies can handle about three hours with their present ordnance load. We don't expect to have to hang around that long before something happens.*

Neither do I, Curt admitted to his air chief.

An airborne force of eight big Chippewa aerodynes accompanied by eight smaller Harpies bristling with ordnance was both a comforting and a frightening spectacle-comforting if they were friendly, frightening if they were not. The Warhawk squadron lifted off and came quickly to cruise configuration, skimming the Nevada grasslands out of Crescent Valley, quickly clearing the peaks of the Shoshone Range, and sweeping across the Reese River Valley toward the Sanctuary main gate. It was hard to see what was going on ahead because the afternoon sun was directly in Curt's eyes. But Phillips was flying by the data fed neuroelectronically to him from the Chippie's sensor suite.

As the squadron came to hover about a kilometer east of the

Sanctuary main gate with the Harpies between the Chippies and the gate, Curt called, *Avenger Leader, this is Grey Head. Update me on the internal chase situation.*

Pursuing vehicles have blocked the road to the main gate, so the pursued vehicle is heading up Copper Canyon toward the Prime Tabernacle. The staff vehicle is blocking the road at the entrance to the park square south of the Prime Tabernacle, was the report from Ellie Aarts. *We've got birdbots over the scene now, and - New data! New data! The two men around the staff vehicle have opened fire on the birdbots! Jenny Volker has taken a hit. Bill Hull's birdbot took evasive action...Someone down there has recognized the birdbots for what they are.*

Calder, Curt thought. Only Calder would spot a birdbot. You had to know what to look for. For use here in the western United States the Greys' birdbots had been configured to resemble indigenous hawks. Even though they looked like hawks, they didn't fly exactly like hawks because of their higher wing loading. Thus, a birdbot could be spotted by the fact that it did less soaring and more wing beating.

But it gave Curt the excuse he needed. The standing rules of engagement prevented him from taking action unless the Greys were shot at. When and if they were subjected to armed attack, they had the right to defend themselves. To Curt, a good defense meant creaming the offender. No sense in slapping wrists only to have the wrists retaliate by carrying fists to the face. The Washington Greys had another traditional saying: "Turn the other cheek, get a second Purple Heart."

Greys all, our birdbots are taking incoming! Activate Bee-For-Blood! Phillips, put us down in that square just to the north of the staff vehicle. Warhawk Leader, I want air cover from Hands' Hawks. One Harpy should be adequate if the pilot's as aggressive as you. The rest of you know what to do. Make it so!

He toggled over to unit tacomm and advised the strike force who had picked themselves in a poker game, *Copper Canyon Companions, we're going to ground in the Prime Tabernacle square just south and downhill from the Prime Tabernacle. Stay the hell away from the fountain. It's got a whopping electric charge on it! I believe the renegade Calder is with a staff vehicle parked at the south side of the square. He's taken pot shots at our birdbots, so he and his companion are armed. We'll take him from behind. Captain Motega is proceeding up from the south and directly into him. She can't help but see us. So let's take this bastard Calder from both sides and squeeze the shit out of him. Then we can handle Captain Motega's pursuers. You've got the data on your helmet visors. Any questions?*

The Copper Canyon Companions were silent. They knew what had to be done. Each of them was engrossed in his or her own thoughts. Just before going into combat, Curt knew that these thoughts would primarily be about getting killed, wounded or maimed. That had been reduced over the years with the perfection of soft body armor, but it didn't eliminate the possibilities, as the Greys knew from tragic experience. The secondary consideration was a fear that one would fail one's comrades and friends. This was more likely in everyone's mind. It came from the fact that a person spent an entire career in one regiment; this enhanced unit cohesiveness in most cases but could also result in arrogant elitism, depending upon the unit leadership. Curt had no worries on that score. He'd learned well, but sometimes it hadn't been easy.

The Chippie went in over the perimeter fence at minimum altitude and flew nap-of-the-earth toward the hulking rocks that made up Battle Mountain. Phillips took it up a broad canyon and over a ridge. Suddenly, the spire of the Prime Tabernacle came into view in the canyon ahead. Phillips was good. He brought the Chippie in fast, flipped it broadside in a maximum-performance stop, then flipped it belly down for a quick landing in the square just south of the fountain.

The instant its landing legs hit the pavement the cargo doors gaped open. Two columns of Greys dashed out, one going east and the other to the west. Because Curt had been up on the flight deck and unable to get to the hold because of the violent maneuvers, he was the last one out. He carried his Novia at the ready and walked directly across the pavement toward the staff vehicle.

Down the straight avenue behind the staff car, Curt could see Dyani's truck careening up the street, dodging from side to side in violent evasive maneuvers in an attempt to provide as difficult a target as possible to the four pursuing vehicles.

Calder was facing the Chippie with his Mendoza SMG in hand while Vargas continued to give his attention to the oncoming truck.

Curt continued to walk straight at Calder.

"Stop right there!" Calder yelled, bringing his SMG to his shoulder.

Its 9-millimeter muzzle was aimed directly at Curt.

Chapter Thirty-Six

"Calder, you son of a bitch, you might as well put down that Mendoza right now," Curt growled in a voice loud enough to be heard over the roar and whine of the Chippie's turbines. "You're through! The whole damned Seventeenth Iron Fist Division is all over you like a rug here."

"Division, my ass! Just because you've put one company in here doesn't mean you've won, Carson!" Calder yelled back.

Curt shrugged. "Have it your way. But in case you haven't checked lately with your cee-pee, your defenses have collapsed. They weren't very good in the first place. Maybe against a warbot ground assault, but sure as hell not against Sierra Charlies with airlift capability."

"One more step and I shoot!" Calder warned as Curt continued toward him.

"Shoot, and you're a dead man! So's your buddy." Curt knew his body armor would probably stop the 9-millimeter Magnum rounds, but he'd likely be knocked off his feet and maybe even get a broken bone or two, depending on where he was hit. "You're the cause of the black burgee flying on the regimental colors right now, Calder. No one here would shed a tear at blowing away a renegade Grey who went merc then supported nuclear terrorism against innocent American people."

"I didn't build the nukes!" Calder objected.

"Maybe not, but your forces were prepared to trigger them," Curt reminded him. "Remember General Ali Akhbar, the most recent *mahdi*? He didn't build the nuke he popped in Chad, either, but he was hung for ordering it to be detonated. Unfortunately, we won't have that privilege in your case, mainly because the United States Army stopped your people before they could nuke Vegas."

"You stopped Colonel von Kampf?"

"Yeah. With full written instructions on his body."

"You can't hang a man for that."

"Maybe not, but you'll get a chance at defending yourself against six counts of kidnapping and one count of first degree murder," Curt advised him. "You might beat the rap. You sure as hell don't have a chance of fighting your way out of here alive. So put down that Mendoza."

"Bullshit! I've got reinforcements on the way!" Calder jerked his head to indicate the bevy of trucks coming up the broad avenue.

Hawk Wizard Seven, take out the four trucks chasing the lead truck up the street to the south of us, Curt tacommed to the Harpy driver whose craft was hovering up-sun to the west of them.

Consider it done, Grey Head. Hawk Wizard Seven rolling in on them now, came the reply in his head from Lieutenant Rick Cooke in the Harpy.

Curt didn't take his eyes off Calder. Thus, he didn't see the Harpy roll in and take out four vehicles in one pass, making use of four M100A Smart Fart tube rockets, one to a truck. The pilot polished off his deadly work with short bursts from the Harpy's two M300A 25-millimeter cannons. The noise was enough to startle Calder. It must have been the final straw for Captain Manuel Vargas, who suddenly put down his Mendoza and raised his hands.

The oncoming truck once being pursued slid to a stop not ten meters from where Calder's staff vehicle was astride the avenue, blocking passage. Three people got out. It would have been a gross understatement to say that Curt was relieved to see that one of them was Captain Dyani Motega.

"Captain Vargas, walk toward me," Dyani called out. "If you're surrendering, get out of the line of fire."

"Vargas, get your ass back here! If we go down, we go down together!" Calder snarled at his subordinate.

"General, maybe your contract obligates you to fight to the death for the Tabernacle and the Prophet, but mine doesn't," Vargas told him and began to walk away toward Dyani.

"You deserting sonofabitch!" Calder swore, whirled, and brought up his SMG.

But before Calder could do anything with the weapon, others who were already primed to shoot acted faster.

Curt brought his Novia to his shoulder, was very careful to get the round target designator on Calder's torso and not Dyani who was behind him, activate the laser ranger, align the pips, and pull off a single round. This he did in a fraction of a second.

But he wasn't the only one.

Two 9-millimeter Magnum rounds went over his head. The third from the three-round burst fired by Dyani was stopped by Calder's body.

Apparently, Calder wasn't hit by just two rounds - one from Curt and one from Dyani. The man's head exploded in crimson mist. Then his body jerked right and left from the impact of dozens of Novia rounds. The kinetic energy of a high-velocity 7.62-millimeter Novia round at close range was enough to pick a grown man off his feet and toss him several meters, but Calder was hit so many times from so many different directions that he finally spun about like a bag of sawdust. What crumpled to the ground was only the ragged bullet-torn remains of a man.

Dyani repointed her Mendoza SMG at Vargas and said cooly. "Hands on the back of your head, Captain Vargas. Around the side of the car - not that side; the other side where it isn't so slippery." As she walked up to Curt with her prisoner, she switched the SMG to her left hand and saluted with her right.

"Captain Motega reporting for duty, Colonel. Sorry I'm out of uniform."

She was so cool, so professional, so tactical that she caught Curt off guard. As a result, he reacted in automatic mode by returning her salute. Her behavior had disarmed his momentary emotional urge to hug her. So he grinned and said, "Captain, I should put you on report for that, except you're still officially on leave...and except I'm damned glad to see you again!"

She glanced up at the sun now low in the western sky. "It's only been about twenty-four hours, Colonel."

The three of them were almost swamped by the Copper Canyon Companions, especially Kitsy and Adonica. Henry Kester and Carol Head were the only two who seemed to retain a vestige of sense at this point, because they took Vargas into custody.

"You look pretty damned good after twenty-four hours in hell, Dyani!" Kitsy told her. "At least, that's the way the colonel described your likely treatment."

"The colonel exaggerated. He wasn't there. I was the one who raised the hell," Dyani replied, beginning to relax for the first time in more than a day.

"And you Americans can have her!" was the comment from Captain Vargas. "She probably killed Dr. Taisha; the woman will be in a mental hospital for a long time. She did kill one of the housemothers. She injured the Prophet's Number One Wife. And I don't know how many people she shot getting out of the Host's main vehicle garage. I am delighted to be your prisoner, Colonel, because I did not look forward to trying to take her prisoner for the Prophet."

"Is he telling the truth, Captain Motega?" Curt wanted to know.

Dyani managed suddenly to look innocent. "Colonel, sometimes a woman's got to do what a woman's got to do..." Then her expression darkened. "Colonel, we've got to get the Prophet."

"Not before we get you out of here, Dyani," Adonica remarked. "Look at your feet! Ginny! Medic!"

"My feet are all right now. I've got two wounded Nevada state troopers in the truck and two others trying to help them now that the shooting's over," Dyani suddenly said. "Send Ginny there first."

"I'll get Ginny and help her," First Sergeant Carol Head said and headed for the Chippie. "Elliot, give me a hand. Koslowski, take over here and help the regimental sergeant major guard this prisoner."

"How about your feet?" Curt asked.

"My feet aren't hurting now," Dyani told him. "But, Colonel, we've got to get the Prophet before he kills one of his wives. Monica Elora doesn't deserve what's likely to happen to her. She's not very bright, but she's not an enemy. She didn't try to stop me when I broke out of Taisha's lab, but she panicked. So, a Host guard robot shot her in the leg. Mathys is the sort of person who will blame her for my escape."

"Colonel," Captain Manuel Vargas interrupted, "it is too late to get the Prophet. He called for an immediate launch of the spaceship *Archangel Gabriel*. He and his wives and crew are probably aboard at this moment. It would be very dangerous to go near the launch silo now. They could lift off at any moment."

Curt toggled the tacomm switch in his helmet and called to his regimental technical sergeant both by NE tacomm and verbally so that everyone present could hear him, "Grey Tech, this is Grey Head. Edie, get on the horn to the Wolfhounds. Tell them I've just got some gee-two that Mathys is about to launch his spaceship out of that silo. Tell Colonel Salley to halt his advance along the west side of Battle Mountain and stay the hell away from that launch silo!"

Roger, Grey Head! Doing it now!

Grey Chief, Grey Head! Curt called to Joan Ward. *Give me a sit-rep, please.*

Grey Head, Grey Chief here. A pushover, sir, was Major Joan Ward's reply. *Reports from Alleycat Leader indicate that the resistance at the main gate collapsed almost at once. TACBATT is inside Sanctuary at this time with no casualties and no losses. No one left in the main cee-pee; but this fracas is being run from somewhere, and he hasn't found it yet. The Wolfhounds have shattered the Host of Michael forces at the mouth of Timber Canyon. The Host robots were no match for Sierra Charlies and Mary Anns once the Wolfhound Saucy Cans took most of them out of action. Otherwise, it's a walk-through. Alleycat Leader reports that his platoons are encountering only sporadic and ineffectual resistance from small groups of Host mercenaries. This wasn't even as dangerous as a war game with the Wolfhounds!*

Maybe for some Greys, but not for all, Curt reminded her.

Did you recover Mustang Leader?

That's debatable. She might claim she recovered us.

Sounds like Mustang Leader! She okay?

In spades. And looking good.

Yes, sir. Not just to you, Curt! To all of us! Orgasmic!

Curt ignored the fact that Major Joan Ward had broken tacomm protocol with her last message. He turned to where Captain Vargas was being covered by Henry Kester and Jim Koslowski. "Captain Vargas, the Host of Michael is beaten and giving up. The slaughter could go on for hours unless you can tell us where the secondary cee-pee is."

Vargas pointed northward to where the Prime Tabernacle's spire loomed up above Battle Mountain and pointed toward the evening sky. "Under the Prime Tabernacle. I can lead you there and negotiate surrender. But I would like special dispensation for doing so. I simply request to be allowed to leave the United States."

"I can't promise that because I can't make good on such a promise, Captain," Curt told him frankly. "All I can tell you is that I'll intercede as best I can on your behalf. Insofar as I know, you haven't done anything an ordinary security guard wouldn't have done."

Vargas sighed. "I'm not in a position to insist. But I'll voluntarily cooperate with you."

"Henry, take Kos and Tullis. Follow Captain Vargas. Take the surrender of the command post of the Host of Michael. And don't hesitate to do what you have to do if something goes wrong," Curt ordered.

"Colonel, you oughta know that if I have any doubts, I'll empty the clip," the old soldier told him.

"Colonel! Another prisoner coming to surrender!" Sergeant Paul Tullis called out.

Walking forlornly down the middle of the avenue from where the Prime Tabernacle's tall spire slashed skyward into the crimson sunset sky came a disheveled middle-aged man, empty-handed, with a tired stoop to his walk.

"Gordon Palmer, Mathys' chief engineer!" Dyani breathed, recognizing him.

Palmer walked right up to them, saw Curt's dull silver oak leaf on his cammies, and announced, "Colonel, I turn myself over to you. I'm Gordon Palmer, chief engineer for the Tabernacle."

"I know who you are, Mr. Palmer," Curt told him. He didn't raise his Novia to cover the man.

"Then maybe you also know that I resigned my position with the Tabernacle," Palmer went on with a sigh. "And that I had absolutely nothing to do with the nukes. When I protested their construction, I was told to run Sanctuary and leave the security up to the Prophet and General Calder. Have you seen the general? I understand he's tearing around somewhere trying to stop Motega - Oh, there you are, my dear. Glad to see you made it out. Really! But General Calder's after you."

"He found us," Dyani told him bluntly, indicating the pile of red meat lying on the pavement.

"Huh? Oh!" Palmer overcame the gag reflex and said, "You're ruthless, young lady. But they all deserved just what you gave them."

"Thank you for the compliment, Mr. Palmer."

"Captain Vargas tells us the Prophet is out at his spaceship in the silo," Curt began to interrogate the engineer, hoping to get some confirmation for Vargas's story.

"Afraid so. That's another reason I decided to leave Sanctuary," Palmer admitted. "I also objected to the Prophet's decision to launch the *Archangel Gabriel* and thus jeopardize the lives of everyone in

Sanctuary. So here I am. Take me prisoner if you wish. I'm the man ultimately responsible for the technology around here that the Prophet and his acolytes misused. I tried not to pay attention to that. For once in my life, I had the chance to do what I wanted to do and apply technology the way I thought it might help people. I guess I was wrong."

Curt let the beaten man go through his catharsis of admission. He had no reason to detain him. However, Palmer could be very useful to the authorities when it came to getting things straightened out. Curt was glad he didn't have to handle the legal mess that would arise out of this. But that wasn't his job.

"You just said that the launch would jeopardize everyone in Sanctuary," Curt asked. "Are we in danger here? Should we get out? Or should we try to stop the launch? The Aerospace Force can come in very quickly and do a job on that silo. Or I could order my tacair to make a mess of things out there."

Palmer shook his head sadly. "I'm afraid you can't stop that madman. He's obsessed. Insane. I was present during his final meeting with his acolytes. I couldn't believe that I'd worked for him. But as for the launch, if the ship blows after it leaves the silo, pieces could land anywhere. However, now I suspect it won't make it out of the silo."

"Why?"

"Most of the automatic control, stabilization, and guidance systems aren't complete. Todd Cartwright, the ship's chief engineer, is going to try to pilot it out of the hole."

Curt decided, "Okay, if we can't stop him, we'll finish mopping up and stand by for a fireworks show. We weren't ordered to stop the launch anyway. We did what we were told to do. And I got what I came for."

Aftermath

The history books tell that the launch of the spaceship *Archangel Gabriel* occurred at 2334 hours, Pacific Daylight Time.

Curt would remember it for years. It was long after evening twilight had darkened the crystal-clear sky over Battle Mountain. The stars above shown brightly as only in the American west.

After locking up their Host of Michael prisoners in Sanctuary, those Washington Greys not guarding them parked their vehicles along the military crest of the western ridge of Copper Canyon and took up positions along the ridge itself. The Wolfhounds had withdrawn with their Host of Michael prisoners to Smelser Pass and the Tobin Range to the northwest. To the south, the Cottonbalers were deployed on Jersey Summit, Golconda Pass, and Wild Range Canyon. Most of the civilian, techie, and religious population of Sanctuary had been told by the Greys to move up onto Battle Mountain to lessen the possibility that a blast might cause buildings to fall on them.

In spite of the fact that the news media weren't there - no time was available to invite them, organize them, and keep them from getting into trouble - Len Spencer had four government video crews who'd been standing by in Carlin just in case. Len wasn't about to face the news media afterward without some sort of goodie in the form of a tape of the launch.

No communication inward to the S.S. *Archangel Gabriel* was possible. Mathys cut himself off from inbound messages. But he established outward communications. For several hours, he ranted and raved on audio-only channels against the governments of the world, against the Department of Defense, and against the Washington Greys. They were all minions of the evil Nibiruan extraterrestrials, according to his ravings which became more virulent and disconnected as the hours wore on.

Interspersed with the preachments of the Prophet of the Galactic Tabernacle of the Human Future were progress reports on the conduct of the launch from the ship in the silo.

Mathys was amazed that no one tried to stop him. He'd expected to have to hold off a siege of the silo.

The word came from the White House, "If he wants to try, let him launch. If he's successful, it will be the first launch of a laser-propelled rocket; we'll likely learn something. If he's not successful, we won't have wasted taxpayer money trying to stop him."

The FAA vectored all overflights well away from northern Nevada, rerouting them hundreds of kilometers north and south of Battle Mountain, along a navigational check point for subsonic jet traffic.

When the message came by radio from the ship that launch was thirty minutes away, the Washington Greys finished up their hot field meal and went up on the ridge to watch.

Curt found himself sitting on the ridge with Dyani, Kitsy, Jerry, Adonica, Henry Kester, Joan Ward, and the rest of his regimental staff - his friends, his colleagues, his subordinates, but not necessarily in that order. He was dog-tired. But he had a sense of anticipation.

So did everyone else.

"I've always wondered what it must have been like when they were shooting those big rockets into space," Major General Belinda Hettrick remarked as they watched the lights twinkle in the valley below. Hettrick was a Grey, and insofar as the regiment was concerned, she always would be one of them.

"You mean before it became commonplace and you had a choice of flights on a schedule?" General Jacob Carlisle asked. He, too, was a Grey, having preceded Belinda Hettrick as the regimental commander before he got his star.

"It must have been like this," Kitsy decided, then gave a little shiver. She was both cold and a little hyped-up because of the launch as well as the aftermath of the battle. "This is exciting!"

"Big rocket launches were circuses," Henry Kester admitted. "Like shooting the man out of the cannon. I saw the last space shuttle launch. It was like the sun coming up underneath this hundred-meter building…then it went up in the sky on a trail of fire."

"Hell, Henry, you've seen everything," Edie Sampson told him.

"Just about," Henry admitted.

"Tell us about when the Pharaoh Thutmose attacked across the Plain of Megiddo, Henry!" Joan Ward kidded him.

"What's to tell? He won. Everyone knows that," Henry kidded back, never cracking a smile.

Kitsy dug her elbow into Curt's left side. "Hey!" she chirped. "Look! The lights are dimming!"

All over the valley below, the brilliant jewellike spots of light were either dimmed or going out.

"Shifting the electrical load to the laser," Carlisle ventured.

"We should have given them back the Valmy power line," Hettrick remarked.

Carlisle shook his head. "Couldn't. Rick Salley's people did a real job on it."

"Besides, Palmer told us they had adequate geothermal and cold fusion reserves," Kitsy remarked. "Pretty place. Too bad what happened to it."

"Oh, you didn't hear?" Carlisle interjected. "Gordon Palmer and Jasper Lyell told me they were going to turn it into a tourist attraction. After all, the nonprofit corporation still owns it. With the sort of media attention it's going to get, they'll probably succeed."

A green flare arced over the darkened mouth of the silo.

"Three minutes," Henry announced. He donned IR night vision imaging battle binocs. He'd seen rockets launched before, so he didn't want to experience it "naturally" like the rest. He wanted to get a close-up look at the bird as it came out of its hole.

A hush fell over the Washington Greys.

"We fought 'em," Kitsy said quietly, "and they hurt us. And I think they're crazy. But, damn, I wish them luck."

"Uh, yeah, people are in that thing," Joan Ward muttered. "Trying to go out to the stars. Are they crazy? Or is it us?"

"They're crazy," Dyani said simply. "Their reality is different."

The valley was now in total darkness with all electrical power apparently switched to the laser propulsion system. The seven-day half-moon hung in the western sky, its dark hemisphere glowing in reflected earthlight:

Suddenly, a caldron lit up on the floor of the valley.

It was at first a glowing orange-red hole.

Within seconds, colored smoke billowed frantically out of vents on several sides of the glowing, lighted hole.

The tip of something appeared in the hole, slowly rising in complete silence, the light underneath it as bright as the rising sun.

It moved upward out of the hole with excruciating slowness, growing brighter and whiter as it rose.

When it became apparent that it was a long cylindrical body, the light under it became almost too bright for the eye to look at.

The ground itself seemed to rumble and grumble. Then the surrounding air took up the noise. It grew louder and louder.

The huge terawatt laser at the bottom of the silo pit was frenetically pumping the energy of pure light into the huge mass of solid propellant in the tail of the ship, converting it into flaming hot gases that now billowed upward, not only through the silo vents, but up and around the slowly ascending spaceship itself.

It seemed to wobble, to hesitate.

"It's hit the side of the silo!" Henry shouted.

"The control and stabilization system! VanDerCamp said it was marginal when he borrowed some of Taisha's equipment for it!" Dyani breathed.

The *Archangel Gabriel*, messenger to the gods in the skies with the fire of the gods beneath it, slowly but perceptibly began to crumple on one side, to bend in the middle. Then it gave in to the inexorable tug of gravity and began to fall slowly back down the silo into the fiery caldron beneath it.

"Look out! It's going to blow!" someone yelled.

As the *Archangel Gabriel* collapsed back onto its driving laser at the bottom of the silo, the chained energy of the stars went out of control beneath it.

The launch silo glowed again, then became a cannon barrel as the ship and the laser exploded.

Curt knew what 150-millimeter artillery pieces looked like when they fired. This must have been something like the old 16-inch naval guns when they fired. Only the silo was more than *twenty meters* in diameter.

A 20,000-millimeter cannon was an unthinkably huge projectile thrower.

But there was nowhere for the energy, the exploding propellant, the gases and the pieces to go but up and out the silo muzzle.

All of these things suddenly came out with an enormous ball of light illuminating a huge shock wave that rippled across the valley floor, driving gases and rocks and sand before it.

It was probably the closest any of them would get to seeing the detonation of a nuclear weapon.

A column of fire projected itself upward into the clear sky, its brilliance wiping out the pinpoint lights of the stars.

In that column of gas and debris was what was left of sixty-six human beings.

The rumbling noise of the launch gave way to the overpressure boom as the shock wave rolled over the Washington Greys.

Then the vertical column of glowing gases and pieces slowly faded and disappeared.

"Holy Mother of God!" Kester breathed, slowly taking off his IR binocs.

Someone was praying. It was Captain Nellie Crile, the regimental chaplain.

Kitsy gave vent to a single sob.

"Well, Mathys wanted to go to the stars. So did Cartwright," Dyani remarked in a shaken voice. It wasn't often that Dyani was shaken, but this was one of those times.

Curt thought he understood as he replied, "They might make it. Their atoms, anyway." That explosion wasn't just another event, a detached occurrence, a mighty spectacle. Curt had known some of the people who'd died instantly in that thundering holocaust and had their elements shot into the sky. He hadn't liked them, but he'd known them.

It was a somber group that trickled off the ridge back to the vehicles.

"Everyone get a night's sleep," Curt ordered.

"I don't think I can sleep after that," Kitsy admitted. "But I'll try. It's been a hard and horny day."

"If you have trouble, give Dr. Ruth a call," Curt advised her. "By the way, I'm damned glad you're back, Kitsy!"

She looked up at him. "So am I. I didn't think I'd dare stay away another day. And I was right."

As people began to walk slowly off toward their vehicles, Curt found Dyani alongside him. He looked down at her and asked, "How are your feet?"

She looked up at him. "I'm all right. I'm used to going barefoot."

"The hell you say. The medicine help?"

"The best medicine for me is you," she whispered.

"You didn't get hurt too badly, did you?"

"I didn't get hurt at all." Dyani smiled. "I kept my priorities straight. Kida, you had trouble, didn't you?"

"At first. Then I remembered who you are. And who I am. Can you really read my mind?"

Dyani merely looked at him. "I don't have to. Colonel, I've been up a long time. I don't think I can sleep. But I've got to try."

"Same here. See you in the morning, Captain?"

"Of course. Did you think I wouldn't fight to make that happen?"

That night, Curt instructed the division megacomputer, Georgie, to play "Taps." Insofar as he was concerned, it was for several reasons.

But after the haunting notes of the music finally stopped echoing off Battle Mountain and out over the flats toward the still-smoking silo, Curt couldn't sleep in his OCV. He dragged his sleep sack out the rear hatch and took it up to the top of the ridge where he spread it out and then lay in the cool mountain air. The stars above were bright. A dim glowing cloud still stretched thinly across the sky, the remnants of the spaceship *Archangel Gabriel* that was now spread across the stratosphere.

He wasn't there very long before someone put a sleep sack down on the slopes of Battle Mountain alongside his. "I didn't think I could sleep. I can't."

"You didn't get any sleep last night?"

"No. I'm cold. Hold me."

He did.

APPENDIX I

ORDER OF BATTLE

OPERATION BLOOD SIEGE

3rd R.I. Special Combat Regiment, the "Washing-ton Greys":
Lieutenant Colonel Curt C. Carson, commanding officer

Regimental staff: ("Carson's Companions")
Major Joan G. Ward, chief of staff
Major Patrick Gillis Gratton, regimental adjutant (S-1)
Major Hensley Atkinson (S-3)
Captain Nelson A. Crile, regimental chaplain
Master Sergeant Major Henry G. Kester, regimental sergeant major
Sergeant Major Edwina A. Sampson, regimental technical sergeant

Tactical Battalion (TACBATT)
("Allen's Alleycats"):
Major Jerry P. Allen
Battalion Sergeant Major Nicholas P. Gerard
Reconnaissance Company (RECONCO)
("Aarts' Avengers")
Major Eleanor S. Aarts (S-2)
First Sergeant Tracy C. Dillon
Biotech Sergeant Allan J. Williams, P.N.
Scouting Platoon (SCOUT)
("Motega's Mustangs")
Captain Dyani Motega
Platoon Sergeant Harlan P. Saunders
Sergeant Thomas C. Cole
Sergeant Joe Jim Watson
Sergeant Donald J. Esteban
Birdbot Platoon (BIRD)

("Brown's Black Hawks")
1st Lieutenant Dale B. Brown
Platoon Sergeant Emma Crawford
Sergeant William J. Hull
Sergeant Jacob F. Kent
Sergeant Christine Burgess
Sergeant Jennifer M. Volker
Assault Company A (ASSAULTCO Alpha)
("Clinton's Cougars")
Captain Kathleen B. Clinton
Master Sergeant First Class Carol J. Head
Biotech Sergeant Virginia Bowles, P.N.
First Platoon: ("Sweet's Scorpions")
Captain Adonica Sweet
Platoon Sergeant Charles P. Koslowski
Sergeant James P. Elliott
Sergeant Paul T. Tullis
Second Platoon: ("Pagan's Pumas")
1st Lieutenant Lewis C. Pagan
Platoon Sergeant Betty Jo Trumble
Sergeant Joe Jim Watson
Sergeant Edwin W. Gatewood
Assault Company B (ASSAULTCO Bravo)
("Frazier's Ferrets")
Major Russell B. Frazier
Master Sergeant Charles L. Orndorff
Biotech Sergeant Juanita Gomez, P.N.
First Platoon: ("Clock's Cavaliers")
1st Lieutenant Harold M. Clock
Platoon Sergeant Robert Lee Garrison
Sergeant Walter J. O'Reilly
Sergeant Maxwell M. Moody
Second Platoon: ("Hassan's Assassins")
1st Lieutenant Hassan Ben Mahmud
Platoon Sergeant Isadore Beau Greenwald
Sergeant Victor Jouillan
Sergeant Sidney Albert Johnson
Gunnery Company (GUNCO)

("Ritscher's Rascals")
Captain William P. Ritscher
First Sergeant Forest L. Barnes
Biotech Sergeant Shelley C. Hale, P.N.
First Platoon: ("Taire's Terrors")
2nd Lieutenant Jerome "Jay" Taire
Platoon Sergeant Andrea Carrington
Sergeant Jamie Jay Younger
Sergeant Pamela S. Parkin
Second Platoon: ("Hall's Hellcats")
2nd Lieutenant Lawrence W. Hall
Platoon Sergeant Willa P. Miller
Sergeant Richard L. Knight
Sergeant Louise J. Hanrahan
Air Battalion (AIRBATT)
("Worsham's Warhawks")
Major Calvin J. Worsham
Battalion Sergeant Major John Adam
Tactical Air Support Company (TACAIRCO)
("Hands' Hawks")
Captain Paul Hands
1st Sergeant Clancy Thomas
1st Lieutenant Gabe Neatherly
1st Lieutenant Bruce Mark
1st Lieutenant Stacy Honey
1st Lieutenant Jay Kennedy
2nd Lieutenant Richard Cooke
Flight Sergeant Zeke Braswell
Flight Sergeant Larry Myers
Flight Sergeant Adam Adams
Flight Sergeant Grant Brown
Flight Sergeant Sharon Spence
Airlift Company (AIRLIFTCO)
("Timm's Tigers")
Captain Timothea Timm
First Sergeant Carl Bagwell
1st Lieutenant Ned Phillips
1st Lieutenant Mike Hart

1st Lieutenant Dorothy Peterson
1st Lieutenant Nancy Roberts
1st Lieutenant Harry Racey
2nd Lieutenant Jess S. Switzer
Flight Sergeant Kevin Hubbard
Flight Sergeant Jeffrey O'Connell
Flight Sergeant Barry Morris
Flight Sergeant Ann Shepherd
Flight Sergeant Richard Cooke
Flight Sergeant Harley Earll
Flight Sergeant Sergio Tomasio
Flight Sergeant John Espee

Service Battalion (SERVBATT)
Major Wade W. Hampton
Battalion Sergeant Major Joan J. Stark

Vehicle Technical Company (VETECO)
Major Frederick W. Benteen
Technical Sergeant First Class Raymond G. Wolf
Technical Sergeant Kenneth M. Hawkins
Technical Sergeant Charles B. Slocum

Warbot Technical Company (BOTECO)
Captain Elwood S. Otis
Technical Sergeant Bailey Ann Miles
Technical Sergeant Gerald W. Mora
Technical Sergeant Loretta A. Carruthers
Technical Sergeant Robert H. Vickers

Air Maintenance Company (AIRMAINCO)
Captain Ron Knight
First Sergeant Rebecca Campbell
Technical Sergeant Joel Pruitt
Technical Sergeant Richard N. Germain
Technical Sergeant Douglas Bell
Technical Sergeant Pam Gordon
Technical Sergeant Clete McCoy
Technical Sergeant Carol Jensen

Logistics Company (LOGCO)
Captain Harriet F. Dearborn (S-4)
Chief Supply Sergeant Manual P. Sanchez

Supply Sergeant Marriette W. Ireland
Supply Sergeant Lawrence W. Jordan
Supply Sergeant Jamie G. Casner
Biotech Company (BIOTECO)
Major Ruth Gydesen, M.D.
Captain Denise G. Logan, M.D.
Captain Thomas E. Alvin, M.D.
Captain Larry C. McHenry, M.D.
Captain Helen Devlin, R. N.
1st Lieutenant Clifford B. Braxton, R.N.
1st Lieutenant Laurie S. Cornell, R.N.
1st Lieutenant Julia B. Clark, R.N.
1st Lieutenant William O. Molde, R.N.
Biotech Sergeant Marcela V. Jolton, P.N.
Biotech Sergeant Nellie A. Miles, P.N.
Biotech Sergeant George O. Howard, P.N.
Biotech Sergeant Wallace W. Izard, P.N.

OTHERS

General Jacob O. Carlisle, JCS, COS U.S. Army, Washington, D.C., United States of America.

Major General Belinda J. Hettrick, commanding officer, 17th "Iron Fist" Division, AUS, Fort Huachuca, Arizona.

Colonel Frederick H. Salley, commanding officer, 27th Robot Infantry (Special Combat) Regiment, "The Wolfhounds," 17th Iron Fist Division, United States Army.

Lieutenant Colonel Maxine Frances Cashier, commanding officer, 7th Robot Infantry (Special Combat) Regiment, "The Cottonbalers," 17th Iron Fist Division, United States Army.

The President of the United States of America.

The Hon. James B. Floyd, U.S. Secretary of Defense.

The Hon. Joan S. Crittenden, U.S. Attorney General.

General Albert W. Murray, USAF (Ret.), Director, National Intelligence Agency.

Admiral Warren G. Spencer, USN, Chairman, Joint Chiefs of Staff.

Major General William J. Barnitz, USAF, National Security Advisor.

Chester Wilfred Martinside, hostage negotiator, State Department.

Leonard W. Spencer, Presidential Press Aide.

Dr. Clark Jeremy Mathys, the Prophet, Galactic Tabernacle of the Human Future.

General Stephen B. Calder, commanding officer, the Host of Michael, Galactic Tabernacle of the Human Future.

Lieutenant Colonel Helmuth von Kampf, the Host of Michael, Galactic Tabernacle of the Human Future.

Lieutenant Colonel Louis DeVille, the Host of Michael, Galactic Tabernacle of the Human Future.

Captain Manuel Sebastian de Vargas e Morales, the Host of Michael, Galactic Tabernacle of the Human Future.

Jasper Lyell, Chief Financial Officer, Galactic Tabernacle of the Human Future.

The Reverend Alastair Gillespie, the Keeper of the Faith, Galactic Tabernacle of the Human Future.

Gordon Palmer, Director of Technology, Galactic Tabernacle of the Human Future.

Dr. Rosha Taisha, Director of Neuroelectronics, Galactic Tabernacle of the Human Future.

Todd Cartwright, Chief Engineer, the S.S. *Archangel Gabriel* spaceship of the Galactic Tabernacle of the Human Future.

Henry VarDerCamp, computer technologist, the S.S. *Archangel Gabriel* spaceship of the Galactic Tabernacle of the Human Future.

Sarah Carmichael Mathys, principal wife of the Prophet.

Monica Elora Mathys, secondary wife of the Prophet.

The Honorable Walter Van Tilberg Hopkins, Governor, State of Nevada.

Wyatt Bloomington, field agent, Federal Bureau of Investigation.

Sergeant Pete Cooker, Nevada State Police.

Sergeant Stan Smith, Nevada State Police.

Officer Harrison Corvus, Nevada State Police.

Officer James Burkhardt, Nevada State Police.

Lieutenant Colonel Arthur M. Boswell, officer in charge, Tiffany security computer complex, the Pentagon, Washington, D.C

Major Anatoly Mikhailovich Zhigarev, chief of watch, Zahvohd military satellite surveillance center, Magnetogorsk, U.S.S.R.

Boris Fedorovich Bugayev, officer in charge, space security watch center, Kaliningrad, U.S.S.R.

APPENDIX II

COSMIC MAGIC TOP SECRET
EYES ONLY
NATIONAL INTELLIGENCE AGENGY
Langley, Virginia
NIA BRIEFING PAPER 35-B-N-007
Prose Text Version
GALACTIC TABERNACLE
OF THE HUMAN FUTURE
BACKGROUND

THE PROPHET AND FOUNDER:

The Galactic Tabernacle of the Human Future was founded by Dr. Clark Jeremy Mathys.

Dr. Mathys was originally an outstanding planetary astronomer. He was recognized as a true genius, although he was never admired for his modesty or manners. He became an extremely popular science reporter whose highly acclaimed television specials about mankind's coming colonization of space made his name widely recognized. He has an incredible TV persona and charisma and is highly attracted to women, although his reputation as a sexually hyperactive man is kept quite quiet by his acolytes.

Professionally, he obtained his Ph.D. and gained recognition for his studies of Mars and the planetoid belt using the latest data from space probes (no humans have yet journeyed to Mars). He was the leader of the scientific team responsible for analysis of the high-resolution photographs of the Martian surface taken by the last planned and funded unmanned space probe to Mars, *Wotan-2*.

According to scientific colleagues, Mathys' metamorphosis from scientist to religious leader began when he attempted to pioneer novel NE techniques to speed analysis and evaluation of *Wotan-2* Martian surface photographs. Thereafter, it is reported that he entered a period of severe depression and deep despondency because the *Wotan-2* probe was the last planned and funded deep space exploration mission. Apparently Mathys was frustrated because the progress in space exploration was far too slow in comparison to the technical capabilities to carry out the missions. Shortly thereafter, he effectively disappeared from public view, abandoning his first wife and two children. He again came to public attention seven years later. Now he claims that when he's in NE linkage with his personal computer, it becomes a channel through which extra-terrestrials he calls Anunnakis speak to him.

Mathys maintains that these Anunnaki extraterrestrials were the original gods who are best known today as the Titans of Greek mythology. However, these same ETs were also part of the earliest religions of Sumer, Akkad, Egypt, Assyria, and Canaan.

He formed the Galactic Tabernacle of the Human Future, a religious space advocacy group.

THE DOCTRINE OF THE TABERNACLE:

The Galactic Tabernacle of the Human Future rests upon the following doctrinal points. This is what they believe to be true:

1. The ancient legends of gods, archangels, and angels are true stories, much distorted from early verbal recountings, of an extraterrestrial humanoid race (ETs) of extreme age and high technology called Anunnakis.

2. The Anunnaki discovered Earth and the proto-humanoids living upon it more than five million years ago. With their advanced biotechnology, they set about altering existing simian life forms on Earth to create a race of star warriors to assist them in the galactic war of good versus evil against a foe Mathys calls the Nibiruans. This work by the Anunnaki. was carried out in biotechnology labs at several bases on Mars to prevent any possible contamination of Earth's ecology with dangerous biotechnological organisms.

3. The biotechnical creation of the human race was interrupted when the Martian labs were discovered, attacked, and destroyed by the evil Nibiruan enemies because of Anunnaki traitors. Some of the Anunnaki managed to remain on Earth until about 2,500 years ago in an attempt to salvage the incomplete experiment that is mankind.

4. The Anunnaki were finally forced to suspend open contact with the human race because of the peace treaty that ended the galactic war. The Anunnaki were charged by the enemy Nibiruans with interfering in the natural development of the germ plasm of a world. However, in spite of the contact prohibition, the Anunnaki have been able to occasionally make surreptitious contact with people. These visits were eventually detected by the Nibiruan enemies who proceeded to plant their own evil human agents on Earth to prevent human progress and mankind's ascent to the stars.

5. The Anunnaki found a new means of communication unknown to the enemy Nibiruans when Dr. Mathys was contacted through his personal computer. Mathys was told that he must build a spaceship and take a host of sixty-six selected humans plus a huge sperm, ova, and embryo bank to the planetoid belt. The Anunnaki have promised that one of their starships will make a clandestine rendezvous and take the spacers to the stars to help fight the interstellar war of good versus evil.

6. In return for the help of the spacers once the war is won, the Anunnaki will return to Earth, save those Tabernacle members who have maintained the Sanctuary base, and place Mathys and his people in control of the whole planet and the imperfect human race.

7. The imperfect humans of Earth can be saved and biologically modified to become the perfect humans the Anunnaki originally designed. But those who believe themselves worthy must prove this and their good intentions by joining the Tabernacle, following the leadership of Mathys and his acolytes, and dedicating their lives to Mathys' goal.

THE ET GODS:

The Tabernacle believes all stories of ancient gods have truth in them and that the ETs put mankind on Earth as a biological experiment using simian stock. The Tabernacle acolytes believe: (a) Yahweh became the Anunnaki winner in prehistory wars of gods and men after the Nibiruan attack on Mars; (b) other Anunnaki who became gods were Amon, Anu, Enlil, Marduk, Ahura-Mazda, Ra, Horus, Osiris, Indra, and Innanalshtar; and (c) these Anunnaki were also the Greek Titans under other names.

THE TABERNACLE ANGELS:

The Tabernacle believes that the archangels and angels were indeed messengers of the gods and were the prototypes of the final products of the Anunnaki biological experiment. Among them are Michael (the warrior), Gabriel (the messenger), Raphael, Lucifer (the traitor), and Moroni (who later broke the peace treaty by visiting America in the nineteenth century).

THE TABERNACLE SAINTS:

The pioneers of space travel are recognized as being the true saints of the Tabernacle because they were the ones who devoted their lives to the task of getting mankind off planet Earth for reasons they may have understood - most were learned men of their time - or may have sensed only as a latent gene-based program motivating them. Among the Tabernacle saints are Verne, Wells, Tsiolkovski, Goddard, Korolev, von Braun, and Heinlein. An annual pilgrimage is made to a Kabbalah-style glass cube at Alamogordo, New Mexico where these saints are venerated. (This, of course, is the International Space Hall of Fame which doesn't like this attention but can do little about it because the Tabernacle members are paying visitors and the small New Mexico town likes the money they bring in.)

THE ORGANIZATION OF THE TABERNACLE:

On this doctrine, Mathys has built himself a huge messianic pseudo-religious empire, raising billions of dollars by television evangelism of a new sort with wide appeal. He is considered to be the father of the hippy like high-technology romantic movement of the twenty-first century, the "spacers." The spacers are many types of people, not only religious fanatics but the grandchildren of twentieth century New Age parents as well as a very large number of brilliant high-technology types who are searching for meaningful application of their know-how for a grand and nebulous cause.

Drugs are not used by the Galactic Tabernacle. NE linkage and programming techniques are used instead.

The technology faction of the Galactic Tabernacle includes the people who will design and build the huge ship in a hidden underground silo at Sanctuary in Nevada and the ones who set up and maintain the high-technology of the Tabernacle and its Sanctuary. They are not as fanatically zealous as the religious or space advocate factions. The techies consist mostly of disenchanted engineers and technicians who believe that the only way they are likely to get to the stars in their lifetimes is to go along with Mathys because the Tabernacle is at least doing something, will give them the free rein to pursue their dreams of star flight, and will also provide for them in the limited, Spartan conditions of the Tabernacle's Sanctuary.

Sanctuary is located about fifty kilometers southwest of Battle Mountain, Nevada, where the Tabernacle owns several hundred square kilometers of a huge ranch. Originally, Sanctuary was housed in old mine tunnels and shafts. Using twenty-first-century technology, Mathys' techies and spacers have apparently expanded this into a prototype planetoid base, developing the needed technologies of such a base as they go along because they realize that the Anunnaki may not pick them up immediately in the planetoids. Energy is supplied by solar power, hot springs, and cold fusion. They have built an underground cold fusion power plant capable of generating several gigawatts of electric power to operate the high-energy ground-based laser that will be used to provide propulsion for the ship. The ship design and construction is under the control of Todd Cartwright while the technical side of Sanctuary is run by Gordon Palmer. Both are brilliant young technical people who are among those Mathys has persuaded to work for the Tabernacle for room and board so they can realize their great technological dreams.

The business and financial side of the Tabernacle is run by disenchanted businessmen and financial types who feel the desperate need for a supportable grand cause in their lives. The business side is run quite well through a series of subsidiary and blind corporations and with an excellent portfolio of stocks, bonds, and other securities. Mathys has taken a lesson from the Reverend Moon, L. Ron Hubbard, and several other Wall-Street-smart twentieth century evangelists. The business-financial affairs of the Tabernacle are watched over by Jasper Lyell, an MBA and former investment broker who appears to be associated with the Tabernacle as a way to ride Mathys' coattails to enormous wealth because Lyell writes the checks. The SEC and the IRS should be alerted to post a watch on this individual.

The religious side is handled by the Reverend Alastair Gillespie, the Keeper of the Faith, the zealous religious expert who enforces the Prophet's doctrines and ensures the religious fervor of the spacers. There is reason to believe that he is the former Gillespie Astaire whose S&M parlor operation was uncovered several years ago in Denver; he was never apprehended and tried for the brutal murders and disfigurations of that grisly incident. Certainly, Gillespie's methods are not benevolent when it comes to recidivism or demonstrated lack of zeal or belief on the part of acolytes, and they show many similarities to those of the Astaire case. Gillespie keeps the acolytes in line by terror or persuasion, whichever works best. He is assisted by the blacklisted neuroelectronics expert, Dr. Rosha Taisha, who was involved in the Zahedan hostage incident and was never apprehended by the Iranians.

Women outnumber men by a factor of at least five to one in Sanctuary. The ship's actual crew will have a ratio of ten to one and will be selected by the Prophet Mathys from among the brightest and most beautiful of his disciples. Every woman is expected to be able to bear as many children as possible, and every man is expected to service at least ten women to expand the ranks of the Tabernacle both in space and on the ground. No gender equality exists in the Tabernacle, and the job of the cult's women is to have babies and to serve the men. Like many messianic religions, the Tabernacle is rife with sexual excesses, and many people join the movement for the psycho-sexual gratification.

The Tabernacle has organized an effective personal army to protect Sanctuary against government intrusions which Mathys predicts will come. General Stephen B. Calder commands the Host of Michael, a brigade-strength warbot guard unit. Calder was formerly a lieutenant and NE warbot combat officer in the United States Army before he resigned his commission.

Those who remain in Sanctuary after what is called the Departure are to reproduce and multiply. They are to protect Sanctuary and keep it ready as an Earth base for the day when the Anunnaki come back to finish the experiment that will produce the final, perfect, angellike form of the human race.

ANALYSIS OF THE BASIC HOFFER ELEMENTS OF THE TABERNACLE:

In his classic book, "The True Believer," the twentieth-century longshoreman philosopher Eric Hoffer pointed out that any great mass or popular movement such as an ideology or even a religion must have the following three elements:

1. A plausible but impossible dream.
2. A glorious, infallible leader.
3. A devil.

A cursory analysis of the Tabernacle indicates that all three elements are present.

The plausible but impossible dream is that the Anunnaki and Nibiruans exist, that a spaceship can be built and launched to the planetoid belt, that the Anunnaki will take the ship's occupants to the stars, and that the Anunnaki will return to give ultimate power over the planet Earth to the followers of Mathys, the Prophet.

The glorious, infallible leader is Mathys, the Prophet of the Human Future.

The devils are the unidentified evil Nibiruans arid their clandestine agents on Earth, the later being anyone who is not a true believer and who attempts to stop the spacers.

The Tabernacle has good business and financial experts so it has money to buy what it needs. Most of its internal affairs can be quite clandestine because of its underground facility. Unlike many religions and mass zealot movements of the past, it relies heavily on high technology and isn't reluctant to use technology to achieve its ends. It is capable of defending itself and perhaps even conducting preemptive strikes with a well-organized, highly disciplined, warbot-assisted army.

This is not a group to be dismissed lightly. These people are dangerous.

APPENDIX III

DYANI'S SONG

Go out against an enemy you see, hear, touch,
And the reward is a feat her upon your coup stick,
Endure pain, thirst, cold,
And the warrior hears the crowd cheering.
But what of the warrior who endures against
Whoever, whatever tries defiling the warrior morals,
Corrupting the spirit? Who will cheer then?
But the warrior who yields neither to angers or lusts
Wears those quiet honors on the heart.
Warrior, learn the staying power to endure
When meat gets scarce, when snow piles deep,
When the enemy sneaks up and denies sleep.
Put your owner stick upon the treasures
Of the sinews of the heart which are truly yours
Against all blood, against all pain, against all death.
I am the wearer of the feather that identifies the scout.
The scout, one familiar with the sky, the voice of cloud, of wind
The scout, someone who remembers all the while watching.
The scout, one who overcomes cold, hunger, pain, and the fear of these.
The scout, eyes and ears of the tribe, bearer of fact, truthbearer.

APPENDIX IV

GLOSSARY OF ROBOT INFANTRY TERMS AND SLANG

ACV: Airportable Command Vehicle M660.

Aerodyne: A saucer-shaped flying machine that obtains its lift from the exhaust of one or more turbine fanjet engines blowing outward over the curved upper surface of the craft from an annular segmented slot near the center of the upper surface. The aerodyne was invented by Dr. Henri M. Coanda after World War II but was not perfected until decades later because of the pre-dominance of the rotary-winged helicopter.

Artificial Intelligence or AI: Very fast computer modules with large memories which can simulate some functions of human thought and decision-making processes by bringing together many apparently disconnected pieces of data, making simple evaluations of the priority of each, and making simple decisions concerning what to do, how to do it, when to do it, and what to report to the human being in control.

Beanie: A West Point term for a plebe or first-year man.

Beanette: A female beanie.

Birdbot: The M20 Aeroreconnaissance Neuroelectronic Bird Warbot used for aerial recce. Comes in shapes and sizes to resemble indigenous birds.

Biotech: A biological technologist once known in the twentieth-century Army as a "medic."

Black Maria: The M44A Assault Shotgun, the Sierra Charlie's 18.52-millimeter friend in close-quarter combat.

Bohemian Brigade: War correspondents or a news media television crew.

Bot: Generalized generic slang term for "robot," which takes many forms, as warbot, reconbot, etc. See "Robot" below.

Botflu,sh: Since robots have no natural excrement, this term is a reference to what comes out of a highly mechanical warbot when its lubricants are changed during routine maintenance. Used by soldiers as a slang term referring to anything of a detestable nature.

Gee-pee or CP: Slang for "Command Post."

Check minus-x: Look behind you. In terms of coordinates, plus-x is ahead, minus-x is behind, plus-y is to the right, minus-y is left, plus-z is up, and minus-z is down.

Chippie: The UCA-21C Chippewa tactical airlift aerodyne.

Class 6 supplies: Alcoholic beverages of high ethanol content procured locally; officially, only five classes of supplies exist.

Column of ducks: A convoy proceeding through terrain where they are likely to draw fire.

Creamed: Greased, beaten, conquered, overwhelmed.

CYA: Cover Your Ass. In polite company, "Cover Your Anatomy."

Down link: A remote command or data channel from a warbot to a soldier.

FIDO: Acronym for "Fuck it; drive on!" Overcome your obstacle or problem and get on with the operation.

FIG: Foreign Internal Guardian mission, the sort of assignment Army units draw to protect American interests in selected locations around the world. Great for RI units but not within the intended mission profiles of Sierra Charlie regiments.

Fort Fumble: Any headquarters but especially the Pentagon when not otherwise specified.

Fur ball: A complex, confused fight, battle, or operation.

General Ducrot: Any incompetent, lazy, fucked-up officer who doesn't know or won't admit those short-comings. May have other commissioned officer rank to more closely describe the individual.

Go physical: To lapse into idiot mode, to operate in a combat or recon environment without neuroelectronic warbots; what the Special Combat units do all the time. See "Idiot mode" below.

Golden BB: A small-caliber bullet that hits and thus creates large problems.

Greased: Beaten, conquered, overwhelmed, creamed.

Harpy: The AD-40C tactical air assault aerodyne which the Aerospace Force originally developed in the A version; the Navy flies the B version. The Office In Charge Of Stupid Names tried to get everyone to call it the "Thunder Devil," but the Harpy name stuck with the drivers and troops. The compound term "newsharpy" is also used to refer to a hyperthyroid, ego-blasted, over-achieving female news personality or reporter.

Headquarters happy: Any denizen of headquarters, regimental or higher.

Humper: Any device whose proper name a soldier can't recall at the moment.

Ice cream cone with wings: What an airborne soldier's insignia looks like to Sierra Charlies. Airborne regiments tend to be special units active only in armies other than that of the U.S.

Idiot mode: Operating in the combat environment without neuroelectronic warbots, especially operating without the benefit of computers and artificial intelligence to relieve battle load. What the warbot brainies think the Sierra Charlies do all the time. See "Go physical" above.

Intelligence: Generally considered to exist in four categories: animal, human, machine, and military.

Intelligence amplifier or IA: A very fast computer with a very large memory which, when linked to a human nervous system by nonintrusive neuroelectronic pickups and electrodes, serves as a very fast extension of the human brain allowing the brain to function faster, recall more data, store more data, and thus "amplify" a human being's "intelligence." (Does not imply that the Army knows what "human intelligence" really is.)

Jeep: Word coined from the initials "GP" standing for "General Purpose." Once applied to an Army quarter-ton vehicle but subsequently used to refer to the Mark 33A2 General Purpose Warbot.

KIA: "Killed in action." A warbot brainy term used to describe the situation where a warbot soldier's neuro-electronic data and sensory inputs from one or more warbots is suddenly cut off, leaving the human being in a state of mental limbo. A very debilitating and mentally disturbing situation. (Different from being physically killed in action, a situation with which only Sierra Charlies find themselves threatened.)

LAMVA: The M473 Light Artillery Maneuvering Vehicle, Airportable, a robotic armored vehicle mounting a 75-millimeter Saucy Cans gun used for light artillery support of a Sierra Charlie regiment.

Linkage: The remote connection or link between a human being and one or more neuroelectronically controlled warbots. This link channel may be by means of wires, radio, laser, or optics. The actual technology of linkage is highly classified. The robot/computer sends its data directly to the human soldier's nervous system through small nonintrusive electrodes positioned on the soldier's skin. This data is coded in such a way that the soldier perceives the signals as sight, sound, feeling, or position of the robot's parts. The robot/computer also picks up commands from the soldier's nervous system that are merely "thought" by the soldier, translates them into commands a robot can understand, and monitors the robot's accomplishment of the commanded action.

Log bird: A logistics or supply aircraft.

Mary Ann: The M60A Airborne Mobile Assault Warbot which mounts a single M300 25-millimeter automatic cannon with variable fire rate. Accompanies Sierra Charlie troops in the field and provides fire support.

Mad minute: The first intense, chaotic, wild, frenzied period of a fire fight when it seems every gun in the world is being shot at you.

Mike-mike: Soldier's shorthand for "millimeter."

Novia: The 7.62-millimeter M33A3 "Ranger" Assault Rifle designed in Mexico as the M3 Novia. The Sierra Charlies still call it the Novia or "sweetheart."

Neuroelectronics or *NE:* The synthesis of electronics and computer technologies that permit a computer to detect and recognize signals from the human nervous system by means of nonintrusive skin-mounted sensors as well as to stimulate the human nervous system with computer-generated electronic signals through similar skin-mounted electrodes for the purpose of creating sensory signals in the human mind. See "Linkage" above.

OCV: Operational Command Vehicle, the command version of the M660 ACV.

Orgasmic: A slang term that grew out of the observation, "Outstanding!" It means the same thing. Usually but not always.

POSSOH: "Person of Opposite Sex Sharing Off-duty Hours."

PTV: Personal Transport Vehicle or "Trike," a three-wheeled unarmored vehicle similar to an old sidecar motorcycle capable of carrying two Sierra Charlies or one Sierra Charlie and a Jeep.

Pucker factor: The detrimental effect on the human body that results from being in an extremely hazardous situation such as being shot at.

Robot: From the Czech word robota meaning work, especially drudgery. A device with human like actions directed either by a computer or by a human being through a computer and a two-way command-sensor circuit. See "Linkage" and "Neuroelectronics" above.

Robot Infantry or *RI:* A combat branch of the United States Army which grew from the regular infantry with the introduction of robots and linkage to warfare. Replaced the regular infantry in the early twenty-first century.

RTV: Robot Transport Vehicle, now the M662 Airporable Robot Transport Vehicle (ARTV) but still called an RTV by Sierra Charlies.

Rule Ten: Slang reference to Army Regulation 601-10 which

prohibits physical contact between male and female personnel when on duty except for that required in the conduct of official business.

Rules of Engagement or *ROE:* Official restrictions on the freedom of action of a commander or soldier in his confrontation with an opponent that act to increase the probability that said commander or soldier will lose the combat, all other things being equal.

Saucy Cans: An American Army corruption of the French designation for the 75-millimeter "soixante-quintze" weapon mounted on the LAMVA.

Scroom!: Abbreviation for "Screw 'em!"

Sheep screw: A disorganized, embarrassing, graceless, chaotic fuck-up.

Sierra Charlie: Phonetic alphabet derivative of the initials "SC" meaning "Special Combat." Soldiers trained to engage in personal field combat supported and accompanied by artificially intelligent warbots that are voice-commanded rather than run by linkage. The ultimate weapon of World War IV.

Sierra Hotel: What warbot brainies say when they can't say, "Shit hot!"

Simulator or *sim:* A device that can simulate the sensations perceived by a human being and the results of the human's responses. A simple toy computer or video game simulating the flight of an aircraft or the driving of a race car is an example of a primitive simulator.

Sit-guess: Slang for "estimate of the situation," an educated guess about your predicament.

Sit-rep: Short for "situation report" to notify your superior officer about the sheep screw you're in at the moment.

Smart Fart: The M100A (FG/IM-190) Anti-tank/Anti-aircraft tube-launched rocket capable of being launched off the shoulder of a Sierra Charlie. So-called because of its self-guided "smart" warhead and the sound it makes when fired.

Snake pit: Slang for the highly computerized briefing center located in most caserns and other Army posts.

Snivel: To complain about the injustice being done you.

Spasm mode: Slang for killed in action (KIA).

Spook: Slang term for either a spy or a military intelligence specialist. Also used as a verb relating to reconnaissance.

Staff stooge: Derogatory term referring to a staff officer. Also "staff weenie."

TACAMO!: "Take Charge And Move Out!"

Tacomm: A portable frequency-hopping communications transceiver system once used by rear-echelon warbot brainy troops and now generally used in very advanced and ruggedized versions by the Sierra Charlies.

Tango Sierra: Tough shit.

Tech-weenie: The derogatory term applied by combat soldiers to the scientists, engineers, and technicians who complicate life by insisting that the soldier have gadgetry that is the newest, fastest, most powerful, most accurate, and usually the most unreliable products of their fertile techie imaginations.

Third Herd, the: The 3rd Robot Infantry Regiment (Sierra Charlie), the Washington Greys (but you'd better be a Grey to use that term).

Tiger error: What happens when an eager soldier tries too hard.

Umpteen hundred: Some time in the distant, undetermined future.

Up link: The remote command link or channel from the warbot brainy to the warbot.

Warbot: Abbreviation for "war robot," a mechanical device that is operated by or commanded by a soldier to fight in the field.

Warbot brainy: The human soldier who operates warbots through linkage, implying that the soldier is basically the brains of the warbot. Sierra Charlies remind everyone that they are definitely not warbot brainies whom they consider to be grown-up children operating destructive video games.

www.ingramcontent.com/pod-product-compliance
Lightning Source LLC
Chambersburg PA
CBHW072125250626
47159CB00007B/2564